Oh! Père Lachaise

Oh! Père Lachaise

Jim Yates

Édition d'Amélie

Published by
Édition d'Amélie

Copyright © Jim Yates 2007
The moral right of James Yates to be identified as the author of this
work has been asserted by him in accordance with the Copyright,
Designs and Patents 1988
ISBN 978-0-9555836-1-2

First published 2007

A CIP catalogue record is available from the British Library

For Niamh, Aidan and Catherine

Contents

Prologue

July 19, 1909.

It was another fine Parisian day as his Hansom cab meandered its way down the boulevard de Ménilmontant, taking him to his legal practice situated on the corner of the boulevard and that of rue de la Roquette. The cab was facing the entrance to the favourite resting place of Parisian's, the cemetery of Père Lachaise.

As he stepped down from the cab and bade farewell to his driver, he noticed a funeral cortège approaching Père Lachaise. Removing his top hat, as good souls do, he stood and watched as it entered the gates. The hearse, a rather grand one, pulled by two well-groomed black horses, rattled its way across the cobblestones, followed by a priest and four gentlemen mourners who walked slowly behind, with heads bowed.

He could not help but wonder why some soul, lying in the plainest and cheapest of caskets, being carried on such a grand hearse could have so few mourners. Curiosity getting the better of him, he decided to let his clients wait and followed the cortège as it made its way along the twisting roads and up the hill to the far extremity of the cemetery. He stayed at a discreet distance, not wanting to be seen trespassing on the grief of the four mourners.

He stood behind a tombstone and watched as the short burial service took place. It was such a brief and simple ceremony that it left him feeling even more curious and perturbed. When it was finished the four mourners huddled together in deep conversation. He began to wonder what they were saying to each other. As he watched, he had an overwhelming feeling that he was not just trespassing on their grief, but shamefully spying on them. He discreetly departed, making his way down the hill, out of the gates and across the road to his office.

As he was about to enter the office, he again heard the rattle of wheels on the cobblestones and turning, saw the grand hearse leaving the cemetery. Again, he wondered whom this soul was that made its last journey in such style, on a fine Parisian day yet had so few mourners to wish it *bon voyage*. It seemed such a sad and lonesome way to go, especially for a Parisian. But then again, he thought, perhaps it is not a Parisian soul, but one from some distant shore.

For the rest of the day, his mind was in turmoil as he wondered who that departed soul was, lowered into Mother Earth, with such little ceremony by four mourners, who for all he knew could have been complete strangers. Who was it? What was the cause of death? He wished he knew. Perhaps he may never know. Perhaps it would

1

remain a secret to all – all except the priest, the four mourners and those good souls of Père Lachaise.

An Odd Revelation

"Bonjour, good souls of Père Lachaise."

Welcome, reader, to this pink-tinted tale of the trials and tribulations of the souls of Père Lachaise.

If you are blessed with a broad mind or have a leaning to the surreal, or can laugh and cry at the ups and downs of this life – better still, at our expectations of the one beyond, then I invite you to turn these pages and allow me escort you through this tale of laughter, sorrow, regret, passion and love.

Imagine if you will, Purgatory – not the kind that first springs to mind, but a pink-tinted Parisian kind with its own quarters, districts and administration. A place that on the surface could be mistaken for life on earth, with all that's needed to sustain a good, happy and healthy life – a place where souls live with the hope of purging their venial sins to reach those dizzy heights of Paradise.

Imagine this place, where flowers have no scent, where the birds are devoid of song, where the fruit of the vine has no intoxicating effect, where the best of cuisine is dull on the palate and the many tears shed are saltless and cold. Imagine this place, a place where sex is but a state of mind – a place where the only sexual release is in the dreams of those fortunate enough to dream.

On a raised marble dais at the Central Reservation, on a sweltering Purgatory morning, sitting under the Laburnum Tree, was Sophie, the mother of Victor Hugo. Next to her, Marie d'Agoult, one-time lover of Franz Liszt and one of the Reservation's most striking beauties. This reader is the setting of a tale introduced by these unlikely companions.

***

"We must do something about Oscar."

"Must we?"

Marie looked at her friend in surprise. "Yes! We must."

"My dear Marie, whatever do you mean, do something?"

"You're telling me, you don't know?"

"Know! Know what for heaven's sake."

"Really, Sophie, are you saying you haven't noticed his odd behaviour of late?"

"No, I can't say I have, but, Oscar's Oscar. If he weren't acting oddly, then that would give us good reason for concern."

"Yes, I agree, but lately he's been acting *really* oddly."

"Is that so?"

"Yes, very much so, not in the way we are so accustomed to, but in a really bizarre way."

"I'm sorry; you have lost me – odd and bizarre! I have no idea what you're on about."

"Surely you must have noticed the drastic change in his behaviour recently?"

"Such as…"

"I don't know how to say this. I find it so distressing. It is so personal. Perhaps I ought to explain the background, so you know what angle I'm coming from."

"If you must," Sophie replied, hoping this was not going to be one of Marie's long-winded sagas.

"As you know, Oscar's been here at the Reservation for a good while now, since 1909, after he was transferred from that horrid Bagneux, where he was first interred. If you recall, he wasn't too happy about leaving his earthly home the way he did, a broken and defeated man, a social outcast dying without dignity in a dingy run-down Parisian hotel. He was distraught that he had left without reaching his full potential as a writer, that the world was being robbed of his undoubted genius. Surely, you must remember that."

"Oh yes," Sophie sighed, "I remember it well. You would think he was the only soul to die before his time. He can be a bit of a whinger at times, but, what's this to do with his odd behaviour."

"Oh! A lot! If you remember, there was more to come."

"Was there?" Sophie groaned.

Marie gave a frustrated sigh at her friend's dismissive attitude.

"He was downright put out that he hadn't gone straight to Paradise. He was so indignant that he ended up here. He didn't half go on and on about it. At the time, he said, 'I'm such a natural for Paradise, so why am I here? My words are pure poetry and isn't poetry the language of God, the language of love, of passion, of life itself? He must have made a mistake. Maybe God is having one of His off days. He must be confusing me with someone else. It is easily done. It is just not fair, not fair at all that a man of genius to be overlooked for the ultimate elevation. An injustice has been committed and should be put right.'

"You remember him shrugging his shoulder, his arms outstretched, and asking, 'Who is in charge of this place anyway? Surely someone must know what's going on.'"

"I know all that. But what about this odd behaviour you're on about?"

"Well, again, I must remind you, Sophie; of how depressed he was when he realised that no mistake had been made and this was his lot. That for him, there would be no Paradise, no golden slippers, no soft divine *pouf* to put his feet upon, just an eternity here on this Purgatory Reservation unless he finds what eludes every soul here: a way of purging his venial sins. His depression lasted for a very long time and we were all worried about him. Even the company of Musset, Balzac and other literary pals didn't help him to recover. It was a very gloomy time, very gloomy indeed."

"Yes. Yes, I recall it well. But did he imagine that he, the sinner he was, was just going to waltz straight into Paradise that his earthly sins were to be of no consequence, that they would just be overlooked? Was he really so naive?"

"Afraid so and still is – where was I?"

"Depressed."

"Oh yes. Anyway, one day, if you recall, Oscar, Chopin, and the sculptor Clésinger were relaxing on Cloud Nine, gazing down over Père Lachaise. Turning to Chopin, Oscar gave a deep lingering sigh and said 'I wonder, Frédéric, I wonder, will I ever get a headstone? My grave looks rather bleak and forlorn. It seems improper and rather insulting that such a genius as I should have no headstone, that there is nothing written in stone to tell the world of my greatness, of who and what I was. Look, people walk past without even a glance. It is not right. I ask you – what is the world coming to when ordinary mortals walk past the grave of a genius without even an admiring glance? It seems that since I left the world, it has somehow lost its sparkle and finesse. Look at your grave, Frédéric. Just look at it. Isn't it just a grand sight, with its beautiful sculptured work? Just look at its figurine. Its finish is divine. A grand piece of art, clearly fashioned by a master craftsman.'"

"'I'll say,' replied a delighted Clésinger, 'All my own work, I'll let you know? Without seeming to be big-headed, I would say it is my finest, my masterpiece, in honour of a *real* master.'

"Oscar, looking admirably at him, said, 'Is that so, my friend? Pity you are dead, for I would certainly have commissioned you to fashion a stone for me. You could have done justice to my headstone. Of course, it would have had to be something fitting a genius. That goes without saying.'

"'Of course,' Clésinger said, 'but don't despair my dear man, I'm certain something is planned. After all, it's not a headstone someone of your calibre is entitled to, but a tombstone, and a grand one at that.'

"Oscar was delighted, grinning from ear to ear. 'What an astute fellow you are,' he cheerfully replied. 'We must be cut from that same delicate fabric.'

"'Without a doubt – a rare piece too,' Clésinger boasted.

5

"Chopin sat up and patted Oscar's head, saying. 'Now, now, my dear friend, you shouldn't fret over such a thing as a gravestone. Does it really matter whether you have one or not?'

"Oscar was horrified. He was up on his feet, hands on hips, fuming. 'Makes no difference?' he bellowed. 'It is all right for you to talk ivory fingers; you already have a fine headstone, so why shouldn't I have one?'

"'Don't worry, my dear friend,' replied Chopin. 'If you're destined to have one that's how it will be – we all get our just desserts in the end.'

"'I think so too. It would be an outrage if I was left without my name in stone,' Oscar replied.

"One day, some weeks later, as we were again looking over Père Lachaise, Chopin jumped to his feet and, pointing down at Oscar's grave, cried, 'Look, Oscar, there seems to be a bit of activity around your grave. Come. Have a look.'

"Oscar ran over to the Viewing Platform and gasped, 'So there is, by God.'

"'Well, Oscar,' said Clésinger. 'It seems like you are finally to get your grave spruced up. It looks like your big day is nigh.'

"'About time too,' Oscar replied. 'It's just not right to keep a genius waiting.'

"'Workmen are preparing the ground. Look at them shovelling away. They seem extremely keen, don't they? In a few days, it will be fully constructed in a few days. By the look of those foundations, you are in for a tombstone, and one of some size, judging by the depth of those foundations,' Clésinger cried as he watched the workers toiling away.

"'Bigger the better,' replied Oscar, thrilled at the prospect. 'All geniuses need good foundations – they carry such heavy burdens. I wonder who has the distinction – nay, the honour – of sculpting it.'

"'Has to be a master craftsman, Oscar, after all, it is for a genius,' smirked Clésinger.

"'How right you are, my dear fellow, how right you are. I can't wait to see what inscription is chiselled into it. It will have to be something fine, something handsome – something in the aesthetic vein to reflect my true image.'

"'Ah! My friend,' Chopin replied. 'Just two words would suffice to sum you up.'

"Oscar recoiled in surprise. 'Just *two*!' he indigently replied. 'Dear me, Frédéric, how could I possibly be summed up in just *two* words.'

'Quite easily, said Chopin.

Oscar, shocked, asked, 'What two words, pray, would they be.'

Chopin laughed. 'My friend, I thought that would be obvious.'

6

"'Well, not to me. I cannot imagine what two words could do me justice. What are they then?'

"'Oscar Wilde! What else?' Chopin announced. 'I can see it before me – beautiful chiselled letters, not too small but large enough to concentrate the mind... Oscar Wilde. There would be no other words needed, as the whole world knows who and what you were. It's all there in those two handsome words.'

"Well, you could have knocked him down with a feather. Oscar was thrilled and cried, 'If you put that to music my Polish friend, you would have the makings of a masterpiece.'"

Marie took a sip of holy water and continued.

"For the first time since his arrival, Oscar had a smile on his face. A few weeks later, we all gathered around to witness the unveiling of the sculpture executed by the brilliant young American, Jacob Epstein. Clésinger was right – it had to be a master craftsman to do such a task and Epstein was just that. When the drape was released, we could see Oscar's depression evaporating before our very eyes. He was overcome as he recognised, standing around his tomb, the small group of friends who had stood by him in the bleakest period of his life. He was delighted at the sight of his younger son, Vyvyan, paying his respects. His elder son Cyril was away fighting in that war to end all wars. The sculpture was a fine piece, as we all know. Everyone present admired it. Chopin, noticing the inscription, looked at Oscar and, smiling, said, 'Didn't I tell you, only two words would suffice.'

"'How right you were. It does look good.'

"'It certainly does,' Chopin said as he gazed at the tomb. 'Those two words sum up the essence of Oscar Wilde. No other words could have said as much. It is a fine sculpture and even finer words to give it that added bit of class.'

"Oscar was thrilled. He could hardly contain his delight. 'My dear friend, what a gem you are. I wish I had known you in life. I am certain we would have got along well – you with your divine music and me with my superb verbal and literary dexterity. What a combination! How could we have failed to be the best of companions?'

"After the ceremony, the only woman present kissed the sculpture, leaving the imprint of her lips on the stone. That was the beginning of a sensual craze, which became one of Oscar's consuming passions. We all hugged and kissed him. Even Chopin, after his fine words, forgot his reserved manner and gave him a hug. Yes, I'm sure you'll agree that seemed to be the end of our dear friend's depression."

"It did, but not quite, for as you know, there was more to come."

"Indeed! Not long afterwards, he discovered a tarpaulin thrown over the tomb by the order of the *gendarmerie*, for there were complaints made to the authorities that it was indecent and offensive to public taste. What an outrage. What a scandal. He was livid."

"Horrified, I'd say. After him waiting so long, it was a terrible blow."

"God, he went on and on until he had us all but demented. You must remember him pacing up and down, his hands clasped tightly behind him, muttering away like some lunatic. 'How could the Parisians of all people be offended by a work of art? It is so unworthy of them. The city of light, that city of art and culture, how could they do such a thing to a work of artistic excellence?'

"He would say this or the likes every time he looked down over Père Lachaise. After a while, he relented, saying proudly, 'The Parisians love me; they adore me with a passion... ah, it must be an aberration. We all suffer them from time to time, so why not the Parisians? They are human after all. They will realise their mistake. It is just a matter of time. They know genius when they see it.'

"You know, Sophie, his vanity knows no limit. Still, the poor soul had waited so long for his tomb that it was heartbreaking to see him still suffering. You know what he was like. He would sit there for hours on end, just staring down at the tarpaulin, muttering away to himself. It was a depressing and disturbing sight and, really, rather pathetic to see a soul in such a state over a piece of stone.

"Poor Epstein," Marie continued. "He was furious and had to do his finishing touches to his masterpiece under cover. How demeaning. The moment the *gendarmes* turned their backs he would be under the tarpaulin chipping away. It had taken two years to complete his work at his studio in London before having it shipped to Paris. He was infuriated to distraction by this insult meted out by the authorities. He argued like mad with them, but to no avail. They wouldn't budge and told him to go away and stop pestering them. It remained hidden from public view for another two years, to the dismay of Epstein and to the horror of Oscar.

"Ah! Poor soul, he descended into the manic stage of his depression. God help him. Whatever we did, it made no difference. He sank deeper and deeper into himself, becoming paranoid and withdrawn – it seemed to be the bleakest part of his Purgatory."

"Then, the terrible news came."

"Oh! Don't remind me."

"Poor Cyril, what a way to die, killed by a sniper's bullet fighting in a war without a cause. Such a waste, such a terrible waste of a young life..."

"Such a waste of millions of young lives," sighed Marie.

8

"It devastated him. It should never have happened."

"The War to End All Wars," Marie cynically said. "The Great War; Fighting for the Freedom of Small Nations – fighting for Little Belgium. They had so many names for it, always trying to sanitise their folly – all those generals playing chess with the lives of innocent young men. Cyril, poor Cyril, he should have been at home rather than spilling his blood on the fields of France for no reason at all. He died in vain, like all the other Cyril's – a useless sacrifice to feed the bloodlust of maniacal generals and ignorant politicians. Men are children for most of their lives, always wanting to play soldiers. They take a lifetime to grow up. When they finally do, they cry into their pillows for their lost childhoods. Pathetic, isn't it? Thank God we women are a cut above all that."

"Yes, I know exactly what you mean. I can't in my life fathom what it is we see in them. They are the pits at times."

"Those two years were the most awful, weren't they? You remember Alfred de Musset trying to comfort Oscar for days on end, but without any success. There was no pacifying him. The wasted life of Cyril preyed on his mind. He blamed himself for his death – said if he'd been a better father and had not embroiled himself in the scandals, perhaps Cyril would never have volunteered in an idle exercise with him throwing his life away. Sometimes I think he's a fool visiting the Knowledge Zone so often, if he hadn't done so, he would have been spared the knowledge of Cyril's fate."

"We all have the freedom to visit the Zone. It's unfair to criticise him for doing what he's entitled to do."

"I'm not. All I'm saying is that he spends an inordinate amount of time there, that it can't be good for him. Sometimes it's better not to know too much of the world you've left behind."

"Maybe you're right. I rarely visit the place. I find it oppressive, all that knowledge coming at you in all directions. Oscar loves it though, can't get enough of it."

"Then one day, without warning, "Marie beamed, "the tarpaulin vanished from his tomb, and so did his depression. He was so relieved he cried for days on end. Yes, it was the end of his depression. It had been a tough two years for him."

"For him, for heaven's sake, Marie, it was as tough for us and all around him who had to cope with him."

"But, give him his due, he put it behind him and did what he does best – he threw a party. You remember that bash he threw to celebrate the demise of the tarpaulin?"

"Do I? How could I forget? It was one of his best. You have to give it to him – he knows how to put on a do. The man has class – a bit off-centre, but real all the same."

9

Cloud Twenty-Two

"It's great reminiscing," Sophie went on, "but what about this odd behaviour you're on about?"

"Patience, Sophie. Don't rush me, I'm getting there."

"At this rate, we'll be here until the cows come home. Come now, let's hear it or forget it."

"Just let me remind you of a few more things first."

"Must you?"

"Afraid so."

"Oh, very well, but don't take forever."

"Well, after the party, as you know, he was his old self, entertaining us with his wit and wisdom. Whenever he had the chance of doing so, he also gave readings of his latest literary efforts. He was at his best. The soul of the party – of any party – but there was still one thing bugging him."

"Which was?" asked her now exasperated friend.

"Dear me, Sophie, you must remember. We were enjoying a picnic on Cloud Twenty-Two, some years after the unveiling. Chopin was there, along with Balzac, Sarah Bernhardt, Musset and our darling, Ingres. Oscar was going on about the injustice of his situation, of him of all people, not going straight to Paradise. He went on and on, driving us mad with his incessant moaning and groaning. We thought he was over that obsession, but no, far from it. He had such an effect on all of us, we kind of ignored him and gave him a little of the old cold shoulder treatment, then, if you remember, he turned to Balzac and said in that matter-of-fact way of his, 'Tell me Honoré, my dear fellow, did you expect to be in Paradise instead of this dive?'

"Balzac looked at him in astonishment and said, 'You're not serious. Me, in Paradise – my God, man, have you completely lost your marbles – Paradise and the likes of me – no! I don't think so. Not a chance.'

"'Why not,' enquired Oscar.

"Balzac looked nonplussed. 'Why not? Well, my dear, deluded friend, to start with, it just isn't me, is it? Can you really imagine me, of all people, with all of my hang-ups being welcomed into Paradise – that is, if there is one? Not likely, I'd say. Really, with my attitude to religion, expecting to go to Paradise would be a non-starter. No, it's not my scene. Surely you must know that.'

"'No. I'm afraid I don't.'

"'Well, Oscar, it's like this. I never considered myself Paradise material. Never gave it a thought for a moment. You know, to be honest, I never believed it existed. I have always been a bit of a cynic when it comes to believing in things one can only experience when one is dead. It is not for me. It is as simple as that.'

"'You, not Paradise material – how very, very odd?' he said, squinting at Balzac.

"'Odd! What's so odd about it?' Balzac replied.

"'Well, you are a writer, for Christ's sake, a man of letters. How can someone so gifted not believe in a higher power, not believe in God or a God of some kind? It just seems so odd. Not right at all for a man of letters not to believe in God or some kind of hereafter, not right at all.'

"'Balls! I never said I didn't believe in God,' snapped Balzac.

"'Well, what did you mean then?'

"'Only that the vision of all of us in some distant Paradise, being good, polite and decent to each other – without any crosswords, seems rather dull and unappetising. Can you imagine, being forever in Paradise with someone you couldn't stand the sight of? Being compelled to be decent and friendly to them? Sounds rather nightmarish to me, sounds more like Hell. I will settle for this, Oscar, even with all its limitations. I would rather believe that Paradise was down there on earth, with the living, being looked over by an ever-loving and caring God, than one sitting on a throne in a distant kingdom of peace and harmony, where we would have to humour our enemies, forgive their tantrums and smile forever at their peculiarities. No thank you, I'll settle for what I've got here if you don't mind,' he replied.

"'Listen here, Honoré, if you don't believe in Paradise, you cannot believe in God. It makes no sense. You can't have one without the other,' Oscar informed him.

"'Is that so? Well, I can,' Balzac replied, as casual as can be.

"'I take it you don't believe in Hell or Purgatory either?'

"'Maybe, maybe not – it all depends.'

"Oscar took a deep breath and cried, 'Depends – depends on *what*? Whatever do you mean, maybe, maybe not? Either you do, or you don't. What kind of crazy answer is that?'

"'An honest one, that's what.'

"'I see,' he said, looking Balzac up and down.

"'Well, some days I do, some days I don't – if there is a Hell, maybe that's on earth too. Maybe it's a matter of choice. If you want your life to be like Hell, chances are that's how it will be. Then again, if you want to live a decent and honourable life – you know, do things that *normal* people do, like working, finding love, marrying, rearing a family and enjoying life – maybe that will be your Paradise. There were times in my life when I thought I was in Hell, and times when I knew for sure I was in Paradise. There were occasions when I was with a beautiful woman and it felt like Paradise. Then again, I can remember women that put me through Hell, and did so with relish.'

"'Very interesting, Honoré – if you are such a philosopher, then what about Purgatory – do you believe in Purgatory?'

"'No... not at the moment,' Balzac replied, as he made for the picnic box.

"'Christ! What do you mean by that?' Oscar asked in an animated fashion.

"'As I said, sometimes I do, sometimes I don't. It's simple to understand. At the moment, I don't,' he said as he rummaged through the picnic basket.

"'I see. But if you don't believe in Purgatory, then what is this?' he said gesticulating with his hands. 'How do you explain *this* place?'

"'I can't – I haven't the faintest idea. To tell the truth, I don't give a toss. It's irrelevant.'

"Oscar turned pale and barked, 'Irrelevant!'

"'Yes. Very much irrelevant,' Balzac said as he bit into a cheese-and-tomato sandwich. 'We're here, whatever or wherever this place is, and really, there's nothing to be done about it. This is your destiny –. Accept it. Accept your destiny. That is what most wise men would do so, if you are wise, Oscar, you should do likewise. Why go on taxing your mind on something like this. It's such a waste of mental energy and so very, very boring.'

"'Are you telling me, Honoré, that you're not curious in any way about why you are here, why you are not in Paradise or Hell?'

"'No! Confused, maybe, but not curious. I've been here a good while now and the curiosity I had in my early days has long gone.

"'What you mean is that you don't have an opinion on such an important issue, 'Oscar said, rattled at Balzac's indifference to his situation.

"'If you say so,' Balzac said as he finished off his sandwich.

"'Indeed I do. I can't believe you of all people are just accepting your situation. I'm amazed that a person like yourself with such an enquiring mind is submitting to the situation you find yourself in and without question. You disappoint me, Honoré, you really do.'

"'Give it a rest will you,' Balzac muttered as he again dipped into the picnic basket for another sandwich.

"'I give up,' Oscar spluttered.

"'Can I have that in writing?' Balzac replied, before taking a big bite of his sandwich.

"Oscar ignored him. He looked around to see whom else he could interrogate. He was out for an argument and determined to have one, if not with Balzac then with some other poor soul. The nearest was Sarah Bernhardt, who was minding her own business

12

reading a slim volume on *Three Simple Ways of Understanding the Complexities of the Male of the Species.*

"'Sarah,' he said, slipping his arm around her waist, 'what about you, my dear? I am sure you, being the angel you are, believe in Paradise. Do you think you should be with the angels instead of in this God-forsaken place?'

"She burst out laughing and could hardly contain herself. Oscar was far from amused. 'What's up with you?' he asked.

"'Me! She replied once she had caught her breath. 'The likes of me, in Paradise, with my reputation – the only place I ever expected to end up in was Hell. Being here is a bonus. Believe me.'

"'What on earth are you saying – bonus? And what reputation are you on about?'

"'You're kidding,' Sarah laughed, dabbing her eyes. 'Where do you want me to begin?'

"'Your reputation isn't that bad. I have known you for years and can't remember you with a reputation of the kind you are suggesting.'

"'Dear me, Oscar, you're such a fool at times,' she replied. 'Your memory's gone dim if you don't remember the kind of reputation I had. But all actresses had a reputation. It was par for the course. One wouldn't get far without one. Shows how little you do remember of me.'

"'Nonsense! I remember you well and without a reputation. I remember you as a great actress and a fine person,' he declared. 'You would have been a perfect candidate for Paradise. Talent, like genius, my dear, belongs in Paradise.'

"'You want to bet?' she laughed. 'I never believed in an afterlife and never gave the concept of Paradise any thought at all. I did when I was a kid, but real life soon put an end to that. Put it this way; I'm like Honoré. Even if there is a Paradise, it's certainly not for me. If anything, I expected to go to Hell if there is one, but my reputation evidently wasn't bad enough, so to my surprise, I ended up here. Purgatory is a bonus to me. I'm a grateful soul.'

"'Then how do you explain this place? God, you are not like, Honoré, are you, not giving a damn and just accepting matters as they are?'

"'Oh, I wouldn't go as far as that. The truth is I don't know. Maybe it's a trick of some kind,' she suggested.

"'A trick!' he yelled.

"'Yes – a trick – a trick of the mind. It is quite common, I'm told. You know what I'm on about, don't you?'

"'No, I'm afraid I don't,' Oscar replied. 'Are you saying we are just imagining this existence? That it's a trick of the mind – that this place doesn't exist, that it is all in the mind, some kind of hallucination – a collective illusion. Is that what you're saying?'

'"Yes. If you put it that way, that is exactly what I am saying. You are right – it's a collective illusion of confused souls. If you think back over your life I'm sure you'll remember many a trick of the mind that left you confused and seeking some explanation.'

'"Confused? My dear, whatever are you saying? I have never suffered such a condition. My mind is always crystal clear. I am never confused.'

'"I'd say you're very confused – a master of confusion,' Sarah replied.

'"He's too confused to realise it,' Balzac giggled as he continued to search the picnic basket for more sustenance. 'If you weren't confused, you wouldn't be talking such *merde*. Be a good fellow, give it a rest, and leave Sarah and the rest of us alone. Can't you see she's reading a very delicate subject matter?'

"Oscar took the book from Sarah and flicked through its thin pages. 'There's nothing simple about the male species, my dear, I can assure you,' he said as he tossed the book back into her lap. 'You ought not to read such nonsense. We men are complicated beings. It will take more than this thin volume to understand us.'

"Sarah burst out laughing and said, 'What a pompous fellow you are.'

"Yes," Sophie said. "He was a bit too much, wasn't he?"

"But he wasn't finished. He looked over at Chopin, who was examining the contents of a sandwich.

'"Ah, Frédéric,' Oscar said as he wandered over towards him. 'My dear chap, surely you expected Paradise as a just reward for your genius and the life you led.'

"Chopin looked up at him. 'Whatever makes you think that? Why should I have expected such a reward? I am, after all, just a mortal blessed with a gift. As for leading a decent life, I'm afraid you're quite mistaken. I'm not quite as you imagine. Why should I expect special treatment?'

"Oscar laughed at his musical friend's protestations. 'Why – that's rather obvious, is it not?'

'"Is it?' Chopin queried, as he picked the chives from his sandwich and disposed of them. 'It's far from obvious to me. You'd better enlighten me.'

'"My dear, man,' Oscar said as he sat next to him. 'You are talking nonsense. Your life has been exemplary. Your commitment to your art is without question. Your intercourse with your fellow beings is that of honesty, honour, and integrity. I would have thought that would have guaranteed you a place in Paradise.'

"'Stop it, Oscar, you're embarrassing me.' Chopin answered. 'Stop fooling about and enjoy this picnic.'

Oscar sprang to his feet. 'So you never had any wish to be in Paradise, to experience the divine afterlife, to play your music at the ultimate venue? Is that what you're saying?'

"'I didn't say that. Of course, I had given it thought. Who wouldn't? If you believe in God, then it is something you think about, something you toss about in your mind now and then and I certainly had, but I was never obsessed about it.'

"'Obsessed! Are you saying I am?' Oscar cried, looking a bit fazed.

"'No! Not at all, but you do get carried away at times. All I meant to say was that I would have liked to believe I was good enough for such an elevation. Unfortunately, it was not to be. However, I'm quite taken by this place. It has a peaceful ambience that suits me. You understand what I'm saying?'

"'I am damned if I do!' Oscar roared. 'Ambience my arse! Dear me, Frédéric, there is nothing is redeeming about this place – ambience indeed. Dear! Dear! How easily you are taken in.'

"'No! You're so wrong,' he replied, 'I always take in my surroundings, and these surroundings suit me just fine. If I am easily taken in, then I am happy to be so. This may not be the Paradise we've all imagined, but it is the next best thing. You need to take things as they come, my friend, and maybe then you'll enjoy your residency here.'

"Oscar glared at poor Chopin and barked, 'Residency! You are talking as though we were doing a summer season at the end of Brighton Pier. As for enjoying the place, I don't have the faintish to enjoy it. I'm not supposed to be here. Can you not see that? How many times have I to tell you. Do you not understand the dilemma I am in? Really, Frédéric, you do surprise me at times. You must know I am destined for a far better place than this. God, does nobody understand me?'

"We all looked up from our picnic and gave a deep collective sigh.

"'Really, Oscar,' Chopin said, 'if you were destined for a better place, that is where you'd be. As for the Brighton Pier, you have lost me. Is it some kind of English joke?'

"He wasn't finished. Looking around at the others, he caught the eye of poor Ingres, who was also minding his own business, eyeing up my dimensions. You know what he is like, Sophie. He has been after me to sit for him ever since he arrived at the Reservation. As you know, I was having none of it for he wanted me to pose in the buff. I am far from a prude, but there is a limit.

15

"'Ingres, old boy,' Oscar said as he sat down next to him, 'surely you, with all your outstanding talents, must have expected better than this.'

"'Never gave it a thought,' Ingres replied, not taking his eyes off me. 'Anyway, what is wrong with it here? Frédéric is right. It does have an ambience about it that is comforting and relaxing. It is so relaxing that I find I'm enjoying my art more here than I did on earth – if Marie would pose for me that would be Paradise itself. No, Oscar, there is nothing wrong with this place. We have all we need. We have all we ever had on earth, even more. We have health. We can't be hurt physically. We have the best of accommodation. You only have to look at your abode to realise that. The weather is suburb – we have excellent entertainment and company. As for money, we have it but have no need for it. We have the advantage of the Knowledge Zone up on Cloud Eighty-Eight, one place you regularly take advantage of. Up there, we don't only study history, but also have the advantage of observing the present culture on earth – another thing that you take every advantage of. We have everything – everything, that is, except sex, which we survive happily without, so, my dear friend, you should take it easy. Enjoy your Purgatory and just, relax.'

"'Relax!' Oscar bellowed. 'Relax, without sex? What kind of idiot are you? You can't be serious. Relax indeed. How can any sane man relax without sex?'

"We all burst out laughing, but Oscar didn't think it at all funny.

"'Really, Oscar,' Ingres continued, 'it's quite easy to survive here without it. I have, and so has Frédéric. It's even improved his music. Isn't that so, Frédéric?'

"'Certainly,' Chopin replied. 'Anyway, sex was always overrated.'

"Oscar shook his head in disbelief. He couldn't believe what he was hearing. 'Overrated? Well, you didn't think so when you were with George Sand, that voluptuous woman from Nohant, did you? By all accounts, you couldn't keep your hands off her.'

"Chopin wasn't too pleased by Oscar's remark. It was clear by the look on his face that he wasn't going to get dragged into talking about George Sand. Oscar trespassing on a part of his life that he knew was taboo, rattled Chopin.

"'And you, Sarah, you've survived happily without it, haven't you?' enquired Ingres.

"'Certainly,' she replied. 'I must confess though I do miss it. It was after all, a consolation for me. It was divine to receive pleasure with little effort. It would be agreeable indeed if it was available here, but it doesn't bother me that much. After all, as Chopin says, sex was always overrated.'

16

"'Overrated!' Oscar gasped. 'How can sex be overrated? It is what we all lived and breathed for, was it not.'

"'No!' We replied in harmony. He looked at us as though we were insane.

"'There you are, Oscar. You can survive happily without it. It's quite easy. It's all in the mind is this sex lark. I don't even think about it anymore. It does me no harm. I've never been happier. I don't need it,' declared Ingres, who I'm certain was enjoying winding up Oscar.

"'Then you can't be normal,' Oscar replied. 'I have never heard such nonsense. All those nude paintings you have painted of women have warped your mind. Aren't we men supposed to think about sex every thirty seconds or so?'

"'That's a myth, for Christ's sake,' Ingres cried.

"'It certainly is not. I think of it continuously,' Oscar bragged.

"'That's your problem.'

"'I beg your pardon, Sarah. Sex is no problem to me. It's the lack of it that is,' he sighed.

"'Sounds like it to me,' she giggled.

"'Nonsense – sex has never been any trouble to me. I can handle anything thrown at me. As I said, I think of it continually, always have and always will,' he boasted.

"'It's alright thinking of it, but do you dream of it, my friend?' Balzac interposed

"'What! Dreams! Why do you ask?' Oscar cried, alarmed by Balzac's question.

"'Because the only sexual thrill you're ever likely to experience here is in your dreams. You won't find it anywhere, but in your dreams,' Balzac laughingly replied.

"Oscar's face dropped. 'But, I don't dream,' he declared as he surveyed our faces for some glimmer of help.

"We all looked at him in surprise.

"'Oh! That's tough,' replied Balzac, unashamedly rubbing it in.

"'Anyway, what do you mean, you don't dream,' asked Sarah. 'Everyone dreams. It's the most natural thing to do. This place would be Hell without them.'

"Oscar turned white and declared, 'Well, I don't, and it is Hell. I did a lot of dreaming in my earthly existence; indeed, night and day, but I haven't dreamt once since my arrival here.'

"'Oh! You're breaking my heart,' laughed Balzac. 'There'll be no sex for you, then. You'll have a monk's existence. Not just for now but for eternity. Don't worry about it, though. You'll soon get used to not having it. Give it time. Abstinence is, after all, the way to salvation.'

17

"'I don't think this is a laughing matter at all,' Oscar scolded. 'This is serious stuff. I need sexual stimulation to survive, otherwise my equilibrium will be out of tilt, and I will end up irritating all around me.'

"'You don't say,' laughed Ingres.

"'I do. I'm here for years without any kind of sexual contact,' Oscar complained. 'It's so unfair. This place is a prison set in beautiful surroundings. I need sex, not abstinence. Does nobody understand me? Does no soul understand my suffering?'

"Again, we all looked at him and sighed.

"'Oh. So that's what's wrong with you, is it? Your equilibrium is out of tilt,' Balzac said, smiling at his frustrated friend. 'We've all been wondering what's up with you. We should have known it was sex. For heaven's sake, you've survived years without it, so why the long face. It's done you no harm, has it – you haven't complained about it before, so why now? There's no reason why you can't spend eternity chaste. It's no big deal. No big deal at all.'

"'No big deal!' Oscar yelled 'Eternity, without sex and you say it is no big deal! I need sex as I need oxygen.'

"'Well you had better start dreaming, Oscar, or we're in for a rough time with you gasping for air every thirty seconds or so,' Balzac replied.

"'It's inhuman not to be able have sex. It's a kind of natural right – isn't that so, Alfred?' he asked Musset who had been sitting there enjoying Oscar's performance. 'It seems rather mean to exclude sex. Having sex in your dreams is no substitute for the real thing. There's never been a healthier pursuit in life than sex. It's an integral part of the Human Condition.'

"'I'm telling you, Oscar, do as Ingres says, and relax. It's no good philosophising about sex here. Forget about it. It's a waste of time fretting over such a thing. Just relax, my friend and take Purgatory in your stride,' Musset advised his friend.

"'Huh!' Oscar replied with a shrug of the shoulders. 'Relax, indeed. Well, Alfred, I suppose you dream.'

"'Take no notice of him, Oscar – he's just showing off,' Sarah said, giving the wit a playful hug.

"'All right, Alfred,' he replied. 'So, you have your dreams to stimulate you. So what – but did you expect your dreams to be in Paradise, instead of here, in this crazy, sexless place?'

"'Really, Oscar,' he replied, 'there'd be no need for dreams of sex in Paradise, would there? For surely Paradise would be on a high plane, a more sophisticated realm. We have everything here, so why be so stressed out about it? There's really no point to it. So you don't dream. It's no real tragedy. As for sex, it's not worth worrying about. All you have to do to satisfy your sexual frustration is to dream.'

"'You are all deluding yourselves,' Oscar snarled. 'Ingres, you are wrong, completely wrong, for things are not as you maintain. You all go on as though this was Paradise itself. It is not. It is far from it. Just listen to yourselves, rambling on about how grand the place is – that the way to sexual satisfaction is through dreams. What rot! The whole place is just sterile, and so are we. All the wonderful flowers that adorn the place have no perfume. The birds that flutter about cannot sing. If there is no song from a bird, then its essence is gone. The food that looks so appetising has no taste. What looks like wine or beer is nothing but water. Even the tears we shed are saltless. If we kiss, it is like kissing cold stone. To enjoy these 'pleasures' we have to imagine them – or, to be more realistic, we have to delude ourselves that the wine is vintage, the foods is exquisite and the birds sing their songs of love as we breathe in the scent of flowers. So don't tell me, Ingres, that all is rosy in Purgatory, for it is not. I should not be here. This is not my true destiny.'

"'You don't say. If you feel so robbed of your rightful destiny, then I suggest you trot along to the Pearly Gates and ask Saint Peter why you're here instead of Paradise and give these poor souls a rest,' suggested Musset.

"'Saint Peter!' exclaimed Oscar. 'You mean to say, Alfred, we can talk to him?'

"We all looked at him. Musset shook his head and exclaimed, 'You're telling me, you didn't know?'

"'I had no idea. How could I? Nobody informed me. You mean to say you all knew?'

"We all nodded. The poor soul, he was crestfallen.

"'Great! Just great – why didn't anyone tell me?' He complained.

"'Are you saying you weren't informed of this at the Reservation Reception Centre when you arrived here?' enquired Ingres.

"'Nobody told me,' he replied.

"'Who was your facilitator?' I enquired; amazed that he was unaware of this right."

"'Seurat.'

"'Seurat!' Musset cried. 'Well, that's typical. He can be as daft as a brush at times. All guides have a brief to explain the Rules of the House. When he welcomed you and showed you to your quarters, he should have mentioned your right to visit Saint Peter.'

"'Rules of the House – he never mentioned any rules to me, never mind Saint Peter,' exclaimed Oscar.

"'Are you sure?' asked Musset.

Oscar, scratching his head, was deep in thought. 'Come to think of it, Seurat did give me a book, yes a Book of Rules he called it. I tossed it in the rubbish where I usually throw rules.'

"'There you are,' Sarah said. 'If you'd bothered to read it you wouldn't be in such a pickle, wouldn't you?'

"'It's like this, Oscar,' explained Musset, 'If you'd bothered to read the book you would have discovered that all souls have a right to visit Saint Peter at the Pearly Gates and to ask any question they wish. You can only have one audience with him. That's your lot.'

"'Right, that seems fair. That's exactly what I will do,' Oscar said, waving his hands in the air. 'But how, what is the procedure?'

"'That's easy,' replied Musset. 'Go to the Pearly Gates. You can see their glow way over there in the distance, at the far end of Cloud Ninety-Nine. It's a good seven-day hike from here, mind you. All you have to do in make an appointment with the secretariat, and then off you go. Would you like me to go with you?'

"'That's very civil of you, Alfred,' he said. 'I would be delighted to have your company. You can tell me of your dreams on the way. Where did you say I would find this Secretariat?'

"'At the foot of Cloud Two,' shouted Ingres, 'but I wouldn't bother. It never does any good. You'll be wasting your time. Now give it a rest and let us enjoy our picnic.'

"Oscar stood there, one hand on hip and the other leaning on his cane."

"Yes," said Sophie, "he can be a bit theatrical at times."

"'Picnics!' he cried. 'I can't think of picnics at a time like this. What do you mean I will be wasting my time? Explain yourself.'

"'Look here, Oscar, I don't want to be a killjoy, but take a little good advice and forget this Saint Peter lark. I'm telling you, it will do you no good at all. Nothing ever comes of such visits – believe me,' Ingres pleaded with him.

"'At the foot of Cloud Two,' shouted Ingres, 'but I wouldn't bother. It never does any good. You'll be wasting your time. Now give it a rest and let us enjoy our picnic.'

"Oscar stood there, one hand on hip and the other leaning on his cane."

"Yes," said Sophie, "he can be a bit theatrical at times."

"'Picnics!' he cried. 'I can't think of picnics at a time like this. What do you mean I will be wasting my time? Explain yourself.'

"'Look here, Oscar, I don't want to be a killjoy, but take a little good advice and forget this Saint Peter lark. I'm telling you, it will do you no good at all. Nothing ever comes of such visits – believe me,' Ingres pleaded with him.

"Balzac waited until the last remnants of the sandwich were gone then put his arm around Oscar's shoulders and said, 'You're reading me wrong, Oscar. I already know. I don't need reminding as to why. What I really mean to say, is that making such a visit is rather a useless exercise, just as Ingres says – it's pointless. Nothing good ever comes of such visits, for if I or any of us were destined for Paradise, we wouldn't be here, would we, we would have been sent directly to Paradise. What's the point of asking Saint Peter such a stupid question as to why you're not in Paradise when you know damned well what the answer will be. If you visit him, you stand the risk, not only of being disappointed but disillusioned and more distracted than you already are. Here, take one of these,' Balzac said, offering him a cucumber sandwich.

"Oscar pushed it away in disgust.

"'What do you mean, stupid?' he cried, tense and agitated. 'There is nothing stupid in asking why a genius such as I, a soul of distinction, is not in Paradise. It seems a natural thing to do. Mistakes are made, you know, and if a mistake has been made concerning me, then it must be put right. It is only fair. Stupid indeed – we'll see.'

"'Well, you've been warned,' Balzac said as he returned to the picnic basket.

"Oscar turned to me and, smiling, said, 'My dear Marie, surely you've visited Peter.'

"'I have,' I sighed, 'and what a mistake that was. I went out of curiosity, of course. It was too much of a temptation, I couldn't resist it, and I wished I had. It was a humiliating experience, not what I expected at all.'

"'Whatever happened?'

"'I'd rather not say. Like Ingres, I suggest you forget the idea and have a sandwich instead,' I said.

"'You can't just leave it at that. What do you mean it was humiliating? What could be humiliating about visiting Saint Peter?'

"'As I said, Oscar, forget it. It will be nothing but a dead-end journey, believe me. You're being given good advice – take it.'

"'Well, damn you all,' he cried, 'I'm off. Come, Alfred, let us make tracks and leave these picnickers to their cucumber sandwiches.'

21

"As I remember, Marie, he didn't waste much time," Sophie said as she fanned herself.

"I'll say. He and Musset were off within the hour, ready to do battle with the saint."

"This is all very interesting, Marie, but remind me, if you don't mind, what's this to do with his odd behaviour? What we have talked about is Oscar's usual odd behaviour, if you know what I mean. Come now; tell me what this is all about before I burst with frustration."

"Dear me, Sophie, you can be very impatient at times… Oh, here comes Alfred. Let him enlighten you."

Alfred de Musset came skipping up the steps towards them without a care in the world. He was in one of his sprightly moods. There was no soul at the Reservation quite like that of Musset, the *enfant terrible*, of the French literati. Even with all the limitations the Reservation threw up it was fair to say, he was enjoying his Purgatory.

"Good day, ladies. You seem to be having a good wag. Am I missing anything?"

"You could say that. It's Oscar. Marie says he's been acting oddly of late."

"Ah! Well, that's nothing new," he laughed. "If Oscar wasn't acting like that, that would be odd."

"But she says he's acting *really* oddly."

"Well, that sounds serious. Tell me more."

"Don't hold your breath. I've been waiting for her to tell me about this odd behaviour and I'm still waiting. She insists on going back in time to when he arrived here before she'll reveal this so-called odd behaviour of his."

"You remember, Alfred, the time you and Oscar visited Saint Peter after Oscar interrogated us all at that picnic on Cloud Twenty-Two way back in 1918? Tell Sophie what happened when you escorted him to the Pearly Gates."

"Oh, that! God, that's some time ago. Give me a moment –Yes, I remember it. If you have the time, I'll tell you the whole story," Musset said as he sat between Sophie and Marie.

"I'm in no hurry," answered Marie. "What about you, Sophie?"

"Well, if it's going to help to reveal Oscar's odd behaviour that you seem reluctant to tell me about, yes, I've got the time."

"We left in rather a hurry. Oscar thought he could just turn up at the Secretariat, get himself an appointment with the saint, and Bob's your uncle. He was a bit deflated when he was told he'd have to wait his turn like any other soul. He can be rather naive at times. When it comes to the practicalities of Purgatory, he is useless. We had to wait a few days, which didn't improve his humour. We then collected a few provisions and headed off. He was in the most confident of moods. I just couldn't tell him what lay ahead.

"On the way, he told me about his ill-fated passion for Bosie, Lord Alfred Douglas, and how he became infatuated with that spoilt upper-crust brat. He told of how he wined, dined and indulged him in every possible way only to continuously be abused insulted by him. He seemed rather bitter about the experience."

"Oh, he was," sighed Sophie. "Look what fate dished out to him?"

"Oh, yes – the trials. Yes, he talked of them. He told how the Establishment and most of his friends turned against him. How one moment he was the talk of the town, invited to the most glamorous and prestigious homes in the land, courted by journals and papers of the day, and the next, a pariah, ridiculed by the very society who had laughed at his witticisms and sought his company. What hypocrites they turned out to be.

"He recalled his conviction and his stay in Reading Gaol. It left a scar on him, a scar never to heal. If there was ever a wounded soul, then it was Oscar Wilde. As we headed off over Cloud Six, he recited *The Ballad of Reading Gaol*. It was very moving. There was passion in the way he recited it, as though he was living and experiencing every word of it. He said he was at his lowest ebb, exiled in France when he wrote it. It had been swirling around his head ever since he was in prison but only found the time and presence of mind to write it down when in exile. He said writing it was a torturous business. A task that should have been so easy for him turned into a burden. He said he knew when he had completed the poem that he had nothing more to give. Unfortunately, as we all know, it was to be his final literary effort of any real worth.

"To my surprise, as we neared the Valley of Tears over on Cloud Six, he stopped at its ivy-clad entrance and peered through the gate. He opened it, and for a second I feared he was going to enter, but he just stood there for a while, looking deep into the valley. Thankfully, he turned and walked away, leaving the temptation of revisiting his earthly sorrows behind. He didn't say, but I believe he was aware that if he ever wanted to attempt to purge his sins, he must travel through the valley.

"As we turned towards Cloud Seven and through the Willow Tree Grove, he began to weep as he talked of his children, Cyril and Vyvyan, his voice breaking as he remembered his wife Constance. It was with sorrow that he had to leave them behind because of his forced exile. He said he loved them truly but he broke their hearts by his outrageous behaviour and humiliated and deeply hurt Constance with his relationship with that brat Alfred Douglas and his many other unconventional associates. He told of his wandering around Europe, lost and unhappy, until his soul passed on in the dingy Hôtel d'Alsace in Paris. He told of his loss of ambition to write while in exile. He tried but was unable to concentrate enough to produce anything of any literary value. He realised that it was all over, that he was a spent force. Time had marked his card, and he would never reach the literary potential that was once within his grasp, which he had believed was his destiny. He would exit this world hated, loathed and misunderstood. A beautiful and sensitive soul is our dear Oscar."

"Sure is," Marie sighed.

"Tell us what happened when you arrived at the Pearly Gates," Sophie pressed Musset.

"As we neared them I detected that he was becoming a bit uncertain as to the wisdom of this visit. He must have wondered why so many other souls hadn't bothered. Perhaps he should have listened to those he had traversed the Reservation with rather than go boldly where his instincts led. We finally reached the summit of Cloud Ninety-Nine and he looked in amazement at the spectacular view before him. In the distance was a golden glow from the Pearly Gates that stretched as far as the eye could see. He couldn't wait to get there. He ran down towards the gates, often skipping as he went. The fool, he didn't know what he was in for. Once near the gates, he calmed down a tad. His gaiety was visibly subsiding.

"As we stood in front of the gates, he was becoming very nervous, twitching and sweating profusely. I thought he was about to turn tail and run, but he took a deep breath, kept his cool and rang the bell. Through the gates, we saw the most beautiful of sights. We could see just a glimpse of that land of milk and honey. That land we all yearn for, but out of reach to us lost souls of Père Lachaise. Then through the haze appeared Saint Peter himself, dressed in a very simple magnolia gown and sandals.

"Oscar stepped forward. 'Good day, brother,' said the saint, offering Oscar his hand.

"'Good day to you, Peter,' he replied as he grasped the holy hand. 'You don't mind me calling you Peter, do you?' he asked. 'I dislike formality – so very English.'

"'Not at all – I believe you have a question to ask of me?'

"'Yes,' Oscar replied. 'Why am I here in Purgatory? Why am I not in Paradise? Why am I denied entry into my rightful home? Why can't you just open these gates and let me in?'

"Peter smiled and asked us to take a seat, which we did. Then he calmly said, 'That's four questions and all without an answer. I'm only the Keeper of the Gate, brother, and the guardian of its keys. It is not for me to allow or refuse you entry. If you were destined to enter, these gates would be open for you. You would not need to ask me such questions.'

"'What must I do to gain access?' Oscar asked.

"Peter smoothed his thick white beard with his right hand. 'Put it this way, brother. It is how you have acted and lived your earthly life that is all-important. That is what determines your destiny, nothing else.'

"'I see!' Oscar exclaimed. 'Well, I would say I have been a rather wayward soul at times, but I always thought I had led a reasonably good life. There were a few diversions and deviations along the way, but nothing to worry myself about. I would say I have led a reasonable and near on decent life. Some would challenge that, no doubt based on my turbulent emotional life, but I would say, in my own way, I lived my life as honestly as I knew how.'

"Peter gave a deep sigh. 'Wait a moment.' He left but returned shortly and placed a large black book on a marble table in front of Oscar, who recoiled at its very sight. 'Every mortal soul has a book in which his venial sins and misdemeanours are recorded,' explained the saint, as he tapped his bony fingers on the book cover on which was inscribed, in bold red lettering, 'OSCAR WILDE'. 'This, brother, is part of the testimony of your life on earth since you became aware of what was right and wrong. Nothing is spared, nothing at all. All the hurt and suffering you inflicted on your fellow beings is listed here.'

"Oscar looked at me in horror.

"'That's some size book, Oscar,' I whispered.

"'I'd say,' he sighed, his eyes fixed on the book.

"'You must remember, brother, what is recorded in this book are only your venial sins that bar your entry into Paradise, not mortal sins, which would condemn you to Hell,' the saint informed him.

"'Oh! I see,' Oscar replied, 'Did I commit any mortal sins, then?'

"'You should know that yourself,' Peter replied. 'No, you didn't, as a matter of fact, but you certainly had a brush with them on several occasions. I am sure you don't need to be reminded of them. It's those mortal sins that you are free of – if you weren't, you wouldn't be standing here, talking to me; you'd be warming your soul at Lucifer's fireside.'

"'Oh! No mortal sins – that's good to know,' Oscar happily replied. 'So all my detractors on earth who condemned me as the foulest sinner ever, a sinner unworthy of forgiveness; a sodomite; a poseur… had it all wrong?'

"'I'm no judge,' replied the saint, 'but yes, it seems so. If they were right, you wouldn't be here. Remember, the entries in this book are serious, serious enough to bar your entry into Paradise. This, you must reflect on. It's these venial sins you must endeavour to purge.'

"'Ah! But it seems impossible,' he replied. 'No soul ever leaves this place, not that I know of. Tell me, how can this be achieved?'

"'Again, brother, I must remind you of my purpose. I am the Keeper of the Gate and nothing more. I have no other function here but to be the keeper and guardian of its keys,' the saint stressed. 'It's not my brief to be your confessor and grant you absolution.' Peter opened the book. 'Would you like me to read out some of your debit entries?' he asked.

"Oscar looked at me for guidance, which wasn't forthcoming. 'No, thank you,' he replied. 'I don't think that's such a good idea. I'd rather not know.'

"'Go on. It could be very interesting,' I cried, just dying to know what his sins were.

"'Are you *mad*?' he said 'I will give this one a miss if you don't mind.'

"'Very well, but if at some time you wish to attempt to purge your sins you have to know the extent of them, as listed in this, your Debit Book,' the saint informed him.

"'If there's no real chance of purging my sins, why bother reading them? It seems to be a worthless exercise.'

"'That's your choice, brother,' said the saint. 'If you change your mind, a copy of your Debit Book can be viewed by you at any time at Alcove 849, at the Knowledge Zone up on Cloud Four.'

"'But I must have some credit? Surely my life has been something more than venial sins?' Oscar moaned.

"'Wait a moment more.' Peter said as he vanished again. He returned swiftly, placing a slim white book, with Oscar's name emblazoned in gold lettering, on the marble table next to his black book.

"'Yes, you do have some credit,' he said as he tapped the White Book with his bony finger. 'This, brother is your Credit Book.'

"Oscar looked at me again in horror. He was sweating profusely, the poor soul.

"'That's some slim book, Oscar,' I whispered.

"'I'll say,' he said as he wiped his brow. 'Maybe we should make our exit... now. I think I'm a loser here.'

"'Would you like me to read out your Credit Rating?' The saint asked.

"'There doesn't seem any point, does there? By the lean look of that book, it seems I am not too creditworthy. Surely, I must have more credit than that,' Oscar sighed, pointing to the slim volume.

"'No, brother – all your credit is here. Every decent act you did in your life is here, in this book, lovingly inscribed by the hand of an angel,' said the saint, again tapping the book. 'You have only one Credit Book and this is it.'

"Oscar was ashen-faced. 'What about my genius?' he forlornly asked.

"'Your genius – what about it?' the saint asked in a soft, calm voice.

"Oscar was baffled by the saint's reply. He looked at me for guidance, but I shrugged my shoulders. This was out of my league.

"'What do you mean; 'what about it? Surely I must have received some credit for my genius?' he gasped.

"'Exactly what I'm saying – what about it – what about your genius? In the scheme of things, is it really of any importance?'

"Oscar looked at me, amazed. He didn't understand what the saint was saying. 'Any importance?' he exclaimed. 'It's of the greatest importance. My genius is everything. It is what I am. It is my very being. What about my genius for the written word, my service to literature, my genius for humour, my ability to make people happy with my wit and intellectual dexterity? Don't these carry any credit?'

"The saint sighed again and, shaking his head, said, 'your use of words, your wit, your intellectual prowess – yes, genius without a doubt, a great gift – given I must remind you, as a gift. You cannot expect credit for a gift given. No, Oscar Wilde, there will be no credit for your undoubted genius. That credit goes to the one who endowed you with your extraordinary talent. It's unworthy to seek credit for something given so generously to you.'

"For the first time, Oscar was stumped for words. He looked at me, then to the saint, then back to me. 'So… there's no credit at all for my genius?' he forlornly asked.

"'No.' replied the saint.

"'Great!' he moaned, 'All that effort for nothing. My genius – that is what I lived for, it's all I have of any worth. Take away my genius and there's nothing left to see.'

"'Not so.' replied the saint. 'Without it you had something far more valuable.'

"'I can't imagine what that could have been. What could be more valuable than my genius?'

"The saint gently laid his hand on Oscar's arm and told him, 'Life, it was life that was of more value than your genius was. Everything else, including your genius, was of secondary value. The quality and value of your life were in how you lived it. If you hadn't been gifted with genius, you would have still lived out your life in some other form and perhaps you may have been far happier and content and at peace with yourself and your fellow beings.'

"'So, my genius was a waste of time?' he sadly asked.

"'No. I didn't say that. All I'm saying is that you haven't received any credit for it. I am sorry. That's the way it is, brother,' the saint sighed. 'I just tell it as it is.'

"'You certainly do. Could there have been a mistake?' Oscar asked. 'Mistakes do happen,' he added.

"The saint raised his thick, white bushy eyebrows and gave a lingering sigh. 'You mean... a divine mistake?'

"Oscar was just about to answer but thought better of it.

"'No, there's been no mistake,' said the saint. 'Although souls may not receive credit for their genius, they can receive credit for how they have used it. There's always credit for how one uses one's gifts.'

"Oscar's ears pricked up. 'Oh! I see. Did I use my genius in a creditable way, then?'

"'You shouldn't be asking me. You should know the answer yourself. Did you, did you use your genius in a credible way? Did you use it to the benefit of others and not for any vain motives? You tell me.'

"'Yes, I believe I did and used it wisely,' Oscar replied sharply.

"'Well... let's see,' said the saint as he flicked through the pages of the Credit Book. 'Here, in Chapter 2, is the history of your genius – very interesting reading. The preamble to this chapter records that from an early age you were inclined towards the wonder of words, that you were marked out from the moment you were born as someone special. When you were ten your parents realised you had the gift for wit and intellectual dexterity and carefully guided you to realise your potential. This you did by application and studies that sent you to the dizzy heights of academia, where you left your indelible mark. You have credit under quite a few categories in this chapter of your life.'

"'I *do*?' Oscar queried.

"'Yes, you certainly do. Let's see, then,' Peter said as he turned more pages. 'Chapter Two – eight to fourteen is very interesting. You have twelve Gold Stars, you know.'

"'Do I? Did you hear that Alfred, I am Gold-Star calibre,' Oscar said beaming from ear to ear.

"'Well, you always did have a thing about stars, didn't you?' I replied.

"'Do I really have Gold Stars?'

"'Indeed you do,' the saint said, a slight smile on his lips.

"'What for?' he asked.

"'For the use of your genius, of course,' Saint Peter replied.

28

"Oscar smiled at me, delighted that he had full marks. He was grinning as though he was top of the class. 'How does it read?'

"'Very well, by the look of it,' replied the saint. 'Oscar, once aware of his ability to digest all knowledge laid before him, puts it to great use,' he read. 'He unselfishly shared his knowledge and talent with the world through literary efforts written with great style, finesse and dexterity. He used his gift of humour to lift spirits and entertain his audiences, whether as readers of his exquisite prose and poetry or as audiences absorbed by his masterful plays, *The Importance of Being Ernest*, for example. His input into the world of literature and theatre stands as a testament to his skill, tenacity and humanity. Rating: twelve Gold Stars.'

"'My, my, Oscar,' I said, 'you have every right to smile. That's not bad at all – twelve Gold Stars for doing what comes naturally – can't beat it.'

"'Do you wish me to read out more of your credits?' asked the saint.

"'Can't see why not, it is better than debits any day,' he replied, still gleaming at his marks.

"'You have another twelve-gold-star rating,' said the saint.

"'Really,' Oscar cried, now bursting with pride. He could hardly contain himself.

"'Yes, but nothing to do about your genius, though. This comes under the category of Civility in Chapter 6, fourteen to twenty-three. Do you wish me to read it out?' asked the saint.

"'Why not, it can't do any harm,' Oscar replied.

"Peter cleared his throat. 'This is one of the thirty-three entries under Civility. It says when incarcerated in Reading Gaol, Oscar while walking the corridors came upon two children imprisoned for stealing biscuits. He was disturbed by the treatment being meted out to them and decided to do as much as was possible to relieve their distress. He enquired about their situation, arranged that their fines were paid and secured their release. He showed compassion and Christian charity to complete strangers, forgetting his suffering and distress and the discomfort of his incarceration. He risked the wrath of and severe sanctions from his jailers but persisted in seeking the release of the unfortunate children. Rating: twelve Gold Stars.'

"'Wow!' I cried. 'If you keep this up, Oscar, you'll be top of the class with all that stardust floating about you.'

"'This is not funny, Alfred. I didn't do it for reward, for Gold Stars,' said our despairing genius. 'I did it because their treatment was unjust, an affront to common decency. These children, they were being ill-treated by what was deemed to be a Christian society. I don't desire any credit for doing what was not just my Christian duty, but also my human duty.'

'"Yes, a decent human and Christian act it was too,' replied the saint. 'That is why you have such a gold-star rating. They are very rare, you know. You are in good company. You may not want credit for it, but as you can see, you are credited for it, and if it was not well deserved it would not be included.'

'"But what is the use of such credit ratings if they can't set me free? I'm a hopeless case with little credit to my name,' Oscar said as he gripped the bars of the Pearly Gates.

'"Now, now, brother, no need to talk like that. You do have some credit, far more than many a soul does,' the saint reminded him. 'As for being set free – well, real freedom can only be found through love.

"Oscar gave a deep regretful sigh. 'Really! Love! What purpose is love in this place? Where my dear saint is love?'

"The saint laid his hand on Oscar's shoulder, giving him a saintly hug, and tenderly told him, 'It's all around you, brother – has been all your life, and on all accounts in abundance around you still. Give and receive love, and you will be on the road to freedom. Look, brother, look through these gates and tell me: what do you see?'

"Oscar stood there, staring through the gates, then gave another deep lingering sigh. 'A peaceful haven,' he said in a voice tinged with sadness, as though he realised that that haven would be forever out of his reach.

'"Very much so – what else?' the saint asked.

"Oscar, with his head resting against the gate's golden bars, observed the sight before him. 'Children, children and more children,' he replied in a quiet voice. 'There seems to be only children and animals playing happily together.' He turned to the saint and asked, 'Are there no adults in Paradise?'

'"Yes. We do have a few, but you must look hard and long to see them. Have you not noticed that on your side of the gates, there are no children?'

'"Yes, I did,' Oscar replied. 'So there is no hope for me? I really am a hopeless case. Are you are saying that if I am not as a child, there is no hope for me. Must I wander forever around this Cuckoo Land without any hope of redemption?'

'"Ah, now, now brother,' replied the saint, 'we're all children of God. There is always hope. You do have some credit, after all. You must now try to increase your credit rating in your new surroundings. It will not be easy, but it is possible. And then these gates will be open to you.'

'"But how do I increase my credit rating?' he asked.

"'That's not for me to say,' the saint replied. 'It's for you to find out. As I said before, I have limited authority. What I do know, Paradise is open to all. How you purge your sins to get there, I don't know. You will have to achieve this by your own means and resources. These resources are there within the Reservation, and only you can find them. All I do know is that your redemption is in your own hands. Now I must take my leave. Take heart, Oscar Wilde. Peace be with you.'

"Before we knew it, the good saint was gone, along with the Debit and Credit books, leaving Oscar rather crestfallen and out of sorts. He sat down with his back to the gates and said nothing. He just stared in front of him as though he was in a trance. I sat next to him but didn't attempt to make conversation. I looked at him as tears trickled down his face. We were there for some time. Then suddenly, he was on his feet. He looked through the gates, then, turning, slowly walked up towards the summit of Cloud Nine with his hands in his pocket and head hung low. I followed, leaving him to his thoughts."

"He must have been upset," Sophie muttered.

"That's what I thought," replied Musset. "As I followed him, I began to wonder what effect the experience would have on him. The thought of the earlier depression he suffered over the matter of the tomb returned, filling me with dread. He'd put such faith in his meeting with Peter that surely it would have a divisive effect on him. However, when we reached the summit of Cloud Ninety-Nine, he turned around and looked down towards the Pearly Gates, now just a haze, and smiled. Putting his arm around me, he said, 'Let us go home, Alfred, my good fellow. Can't understand what I made such a fuss about. Me! – In Paradise – did you ever hear of anything so outrageous in your life? What a preposterous and blasphemous thought! I think I will settle for this near-heavenly experience. It seems that all the interesting folk are here in Purgatory anyway, and likely to be for eternity. Let us enjoy it. It could very well have been worse.'

"'Could it?' I replied.

"'Oh, yes. We could have ended up in Hell, stoking the Devil's fire with our genius and inflaming it with our inflated egos,' he replied.

"We continued our journey home. Oscar was in great form. We talked about each other's experiences, and when I was telling him about my ill-fated love affair with the *outré* French novelist, George Sand, his eyes lit up. She fascinated him and was keen to know all about her. I should say more than he already knew, for he seemed well versed. The impression I got from him was that he thought she was a nymphomaniac who also happened to be a mediocre writer.

"Suddenly, he burst out in uncontrollable laughter. After he regained his composure, with a twinkle in his eyes said, 'Just imagine Alfred, imagine if George were here, in this place, with everything she could possibly need – everything except the one thing she craved for and needed as if it were a drug.'

"'Which was?' I asked.

"'You know full well. You provided her with enough of *it.*'

"'Did I? What was that, then?'

"'Sex!' he laughed.

"'Oh, that,' I replied. 'Yes, I wasn't shy about providing her with it, and she was always grateful – very, very grateful.'

"'Can you ever imagine her surviving here without it? She'd go crazy.'

"'Go crazy!' I replied. 'She was crazy. If she was here, we would all go crazy. I'd be off, seeking fresh pastures, like a safe passage to Hell. It would be preferable to spending eternity with her. If she were here, you could guarantee one thing; the sex ban would not deter her, oh no, not her. She would look at it as another challenge. She would relish the idea of finding some way around it – not that there is one, as she would finally realise. I'm telling you, she'd have a field day here. There are quite a few of her former lovers at this Reservation, including me, her most virile one. There's Chopin, of course, then there's Félix Nadar and Eugène Delacroix and the politicians Louis Blanc and Alexandre Ledru-Rollin.

"'Did she really have an affair with Ledru-Rollin?' Oscar asked.

"'Yes,' I acknowledged. 'She always maintained she didn't, but she did. She had a sharp political mind and certainly physically attracted to him. He set her alight in more ways than just politically, but she was so political at times, she'd bore the life out of you. She wasn't shy about airing her political views that at times could be pretty strong. It used to turn me cold but she loved it, and ran after Rollin like a love-struck schoolgirl.'

"'Unusual for a woman to be so politically vocal, is it not?' he asked.

32

"'She was ahead of her time all right. She was a woman who knew what she wanted and went after it with determination and woe betide anyone who got in her way. She denied having affairs with Delacroix and Nadar, but I wasn't convinced. When it came to men, you just couldn't believe a word she said. As for Delacroix, I'm certain he used more than his brushes on her. She was unlike any woman I had met before. People used to say I was wild and outrageous, but she left me standing.'

"'A liberated woman, I'd say.' Oscar said.

"'Yes, not just politically but sexually and intellectually,' I added.

"'What other way is there?' he smiled.

"'Indeed,' I replied, 'but she wasn't seeking liberation for women in general – no, not at all. All she ever wanted was liberation for herself, sexually, materially and politically, and to hell with any of her downtrodden sisters.'

"'I was reading her autobiography, *Histoire de ma vie*,' he commented. 'According to her, she got through quite a few men and women by all accounts, and intimates that it was you, my dear fellow, who were the true love of her life.'

"'No, no, Oscar, I disagree. You've got it all wrong,' I retorted. 'She hardly refers to our relationship and never uttered words of true love about me. As I see it, she didn't think too highly of me; rather bitter in her remembrance. You're reading too much into it. Love – I don't think poor George, God bless her soul, ever knew what love really was. It had come upon her several times, but unfortunately, she was looking the other way at some other beau and missed it. Even when Chopin came into her life, she didn't realise she was in the presence of true love. She was too intense for me. Come to think about it, she was too intense for most people. I'd say you would have suited her, rather up her street. Pity you never met. I would say you were kindred spirits, literary soul mates.'

"That got him aroused. He began breathing erratically. There was a sparkle in his eyes.

"'You think so?' he asked in a rather self-satisfied way.

"'I know it,' I replied, 'I'm telling you, my friend; you were made for each other, in an odd kind of way, of course.'

"'I must admit, Alfred, I'd loved to have met her. Something about her fascinates me, something that gets my intellectual juices flowing. I must confess; I would not have minded trying my hand with that woman. Indeed, she would have been a challenge, perhaps one of the biggest challenges of my life.'

"'Without doubt,' I replied, knowing he wouldn't have stood a chance with her. She would have devoured him in one sitting.

"'I would have given her a good run for her money. Do you think she would have fancied me, not just intellectually – that goes without saying – but in an emotional and physical sense?' he asked.

"'No doubt, you'd have had her eating out of your hands. You'd have such a hypnotic effect on her; you'd send her blood rushing through her veins in uncontrollable passion,' I replied teasingly.

"'Ah, go on, you are not serious now,' he said giving me a playful push.

"'I'm telling you, you were made for each other. She'd take one look at you with her large smouldering dark eyes, and she'd have you so mesmerised you'd be lost for words.'

"'Now, that would be some feat,' he quirked.

"'She'd have whispered sweet nothings in your ear in that husky voice of hers and she'd have had you by your short and curlies in no time at all; she'd let that bottom lip of hers quiver, and you'd be like jelly. Yes, she'd have mesmerized you, just as she did me – just as she did Chopin and that never-ending line of suitors,' I said, mercilessly teasing the poor soul.

"'Ah! I would be different,' he assured me. 'She wouldn't have wanted another after she fell for me. Ah, but it is not to be, Alfred,' he sighed as he put his hand on my shoulder. 'I will have to content myself with yours and Chopin's reminisces about her, that's if he ever gets around to talking about her. You know how secretive he is about anything to do with her, how over-protective he is of their relationship. He will talk about her one of these days, just wait and see.'

"'I wouldn't count on it,' I replied.' All the time I've known him he hasn't mentioned her once.'

"'Ah!' he exclaimed. 'There will be a time when he will reveal all. I would stake my life on it, if I had one.'

"'Never – if he hasn't done so by now it's highly unlikely he'll ever will.'

"'Do you know why he's so secretive about it?' he asked.

"'No – he just is,' I replied. 'But he's not alone in not wanting to talk about his past. I know there are some parts of your life you don't want to talk about. I'd say there are some you'd wish to eradicate from your memory and the public record. I know there are some elements of my life I will never talk about, so it's a waste of time pestering him about it, for he won't talk about her.'

"'If you say so,' Oscar sighed. 'What a pity, though. I would love to really understand him, understand what makes up that complex and fascinating nature. Come now, my dear fellow, tell me more. Tell me how you treated poor George. Tell me everything – every minute and scintillating detail. Spare me nothing.'

"'You know, Oscar,' I continued, 'Looking back, I must admit, I didn't exactly treat her well. I was a bit of a rogue, a bit of a bounder back then. Couldn't leave women alone, you know. I wasn't too fussy either – anything would do. Some mornings I'd wake up, look at the unfortunate woman next to me, and not recognise her – a complete stranger. I blame the drink. It's to blame for most of life's ills. It dulls most of the senses but does enlighten the imagination. You know what it's like after a few drinks. Every woman you meet, is the most beautiful you've ever cast eyes on and as the night goes on she turns into Venus, and you're in seventh heaven, only to discover in the light of day, you're in bed with a Siren. I know decent women don't hop into bed with a drunk like me, yet I spent night after night with Venuses, believing them to be good and decent women, only to wake up disillusioned and many a time rewarded with a dose of the pox. I never did learn. I'd suffer severe headaches if I stayed with the same woman for too long. Poor George, God love her, gave me a permanent one.'

"'Ah, now, that is a cruel thing to say,' Oscar exclaimed. 'She couldn't have been that bad, could she?'

"'I'm telling you, the woman was overbearing. She may have suited you, but she was too much for me. I prided myself on my stamina, but by God, I couldn't keep up with her. She demanded full-time attention, and if you didn't give it, she let you know about it. Don't know how Chopin, being the quiet fellow he is, put up with ten years of it. The man's a martyr.'

"'Perhaps he didn't suffer from headaches,' Oscar tittered.

"'Maybe, but he must have suffered from something to survive a decade with her.'

"'If she was as bad as people made her out to be, then how come he stayed with her for so long?' He asked.

"'I can't imagine,' I said. 'It couldn't be his potency – I couldn't imagine him ever getting too sexually exited – far too delicate a chap, far too reserved. I am a hard act to follow. I doubt sexual magnetism kept them together. As I said before, maybe he was just a martyr and will be rewarded sometime for his tolerance and forbearance of such a demanding woman.'

"'Not much of a reward for being a martyr, ending up here, is it?' Oscar cried.

"He was getting serious again, so I thought I'd better distract him. 'Did I ever tell you of the time I visited Venice with George on what she liked to call our honeymoon?'

"'No, but I'm sure you're going to.'

"'For some reason, we decided to visit Venice,' I said as I began my tale. 'Don't know why, but at the time it seemed like a good idea.

We were so wrapped up in each other we were inclined to do the craziest of things, like heading off to Venice on a whim. I didn't have a bean to my name, so I talked my parents into financing the trip. They didn't like the idea of my association with an older woman, especially a married one with a dicey reputation. They did, however, reluctantly, give me the funds with a few stipulations and off George and I went on our Venetian sojourn, like two love-struck fools, which was exactly what we were. On route from Lyon to Avignon, the first leg of our journey, we had our honeymoon disrupted, by that pretentious poet, Stendhal. George hinted to him that he wasn't welcome, but he didn't take the hint. I didn't mind his company in the least, but she was getting bitchier about it. What made it worse, he thought he was a grand chap, and she desired his company. More fool him – she couldn't stand the sight of him or his amateurish verse. She thought she'd be burdened with him for the entire journey. To her delight, he parted company with us at Avignon and headed for Civitavecchia to take up his new position as French Consul.

"'We sailed to Genoa, then to Venice. We hadn't been there that long when George became violently ill – I thought she'd had her lot. She was no fun at all, was a bad and contrary patient and the thought of nursing her back to health filled me with dread. I wanted nothing to do with it. I should have been the gentleman and nursed her, but being the cad I was, I headed off to those seedy alleyways of Venice and the ladies of the night and left her to get well on her own. You see what I mean – I just couldn't leave women alone. It was a disease without a cure. Women, they were my Achilles heel,' I said. By the look on his face, he thought I was boasting. He glared at me with absolute revulsion; then said in a raised, scornful voice, 'My God, Alfred! Are you saying you just left her there, in a strange city to cope on her own? That's a bit rough, I must say. Have you no shame? Have you no breeding at all?'

"'Breeding! Certainly not! What a disgusting thought,' I replied.

"'Well, what happened when she recovered?' he asked.

"'She let me have it. Called me everything under the sun – philanderer, bastard, low life, poseur. She wasn't impressed by my lack of compassion towards her. I thought she must have been mad going on such a journey with someone like me. When she let loose, there was no holding her back. Then I became violently ill. It was my turn to suffer. At first, she said it was my fault and that I was being paid back for my gallivanting and gorging myself on the ladies of the night while she lay alone in bed for a fortnight sweating and shivering. But good old George, after having her say, looked after me and nursed me back to health in the most loving and caring way. It was a hard slog. She tended me day and night and for a time forgot my bad treatment of her. She found a young Venetian doctor who worked hard to cure me of my illness. With his dedication and her nursing ability, I made a good recovery. She had a motherly instinct about her that most of her lovers appreciated.'

"'You're a lucky fellow. It's a wonder she didn't toss you into one of those stinking Venetian canals,' Oscar said.

"'Don't think it never crossed her mind, because it did,' I replied. 'Apart from tossing me in the canal, I'd say she would happily have throttled me as I went under.'

"'Maybe she'd have done you a favour,' Oscar laughed

"'Maybe, but guess what happened when I was suffering and fighting for my life?'

"'I hate to think,' he replied.

"'Come now. Guess.'

"'Let me see now. You discovered you were dying from the pox after your exertions with those ladies of Venice and she wouldn't let you touch her,' he replied with a cynical edge to his voice.

"'Oh, very droll, Oscar – guess what happened?'

"'As I recall from one of those many biographies about her, there was a bit of a problem with the young Venetian doctor as he attended on you,' he replied.

"'Attended on – you bet, but not just on me,' I exclaimed. 'She had a dingdong with him behind my back, the Jezebel. Dr Pagello was his name – a handsome quack if there ever was one. He had saved my life when I was ill, so I had a lot to be thankful to him for, but in lieu of payment, he took a good taste of George, the rotter. He liked the taste so much that from then on I didn't stand a chance. Even with all my charm and sexual magnetism, I couldn't compete with him. When he was attending to me, I noticed he couldn't keep his eyes off her. I thought at first that his continuous attention to me was that of a dedicated physician, but he had other things on his mind. He had that look of lust stamped all over his handsome features.'

"'Being who you are, no doubt you recognised the symptoms,' Oscar quipped.

"'Certainly – I know lust when I see it, and he had it in abundance,' I replied. 'He couldn't keep his eyes off her. That's nothing unusual per se, for most men when they see or meet her, have palpitations and cold sweats – but this was different. At every opportunity, he would touch her in some way or another. You know the kind of thing – a gentle touch on the hand, a tug at her sleeve or a sly touch to her hair. He would look at her as though he'd seen an angel. When I was lying there feeling like death warmed up, I noticed them sitting at the table, talking. He would hold her hand and play footsie with her under the table. I thought it was just flirtation. It didn't cross my mind that she'd be off having an affair with him, for I thought she was in love with only me – big mistake. He was besotted with her. He thought she was God's gift, but soon found out she was far from it. He was at her beck and call and was more like a love-struck schoolboy than a lover was – he was so bowled over by her that he deserted his medical practice, to the despair of his father, and followed her back to Paris, the silly bugger. Guess what?'

"'What?' Oscar echoed.

"'I was deeply jealous,' I confessed.

"'What!' he scowled.

"'Yes... Jealous,' I repeated. 'After abandoning her for the ladies of the night, I was jealous...I was violently jealous of the doctor. I could find no rational reason for it, but by God, I was so jealous. I was seething with rage every time I thought of them together. I could have throttled him, but it wouldn't have looked right, throttling the man who'd saved your life, even if he was making love with the woman of your dreams. Crazy, isn't it?'

"'You're a ratbag, you know that?' he said, looking down his nose at me as though he had never been guilty of jealousy.

"'Well, we're not all perfect,' I replied. 'When I challenged her over their dalliances, she just laughed and told me to grow up, that I was just a mean, jealous little man. In a moment of rage, I pushed her against the wall wanting to choke the life out of her – but I thought better of it. God! She could get my temper up.'

"Oscar grabbed hold of my lapels and looked at me in a rather curious way through squinted eyes. 'Violence! Very interesting indeed,' he said. 'Didn't I read that you had a violent streak in you, especially with women? That your relationship with George was violent, not just emotionally but physically, that you indulged in a bit of sadomasochistic behaviour. Has not what you have just said confirmed that you were violent to women? That behind that clean-cut image, you are a thug – a woman beater?'

"I didn't know what to say. It's not one of my proudest moments. 'That was a long time ago, Oscar, a very long time. I'd rather not talk about it,' I said, hoping he'd forget it.

"'I bet you wouldn't,' he said. 'That's the lowest any man can fall to. There can be no justification for such demeaning behaviour. However much a woman annoys or irritates you, hitting her is not the answer. Why did you do it? Did it give you some kick, some exaggerated sexual thrill or power?'

"'No, it didn't,' I replied, angry that he thought I was so inclined. 'You are being carried away with that sadomasochistic nonsense. It never happened, for Christ's sake. It's one of the numerous historical inaccuracies about me. You won't believe the nonsense attributed to me. Anyway, George wouldn't have put up with that kind of carry on. She was quite conservative underneath her lusty image. I admit I had a violent streak in me, but it only raised its ugly head with certain people around me and one of them was poor George. She could rattle me so easily with her persistent demands, that I'd lose my temper. Yes, I hit her and pushed her around. I'm not proud of it, but it was never this sadomasochistic nonsense I'm always accused of. She didn't just stand there and take it either – she hit back. She was no pushover. She knew how to stand up for herself. Yes, I suppose my violent streak gave me a feeling of power. To be more precise, of a power I thought it gave me. There's no rationale about it. You could say it was a flaw in my character. We all suffer one way or another from such flaws, as you know damn well,' I declared.

"I had touched a nerve; by the look on Oscar's face, I'd rattled a few skeletons in his closet. All his faults seemed to be swimming before his eyes. He took the easy way out and said, 'As I said, you're a ratbag, Alfred.'

"'Oh, I know. I can't help it – it's in the blood,' I laughed.

"He wasn't amused. 'It is nothing to be proud of, you know – it's not a badge of honour to be a cad and a bounder and certainly no glory in being a woman beater,' he snarled.

"'At the time it was. My prowess with the ladies was indeed a badge of honour. It was all part of my image. Image was important to me back then. My literary efforts were of little value – almost worthless, I'd say, for they were overshadowed by my obsession with image and ego that dominated my thinking and my very actions. I should have produced more work than I did, and better. I could have if I hadn't spent so much time seeking and enjoying the pleasures of life and losing myself in an opium haze. But that's me – nothing in half measures. God, Oscar, George was an extraordinary woman. I may joke and say our relationship was only about sex, but I loved her in my own special way. The problem was she was so obsessive, so domineering that it became claustrophobic. I couldn't breathe around her. She was impossible to live with. Our passion was so intense it was debilitating. I always prided myself by my staying power, but she was never satisfied. I just couldn't keep up with her. Of course, looking back across all those years, I now realise how shameless I was, that I had nothing to be proud of, nothing at all. My treatment of women, especially George was unforgivable.'

"'You're still a ratbag,' Oscar reminded me.

"'God, lighten up, will you? Don't get so hot and bothered, Oscar. I'm a cured man now. I've learned my lesson and put my shameful past behind me,' I proudly boasted.

"'I'm relieved you feel some shame.'

"'Very much so,' I said. 'When I recovered my health George wanted nothing more to do with me. Told me to go back home to mamma, as if I was a child in need of a good spanking. I let her know how I felt over her affair with the quack, and she yelled blue murder over my disappearance whilst she was ill. The tension between us became so unbearable that I departed for Paris as soon as was practicable, leaving the lovebirds to get on with it, and they did.'

"'So that was it,' Oscar asked.

"'Not quite. We tried again when she finally returned to Paris. The Venetian was soon out of favour and flavour with George,' I continued. 'He was way out of his depth in Paris. Her passion for him didn't take long to evaporate. The moment she was back on her old stamping ground, she didn't have time for him. Once she was surrounded by her kind of people, who did not warm to him, it wasn't long until he realised that instead of being her lover he was more like a curiosity to be shown around the salons of Paris, as an acquisition she'd picked up on her travels abroad, just like a trinket. His pride being injured, he headed back to Venice with his tail between his legs and George not long after came running back to me, professing undying love. It was doomed to failure, of course. It was a grand passion at first. We'd be all over each other like a rash, but then she'd go on about Venice and how I left her when she was ill; deserted her when she needed me most. God, she would never let me forget it. She would whine on like a wounded animal. When she was in one of her moods, there was no stopping her. In return, I would tease her about the doctor, at how easy she was at picking up stray men to take home to show off like a prized possession. It didn't take long to end. It was quite painful, full of spiteful jibes. We parted and avoided each other as much as we could for the rest of our lives. The last time we met, I was so drunk she was just a blur.'

"'Did you miss her?' Oscar asked.

"'Not really,' I said. By the look of him, he didn't believe me. 'But according to many of her friends and acquaintances, she missed me greatly, and why wouldn't she, I was, after all, an electrifying lover,' I bragged, 'But But I was not the love of her life, that distinction goes to the divine Chopin, that martyr of martyrs.'

"'If you say so.'

"'I do,' I replied. 'She soon got over me, you know, for within a short time she was deeply involved with Chopin. She took one look at him, and that was that. At first, he found her repulsive, thought her too masculine. He soon warmed to her, though, and within a short while, they were together. He may not have been as potent as I was, as few were, but she doted on him. Poor man – he deserved sainthood for his tolerance of her. Don't know how they ever got it together –

he, a perfect gentleman, but weak, retiring and unhealthy, she, as fit as a fiddle, sex mad and far from a lady. They had nothing in common, yet got on extremely well – quite amazing.'

'"Come now, Alfred, they were both artists. Surely that was the main attraction.'

'"Maybe,' I replied. 'But apart from the artistic appreciation of each other's work, they were just so different. He was the soul of respectability and she, France's most outrageous and notorious woman.'

'"And isn't it true that she mothered poor Chopin,' he asked. 'You must admit that's an attraction to many a fellow. All fellows love being mothered – they all want to be mothered one way or another by a woman, as long as they're free to have sex whenever it suits them. They expect women to change from mother to whore at a moment's notice. Isn't that so?'

'"Certainly,' I replied. 'She mothered and smothered him as she did me. She smothered me so much I could hardly breathe.'

"Oscar laughed. 'There is no satisfying you, my boy. You search out sex with George, like seeking out your opium, and then, when you find it you complain that you cannot stand the pace – that you were being smothered – I must say, Alfred, I find it hard to feel sorry for you. You are continuously bragging about your prowess with women, yet when it comes to a woman with real passion, you wilt like a dying flower. Sorry, I'm not sorry for you at all.'

'"Well, you ought to be, after my suffering at the hands of Madame Sand. It wasn't easy; I can tell you, and what about Chopin? After suffering a decade of her mothering and smothering, surely you can feel compassion for him?' I replied.

'"I certainly do, but not for you. At least he was able to keep up with her for ten years, whereas you ran, abandoned her after only two years. So much for your potency,' he replied, then burst out laughing.

"I don't find that funny."

'"But just imagine,' he chuckled, 'if Chopin woke up and found George here. How would he react? They didn't exactly part on good terms, did they?'

'"I don't think it would worry him too much,' I replied. 'A long time has passed since their romance, and maybe it has mellowed his feelings for her. Their parting may well have been frosty, but I'd say they would have melted into each other's arms if they had ever met up again. I believe Chopin was the love of her life. I was just a passing fancy, a bit of light relief. Chopin was in her blood. She lived and breathed him. They inspired each other. Some of Chopin's greatest works were composed in their time together, mostly at her home at Nohant, down in the Loire Valley, as well as at their various love nests

41

dotted around Paris. You can just imagine her scribbling away at her desk with Chopin in the background playing his divine music, his bony fingers dancing across the keyboard. They were good together and good for each other. The breakdown of their relationship was the fault of her daughter, Solange, whose relationship with Clésinger was causing a domestic rift. George asked Chopin for his support against her daughter, but he took Solange's side. That's what caused the rift that ended their relationship. She wanted support from her lover, and none was forthcoming. She demanded loyalty from him as she did from all around her. Instead of compromising with Solange and Chopin, she took a rigid stance and lost Chopin in the process. Nothing good ever comes from being too rigid in life. They were each too proud to give into each other and apologise. Instead, they preferred to stay in a huff and in doing so ended a beautiful association. People in love do stupid things.'

"'As Chopin lay dying,' I continued, 'she visited Paris to see him, but lost her nerve. She wandered up and down the quays, not certain whether she should visit him or not. She didn't and regretted it for the rest of her life. When he died, she was so devastated she was unable to attend his funeral at the Madeleine, instead stayed grieving at Nohant. She was never the same again. No other man ever compared to Chopin. Many tried and failed – Manceau, Blanc, Mérimée and Flaubert – but they could never replace him. He was dead before she realised she had had the love she'd been searching for all her life. She had had it but foolishly let it go and could never retrieve it. Chopin was in her blood and she in his. Without any doubt, he was the true love of her life, and she of his.'

"Oscar looked at me with amazement. 'Then why do you think she and others wrote that it was you, who was that love of her life?'

"'Really, Oscar,' I said. 'I've already told you – I'm not the one. You shouldn't believe what anyone writes in their autobiography. It is guaranteed to be shaped, coloured and, without doubt, self-serving. If you study George's autobiography, it is evident that she is rewriting her life to suit her image of herself, an image by which she wanted posterity to remember her. She hardly mentions me. Her other lovers are just a by-line. As for Chopin, she rambles on about him as though he was a child, and she, his devoted mother. There is not a mention of the fact they were lovers sharing a burning passion. She could be vain, you know. Little like someone else I know.'

"'Steady on, dear fellow,' he cried.

"'I'm telling you, she was a vain, vain woman,' I emphasised.

"'Then why were you attracted to her?'

"I couldn't help but laugh. 'Sex! Sex! Nothing bet sex,' I bragged.

"'That's it? You wanted her for nothing more than sex?' he said in a high moral tone. 'That is disgusting. To use a woman solely for sex is sick – demeaning and offensive.'

"'Now don't go all moral on me. It won't wash. You used young men for sex and had no scruples about it,' I teased. 'What's the difference?'

"For a moment, he was speechless. He didn't like to be reminded of his own moral lapses. He walked away from me, his hands clasped firmly behind him. He swung around and glared at me. 'Surely you believe there's more to women than sex.'

"'Yes, I do', I assured him. 'Just as you no doubt believe there's more to men than sex. As well as sex, her intellect attracted me. Intellectual women always excite me. The only problem was she was too domineering for my taste.'

"'You're most generous with your compliments,' he jeered. 'Of course, what better companion is there than one who intellectually stimulates and sexually excites?'

"'I'm a changed man now. You may not believe it, but I am,' I continued. 'These days I have the greatest respect for women, even plain ones. You could say I've been liberated, that I've seen the light. I had no respect for her as a person. To my shame, I could see her only as an intellectual sex object.'

"'Indeed. It seems to me that you had no respect for any woman,' Oscar retorted.

"'That's not so, or fair. I did for my mother, and *she* was a magnificent woman,' I replied.

"'What a saint you are, Alfred, respecting your mother,' he growled.

"'I'm telling you, these days I have the highest respect for the opposite sex,' I replied, but by the look of him, he was far from convinced.

"He gave a cynical laugh. 'You now discover that you have respect for women, now that you can't get your hands on any. George was wise to fall in love with Chopin, instead of you! You seem to be a scoundrel when it comes to women – you, a poet of the Romantic Movement. You wouldn't know romance if it slapped you across the face a dozen times. You are just a scoundrel – a literary one at that.'

"'I'm not,' I said, hurt by his words. 'Since I've been here, I've had time to concentrate my mind on my past and reflect on the way I treated and used women. I'm telling you, I'm a changed man. I have the utmost respect for them now, even in my dreams. At one time, I'd waste no time in heading for the nearest bed to make love to them, many a time not even bothering to ask their names. Now, in my dreams, I always ask their names, court, wine and dine them, then wait until I'm asked before I make love to them – real gentleman's stuff. That's the sign of a changed man, wouldn't you say? I'm a good boy now, no longer the *enfant terrible* in any way whatsoever. I'm an absolute gentleman in my dreams as I ought to have been in my earthly existence.'

'"You don't say,' Oscar mockingly replied.

'"I certainly do, and they love me for it,' I proudly said. 'In my dreams, I experience erotic sex, something I never did in my earthly life, even with George.'

"He gasped. 'Are you saying sex with George was dull?'

'"No... not dull at all, but certainly not erotic. George, she was out on her own when it came to sex. You know, the first time I made love to her she nearly gave me heart failure,' I informed my curious friend.

"His eyes widened – really!' he cried.

'"Indeed,' I replied. 'She was very responsive to my masterful technique as most women are, when all of a sudden she tensed up, gave out a mighty cry, then bawled her head off. God, I didn't know what to do. I tried to pacify her, to no avail. I panicked, fearing she'd had second thoughts about our liaison, so up I got and off I ran as fast my legs could carry me.'

'"You left her there, crying. What a rat you are,' he replied, absolutely disgusted with me.

'"You don't understand, Oscar. I panicked, thinking she'd cry rape, but I had misread her, as many did before.' I informed him.

'"Whatever do you mean?' he asked.

'"The next day a letter arrived from her, apologising profusely, asking me to return to her that evening.'

'"Why did she apologise when she was the victim?' he asked.

'"Victim – there was no victim! It was all a misunderstanding,' I said, taken aback that he thought she was a victim, that he imagined I did something to her against her will.

'"That's what they all say,' he replied.

"He looked confused, so I explained what happened. 'When I arrived, she was embarrassed and tongue-tied.'

'"George Sand, embarrassed and tongue-tied – highly unlikely,' he laughed.'

'"I asked her why she was so distressed. What had I done to make her so distressed? She informed me I had done nothing wrong. She revealed that sometimes when she became aroused, she couldn't help but scream and cry. She had no control over this and hoped she hadn't scared me off. She had not. If she hadn't explained, I certainly wouldn't have pursued her. After that initial jolt, we got it together. It was plain sailing, apart from the fights, but nothing erotic.'

"'Most historians believe she was frigid, that throughout her life she failed to achieve sexual satisfaction, so you must be having me on. With all of your talk about virility, you're probably a dud,' Oscar declared.

"'What!' I cried, startled that he could have questioned my virility. 'That's nonsense – no woman I've ever been with suffered such a condition, and George certainly didn't – frigid indeed. She had no complaints about my performance, I can tell you.'

"'I was always told I was as vain as they come, but you, dear Alfred, take the biscuit.'

"'I do try,' I laughed.

"We walked further without talking. He seemed deep in thought; I wondered what he was thinking. I was soon to find out. 'These erotic dreams,' he probed, 'you have them… every night.'

"'Most nights…'

"'Are you bragging?' he snapped.

"'No, just informing you of my nocturnal habits. They're always sexual and always involve women.'

"'No men then,' he asked, tittering.

"'Certainly not," I cried. 'You may be that so inclined but I'm not – not even in my dreams.'

"'Only wondering,' he said, shrugging his shoulders.

"'You can wonder as much as you like, but you're wandering down the wrong road. I'm one hundred percent heterosexual, I'll have you know,' I said, eying him up and down, wondering if he was making a pass or contemplating one.

"'Well, bully for you, that's some percentage,' he replied

"'Yes, it's only women I dream of,' I snapped.

"'Such, as?'

"'You really want to know,' I asked, already knowing the answer.

"'Don't be daft. Yes, of course I do. Seeing that I don't dream, the only pleasure I'm likely to get is from your account of your erotic ones and my own imagination,' he said.

"'All right,' I said, 'let's take a break. My legs are killing me. I'm not used to all this walking. Here, over there, on that ridge near that elm tree, it will be a perfect spot. There's a place I want you to see before I tell you of my dreams.'"

"I thought you were going to keep this short," Sophie muttered as Musset took a drink of water.

"I am. I'll stop if you wish."

"No, it's very interesting. But I just want to know about Oscar's odd behaviour."

"Sophie, what Alfred's on about has a lot to do with it."

"If you say so – Alfred, you were on about erotic dreams."

"So I was. We sat down and leaning against a tree had a sandwich and fill of divine wine we had picked up as we left the Pearly Gates.

"'Come now, these women. Who are they?' Oscar impatiently asked.

"'Where do I begin? There're so many,' I bragged.

"He was very flushed and excited. 'Do I know any of them,' he asked.

"'No, I wouldn't say so. I do have the *odd* dream about some I knew in life.'

"His eyes were alight. 'Who,' he keenly asked?'

"'My schoolmistress, Mademoiselle Miromesnil to start with...'

"'I say, Alfred that is rather kinky, dreaming sensually of your teacher.'

"'It's not what you think, I said. 'She was, as I knew her at school, a dark-haired beauty with luscious lips and dreamy blue eyes, who tickled me under my chin if I got my maths right. In my dream, I was no longer a schoolboy in short trousers but a strapping virile young man, and she took a shine to me. She ran after me and made no secret of the fact that she had in mind lessons of quite a different nature. Of course, I couldn't resist her advances. She was delicious and taught me some valuable lessons in love. She was far from shy. She was into everything Greek. When tired of that, she showed her dexterity in the oriental technique.'

"'Wait a moment,' he cried. 'Are you telling me you used to fancy your teacher when you were five or six years old and that she was into erotic acts but waited until you were a strapping young fellow before seducing you?'

"'I didn't know what sex was then,' I laughed, 'but I remembered her so well that I ended up dreaming about her in a way I'd never imagined I would. God! She was a revelation.'

"'I still think it is kinky, having erotic dreams about one's teacher,' Oscar announced.

"'I believe you're jealous,' I teased.

"'Rubbish,' he snapped – 'who else?'"

"'Let's see,' I continued, starting to enjoy his attention. 'There was the delectable Pauline Tristan, though she wasn't that delectable when I knew her in life. She was a bad-tempered nasty piece of work, known in the local village as a right old sour-face with the manners of a pig. Nobody liked her, not even her mother, who was only a slight improvement on her surly daughter.'

"'You did,' Oscar laughed.

"'No, not then – I was like everyone else in the village – I couldn't stand the sight of her and tried to avoid her at all costs. She hated the sight of me. She would run after me through the village brandishing a stick, ready to beat the living daylights out of me. She was a mean, nasty woman.'

"He was looking confused again. 'If she was so horrid, why did you end up dreaming of her in an erotic way?' he asked.

"'Ah, now, Oscar, you're asking me to interpret the meaning of dreams – which I can't. What I do know, is that I dreamt of a woman I couldn't stand the sight of. The very thought of kissing, never mind making love to would make me sick. In my dream, I saw her in a completely different light. I chanced upon a woman sitting amongst the *Aster alpinus*, reciting my poem, 'La Nuit de mai'. I sat down and listened to her perfect diction. She was word perfect and recited from memory. She was so startled when I introduced myself that she fainted. As I fanned her, it dawned on me who she was – Pauline Tristan, the village demon. Yet as I held her, she looked far from the village demon I had known. She was beautiful, with a soft delicate complexion and her gorgeous red hair was tied up with a green ribbon in a ponytail. She came to and looked me straight in the eyes. The moment she realised who I was, she had her arms about me then gave me a deep, passionate, lingering kiss. I tingled from head to toe. She told me she had been searching for me since discovering my poems and believed they were all dedicated to her. They had such an effect on her she swore they had transformed her life. I didn't want to disappoint her so I let her believe all she thought was true. She was so passionate amongst the *aster alpinus*; I just couldn't believe my luck. As I made love to her, she recited my poems. I had never experienced such joy and pleasure. I won't tell you the details of our lovemaking, for they would only leave you more frustrated than you already are. She bore no relation to the surly person I had previously known – God, what a dream.'

"'Very interesting indeed,' Oscar drawled. 'Do you have *more* examples?'

"'Aye, here's one for you,' I said. 'There was a friend of George – the actress, Marie Dorval, whom I'd had met on a few occasions. I never thought she was anything special and had little interest in her, so I was surprised that I ended up dreaming about her.'

"He looked at me in astonishment. 'Was she not one of George's lovers?'

"'So they say.'

"'She was a lesbian.' Oscar exclaimed. 'She wouldn't have been interested in a man, especially your kind.'

"'You're wrong, she was very interested,' I replied. 'In life, she didn't interest me in the least, but in my dreams, well, that was another story. I've had quite a few erotic dreams about her, and each one is better than the last. I'm a lucky soul when it comes to dreams.'

"'You don't say?' he sighed, clearly not convinced by my claim.

"'Oh, yes, better and better. I dreamt I was at the theatre with George and a few others on a cold December evening to watch Marie in her most recent play. It was freezing throughout the performance, not helped by the fact that it was far from one of her best. Afterwards, we were invited to a reception to celebrate her success. George cried off because she was frozen stiff. The others followed her. I was about to leave but thought about the hot toddies that would be served at the reception, so I made a beeline for it. I was glad I did. After downing a few cognacs, I was ready for action. Marie came over and asked if I liked her performance. I lied. I told her it was the best I had seen for years and that her performance was superb – in a class of its own. It seemed to do the trick. Her eyes lit up, and she was mine. She was delighted, and after all the guests had departed, she asked me if I would accompany her home. Being the gentleman I was, I told her it would be a pleasure – which as it turned out, it was. On the way, she complained that George had let her down, for she always accompanied her home if she was at the theatre. At her apartment, she soon forgot about George. Before me, was a woman I hadn't noticed before. I had thought her plain and unattractive. Ah, but that night she was a revelation. I whispered a few romantic stanzas, as any self-respecting poet would do in the circumstances, and she was mine. She was all over me in no time. She certainly knew what she wanted and headed straight for it. She was so hot; I sizzled at her very touch. The next morning, I was still sizzling and deliriously happy and contented. She was ready to go again. So was I, but dreams being dreams, I woke up. There's nothing worse than waking up from a sensuous dream.'

"'If this is true, you are a lucky soul, Alfred. It is so unfair I can't dream. It is as though I am being punished for something or other,' he sighed.

"'You've never dreamt all the time you've been here?'

"'No. Not a hint of one,' he sighed.

"'That's tough. I think I can help you, though.'

48

"'What!' he exclaimed, 'To dream?'

"'I'm never short of a trick or two – that's why I'm always a success with women. Let me help.'

"'When do we start,' he keenly asked?

"'Right now will do – telling you of my dreams and my reminiscences of the Erotic Zone up on Cloud Sixty-Six will be a great help. You could say these are your first steps to your sexual healing or, should I say, rehabilitation, albeit, only in your dreams.'

"His eyes nearly popped out of their sockets. 'The Erotic Zone – where on earth is that?'

"'You don't know? You don't know much, do you? It's not on earth, but here. The Erotic Zone is the place of sexual enlightenment and pleasure. I only visit it in my dreams. But it does exist,' I informed him, 'although now, strictly out of bounds to us souls of Père Lachaise. It's on Cloud Sixty-Six. Most of my dreams take place there, apart from the odd ones I've already told you.'

"'Over there, that's the place I want to show you. You see that large gate, there between those two mounds of larva on the foothills of Cloud Sixty-Six. Well, that is the entrance to the Erotic Zone. The Facilitator has barred it to the souls of the Reservation since the reassessment, well before I arrived here. Pity – it was the nearest place to Paradise, they used to say, for those inclined to pursue sensual pleasure.'

"'Are you telling me there used to be sex here at the Reservation?' he asked.

"'…Until things got out of hand.'

"'Whatever do you mean?' he cried.

"'Dreadful scenes, apparently… It seems the Zone was there to tempt those trying to purge their sins, but it became an obstacle to redemption and subsequently closed. If you want to, we'll make a little detour on the way home, and I'll show you the entrance.'

"'Very well – what dreadful scenes do you refer to?' Oscar asked.

"'Oh, there was one in particular that caused its closure,' I said. 'It was there to be a temptation for those serious of purging their sins, but the temptation was too much for them, as the experiences there were so superior to what they had on earth, that they became obsessed with it and soon forgot It seems temptation had more to offer than redemption.' about purging their sins.

"'Wait a moment. Are you saying there was wholesale sex there?' he asked.

"'Yes.'

"He became very quiet as he stared at the Zone. 'Only heterosexual sex,' he blurted out.

'"No, not at all, you name it; they had it and did it. Anything went – everything in excess. There was nothing in half measures. It was always party time there,' I replied.

'"Just a moment – there's something that doesn't add up,' he said, scratching his head. 'If we can't experience sexual pleasure here, why is there an Erotic Zone?'

'"This place is more sophisticated than you could imagine,' I replied. 'You see that humpback-bridge at the barricaded entrance to the Zone. Well, it seems that when the Zone was in operation, the moment you passed over it you regained your human emotions, especially your sexual drive – that is why everyone made a beeline for it at every available opportunity. You could say it was Purgatory's red-light district.'

'"No wonder they went wild,' Oscar exclaimed.

'"The whole idea of the place was that as part of your purging, you had to travel through the Zone without giving in to the temptations that were thrust in your face. Of course, very few ever managed it. I don't think I'd have got past the first few pleasure houses. It was, according to those who experienced it, an extraordinary place.'

'"But these scenes, these wild scenes, how did they happen? You must tell,' he insisted.

The main attractions at the club were three sassy women, Jacqueline, Ségolène, and Lesley, who set the place alight night after night. They say they were the most delectable women you were ever likely to see. When gazed upon, they turned into whichever woman the viewer fancied and then looked after all of their needs. What more could a man want? No wonder few ever reached the other side. You could say these women became the flavour of the moment and the souls were always fighting over them. Even some of those from the Moral High Ground up on Cloud Eighty-Seven, who came to condemn the girls and their customers for their outrageous behaviour, fell for their erotic charms.

'"One day one of the Moral High Grounders grabbed hold of Jacqueline, put her over his knee and began to slap her hard on the arse, screaming at her to repent for her scandalous behaviour. However, it soon became clear that he was enjoying himself. The customers thought he had overstepped the mark and grabbed the Moral High Grounder by the scruff of the neck and threw him across the floor towards his fellow moralists, who were also becoming hot under the collar. They picked up their companion and with rage in their eyes ran over to the girls, screaming holy murder. They grabbed them by their hair and were about to drag them out of the club when the rest of the revellers turned on them. They say it wasn't a pretty sight. The three girls had often had men fighting over them, but never like this. It seemed as though the whole Reservation had lost control and as well as beating the hell out of the moralist, they fought between themselves for the favours of the girls. It was a shambles. Within, days the Erotic Zone was closed and has never been open since.

"'The Facilitator ordered an immediate report on the disturbance. After studying the results of the investigation, he submitted it to the Divine Council with the recommendation of the permanent closure of the Zone. It was a hindrance to the good government of the Reservation. They had been considering reform of the structure of Purgatory for some time, so this disturbance was the green light to implement the reforms.'

"Oscar sat there looking rather confused by what I'd revealed. He hadn't yet taken his eyes off of the Erotic Zone. I certainly had his attention. He was in a kind of trance. 'It is such a pity,' he sighed.

"'What is?' I asked, offering him more divine wine, for he seemed in dire need of some.

"'The closure of the Erotic Zone,' he replied as he sipped his wine. 'Surely it would have been more beneficial to have kept it open rather leaving the tenants frustrated? Surely, an odd brawl was preferable to having frustrated souls running about the place. There must be many sexually disturbed souls here now because of its closure.'

"'That's what's so odd about it,' I replied. 'You would have thought that would have been the case, but after the initial shock of its closure, they got over it. As you can see, the lack of sex doesn't bother the tenants at all – apart from you, of course. Well, I must say, Oscar, you are the only one I know who is bothered about sex. There again, you are the only one I know of who is unable to dream.'

"'Am I?' he sighed.

"'It seems so. So, you want to know how to dream, do you?' I asked as I put my arm across his shoulder.

"'Indeed I do. My last dream was of seeing my mother dancing with my father at a ball in Saint George's Hall in Dublin Castle.'

"'When was that?' I asked.

"'A few days before I died – the odd thing was they were in their twenties, without a care in the world. Of course, that was before I was born. They just sallied across the floor – knew every step of every dance. I suppose I inherited my finesse from them,' he proudly announced. He was serious.

"'One of my regular dreams is about dancing. Very erotic it is,' I teased.

"'Really!' he panted. 'You must tell me.'

"'All in good time – forget about dancing – you have to dream first,' I told him. 'It's essential for your emotional survival.'

"'You never said a truer word,' he cried.

You may have realised that Alfred de Musset is a bit of a braggart. Once he gets started, it's hard to shut him up.

Sophie, who usually suffered from a short attention span, somehow forgot about Oscar's odd behaviour as she listened intently to Musset. His retention to detail intrigued her, and he talked as if everything he said were gospel.

Marie however, had heard it all before. Was she aware that there was something hidden within Musset's words that had a bearing on what she was calling Oscar's recent 'odd and bizarre behaviour', or was this just more of Musset's tall tales? Let's find out.

We rejoin Marie and Sophie as they listen to Musset describing how he administered his magic potion to our frustrated genius as they sit under an elm tree looking out towards the defunct Erotic Zone.

***

"'What do you think of when you are trying to sleep?' I asked my keen patient.

"'Everything – I have so many unresolved matters flying around in my head they exhaust me and I normally nod off,' he replied.

"'The classic sign of a non-dreamer, having too much rubbish floating around in the head – does you no good at all. To dream, one must empty one's head of all that garbage we accumulate throughout the day. If one doesn't, one will end up with nothing but nightmares,' I informed him. 'So you don't dream. We'll soon put that to rights.'

"'How?'

"'Simple. You see this,' I said as I withdrew a small blue bottle from my coat pocket. 'This is my magic potion. If this can't help you, nothing can.'

"Taking the bottle, he looked curiously at it. 'That! A magic potion?' he howled, pointing at it, unconvinced by my claim.

"'This, my good man is my Dream Enhancer. When my dreams become a bit stale, as they do now and then, I take a drop of this, and they return to their most sensuous splendour. I never let this precious bottle out of my sight,' I said.

"'But how can it help me? I have no dreams to enhance,' he reminded me.

"'I'm serious. This blue bottle is the answer to your dilemma,' I replied. 'This was mixed by a herbalist over on Cloud Eighty-Six, whom I visited not long after I arrived at the Reservation. Fontaine, who directed me to her den deep in the Forest of Thyme told me about her. She was a difficult woman who took some convincing that I was sincere in my belief in herbal remedies.'

"'Were you?'

"'Not at all,' I replied. 'But I soon convinced myself at the thought of what the formula could do for me. She had a strict requirement to be satisfied before she parted with her magic, for it was potent stuff. It was so potent, she said, that if you were unfortunate not to dream, it would do the trick. I had to make twelve visits before she gave it to me. She doesn't give away her formula to any old soul. She's very selective.'

"'Why, then, did she give it to you?' he cynically asked.

"'Now, now, Oscar, behave yourself, or I won't help you to dream.'

"'Don't be daft,' he sneered. 'Nobody can teach or make people dream.'

"'I intend to prove you wrong.' I said.

"He didn't look too convinced as he examined the bottle and said, 'This herbalist, are you sure she didn't see you coming, that she was just having you on, just as you are with me? It seems a bit far-fetched to believe there is such a tonic as a Dream Enhancer or one that can give you erotic dreams.'

"I laughed at the silly ass as he again examined the bottle. 'Well, there is, and you have it in your hands. Go on, be a brave soul and have a taste.'

"He looked at it for some time; then took a swig. He shivered at its foul taste; his face contorted as he returned the bottle to me.

"'Well done,' I said. 'The next time you lay down your pretty head to sleep, you will wake up a new man. Trust me.'

"'So that's it?' he said as he sprang to his feet.

"'Yes. Wait until your next sleep, you may well be in for a pleasant surprise.'

"'I must say, it's a foul-tasting concoction,' he moaned.

"'It has no taste. You're imagining it.'

"'I am telling you, it is foul,' he stressed. 'I know we are not supposed to have any sense of taste, but that tasted foul.'

"'It's all in the mind. Anyway, sometimes you have to suffer for the sake of pleasure,' I said, as we continued our journey.

"We walked on for a while, not saying anything; then suddenly he stopped in his tracks and was back to the subject of George Sand and Chopin.

"'You think Chopin was the love of George's life?'

"'Certainly,' I replied.

"'Odd, though,' he mused as he stood in front of me, with his hands on hips. 'That journal she wrote.'

"'*Journal intime*. You've read it, then?'

"'I have. She seems to have been fixated on you. Argue all you want about not being the love of her life – but by God, going by her journal, you certainly were. You didn't know she was writing it?' he asked.

"'I had no idea until in a moment of madness she sent me the original,' I answered. 'Once I read it, I was a bit disturbed that she could put such sentimental stuff to paper. Shocked I was by what she wrote about me, things she never said directly to me. If she had, maybe our affair would have lasted longer. Maybe I would have seen a different side to her, a softer, more loving side, not simply an object of sexual desire, for that is all I considered her. Instead, I used the journal to humiliate her. I sent copies to all my friends and to those who knew her well. My friends thought she had made a stupid mistake – not just in writing it, but also in sending it to me. I was annoyed that she could have penned such drivel and I wanted to embarrass and belittle her, which I did.'

"'Why do you think she wrote it?'

'I don't know,' I replied, hoping he'd forget all about it as it was embarrassing talking about it, seeing as I used it against her. 'She did go overboard. It was a bit too descriptive when it came to our tempestuous relationship.'

"'Perhaps she was more attracted to you than you think. After I read it, I got the distinct impression that she loved you with a passion. You could say she was obsessed by you,' he continued.

"'Rubbish. It was Chopin she was madly and hopelessly obsessed with,' I reminded him.

"'Seems odd, though, that she wrote with such passion about you,' he said.

"'For heaven's sake, Oscar, it was a fantasy, nothing more,' I laughed. 'Did you not read her final comment at the end of the journal she wrote in September 1868, before she died? She begins by saying that she had hoped it would have been full of beautiful things, but what she had written was nothing but foolishness. That doesn't sound like true love, does it? Surely you wouldn't describe the love of your life as foolishness, would you?'

"'I don't remember reading that,' he said, confused.

"'You shouldn't skip pages. It is a bad habit. You end up missing all the juicy parts. It's as clear as day, throughout the journal, that it's nothing more than fantasy. It's well written, probably one of her finest works, and an interesting read, but nothing more – and certainly not a declaration of undying love. It's Chopin you should be talking to, to understand just whom George really loved and why.'

'"Very interesting you should say that,' Oscar said. 'You know, every time I try to talk to him about their relationship, he goes very quiet – as quiet as a mouse. I've tried every trick to get him to open up, but no, he won't. He will talk forever about the rest of his life, but not about her. Strange, is not it? Have you noticed how he will stand up for her when anyone says anything nasty about her? I wonder what that is all about.'

'"Never noticed,' I replied.

'"What! Are you saying you never discussed George with him?' he asked.

'"No. We talk about everything else but never about her.'

'"How very odd, how very, very odd indeed,' he replied, surprise lacing his words.

'"No, there was nothing odd about it,' I said. 'We were well aware of the connection between us. But for Christ's sake, we never exchanged notes on each other's sexual performances, if that's what you're getting at. He never mentioned her, and neither did I. We get on very well with each other, so why spoil a good relationship with idle talk about George.'

'"Even so, it's a pity he won't talk about her. I wonder what cloud she ended up on,' he mused.

'"Not this one, thank God. I do know however on which one she resides,' I replied, knowing that I'd get a reaction.

'"You do?' he asked, surprised.

'"Yes. When we reach the summit of Cloud Twenty-One, which is on our route, I'll show you. Don't worry, though, there's no transfer system between the sectors. We are quite safe. No chance of coming face to face with her.'

'"What a pity,' he replied. 'I'd loved to have met her.'

***

Now reader, isn't that something to whet the appetite, Oscar Wilde meets George Sand? Imagine these two getting to grips with each other. Who would have won the intellectual battle? Whose ego would have dominated? Would they have liked each other? I feel a thesis coming on. However, I digress. Let's return to Musset as he continued escorting our wayward genius towards the summit of Cloud Twenty-Two.

***

"We continued on the way home, passing through the Cyprus Tree Grove, until we arrived at the tunnel, leading to the Valley of

Happiness. Oscar stopped and peered through the clematis-clad entrance.

"'What happens if we enter, Alfred?' he enquired.

"'We relive the happiest times of our lives.'

"'Oh, I'm all for that,' he beamed.

"'Ah!' I replied. 'It's not as straightforward as that. There is a penalty to be paid if you pass through the tunnel.'

"'What kind of penalty?'

"'I don't know. What I've been told is that a penalty is applied and you don't know what that penalty is until you return through the tunnel.'

"'Is that so?' he said in one of those odd voices of his. 'Seems unfair, to be penalised for being curious. Come now; let's see what the penalty is?'

"'Are you mad?' I replied. 'Nobody with any sense enters. Let's go home.'

"'Don't we have to pass through here as part of purging our sins?' Oscar asked.

"'Yes, but most souls have more sense than to try.'

"'Come here,' he said, grabbing my sleeve and pulling me towards the entrance.'

"'Only fools are foolish enough to revisit their past. If you are foolish enough, then go by yourself. It's a waste of time trying to get me to go with you, for a soul can only do the journey alone. Go, if you wish, I'll stay here. Everyone who goes there always regrets it. Remember that, Oscar.'

"'Right, if you are going to be like that I'll go on my own. My enquiring mind will not allow me to pass an opportunity to broaden my horizons and help to purge my sins,' he replied.

"'Some things are not worth knowing about, and this is one of them. You don't even know what your venial sins are, so it's insane trying to purge them,' I said, angry that he was too blind to see the danger before him.

"He entered the tunnel with a swagger and as I looked through it, I could see him vanish as he reached the far side. I sat down at the foot of a cypress tree and before I knew it, I was fast asleep, dreaming of better things than unwanted penalties. The next I knew – I was being shaken violently.

"'Wake up, Alfred, wake up,' a voice cried.

"I looked up, and there was Oscar returned from his journey. He looked rather shaken. He had been crying.

"'What happened?' I asked.

"'Oh... nothing much,' he whispered. 'Come! Let's go home.'

"'The penalty – were you given one for your troubles?' I asked.

"'I don't want to talk about it.'

"'Did you get a penalty?' I repeated.

"'Yes,' he mumbled.

"'What was it?'

"'Another time – I really don't want to talk about it,' he said. He turned and headed for home.

"I ran after him, keen to know what happened. I tried to get it out of him, but he wouldn't tell. As we continued our journey, he seemed rather distracted, and I knew deep down it had been a mistake to let him enter the Valley of Happiness. I hoped it wasn't going to prey on his mind. It didn't seem to, for as we neared the road to the summit of Cloud Twenty-One, he was back to his breezy self. There was a spring in his step as we carried on our journey home.

"He resumed our conversation about George Sand and wanted to know more and more about her. She fascinated him. His meeting with Saint Peter and whatever he'd experienced in the Valley of Happiness was soon forgotten. He was relaxed and peppered me with questions, most of them about George. I answered as best I could, but he was never content with my answers and would find another approach. By the time we reached the summit of Cloud Twenty-One, he'd mentally drained me.

"We settled down for the evening, sleeping under the stars. The summit was a popular resting place for those on route to and from the Pearly Gates. Up there are the best views of the whole Reservation and the best hotels and watering holes. From there you could see the beauty of the Reservation and many of the other Reservations, which stretch as far as the eye can see.

"We awoke to a glorious day. Jumping to my feet, I had a good yawn and stretch and gave Oscar a gentle nudge with my foot. 'Take a look at this. Wake up. What a view!'

"'It's too early to view anything,' he groaned. 'Go back to sleep.'

"I gave him another nudge. He sat up and rubbed the sleep from his eyes. The view before him took his breath away. He sprung to his feet and gazed about him.

"'What a scene,' he enthused. 'You could be forgiven in thinking this was Paradise itself.'

"We just stood absorbed in the spectacular view. I'd been there many times before, but this splendid sight never failed to impress. Indeed, this was the nearest any of us souls of Père Lachaise would ever get to Paradise. Many a time, when I was feeling out of sorts, I would walk up here just to experience the dawn rising over this special place. It wouldn't take long for my sprits to revive and I'd wander off home with a feeling of exhilaration that would stay with me for a good while. Sharing with Oscar this sight would make an impression on him so that he'd want to return time after time. On our outward journey, I deliberately took the less scenic route, so if all went pear-shaped with Peter, as it did, this scene would revive his spirits.

"'Where did you say this place was?'

"'Cloud Twenty-One. Most call it *Faux Paradis,*' I replied.

"'Most impressive – I wouldn't mind living up here.'

"'Sorry, no soul can reside here, only visit. That's the rule, I'm afraid,' I informed him.

"He looked at me scornfully. 'Why ever not?'

"'Rules,'

"'Rules! Are these more of the rules nobody told me about?' Oscar asked.

"'It's your own fault for not reading the Book of Rules when you arrived,' I replied. 'Look, way over there,' I said, pointing to a distant cloud. 'That is the Pantheon Reservation.'

"'There must be good company there. I wonder if Victor Hugo is there along with Voltaire.'

'I'd say Victor's in Paradise,' I nonchalantly replied.

"'Would you now?'

"'Yes, I'm sure of it,' I replied.

"'Why?'

"'Why! That's obvious, isn't it?'

"'Is it?' he muttered as he gazed over towards the Pantheon Reservation.

"'Of course it is. He's a genius, that's why,' I replied.

"He stood back and glared at me. With hands on hips, he looked me up and down with abhorrence. 'Well, I'll be damned,' he cried. 'Didn't Saint Peter just say that there was no credit for genius and now you say Victor is in Paradise because of his genius? I'm a genius too, you know. Maybe not up to Victor's standard, but a genius all the same.'

"'Aren't we all?' I sighed.

"'No! No,' he snapped, looking very agitated. He wasn't far from stamping his feet like some spoilt child who can't get its way. 'Some just imagine they are. Geniuses are thin on the ground. We are a rare species. Why, for heaven's sake, should Victor be treated better than any other genius, better than my good self?'

"'Because he's a cut above the rest, that's why.' The second I uttered the words I knew I was for it.

"'Oh! And how, pray, do you work that one out?' he snarled.

"'Saint Peter said it was not your genius you receive credit for – but how you used it, and Victor used his to great effect.'

"'You're saying I didn't?'

"'Only you can answer that.'

"'Do you think I made a hash of my genius? Come now, spit it out. No need to be shy with me,' he cried.

"'It's not for me to say. You tell me.'

"He scowled as he looked at me, as though he was trying to read my mind. He bit his lower lip, squinted at me, shrugged his shoulders and said, 'What about the Gold Stars in my Credit Book? I received most of them for the use of my genius. If you are so smart, then answer that.'

"'So what, you've got Gold Stars. Maybe Victor has got a book full,' I laughed. 'And by the way, you didn't receive all your Gold Stars for your genius – you got them for your humanity. You heard Peter say you receive no credit for your genius.'

"'You're just being pernickety now,' he snarled. 'Peter may well have meant that all of my actions were because of my genius that everything I did and achieved was because of it. I'm surprised you didn't understand what he was saying.'

"'I understood exactly what he was saying. You're twisting his words,' I said. 'Only you would try to manipulate the words of a saint. You certainly didn't receive enough Gold Stars to put a foot inside the Pearly Gates, that's for sure.'

"He stepped back in surprise. 'So, are you saying, to secure your place in Paradise, it is all down to how many Gold Stars one has? Is that really the determining factor to see the face of God – a book full of Gold Stars?'

"'Now… you're being silly. The truth is, Oscar, I don't know if Victor is in Paradise or not, so it's a waste of time even speculating, as for Gold Stars, I have no idea.'

"'Then why did you say he's in Paradise?' he asked.

"'I thought I'd better get myself out of this mess. He was getting a bit too serious about his genius. Instead of it being a blessed gift, it was becoming a burden to him. 'What an idiot you are at times. I was only teasing. I thought you were known for your sense of humour.'

"'I am,' he replied, 'but one can't laugh at genius – it's a serious subject. What about Voltaire, is he at the Pantheon?'

"'Why not!' I replied. 'It's as good a place as any. I'd say, along with Zola and all the heroes of the Republic, good old Voltaire is there amongst them, having a good laugh at his Purgatory and the company he is keeping.

"'Not in Paradise then?'

"'Highly unlikely – like Honoré and Sarah, he's not the kind,' I replied.

"'Apart from Voltaire, then, the company doesn't seem too wonderful, does it? I think we're better off here,' he said.

"'Certainly – there's more variety here. I imagine it being rather stuffy and overbearing on that cloud with all those military heroes and the likes that reside there, all polishing their brass and screaming orders at each other. Not exactly a belly full of laughter. It wouldn't suit us.'

"'It's certain to be devoid of any humour,' he added.

"'I don't know about that. I'd say Voltaire wouldn't be shy about cracking a few racy jokes, but forget about Victor – he has no sense of humour at all - never had. A bit of a sourpuss,' I said.

Sophie gave a riotous laugh at the description of her famous son.

"Sorry, Sophie – didn't mean to insult poor Victor."

61

"Don't apologise. That's our Victor all right – a genius, and yes, a sourpuss of one – a bit like his father."

Oscar continued, 'Victor may very well be a fine writer and poet, but he is not the kind you would bring to a party to set it alight, is he? Did you know I went to see him when he was dying? I made a few witty remarks, but he looked at me as though I was mad. He said nothing, just closed his eyes and went to sleep. Not long after, he was dead.'

"'I didn't know you knew him.'

"'I didn't,' he replied. 'A friend had said poor Victor was ailing and that a visit from me would perk him up. The only effect I had on him was that I sent him to sleep.'

What about George. Where is her cloud? He wistfully asked.

"'It is so far away you'll need binoculars to see it… Here,' I said, handing him a pair. 'It's way, way over there on the northern horizon.'

"He stood for some time, gazing at a far away cloud. I wondered what he was thinking. I soon found out. 'If you had happened to have been on the same cloud as George,' he mused, 'do you think you would have settled your differences with her and became friends again or even lovers?'

"'That would depend on how she'd adjusted to her new surroundings, wouldn't it. To tell you the truth, I doubt she'd have the mental capacity to do so. I say she'd be a perfect candidate for Cloud Eighty-Seven with the rest of those souls who can't hack it. Now, if she had you, Oscar, for intellectual company, matters would certainly be different,' I teasingly said, knowing how he'd react.

"'You think so?' he exclaimed. 'You really think she'd connect with me, not just emotionally, but physically?' he asked, still looking over at her cloud.

"'Without doubt,' I replied. 'You would have been a challenge to her. Just as I said, she would be the one for you. It would have been a battle of emotional and intellectual prowess. You would have been electric together, that I know for sure. You would both sizzle at each other's touch. Yes, my friend, I can see you both bouncing off each other like sensual ping-pongs.'

"'The more I turn it over in my mind, the more I think you are right, Alfred. Yes, George and I are kindred spirits. I can feel it. Alas, we were destined never to meet,' he lamented.

"'Perhaps you might dream about her – you never can tell.'

"'Ah, a poor substitute for the real thing,' he replied.

"'Well, if your dreams are explicit, I can't see why they can't be as good as the real thing.'

"That's what it was like all the way home. He wanted to know every scintilla of information about her. He was obsessed by her and couldn't get enough of her. For a fellow with a reputation for having eyes for Greek looking young men, he had a powerful attraction to the fairer sex, especially dear George. I don't know if his attraction was of her dressed as a man, smoking a cigar or because she was an attractive female. Perhaps he'd be happy with either. After all, he always wanted more than his fair share of the sexual cake."

Now, reader, as Musset was talking, he noticed a soul he hadn't seen before, sitting not far from him scribbling notes like it was going out of style. The soul didn't miss a word he was saying. Musset, being the Reservation's number one teller of tales, either short or tall thought the stranger was just a keen fan hanging on his every word.

Ah! How wrong he was.

***

He continued his tale. "As we were nearing the Buttercup Vale, which leads down toward the Literary Quarter, Oscar tapped me on the shoulder. 'These dreams of yours – tell me more.'

"'Perhaps it's not a good idea. They'll only make you more frustrated and hot under the collar than you already are – that will never do.'

"'I can take it,' he assured me.

"'Are you sure?'

"'Certainly,' he replied.

"'Very well, but we should wait until you're dreaming again. With a bit of luck, you should experience your first one tonight.'

"'Are you sure this tonic, this magic potion of yours, will work?' he asked. 'It sounds unlikely.'

'Of course! Never fails. When you wake in the morning, you'll be forever thanking me. Trust me.'

"He didn't look too convinced. 'Tell me about your dancing dream. Tell me now. I can't wait until I dream, that's if I ever do.'

"'Oh, all right!' I said, feeling sorry for the frustrated soul. 'Let's sit down here amongst the buttercups and I'll tell you of the dream I call The Waltz of the Fleurs. To date, I have had the pleasure of this dream on about twenty-five occasions. Apart from a few deviations here and there, the dreams have been very much the same.

"'As you know I'm a real lover of Paris – one of her most passionate and dedicated sons. Paris to me is like a tantalizing woman off whom I can't keep my hands. The more I see her, the more I want her. The more I have her, the more possessive I become. I'm a slave to her beauty. Because I miss her so much, and I'm so far away from her, I can't help but see her in my dreams. Most of my dreams outside of the Erotic Zone are always about Paris. And would you believe it – dancing? Why dancing? In life, I wasn't that mad about it. You couldn't exactly call me twinkle toes when it came to the light fantastic, but I'd make a few turns around the dance floor if there were a possibility of passion for my efforts, which there usually was.

Dancing to me meant nothing more than an avenue to getting my arms around the female form. I just can't help myself. It's a kind of illness. Can't put a name to it but I'm sure there is one.'

"Oscar laughed. 'Rake springs to mind.'

"I ignored his remark. 'I dream that every Sunday evening there is a gathering on the bridge of Pont d'Arcole in preparation for the dancing competition of the Waltz of the Fleurs. It begins with a barrow load of flowers being delivered to the corner of the quai aux Fleurs and the bridge of Pont d'Arcole, where a multitude of dancers limber up for the evening's event. The rules for the occasion are simple: all women must turn out in long dresses, with blouses of any hue and hair ribbons in red, white and blue or a combination of the three and must wear a flower in their hair. The main attraction for women is showing off their shoes. There is always something very sensual about shoes, especially those worn by gorgeous Parisians women. When I meet a woman for the first time, I look at her shoes. Then her figure, then her breasts, then her eyes and to her shoes again. I can always detect the level of their sensuality by a quick look at their shoes.

"Oscar raised his eyebrows in amazement.

"'The chaps have to be decked out in black suits with white shirts and shoes, any colour tie or cravat with a flower in their lapel. They must all wear a sharp false nose, so they all look like me,' I continued.

"'Why?' Oscar asked, laughing.

"'Because they're the rules – they love and worship me so much they endeavour to look as I do.'

"'You certainly love yourself,' Oscar cried. 'I thought I was bad enough, but you are the limit. It's bad enough dreaming about yourself, but to have hundreds disguised as you is sheer egomania.'

"'Don't be petty. It's not becoming,' I replied. 'Each couple waltz across the rue d'Arcole, finishing on the bridge of Pont au Double, opposite Notre Dame. The judges spread out along the route judging the dancers' dexterity and pose. The winners receive the freedom to dine for a month at any restaurant in the city at the expense of Monsieur, the Mayor of Paris.

"'The event begins with the gentlemen selecting flowers for the ladies – there's always a choice of roses, violets or carnations – and the ladies picking buttonholes for their partners. Then the ladies inspect their partners' false noses to see if they are up to scratch, nothing bent or leaning the wrong way. They must be as perfect as I am. It's most important that they are sharp and smooth without any blemishes. Then, ten accordion players line up across the road, and the dancers get on their marks, three abreast, waiting for Monsieur, the Mayor of Paris to drop his handkerchief to begin the waltz. Off they go at a steady pace with the judges watching their every move. Then at random, a couple will be halted and asked to recite a stanza of one of my poems or plays. If they can't, they have to leave the waltz. If they recite it word for word, they receive a rosette. It's all done I must say, in the most cultivated and civilized Parisian way. The crowds encourage them and all in all it's a festive evening.'

"Oscar looked at me, his eyebrows raised and enquired, 'There was no sex involved?'

"'No… not at all – but it's always a very sensual display,' I was pleased to inform him. 'There's always passion and close-quarter dalliance throughout, but no sex. However, you can feel the sexual tension vibrating along the route.'

"'You never participate?' he asked.

"'No. I'm always an onlooker. I have no need to join in as all the men look like me. Whatever happens, I'm always a winner; always the centre of attention?'

"'If it's true what you say, then you're an incredibly egocentric poseur, imagining yourself waltzing with all the pretty women of Paris!'

"'Take it or leave it,' I replied. 'Once my magic potion takes effect you'll begin dreaming, then you'll discover that it's far from nonsense.'

"'I won't hold my breath,' he grunted. 'What about your dreams of the Erotic Zone – I suppose you're just dying to tell me about them too.'

"'I certainly am,' I replied. 'Look, we are nearing the Zone's entrance now. Come, let us sit on the fence and I will tell you all about the Zone and, if you are a good chap, I will tell you of my dreams. '

"We sat on the fence, looking at the barricaded humpback bridge that led to the entrance of the Erotic Zone, the now-defunct Purgatory Pleasure Park," said Musset as Sophie and Marie sat eagerly waiting for him to continue.

"Oscar was quiet for a while as he surveyed the entrance that was smothered with overgrown passion flowers. He gawked at the run-down pleasure houses and sighed. 'For someone who's never been to the Zone, you know a lot about it, Alfred,' he said as he jumped off the fence and walked over to the barrier. 'How come you know so much about this pleasure park?' he asked as he observed the place.

"'I take a lot of interest in anything erotic; it's in my nature. Once I was aware that the place existed, I naturally sought it out. I asked around to find out what it was all about; I even tried to sneak in a few times, without success, I may add. Molière educated me about the place. He's the Reservation's expert on the Erotic Zone. He described the place in detail to me when he was in one of his better moods. He's into eroticism in a big way. You could say he's the historian of the Erotic Zone.'

"'So you know the history of the place?'

"'I spent hours listening to him describe it. This wasn't a fable; this was the real thing. I just couldn't believe that such a place existed. It was the most visited place on the Reservation by a long shot, even beating the Pearly Gates.'

"'You don't say!' Oscar replied as he took a good look at the carved panels at the Zone's entrance. 'Have you seen this?' he asked as he guided his fingers over the carved figures that decorated the huge entrance panels standing at either side of the large wrought-iron gates.

"'Many a time,' I said. 'It's very graphic.'

"He let his fingers pick out the contours of couples contorted into the positions of the *Karma Sutra*.

"'You're not the first one to run their fingers over those seductive panels, I can tell you. According to Molière, when souls arrived here, the first thing they did before walking over the humpback bridge was to caress the panels. It was a kind of religious ritual, you know, a form of foreplay before they entered the Zone. The panels were just a taste of what was yet to be experienced once you passed through the gates.'

"Oscar licked his lips. 'How did it all begin?' he asked.

"'As Molière described it, it looks like whoever governs this place decided that the best way of testing the inhabitants' sexual control was to set up an Erotic Zone. Here, they would have to confront sexuality to see if they could resist it. Those guilty of sexual excess in their earthly existence who had a desire to purge their venial sins were always on to a loser. They didn't stand a chance. You see, instead of resisting the urge to visit, they took every available opportunity to head off to the Zone and indulge in anything that they desired. Even those not into sexual excess on earth fell victim to its delights. It was like a magnet to them – and I'm telling you, anything went.'

"'Really, such as?' he excitingly asked, his eyes wide with anticipation.

"'The Zone was set out in separate spheres, which accommodated all kinds for sexual persuasion,' I teased. 'You name it – it was there. There were so many saloons, houses and gardens one was spoilt for choice. Molière gave me a map of the place. I have it in my study. I'll let you have a look when we get back. Let's see if I can remember the layout. Oh, yes. You see the cloakroom there?' I said, pointing to an area just to the right of the bridge. 'Well, just behind it was the Titillation Saloon. It appears that this was pretty mild – beginners place, a place to find one's feet, you could say. Those who'd never indulged in sex on earth could be found hanging about there, dithering about as to whether to come or go. Sounds sad, doesn't it? Leading from that was a red bridge that was lined with pots of yellow tree poppies that led to the Mud Baths, where couples got down to business in the warm mud, splashing and sliding all over the place. Not my kind of thing, I may add, but they say it was popular. There was also a viewing room if you were that way inclined. A very popular place, I'm told. Next to it were the Mud Baths for the likes of you. It accommodated all tastes. No prejudices there.'

"His eyes widened. ' I'm glad to hear it. But is all this true?'

"'So Molière says,' I replied. 'Then, at the far side of the Mud Baths was the Cross-Dressers Club. That was supposed to be something to see. It was a huge barn-like place with a raised stage. In front of the stage was a horseshoe bar. After every ten minutes of serving drinks, a bell would ring. The bar quickly cleared, the curtains would open, and a ten-minute musical revue would take place, with the men dressed as women and women as men – a kind of pantomime thing. As well as dancing and singing on stage, they would also dance across the bar, high kicking as they went. This was repeated every twenty minutes – raunchy stuff indeed.'

"He looked at me in his Wildean way. 'Are you having me on again? This seems too good to be true.'

"'I'm only telling you what Molière told me. He was pretty keen on the place. I've also talked to numerous souls who'd spent many satisfying hours there, and some of their stories would make your hair stand on end. The stories were so good I wrote them in a journal I called *Short and Tall Tales of the Erotic Zone*. Grand title, isn't it?

"'Ah! Opposite the Cross Dressers Club was the place itself, the place to be seen in – Club 88 with all its wonders. Molière bragged that he spent most of his time there. He had a thing about Jacqueline. He liked her as she was and never envisaged her as any other woman. This club was the heartbeat of the Zone. Even though a soul may be on his way to some other house of pleasure, he or she would always stay a while here to down a few drinks before their exertions. The club was a mass of greenery growing in terracotta pots of every size, festooned with varieties of passion flowers with a sprinkling of busy Lizzies and geraniums. Molière was so taken with the place that he'd spend every available moment there. That is why he is such an expert on the Zone. He was so keen on the place that he wrote many of his new plays there. He sat at a table in an alcove, just inside the main entrance, and as he eyed up Jacqueline, he scribbled away on his script.'

"'How come I've never encountered Molière?'

"'When the Zone was closed down he went loopy and after a while went off in a huff to the marshes up there on Cloud Thirty-Three. He's now a hermit there and never leaves the place. I had a job getting to see him. When I did, he took a shine to me, and we got on as though we'd been lifelong friends, meeting on a regular basis. It was at these meetings he revealed to me the history and secrets of the Zone.'

"'Do you think he'd meet me?'

"'You never can tell,' I replied. 'Maybe you should try on one of his better days; he's turned into a cranky bad-tempered sod since the closure. Anyway, let me continue. After leaving Club 88, there was a choice of venues. To the left was the Bondage Club, to the right the Masochism Revue Bar.'

"Oscar's eyes lit up again.

"'The Bondage Club was in a round red-brick building with ivy gripping it tightly, as tightly as the chains that bound the clients of the club to their addiction. This was a favourite spot for the religious. I don't know what it was all about, but priests and monks had a whale of a time there, along with nuns letting go of their virtue. The more chains that bound them, the happier and more gratified they were. Odd, isn't it, what some souls get up to for a bit of pleasure?'

"He gave a hearty laugh. 'What is odd to some souls is normal to others. There is no accounting for taste.'

"'How right you are,' I replied. 'The Masochism Revue Bar... well, that was a place one had to be desperate to visit, and there must have been many desperate souls about as it was always bursting at the seams.'

"'It would have suited you, all that rough treatment,' Oscar laughed. 'I know you said you were not into it, but I would say you would have been a permanent fixture there if it were still open.' He chuckled and looked at me with a twinkle in his eyes. 'I would have thought it would have suited you just fine.'

"'I've already told you that I'm not and never have been a masochist. Violence in sex is demeaning. I love women too much to demean them.'

"Oscar gave a hearty laugh. 'You don't mind giving them a straightforward whack like you gave poor George but you stop short of sexual violence, is that what you saying?' I took no notice of him. 'You treated women as sexual playthings,' he continued. 'What do you mean you never demeaned them? You were an expert at it. You have already confessed to treating poor George as a sexual plaything?'

"I refused to answer him. 'Then there was the Fetish Cellar,' I said, continuing my verbal guide. 'Now, this was the place that attracted the cream of the legal profession. Judges, barristers, and certain solicitors had an addiction to its seedy goings-on.

"'The judge that sent me down would have had a field day there. If ever there was a judge who had a fetish, it was he,' Oscar laughed.

"'Once outside of the Fetish Cellar, if you survived the antics of the legal profession, you would come face to face with the tastiest place of all – the delectable Chocolate Spa.'

"Oscar's eyes widened, and he began to pant. 'I've never heard of such a place. What's chocolate to do with erotica?' he asked, his eyes watering at the prospect of some sensuous explanation. God, he was easily aroused. I continued to tease him.

"'Oh, it wasn't like any other spa. This place was different in every aspect – no waters to refresh the soul and one's sensibilities. No, no, what refreshed the soul there was something out of this world, something tasty and delicious; something to get one's tongue around. At its entrance, some golden-skinned beauty would offer you a seat in her silver parlour; then spread before you a selection of well-endowed chocolates. The secret of these was to suck them slowly. It would take seven minutes to finish one, and in doing, so you would experience the height of pleasure. You were only allowed one at a time mind you; no overindulgence of these erotic sweeties was allowed. The slower you sucked the clearer your vision of perfection would be...'

"'Vision!' he gasped. 'What kind of vision?'

"'The best kind – the most desirable person you could ever imagine became clearer and more sensuous with every suck. The one soul who was forever out of your reach on earth was in your grasp as you sucked away in that silvery parlour of chocolate delight. This was the ultimate experience. This parlour wasn't for those who were

70

sexually faint-hearted. Better still,' I continued. 'After you had devoured the chocolate you were then escorted into a spa room, where you'd have to strip off and stretch out on a silver raised podium. Then, for a solid two hours, warm chocolate would be spread over you, scraped off, then repeated until you were completely satisfied. Another erotic sweetie rounded off the session – a kind of dessert to send you on your way. Yes, a very special treat.'

"He licked his lips but didn't say anything, just gazed over at the Zone. I had him transfixed.

"'After the delightful chocolate experience, came the Whipping Paddock. Barrister Bar, who loved nothing better than trying to take a strip of you, ran this house of ill repute and did so with devilish delight. They say he had the sharpest flick of the wrist when he let fly with his whip that would leave the flesh sizzling. Even Molière found this place hard to take. He couldn't understand why any soul would want to willingly be whipped to within an inch of their life and take pleasure from it.'

"'Who visited?' he curiously asked.

"'Mostly those from the legal profession – after their exertions at the Fetish Cellar, they headed for the paddock for a little extra pleasure. You know, those legal eagles seemed to feel at home there. Then there were priests, nuns, and captains of industry who could never get enough of the place. Not my scene, mind you, but many thoroughly enjoyed being whipped by a legal eagle. Across the road from the Whipping Paddock was the Sadists' Château.'

"The moment I mentioned sadism, he was agog and began to perspire. He took another swig of divine wine.

"'You'd never believe how many make a dash for that hellhole – at least, that's how Molière described it. He wasn't too impressed by it.'

"'I suppose you weren't into sadism either,' Oscar sneered. 'Just as you weren't into masochism…'

"'I wasn't, but the next place would have been more to my taste.'

"'Oh? And what was that?' he asked.

"'If you were still on your feet and still mentally intact after the exertions the Sadists' Château offered, you then had to swim the length of the Nymph's Lake to continue your journey to redemption. It was extremely difficult to achieve, for once in amongst the reeds and lilies the nymphs were all over you. Molière maintained that most souls never got any further than here for the nymphs were so seductive and alluring. I must say, I couldn't see myself wanting to leave such a delightful place.'

"Oscar scratched his head in bewilderment. 'What about women, what was on offer to them in this Nymph's Lake?'

"'The same,' I replied. 'Whoever they looked at was male, unless they were lesbian of course. In that case, all they looked at were women. There was absolute equality in the Erotic Zone. Instead of nymphs swimming in between the water lilies, women came face to face with young men looking like Greek gods. No woman could ever swim past them without falling for their charms. Even the most prudish succumbed, and the Lady in Blue, with all of her repressed feelings, fell for their charms. She was so disgusted with herself for giving into such erotic pleasure; she turned sour and became the paragon of morality she is today. Yes, Oscar, this was the place to be.

"'If you did manage to survive the lake, once you come ashore you came to the colourful entrance to the *Karma Sutra Gardens*. Now, this was a delightful place. Standing amongst a mass of campanula were two well-endowed statues that stood guard over this garden of sexual delight. The man was to the left and the woman to the right, with their arms reaching out to each other, making an archway into the gardens. What I have heard about this place would turn the head of any straight-laced or puritan soul. The tales of this place are legendary, so Molière says.'

"'These gardens, do you know what they were like?' Oscar asked; keen to know all about the place.

"'Only what Molière told me,' I answered. 'It was about these delightful gardens I had another of my dreams.'

"'Really! What was it about?'

"'All in good time,' I replied. 'Anyway, the way into it was through the Satin Curtains. These curtains, scented with oriental spices enhanced your senses, ready for what was about to come. Once inside it was a revelation – before you were villas with cascading gardens of mixed lobelia, intermingled with hanging geraniums. In each of these villas were the artists of the Karma Sutra, waiting to put you through your paces.'

"'Paces!' he cried. 'What paces?'

"'Sexual paces – you know the positions of the *Karma Sutra*. In each of the villas, a couple demonstrated how to do it done. Like a rehearsal room, you could say. You were kept at it until you had it right.' I informed him.

"'How many villas were there?' he asked.

"'One for each position of the *Karma Sutra* – I can't remember at the moment how many there were. Each one was dedicated to a position, its purpose, reason, and practice. Makes the mouth water, does it not?'

"'Indeed. You would never get that kind of service on earth. How long did it take to get through the gardens?' Oscar asked.

"'Ah, that would depend on what your sexual appetite was like... If you were greedy sod like I am, you'd never leave the place – you'd try every position and do so over and over again until the bell rang.'

"'Bell! What bell?'

"'The Goodbye Bell,' I informed him.

"'What on earth is the Goodbye Bell?' he muttered.

"'At ten each evening they'd ring a bell and that was it. The Zone emptied in no time at all. Once the bell rang, the nymphs disappeared as well as the *Karma Sutra* artists and the other purveyors of pleasure. Then all souls would have to exit the Zone whether they wanted to or not.'

"'Were the gardens the end of the journey?' he asked.

"'Not quite,' I replied. 'If you managed to get out of the gardens intact you had to cut across the Swamp of Desire to finish the course.'

"He gave out a riotous laugh. '*Desire!* What kind of desire can you find in a swamp?'

"'You'd be surprised.' I replied. 'The swamp covered a good mile,' I informed him. 'What one had to do was plough through it without succumbing to the temptations that lie below; and believe me, they were extraordinary temptations.'

"'What kind?'

"'Every kind,' I replied, handing him a handkerchief to mop his brow. 'Once you had your feet in the swamp, arms would reach out, beckoning you to come under and sample their wares. If you were a smart soul, and got that far without hearing the bell and without succumbing to the temptations of the Zone and were determined to reach the end, you would ignore their charms. But few ever did. Their arms reached to the very root of your sexuality and come what may, you couldn't escape or resist once they touched you with the tip of their titillating fingers. If they did, they dragged you down into the quagmire and into the Pleasure Caverns that honeycombed the entire area.'

"By the look on Oscar's face, he was far from convinced. 'What kind of pleasure caverns?'

"'All kinds,' I replied. 'You had no hint at what was on offer but you would certainly find out once inside the caverns.'

"'How did a soul get out of the place?'

"'Like all of the pleasure gardens, taverns, bars and the likes, there was always an exit that would take you back to the humpbacked bridge,' I said.

"'What happened if you managed to complete the journey through the Zone?'

"'That all depended on whether or not you gave in to the temptations they presented to you,' I replied. 'It seems to me that if you did get through without giving in to the temptations, then a saint you would be and really, there are no saints in Purgatory. Then again, if you did give in and managed to get through, because of your extra indulgences, you'd find it twice as hard to purge your sins and your Debit Book would become thicker and heavier. It was supposed to be a temptation to resist, but being the weaklings human beings are, we succumb easily and pay dearly for it. The whole idea of the Zone was to resist the temptation, but according to Molière, no soul ever did.'

"'Do you think you would have succumbed if the opportunity was presented to you?'

"'Without doubt, and so would you – no question about it. That's the Erotic Zone for you, Oscar, the ultimate temptation,' I said, pointing towards the dilapidated pleasure houses. 'A place of past pleasure – all washed out and jaded.'

"'Do you think it will ever be revived?' he asked.

"'Unlikely! Come, let's go,' I said, dragging him away from the entrance. He resisted.

"'There is no big hurry, is there? Let's stay a while longer,' he replied as he loosened my grip.

"'Oh, very well – let's rest here between these two palm trees,' I said as I plonked my arse on the soft grass. He was still standing there gawking at the entrance, his mind racing at the very thought of the place, at the thought of what he was missing, what he was being deprived of. What a sad case he was, standing there mesmerized by something from the past.

"We left the Buttercup Vale and continued our journey home with him looking back yearningly every so often towards the Zone. We parted company at the foot of Literary Way, where he thanked me for my company and told me he will be in contact if my magic potion did not work. He cheerfully headed off to his home. As we all know, he was in great form from then on – apart from his reaction to my magic potion, which turned out to be a disaster. After resolving his dream problem he settled down and became a model tenant of the Reservation. In a very short time, he became a Trusted Soul, a rare achievement indeed, and as you know, he became one of the most popular and respected of souls. Any talk of odd behaviour, Marie, seems rather far-fetched. "

"You have a good memory, Alfred," Sophie exclaimed.

"Oh, I forget very little. I remember everything about Oscar – his silliness, his good nature, and his odd behaviour whenever it raises its crazy head – to be fair it rarely does."

Marie sighed. "Oh yes, his odd behaviour, his very odd behaviour. Well, I'm sad to say it has raised its head."

74

"Interesting you should say that, Marie," replied an impatient Sophie. "Will you now, please tell me about this odd behaviour you accuse him of?"

"Yes, I will."

As you may have gathered, the Central Reservation is the meeting place for all the bright souls of Père Lachaise. Here they meet, debate or just gather to gossip. It is the Speaker's Corner of the Reservation. Being in the most central location, it never takes long for the residents to notice what is going on. Sophie, Marie and Musset huddled together soon attracted other souls who were passing by. The stranger was still there scribbling away and a sprinkling of other souls, realising it was Musset talking, had stopped to listen.

Up the steps of the Central Reservation came actress Sarah Bernhardt, arm in arm with the Jane Avril, the Moulin Rouge dancer, followed by artists Eugène Delacroix, George Seurat and the sculptor, Augustine Clésinger, who were deep in conversation.

"What's going on?" said Sarah.

"Just having a gossip, Sarah," replied Sophie, rising to meet them.

"About what, may I be bold enough to ask?"

"Oscar!"

"Oscar! Oh dear," Sarah exclaimed. She had known Oscar from the days when she was one of France's finest actresses. Oscar had once said that if there were one woman he would have married if he had had the chance, it was the Divine Sarah. That was well before Constance was on the scene. Since Sarah's arrival at the Reservation, she had continued to nurture the friendship that first begun when they met in Paris way back in 1889. Their friendship had been temporarily fractured following her refusal to help him when he was down and out in Paris on his release from prison. He forgave her, and the friendship bloomed again. They had no secrets.

"Oscar!" yelled Seurat. "He's not here... is he?"

"No."

"Thank God," he said, crossing himself. "That man is just too much. Why must he always dominate everything? Why must he always be the centre of attention, and why must he always be the main attraction? Why – why are we not spared his presence? I don't understand why you bother talking about him. He's a loser."

They ignored him. Seurat had developed a certain problem with Oscar recently that no other one could fathom.

"Is he in trouble?" asked a worried Jane Avril, who since her arrival in 1942, had become Oscar's closest female friend.

"Without doubt," Marie sadly replied

"Dear, dear, I hope it's nothing too serious."

"Well, Jane, it's like this,' said Sophie. "Marie says he has been acting oddly of late. She and Alfred have been going on and on about his past, but not about the odd behaviour she accuses him of. So far she has failed to say how this has manifested itself," she moaned. "When are you going to tell us about it? All I've heard so far is how Oscar was when he arrived here, and that is already so well known. Alfred has added some interesting detail that I was unaware of, but what about this odd behaviour. Are you going to tell us or not?"

The new arrivals sat down in the ever-growing circle, ready to hear Marie's revelation. She was just about to begin when interrupted again, this time by the appearance of Isadora Duncan, the sleek American, who skipped up the steps towards them.

"Well, hello, you bunch of breezers. What's up, what are you all up to? You do look extremely serious."

"Here, Isadora, take a seat," Musset said, directing her to a space between himself and Jane Avril.

"Why the big gathering and why the solemn faces?"

"It's Oscar," muttered Sophie.

"Oh!" exclaimed Isadora. "You know, then?"

"Know? Know what?" asked a baffled Musset.

"That he's flipped… lost it. That he's gone on an emotional walkabout."

Sophie jumped to her feet and stood there hands on hips. "For heaven's sake, this is just too much. Are you lot going to tell me what's happened to him or not?"

"It's a long story," sighed Isadora.

"I'll say. I have been sitting here all morning waiting for it to begin. I've listened to Marie alluding to his odd behaviour and Alfred rambling on about Oscar's early days here, so perhaps you can enlighten me on just what his problem is."

"Come on, Isadora; tell them what you told me last week before I tell my story. Yours is of more importance. What you witnessed seems to be the beginning of his troubles."

"Do I have to?"

"Yes!" they all cried.

"Oh, very well then. You all know that Oscar loves the idea of visitors to Père Lachaise stopping at his tomb and singing his praises and leaving their little mementos, and that he is thrilled to bits when they kiss his tomb. He loves it. He always teases us that his is the only one where this happens, that they do this because he's irresistible, and they have a deep need to be near his soul."

"God, give me strength," cried Seurat. "His ego knows no bounds. The man never stops. His self-regard is becoming obsessive and boring."

"Its harmless nonsense," Eugène Delacroix replied, Oscar's closest male friend at the Reservation. "It's just a game with him. You take him far too serious, Georges."

"Seurat is right," continued Isadora. "Although we all love him, his vanity is a problem. At times, it is too much to take. Recently, however, he has been spending a great deal of time on Cloud Nine observing the visitors to his grave. I caught him screaming down at a visitor who walked straight by his tomb without even a glace, never mind a kiss. Of course, it would never have dawned on him that perhaps these visitors have never heard of him. He thinks the whole world knows who he is, what he's done, and what he is."

"We all know what he's done and certainly what he is," laughed Seurat.

The others did not think it funny and looked at him with contempt.

"He was in such a foul temper," continued Isadora. "He jumped up and down with his fists clenched in anger and cursed like a trooper, which you must agree, is not him. I stayed awhile, sitting behind a yew tree, and listened to him talking to himself.

"'What's wrong with some people, walking past me like that?' I heard him moan. 'They didn't even glance at me. Don't they know who I am? Don't they know they are walking past the resting place of a genius? Have they no respect? Have they no class at all?' He took a drink of water, wiped his face, and then gave a cheerful cry. 'Wait a moment,' he exclaimed. 'Here come seven girls, seven beauties by the look of them. They look like sisters. Look at them, all dressed so colourfully. This is more like it. Are they going to stop? Go on, girls, stop and look at me. Talk to me, kiss me, pass some remark or other – but please, please, don't pass me by. Don't ignore me.'

"They didn't. I looked down, and yes, he was right, they were certainly sisters. They stopped and huddled up together, deep in conversation.

"'I wonder what they're talking about,' he pondered.

"They all had very distinctive noses with very pale faces, so pale, that if it weren't for their noses and colourful lips you'd swear they had no features at all. They were all black-haired apart from the smallest, which was blonde. They stood there for a long time talking between themselves. Then the one dressed in a pink dress and a hat with sky blue trimmings took out her lipstick and compact case and carefully painted her lips the same shade of pink. She knelt down and lovingly kissed the tomb.

"Oscar gave a submissive sigh.

"The next, the fair one was dressed in a canary-yellow skirt with a brown petticoat showing, her white blouse highlighted with a brown collar – very attractive. She looked into the compact mirror and seductively applied a matching shade of brown. She too knelt, and giving out a giggle, kissed the tomb with relish. The third, an absolute stunner with her green dress with a scarlet flounce, belt, and hat, carefully applied a crimson hue to her pouting lips and, kneeling, passionately kissed the tomb as though she was kissing her lover.

"By this time, Oscar had calmed down and gave a satisfied smile as he observed this colourful scene.

"The fourth sister, who seemed to be the eldest, was dressed in an orange skirt and ochre blouse and she applied an ochre shade to her lips and kissed the tomb, letting out a cry of delight when finished.

"Next was the tallest, dressed in a bright red silk dress set off with a green bonnet and a matching green leather belt and red leather boots. She took her time applying green to her pouting lips as though she was keeping a lover waiting, before giving the tomb a good lingering kiss. The others giggled their approval.

"I looked at Oscar. He was mesmerised. I don't know what he was making of it, but they certainly had his attention.

"The penultimate girl applied lipstick of a purple shade that matched her blouse, hat, and boots. She hitched up her yellow skirt and gently leaned over the tomb and left her mark with a smack of her lips. The last to plant a kiss was the youngest. She was dressed in a blue dress with dark blue stripes. She applied a thick layer of dark blue lipstick to give maximum effect.

"The imprint of their kisses formed the figure seven. They stood around, arms linked, swaying to and fro, looking adoringly at their work as though they had just produced a masterpiece.

"Wow! That's surreal," said Jane.

"Nuts, I'd say," replied Seurat, barely containing his laughter. "They must be from the same fruit cake factory as Oscar – kissing tombs, indeed?"

"Very colourful, though. Like a piece of art."

"Yes, Sarah, it may well be artistic, but what does it mean?" asked Jane.

"It means they are as stark raving mad as he is," laughed Seurat.

Again, they all ignored the artist.

"It must mean something, but what?"

"Haven't the foggiest, Jane," Isadora replied. "All I know is that Oscar was thrilled to bits. He stood up, with his hands on hips, and nodding his head, smiled to himself saying, 'That is more like it. Aren't I something? Look at all those pretty girls. Aren't they just grand? Aren't they a picture of delight? They know a good thing when they see it and, by God, they have just seen and kissed it. The truth is there is nobody quite like me. I know it, they know it and the whole world knows it. Forget about Chopin and the rest – I am destined to be the main attraction at Père Lachaise. Oh! Père Lachaise, how lucky you are, to have such a soul in your care.'

Sophie laughed. "You can't be serious. What, Oscar, talking to himself. Pull the other one."

"It takes some believing," remarked Delacroix. "I'd say I know him as well or better than most, and I don't ever recall him losing his temper. I never recall him talking to himself. It is not his style – as for him cursing – no, never – not him at all. It is hard to take what you say seriously, Isadora. Let's face it; what you've described is not the Oscar we know."

"I'm serious – very much so. There was more to come," sighed Isadora.

"Like men in white coats," Seurat cracked.

"That's not funny, Seurat, not funny at all," Jane angrily retorted.

"As I was saying, there was more to come," Isadora continued. "I was a bit concerned by his manner, so the next day I returned and sat behind the same yew tree. When I arrived, he was not there, so I waited. My mind was in turmoil as to what was causing him to act so strangely. I was about to leave when I saw him coming up the hill. He looked out over Père Lachaise, sighing and nodding his head. He paced up and down with his hands behind his back, mumbling to himself. I couldn't make out what he was saying this time, but something was annoying and bothering him. Then, suddenly, he let out a mighty scream. He frightened the life out of me. The poor man was red in the face and ready to pop. 'You rotten blackguards; you bastards!' he hysterically screamed.

"I looked down to see what was infuriating him. Around Oscar's tomb were four cleaners, escorted by four *gendarmes*. The cleaners set about their task, scrubbing like demons, with stiff brushes and cleaning solutions, trying to rid it of the hundreds of lipstick marks and other graffiti. I looked over towards Oscar, and he was near apoplectic.

"'What are you playing at? Get away! Get away. Leave my tomb alone,' he yelled.

"He slumped to the ground and lay flat on his back, panting and sweating. I thought he was having a seizure. I wanted to comfort him but decided maybe it might be better to let him be and allow him to recover his composure. Under the circumstances, it seemed the most decent thing to do."

"My God," cried Sophie. "You mean to say you did nothing to help him, just left him lying there."

"I didn't want to embarrass him. You know what he is like. He can be so proud. He would have felt awkward if he had realised I had seen him in that condition. Anyway, afterwards, he got to his feet and had another look. He had calmed down and stood looking down at Père Lachaise, wiping his sodden brow. The cleaners and the *gendarmes*

80

had gone and his tomb was spick and span, without a trace of lipstick, and that seemed to depress him even more. He shrugged his shoulders muttering 'bastards, bastards' as he turned and walked slowly down the hill with his hands in his pockets, head down, kicking up stones as he went."

"Poor soul," Jane sighed. "Whatever can be wrong with him? Did you go back?"

"Indeed, I did, for another three days. I must say I did feel a bit guilty spying on him like that, but I did so solely out of concern for him. The first day he just sat there for hours, his knees tucked up to his chest and stared down over Père Lachaise. I couldn't help but wonder what he was turning over in his mind. He sat there all day, oblivious to others saluting him as they passed by. I was tempted to go and sit with him but thought better of it. Maybe I ought to have."

"The next day was very disturbing. As he passed the yew tree I was hiding behind, I noticed he was carrying a fancy bound journal and looking extremely agitated. Over his shoulder, he carried a pair of binoculars – not the ordinary type but a pair of the divine binoculars. You know the ones I mean, those with infinite magnification. For a few hours, he sat there, his eyes fixed firmly to the lens, observing his tomb. He then took out the journal and made notes."

"Do you know what he was writing?" asked Musset.

"Probably a letter to the fairies…"

"Shut up, Seurat. Give it a rest, will you."

"For heaven's sake, lighten up, Jane, will you? You've got to see the funny side of it."

"Have I now? I suggest you keep your wisecracks to yourself and allow Isadora to continue her story."

"Well, as he was writing he was saying to himself, 'Light pink – thin lips; crimson – full lips; orange – round lips; brown – full lips. That makes twenty-four today.'

Musset burst out laughing. "You're having us on!'

"I wish I were."

"This is crazy. I'm confused. I just can't fathom what is wrong with him. This obsession with the cemetery is perplexing," cried Jane.

"Go on. What happened next?" asked Sophie, her impatience now turning from curiosity to concern.

"Oh! This continued all day. By the time he left, he was at sixty-seven. As he put away his journal, he seemed rather pleased with himself as though he had one up on somebody.

"The next day it was the same routine, with the count now up to one hundred and twenty-one."

"Wow! What was he counting?" asked Seurat.

Isadora looked at him as though he were an idiot…"Kisses, you ass."

"Kisses? I thought all the lipstick was cleaned off by the cleaners."

"That's right – it was. But on the second day as he sat looking at Père Lachaise, he was watching the throngs of visitors who were replacing the vanished kisses. It started with two golden-haired and white-faced women kissing the cleaned tomb. Having made their mark, they held hands and kissed each other. Even the seven sisters made a return visit and again lovingly left their mark, this time having their photographs taken, standing on each side of the figure seven."

"What happened on the last day?" asked Nadar, the nineteenth-century Parisian society photographer, who had joined the gathering.

"When I arrived, he was already there, again with his binoculars and journal. Colette was talking to him. They were deep in conversation about something or other. I was too far away from them to hear, as the spot where they were standing was further away from the yew tree than on previous occasions. She took his binoculars and was calling out something to him that he then wrote in his journal. Every so often, she let out a burst of laughter. When she did, he turned and looked at her with scorn. She said sorry, fluttering her eyelashes to pacify him, and continued looking through the binoculars."

"Surely Colette must have found his behaviour odd? She must have questioned him about what he was playing at," enquired Seurat.

"Maybe she did," said Musset.

"They were together for most of the day," continued Isadora, "then left together, Colette linking arms with him as they passed my hiding place and headed off down the hill, followed by his dog, Dubliner and Colette's pussy, Kiki-la-Doucette. That was it. I didn't return as I thought it was wrong to be observing him in such a secret way."

"Wrong?" said an exasperated Seurat. "The only wrong thing is his behaviour, not yours. He's as crazy as they come."

"God! Seurat, you can be an insensitive sod at times. Have you no compassion? He's suffering, and you want to put the knife in," Sophie remarked, clearly annoyed with the artist, who she seemed to think was taking some sadistic pleasure in his former friend's discomfort.

"Yes, I do, although you might not believe it. Let's be honest, some people are beyond redemption and Oscar's one of them. Compassion, it is wasted on the likes of him. There is nothing we can do to help him – it would be kinder to send him to Cloud Eighty-Seven with the rest of the other head cases."

"That's nonsense," cried Jane. "He's not a head case, and your bitterness towards him is not warranted. You demean those on Cloud Eighty-Seven by your cruel comments. Whatever you may think, Seurat, there must be something we can do to help him. What, I don't know, but something must be found. Sarah, have you any ideas?"

"I haven't a clue, but I agree something must be done. To leave him as he is would be cruel and unseemly. Maybe what Isadora has revealed is just an isolated incident."

"I don't think so," Delacroix replied as he stood up and looked around at the circle of concerned faces. "It would be a mistake to believe what we've heard so far is an isolated incident – far from it, as I can sadly testify too."

Eugène Delacroix walked slowly into the centre circle, leaned against the Laburnum Tree, lit a cigarette, slowly inhaled, and then blew smoke rings. There was sadness etched into his strong features as he began to tell his tale. "I had a run-in with Oscar not long ago."

The circle all looked at each other in amazement.

"You know how impossible it is to get really annoyed with him," he continued. "Well I did and he with me. It was very disturbing."

"I can't believe it," said Sophie. "You two never argue."

"That's right. In all the years I've known him we've not had a cross-word, but we did this time, much to my surprise."

"Well, how about that," exclaimed Sophie, "There really must be something ailing him if he took umbrage with you."

There was a nod of acknowledgement from the circle of friends.

"I was busy in my studio early one morning cleaning my brushes – you know, preparing for the day's painting – when there was a sharp rap on the door. To my surprise, there stood Oscar, all dressed up as though he was going out on the town.

"'Good morning, Delacroix,' he said, doffing his hat with his cane.

"'Good God, Oscar,' I cried, a bit surprised at him addressing me as Delacroix – he always calls me Eugène. 'You're up and about early –something wrong?'

"'Wrong!' he said with a sharp edge to his voice. 'Why ever should there be anything wrong?'

"'Sorry… you seem a bit touchy this morning,' I answered.

"'Rubbish! You must be imaging things, my friend. You ought to see a doctor,' he nervously laughed.

"'There's nothing wrong with me,' I replied.

"'Likewise, there's nothing wrong with me, nothing wrong at all. How could there possibly be, on such a fine day as this?'

"He entered and slumped into a chair, took off his gloves and threw them on to the table. Leaning his cane against the chair, he put his feet up on a stool and gave a good stretch.

"'I adore your studio, Delacroix; it's full of anticipation and artistic vibes. There's something, something special about the place.'

"'It does have a certain feel to it,' I replied. 'Far better than any of the studios I had down there.'

"'I always imagined your studios to be of the highest standard, well organised and tidy like you are.' he replied.

"'Well, you're wrong. This is my finest by a long shot. The best I have ever had. Apart from my studio on the rue de Furstenberg, the rest of my studios in Paris were dives compared to this. It's the most inspiring studio I've had.'

"'Indeed. Be inspired then, my good fellow, and paint another portrait of me,' he said, waving a hand as if he was an emperor ordering about his subjects.

"I looked at him with some surprise. 'Another?'

"'Yes, another,' he answered, near enough spelling out the words, obviously annoyed by my reaction.

"'I've only just completed one. Why do you want another?'

"'Ah!' he replied. 'That was my right profile. It's the left I fancy now – be a good fellow now and get on with it.'

"'Oscar, this will be the fifth I've done for you in as many weeks,' I reminded him.

"'So?' he bellowed.

"'So! Is that all you have to say to me?' I said through clenched teeth, really disturbed by his manner.

"'My dear boy, what are you expecting me to say?' he said as he stood up, admiring himself in front of my studio mirror.

"'To start with, some explanation wouldn't go amiss,' I said, putting down my brushes.

"'There's nothing to explain. All I desire is to have my portrait painted. It's no big deal, is it?' he sighed as he admired his profile.

"'That depends.'

"He turned around and glared at me. 'Depends? My dear fellow, whatever do you mean? Depends, depends on what?'

"'Depends on a reasonable explanation…'

"'Does it now?' he growled.

"'David told me you sat for him on six occasions – worse still, in the most bizarre of poses.'

"'Did he now? So bloody what?' he snarled.

"'So what! Is that all you have to say, so what?' I explained.

"'Huh! I fail to see what else there is to say to your ridiculous questions,' he retorted.

"'What about Modigliani then? He says you had eight paintings commissioned and again in the most peculiar of poses.'

"'So?' he replied as he continued admiring himself.

"'What about Ingres? He did a nude painting of you – a reclining nude on a couch, for heaven's sake!'

"'So!' he replied again in the same matter-of-fact way.

"'That's all you can say to me – so?' I said, really annoyed at his manner. 'Oscar, men don't pose as reclining nudes. It's just not done.'

"'What's wrong with you, Delacroix? You are talking like a right little prude. What do you want me to say?' he asked.

"'As I said, an explanation wouldn't go amiss. I need to understand. I need an explanation.'

"'Well!' he sneered. 'That is tough luck, now, seeing you are not getting one. You have never asked me to explain anything, now suddenly you get all inquisitive and boring. Whine as much as you like you are not getting an explanation.'

"'I suppose it would take some explaining – you, a reclining nude – Heaven help us.'

"'What are you saying?' he asked as he turned again to admire himself in my mirror.

"'Come on, Oscar, you're no Adonis. Ingres must have had a tough job keeping a straight face with you, spread out on his couch.'

"He turned and looked me up and down. 'You are no beauty yourself, so don't laugh at me, you half-baked frog.'

"I was shocked. He had never insulted me in such a fashion before. I was at a loss to know what was ailing him.

"'It's nothing to do with beauty. It's all a matter of taste,' I replied as I tried to regain my composure.

"'Taste… not taste, my dear fellow, but class, real class,' he replied as he sat down with a smug look stamped all over his face. 'And as you know, I have class in abundance. Even in the nude, I have it stamped all over me. What Ingres was applying on canvas, was a reflection of style, sophistication and of course, real class.'

"Believe me: he said this with a straight face.

"'Seurat refuses to do any more paintings for you; he thinks you're mad. Come now, why so many portraits?'

"He spun around and glared at me. I had never seen him in such a state. The veins in his neck were raised. There was fire in his eyes. '*So!*' he yelled at me. 'What about it? It should be of no concern to *you*, how many portraits I wish to have commissioned. I am sure you don't quiz other clients on why they need their portraits painted, so why quiz me. As for Seurat, he is a useless artist anyway, a Sunday artist at the most – mediocre and over-rated. I let him know it, too.'

"'Oh, that's really big of you. If he's so useless, why did you ask him to do so many portraits?'

"'Just to annoy him, as simple as that,' he said in a lofty tone.

"My God, I was ready to throttle him, but I thought I'd better keep my temper and let him get whatever it was that was annoying him out of his system. 'But why do you want so many portraits?' I asked after I calmed down.

"'You mean to say there's a limit?' he sharply replied.

"'No, but whatever do you do with them?'

"'None of your damned business,' he retorted.

"'All the time I've known you, you've never had a portrait painted. Now you seem to have commissioned one near on every week – Why, why now, why so many? Seems like obsessive behaviour to me.'

"'My, my, you're a psychiatrist as well, are you?' he sneered as he again turned to admire himself from another angle in my studio mirror.

"'You're being sarcastic now,' I said as I spun the mirror around.

"'Oh, am I now?' he replied, taking umbrage because his precious reflection had been snatched from him.

"'Yes, you are. You are acting like a prima donna. All I have done is to ask you why you are having so many portraits done and you get all aggressive. Whatever is wrong with you?'

"He snarled at me. 'You're becoming a nosey little painter, Delacroix, you know that.'

"'No, not nosey, Oscar, only concerned,' I calmly replied.

"'Concerned? With what?' he snapped.

"'Your behaviour…'

"'Huh! Nothing wrong with my behaviour,' he stated quite firmly.

"'I'm also concerned about the way you want to be represented in your portraits.'

"'Indeed?' he replied. 'You are a concerned little fellow, aren't you, Delacroix? What is wrong with my portraits? Come on, out with it.'

"'Well, seeing that you've asked; what about that first commission I did for you? You were dressed as Salome.'

"'And… what is wrong with that?' he asked.

"'Oh, nothing at all,' I replied. 'I suppose it is natural for a fellow to dress as a biblical whore who collects heads on silver platters for a hobby. No. I suppose there's nothing wrong with that at all.'

"'Don't try to be cynical, Delacroix, old boy. It really doesn't become you. Leave cynicism to its masters. We are the only ones who know how to apply it thick and dry,' he said, laughing at me.

"'It's what followed that bothered me, Oscar. Don't try to look the innocent with me. You know what I mean.'

"'Do I?' he said, dragging out the words.

"'You know damn well, what I'm on about. The portrait which I executed with you decked out as a pompous judge.'

"'Well, my dear fellow, again, what is wrong with that?' he asked.

"'What's wrong? Jesus, Oscar, it is a series of wrongs. First, you pose as Salome, then a judge, then as the Marquess of Queensbury of all people! I would have thought you had had a bellyful of him… but you go and have your portrait painted with you dressed as that idiot. Then there was the series of you as Justice, Fraternity and Liberty. Then to cap it all you posed as the Grim Reaper. And you wonder why I think something's wrong? You must be having the portraits done for a reason. What is it? Tell me. I need to know,' I pleaded with him.

"'As I said, it is really none of your business!' he yelled back at me.

87

"'Well, maybe it's not. However, I am the one who is doing the paintings. Therefore, if you don't like my questions, you can take your custom elsewhere. Let me be, Oscar, you're really starting to get under my skin.'

"He was fuming. He poked me repeatedly in the chest with his index finger. 'Do not talk to me like that, you jumped up little mountebank?' he cried. 'So… you won't do it. You won't paint the face of a genius?'

"'No! Not even if you were a saint.'

"'Are you serious? You refuse to paint me?' he said, as he once more poked me in the chest.

"'Yes.'

"'Very well, I'm off,' he yelled. He grabbed his gloves and cane and headed for the door. In a way I was delighted he was leaving, but then I felt a twinge of remorse. I just couldn't let him leave whilst so upset. Whatever it was that was distressing him, I did not want to exacerbate it.

"'Oscar! Oscar! Come back. Don't leave. I'm sorry I've upset you. I'm just having an off day,' I lied. 'Of course, I'll do another portrait of you. Please. Come back. You don't have to go.'

"He didn't need much coaxing. He stopped, turned, gave me one of his winning smiles, returned and flopped back into the chair, resting his feet back on the stool.

"'Any chance of starting it now?' he asked. 'Had my hair specially groomed for the occasion. Suppose you haven't noticed the delicate tint and my New Wave curls,' he beamed as he slid his fingers through his well-groomed hair.

"'Can't say I have and what are New Wave curls?'

"'You haven't heard?' he asked. 'Tut, tut – you are out of touch, dear boy – it is all the rage. I heard it at the Knowledge Zone. Apparently, it was a term used in the 1990s when everyone was bored and looking for something new. There were a series of new sensations – you know: the New Black is Grey, New Kids on the Block (they were a kind of singing troupe) and best of all, the New Man. Sounds real cool, does it not?'

"'*Cool?* You are starting to sound like the Morrison boy – New Man, indeed. What is a New Man, if you don't mind me asking?' I replied as I set up my easel.

"'A chap in touch with his feminine side,' Oscar proudly informed me. 'One who knows and appreciates the feminine mind and understands the subtleties and complexities of the fairer sex?'

"'What! Never heard such rubbish,' I cried. 'I must say, Oscar, you do know how to come out with them.'

"'You should try it,' he suggested. 'Being a New Man may improve your image and your sense of importance.'

"'So that's it. That's what all the portraits are about, you and your New Man image thing.'

"'Certainly not! I don't need a new image. It would be impossible to improve on perfection,' he smugly replied. 'I don't want to brag, but you could say I was the original New Man. What a hit I would have been in the 1990s, there would have been no stopping me. I would have been the standard for all to attain. Yes, there is something about this New Man thing, something very liberating, something very me.'

"'You spend too much time up at the Knowledge Zone,' I exclaimed. 'I don't know why you want to fill your head with so much useless information. You and your New Man,' I said as I indicated to him to take his position.

"'Just because we are in Purgatory doesn't mean we should lie back and stagnate and dry up altogether,' he said as he ran a comb through his New Wave curls.

"'If you say so, Oscar – it's a waste of time disagreeing with you, as you seem to know everything. You are like some walking, talking encyclopaedia. Now, be a good chap, sit still, and let me get started,' I replied as I picked up my pencil, ready to do battle with this New Kid on the Block."

"So, Eugène, you painted his portrait after all of that?" Sophie asked.

"I did, and very good it turned out to be. It was a match for the right- hand portrait I did some weeks earlier."

"How was his demeanour during the sitting?"

"Well, I did a primary sketch as is my practice and showed it to him.

"'You need to sharpen my nose a bit,' he said as he glanced at it. 'And my eyes are set too deep and my chin is slightly out of place. It has taken that unique character away from my face. I should not have to explain it to you. I am sure you know exactly what I mean?'

"'I'm damned if I do,' I retorted, feeling insulted that he had criticised my work, something he'd never done before.

"'You have to get it right. I must take care of my image – it is most important. It has taken a lifetime to perfect,' he proudly announced, 'and I don't want it marred by a careless wielded pencil.

"'If you don't like it, you can leave. You and your stupid image,' I said crossly. Once again, he had managed to infuriate me.

"He realised he'd riled me and sat down again. He began laughing. 'You surprise me, Delacroix. Since when did you ever take anything I have said seriously?'

"'When you attack my art, that's when and haven't my entire portraits of you been accurate? I made you even more Oscaresque than you really are.'

"'I'm sorry. Only messing about,' he said, but I could see that there was something seriously wrong with him. He was out of sorts. I had never seen him in such a state before.

"I put the sketch aside and began the portrait. Throughout the sitting, he prattled on about his latest play. I only half- listened to him as I was still rattled by his insulting behaviour and annoyed that he kept on calling me Delacroix as though it had been our first meeting.

"After I had finished the portrait, he looked at it and smiled. 'Very good,' he said. 'A pity, though.'

"'What is?' I asked, wondering what he was up to now, what rubbish he was about to throw at me.

"'The eyes, pity about the eyes,' he said in a matter-of-fact way.

"'What's wrong with them? I cried.

"'My eyes seem to have blankness about them. No sparkle, no depth or feeling – features that are my trademark.'

"'God, give me strength,' I exasperatedly replied. 'It is as good as you are going to get. You moan because your nose isn't sharp enough, your chin is out of place, your eyes are set too deep, now you have a blank look. Is there no pleasing you?'

"'Certainly,' he laughed. 'I am so easy to please. Doesn't take much to humour or please me. Everyone knows that.'

"'All right, Oscar, we all know you're God's gift to artists, we all know how good you are, now piss off. Go, and leave me in peace,' I snapped back at him as I pointed to the door, annoyed that he had made me curse.

"'You really do take constructive criticism a bit too seriously, don't you? Be a good fellow now, calm down, and make me some tea before I go. I am parched. A few crumpets wouldn't go amiss either.'

"He can be so infuriating at times. I tossed my brushes in a jar and reluctantly prepared his refreshments. 'I hear you once had a studio in George Sand's home at Nohant, down in the Loire Valley,' he suddenly blurted out.

"I looked at him and wondered what he was up to now. 'Yes, I did for a while. Afraid it didn't last long.'

"'Why?' he asked, giving the impression he already knew.

"'I'd rather not say. It's something from a long time in the past, that I'd prefer to leave there,' I replied, just hoping he would finish his tea and leave. He was becoming very wearing

"'Come now, I can't see the purpose of blocking out the past. It is a part of who and what we are.'

"'You would, wouldn't you?' I snapped back at him. 'You should try it. Forgetting the past sometimes allows you to see the future more clearly. You are obsessed with the past – you always have been. It seems to be a preoccupation of many of your Gaelic cousins. It does you no good at all. Look to the future and forget about the past and past ghosts, like the much-maligned George.'

"'George!' he cried. 'How could I ever forget about such an intriguing woman?'

"'Jesus... you never even met the woman. You talk and act as though you knew her intimately.'

"'Well, in a way I do, but apparently not as intimately as you did. You fancied her, then?' he asked.

"I must say, I was astounded by such an intrusive question. 'What do you mean, fancy her? You do use some odd phrases at times.'

"'Not odd at all,' he laughed. 'It is a reasonable question. It is a simple question – did you fancy that notorious woman? Or, to be more precise, did you fuck her?'

"I nearly choked on my crumpet. I had not heard him use that kind of language before. 'Really, you're being downright offensive. That is crude and you, a professed literary genius, spitting out such crass words! You're just too much,' I replied, feeling disgusted by his phraseology.

"'Tut, tut,' he replied. 'You seem very touchy on the subject... as though you had something to hide.'

"'Listen!' I bellowed at him. 'I don't know what you're up to, but you're not just becoming offensive, you're becoming a bloody nuisance. George's home at Nohant was a centre of artistic excellence. There was nothing-untoward going on, as you seem to be suggesting. As well as Chopin being in residence, producing his masterpieces, Liszt and Marie d'Agoult were regular visitors. Liszt was able to compose in the peaceful and idyllic surrounding that was Nohant. Literary folk like Balzac, Dumas, Gautier, and Turgenev visited, adding that extra pinch of artistic spice. The place was always throbbing with artistic activities. That, Oscar, was the only thing that was throbbing, so keep your dirty mind to yourself.'

"'Why, then, if it was throbbing with artistic activities, did you suddenly pack up your easel and brushes and leave Nohant and head off back to Paris?' he asked. 'There must have been some reason for your sudden departure. You don't just get up and leave without any reason. Was she fed up with you – could you not stand the pace, or could you not satisfy her needs as all her other lovers could?'

"That was it. I'd had enough. 'Here, Oscar, time to go,' I said, handing him his hat and cane. 'You really are becoming a bore and a nuisance. Off you go.'

"He took the hat and cane and walked towards the door. He turned and offered me his hand. 'I was on my way anyway. Goodbye, Delacroix, give me a call when the painting is dry and ready for collection,' he said as he shook my hand. To my horror, his hand was as cold as ice and as he looked at me, I was startled by the blankness of his eyes, blankness I hadn't noticed when I was actually doing the painting. One thing I was sure of – this man before me was not the Oscar Wilde I knew, but a strange, haunted creature, which sent a shiver down my spine."

"Are you telling us, he's a bit touched?" asked Jane, tapping her forehead. Delacroix shrugged his shoulders.

"Sounds way over the top to me," said Seurat. "Who would want to keep on having their portrait painted?"

"A maniac, by the sound of it, a lost soul, that's who," a voice came from behind the Wisdom Stone.

"It's that boy, Morrison," cried Sarah.

Jim Morrison, the Rock phenomenon of the late 1960s, peeped around the stone, smiling at the gathering. He edged around and, leaning against the stone, dragged on his second reefer of the day, the only habit of his former life in which he still indulged. Of course, the joint had no effect – he just imagined it did. He was adept at getting high in his imagination. He was a cool dude, was Morrison. He took his Purgatory as it came. He was one of the Reservation's most relaxed residents.

"Man, he's freaked out," Morrison said, "ought to do somethin' about him. Been sittin' here a while listenin' to the downfall of our genial genius. Afraid he has it bad, man. What old Delacroix described is only one of the symptoms of his malaise. Man, he is a sad, sad case. I'd say a hopeless case." He took another long drag at his reefer. "The man needs love and understandin'. I have been worried 'bout him for a good while now, especially after our conversation last fall up on Cloud Nine. Man, it was way out, way, way out."

"What conversation was that?" asked Sophie.

"Dunno if I should say," he replied as he took a last drag on his joint. "It's kinda personal."

"If it will help us to understand what's ailing him, maybe you ought to say?"

"Yea, Marie, maybe yuh right," he replied, as he flicked the remains of his reefer away.

"Go on, Jim," said David, the neoclassical artist, who had joined the circle, said as he tapped Morrison's arm. "Let's have it. Tell us what transpired."

"All right, it's like this. I was wanderin' up View Point Hill on Cloud Nine when I came upon Oscar, and Dubliner, his red setter. At first, he seemed his same old self, just talkin' about this and that. He was tickin' me off for not creatin' any poetry, that I had a duty to use the talents I was blessed with, but when we got to the summit he kinda changed."

"In what way?" Sophie asked.

"His demeanour was kinda 'different'. The moment we reached the top of View Point Hill, you could see the change in him. He sauntered over to the Viewin' Platform and peered down over Père Lachaise and became very animated."

"Musset laughed. "He is always animated. He was probably born animated."

"Oh no, this was different, man. This wasn't his normal theatrics. This was different, very different. He turned to me and said, 'Tell me Jimmy, my boy, do you ever look down at your grave?'

"'No. Never!' I said. 'Who wants to be reminded how we got here? – got better things to do, far better things to concentrate my mind on.'

"'You do. Such as?' he asked

"'Growin' roses.'

"He looked at me as though I had the plague.

"'I thought you were an artist,' he said, not taking his eyes off me.

"'I was. Now I am a former rock artist who grows roses and I have never been happier.'

"'Rubbish! Once an artist always an artist,' he said. 'Surely there is an art, even in the growing of roses'

"'No. I wouldn't say there is. All I'm doin' is nurturin' the original artist's work.'

"'So, former rock artist who grows roses, you are not interested in who visits your grave?'

"'No, not really,' I replied.

"'You ought to. It is very educational, you know.'

"'Is that so,' I said with a sigh.

"'Indeed. I have flowers and kisses planted on mine along with loving letters and mementos,' he informed me.

"'Man, aren't you just one lucky soul?' I replied.

"'Yes, I am. You want to see what's on yours?'

"He said this in a kinda smug way. Like most of us, I've never bothered to look down over Père Lachaise. I just couldn't see the purpose of it. I was aware that my old admirers visited, but that is all I knew and really all I wanted to know. I wasn't interested in any way, why they visited or what they did when they got there. It was all of little importance to me, but Oscar thought it was of the greatest importance. Man, to him, observin' his restin' place was like a way of life. He reads so much into it and what those visitin' do or say. Man, I find it all ghoulish and borderin' on the satanic. It would be a waste of time pointin' this out to him, for you'd be guaranteed that he'd turn the argument around and make you feel an ass. He is so good at that.

"'Here,' Oscar said, handing me a pair of binoculars. 'If you don't want to look at your grave, I will give you the privilege of looking at mine. Here, have a look – it's something special.'

"'I'm really not that interested,' I said, pushin' the binoculars aside.

"'Don't be such a prig. Have a look,' he insisted, brandishing the binoculars in my face.

"I reluctantly took them and looked down at his tomb and, yeah he was right, he did have loads of flowers and it was festooned with kisses of every hue. The imprint of the kisses made his tomb a kinda canvas – very impressive in its own *odd* way, but not my scene. 'Very interestin', Oscar, now, if you don't mind, man, I'm off,' I said handin' him back the binoculars.

"'Where to?' he asked.

"'The rose garden.'

"'The rose garden!' he cried.

"'Yes, it seems far more appetisin' than lookin' at graves,' I said, just dyin' to get away.

"'Don't be daft, the rose garden can wait,' he said as he laid his hand on my shoulder. 'Look over there at Chopin's. Here,' he said, thrusting the binoculars at me again. 'You see, his tomb is smothered by flowers, and look at that woman standing on the step at the side of it. Look and listen. She is humming his Lento assai. He's surrounded by love and devotion.'

"I took a reluctant look. Oscar was right. Chopin's grave was ablaze with colour and a young woman, dressed in a white skirt and red blouse holdin' a red and white carnation against her heart was hummin' the Lento assai. There was a steady stream of visitors makin' their way up the narrow pathway, most of them clutchin' a bunch of flowers, bringin' them to their master's grave. It was a kind of pilgrimage. Well, he does have that saint-like quality about him.

"'Beautiful, is it not?' Oscar said, slapping me on my back.

"'Very much so,' I replied, hopin' he'd go home and give me a break, 'but I still don't see the point or any purpose bein' served by continuin' this nonsense of observin' graves, especially your own. It seems rather crass and touchin' on the irreverent. Man, what am I sayin', it's downright irreverent.'

"'Nonsense! There is nothing indecent or irreverent in viewing one's final resting place. It is an opportunity of which all souls should avail themselves. Come now, my boy, have a look at yours,' he said pointing me in the direction of my grave.

"'Man, don't yuh get it? I'm not in the least interested,' I replied. He was really startin' to bug me, but he would not give up.

"'Come now, don't be so dreary – you don't know what you're missing. You will be surprised at the sight. It will be a revelation. It'll be illuminating *and* liberating.' he promised.

95

"'I'm tellin' yuh, man, I ain't interested in your stupid obsession,' I said as I felt the anger in me grow. I turned to leave and he teasingly cried, 'What, you are scared of what you will see?'

"I stopped dead in my tracks and cried, 'Rubbish! There's nothin' there that will bother me.'

"'Then look,' he insisted, again thrusting the binoculars at me.

"I suddenly became very curious and decided to take a peep. Don't know what came over me. I did what I said I would never do, probably just to get him off my back. He sayin' I was scared really got under my skin, so I looked. I wish I hadn't. As I surveyed my grave, I could hear him sniggerin' behind me.

"'Impressive, isn't it?' he said.

"I was in shock. I couldn't believe what I was seein'.

"'My grave,' I gasped. 'It looks like a cesspit.'

"'It is a cesspit,' he laughed.

"I threw the binoculars to the ground in disgust at what I saw. He was enjoyin' my discomfort. 'You knew this, so why did you want me to see it?' I shouted at him, horrified by the sight. 'How long has it been in this state? It is a disgrace. It's sacrilege, an insult to my memory.'

"'My dear boy, did you not know?'

"'Know, know what?' I cried.

"Putting his arm across my shoulders he whispered in my ear. 'You are a god! Did you not know, my dear boy, that you are a god, yes, a god? You have been elevated, don't you know? That rabble down there – your fans, I believe they are called. They worship you like you were some kind of god, like a messiah. You, my dear rock star turned rose grower, have a fanatical following. You are a superstar or, should I say, a megastar? That is the modern term, I believe. Sounds great, does it not – megastar – got a certain ring about it. It has been like this since your interment. You have devoted followers – not like mine, of course, who have style and sophistication stamped all over them, nor like Chopin's, who show absolute love and dedication. The wardens down there have had enough of you and your frenzied followers. I would say if they had any chance of getting rid of you, they would jump at the opportunity and dump your remains in the Seine.'

"'Why?' I asked, amazed at his cynical manner.

"He chuckled. 'Let us see. This is what your followers leave as a mark of respect for you, my dear rose grower. Photographs – mostly pornographic, I must say; cigarette of the *cheapest* kind; condoms, in every possible flavour and design, often used; reefers, mostly hashish; metro tickets; handkerchiefs, soiled of course; beer and whiskey bottles; obscene letters and wait for it, money. How vulgar can they get? Last week I observed a couple making love on your grave – fucking like rabbits and being cheered on by some of your deranged fans.'

"'Man, that's sick. That is my restin' place they are desecratin'. What kinda morons are they?' I complained. 'And what kinda moron are you to want to put me through this sick spectacle.'

"Oscar gave my shoulder a squeeze and smiled at me. 'Fans, my boy, I believe they are called fans,' he sneered.

"I pushed his hand away. 'If they're so devoted to me, why do they wanna' do such things, such hurtful things? Have they no respect?'

"'Yes, in their own, sick way,' he replied, clearly wallowin' in my discomfort.

"'What do you mean, respect? They have no respect for me – just look at my grave. It is a disgrace. If they had any respect, they wouldn't desecrate it. If what they were genuine in their devotion, they would leave flowers and not the debris they've festooned my restin' place with. I feel sick.' I replied as I sank to the ground.

"He knelt down and patted my arm. 'Apparently, they believe you would appreciate this kind of offering, that you crave this worship. They idolise you, my dear boy. They think you are a god and treat you as such.'

"'Worship! Worship!' I cried. 'Man, this isn't worship, this is a sickness. It seems satanic to me. I may have been outrageous in my day, but never like this. This is sick. I want nothin' to do with this kind of indecency. If that's the kind of fans I have, I'd rather not have them,' I said, annoyed, not just at my so-called fans, but at Oscar for persistin' in showin' me somethin' he knew would upset and irritate me.

"'Now, now, my dear boy, it's their idea of love and devotion. Enjoy it,' he said.

"'You're as sick as they are if you could ever imagine I could enjoy such a corrupt form of devotion. I'm tellin' you, man, I want nothin' to do with it,' I repeated as I got to my feet to leave. 'Out of my way, I'm goin'. I've had enough of you and your nonsense,' I said as I attempted to leave.

"'There's more,' he said, grabbing hold of my sleeve. 'There is so much more.

"'Is there?' I asked, horrified at what could be worse than what I had just witnessed.

"'Some of your followers have defaced other graves by painting arrows on them, indicating where you are to be found so they can find their God and pay their respects,' he continued. 'And, they didn't just paint arrows, but slogans of every kind: "Lizard King"; "Jim This

97

Way"; "To the Greatest" and "Rock Heaven". Every evening the wardens have to clean up the mess. There are no fans quite like yours, I can tell you. There are in a class of their own, head-bangers, one and all.'

"'I feel sick.'

"'You look it,' he sneered.

"'It's horrendous. How can they desecrate my grave and believe it's done in my honour?' I cried – my mind in turmoil.

"'There is even more. Focus on that message,' he said, handin' me the binoculars again and directin' my view towards a piece of paper lyin' next to a half full-whiskey bottle. 'What does it say?'

"I read it. Lettin' go of the binoculars I sat down, feelin' drained. Why was he doin' this to me? It was a nightmare.

"'What does it say?' he repeated.

"I refused to answer.

"'I'll read it,' he said snatching the binoculars from my grasp and focusing on the paper. "Out there we is stoned." Great, is it not? Great grammar – has real style about it, don't you think? The one next to it is even better: "Jim Says People Love Freedom, Sex, Drugs and Rock 'n' Roll". My, you do have some first-class head-bangers on your trail, my dear boy,' he mockingly said, intent on further humiliatin' me.

"'Why did you want me to come here?' I sadly asked, tryin' to get eye contact with him, but he was shifty. He didn't reply. 'Tell me?' I said as I got hold of him and tried to make him look at me. 'What's the purpose of this nonsense? What are you tryin' to say to me, man?'

"'My dear boy, whatever do you mean?' he replied, still refusin' to look at me.

"'You know damn well what I mean and stop callin' me your dear boy!' I cried. 'I'm not one of your rent boys.'

"He recoiled in astonishment, throwing the binoculars to the ground. I shouldn't have said it, for it hurt him. He tried to ignore my comment, but the pain it was stamped all over him. However, it didn't last long.

"'Don't be so touchy,' he muttered. 'You know exactly what I am saying about you and your deranged fans.'

"'No, I don't, Oscar. I find your manner and attitude disturbin'.'.

"'Disturbing?' he laughed. 'My, my, you really are touchy today. You should not be, you know. On occasions, you get more visitors than Chopin and I put together, so why be so touchy? You are a hero, a god, a megastar. What else could you possibly want?'

"'Peace!' I barked at him. 'I don't give a shit how many visit, I'd rather have none than be subjected to that kinda sickness. I'm tellin' you, I want nothin' to do with it. Man, how many times must you be told? You're a real demon today.'

"'But you are a megastar. You cannot get better than that, can you? There were no megastars in my day; you were either a success or a failure. Of course, a success I was. I wish I were a megastar, though. If I were, I would not have such a long face about it. Surely, you must be pleased that so many visit you to pay their respects. But then again, it is not the quantity that counts, is it?' he sneered.

"'Oh? What do you mean by that?' I asked.

"'You may get a lot more visitors than I, but you see I get quality, not trash like that,' he said pointing down at the crowd mutilating my grave. 'Why? Because that is what I was on Earth and still am in this domain, quality through and through – a thoroughbred – one of nature's blue bloods. There is no rubbish thrown on mine – no visits from trash like your drugged admirers. Only those who see the beauty of life visit my tomb, those connoisseurs of artistic life.'

"'You talk a load of shit at times, Oscar,' I said furiously.

"'No,' he snarled back. 'It is that kind of expletive that visits your grave, not mine.'

"I looked at him – this wasn't the same Oscar Wilde I knew, the one I admired and respected. No, this was a stranger in thought, manner, and deed. Man, how shocked I was by what had become of my grave, but more so by what had become of the soul of this talented and special man. He seemed to be gloatin' at my distress as though he wanted to wound me. Why would he want to do such a thing?"

"Because he's nuts."

"For pity's sake, Seurat, let Jim finish," Sarah said, nudging the painter in the ribs.

"'You are annoyed with your fans for their misguided way of showing respect, aren't you?' Oscar continued.

"'Listen,' I said, tryin' to contain my anger. 'I don't know why they act like that. It is a waste of time even speculatin' on the reasons, for there is nothin' whatsoever I can do about it. I was a fool to let you talk me into lookin' over Père Lachaise. I had never done so before and that is how I should have left it. Some places are not worth visitin' and Père Lachaise is one of them. It may be an interestin' place to visit for the livin', but it's a bore for the dead.'

"'It is getting to you, is it?' he gloatingly asked.

"'It means nothin' to me. Just let it be, Oscar. Give it a rest.'"

"You mean to say that after all your time here, you never once viewed Père Lachaise?" asked Marie.

"I never had the need to. Most souls don't. I accepted my fate and had no desire to relive my earthly existence in any way. I can see no purpose in doin' so. I made too many mistakes in life; I really have no desire to revisit or repeat them. Man, my life was adrift with drugs, drink, and sex, and because of that abuse, my time was cut short. I denied myself the meaningful experiences of life, like love, marriage, the pleasure of bein' a father and most of all, livin' out my life to the full. I hadn't been here that long before I realised that I'd fucked up my entire life. Lookin' at my grave brought it all back in a vividly disturbin' way.

"I noticed when I arrived here, that most of us carried on with the profession or trade we had on earth. That was not for me. I didn't take the option of viewin' Père Lachaise or tryin to relive my life. Instead, I settled for a more tranquil existence, now shattered by Oscar's behaviour. This is my home now and it was a mistake to give in to his pressure and my curiosity and take a peep at what is nothin' more than a bad memory of not just a wasted life, but a wasted talent. I was always fully aware of it and certainly didn't need remindin'. That is why I never viewed Père Lachaise or visited the Knowledge Zone. I'm happy and contented with my existence, but Oscar thought he knew better and set about humiliatin' me. He cajoled me into his silly game of gawkin' down over the graveyard. How I regret it. Whatever could it be that's turned his mind?"

"Wish I knew," sighed Sophie. "What happened next?"

"Man, he went on and on about my music. What was it all about? Was I really a poet or just an amateur? Did my work have any aesthetic value? You know the kinda stuff. Man, he was really startin' to bug me. I have known him since I arrived here. He did all that was possible to help me settle into my new surroundin's. He couldn't have been nicer. Man, we would sit for hours talkin' about music, poetry, and literature. Man, oh man, he wanted to know everythin' about my life. What was it like bein' a superstar. It absolutely fascinated him. Rock music really got him goin'. He couldn't get his head around it. He wanted to know if it was satanic or mystic. Man, he just would not accept that it was only an alternative way of performin' music. He was seein' more in it that really existed.

"He was never into drugs himself so he said, and wanted to know why I took so many and whether my lyrics were composed under the influence of either drugs or drink. I would wind him up by sayin' I couldn't remember anythin' when I was out of it. He took such a genuine interest in me that his behaviour up at the Viewpoint came as a shock."

"What did he say about your music?" enquired Delacroix.

"Man, do I have to say?"

"I rather think so, if we want to know what's wrong with him," replied Marie.

"He said that, unlike his work, mine would be forgotten and buried by future generations in a cesspit, like the one I have down in the cemetery. All I would be remembered for was being an alcoholic drug abuser and first-class loser."

"That's a bit rough, I must say," gasped an indignant Isadora. "I'm sure he didn't mean it."

"You could have fooled me. He said my lyrics were unintelligible diarrhoea and better off in the sewer."

"Jesus!" Jane cried. "That doesn't sound like him at all, criticising a fellow artist. Are you sure you didn't give him one of your reefers?"

"Man, there was more to come. Oscar insisted that rock music was the music of the mentally challenged, had no merit whatsoever and was demented in its content and conception. What he was meanin' to say was that it's all a load of crap, and so was anyone who indulged in it. Then he went on and on about the Doors, my band. Man, he can go on. He wanted to know if the use of the word Doors had a sexual connotation. I told him to give it rest, go home and sleep it off. He wouldn't give up, though. He insisted that behind The Doors was a cell of sexual decadence that only opened to those who passed a Doors test. By this time, I'd had enough of him. I tried to get away but there was no stoppin' him. He pulled me back. There was more on his mind. 'Why did you kill yourself?' he blurted out.

"'I couldn't believe my ears. 'Man, what the hell are you on about?' I screamed.

"'You killed yourself. You took a cocktail of alcohol and drugs and lay down in your bathtub to die. At twenty-seven, you had had enough of life ...' he sneered.

"'You are talkin' a load of shit again. Man, where do you get such crap from?' I asked.

"'I have my sources.'

"'Well,' I replied, 'you should check your sources, 'cause they are way off the mark.'

"'You telling me you didn't kill yourself?' he asked, surprise in his voice.

"'Yes. Now give it a rest.'

"'All right, then, how did you die?' he asked.

"Man, he was really buggin' me now. He was stretchin' my patience to the limit with his obscene probin'.

"'You are really chancin' your luck,' I cried, as I got up to take my leave.

"'Come on,' he sneeringly said, grabbing hold of my arm. 'If you didn't kill yourself, how did you die?'

"'What makes you think I topped myself?'

"'It's a matter of deduction,' he answered.

"'Man you startin' to sound like Sherlock Holmes. You are talkin' garbage again. I ain't gonna answer any more of your ridiculous questions. Now go away,' I cried, as I tried to loosen his grip on me. 'By the way, it *was* an accident.

"'An accident,' he jeered.

"'It was an accident,' I stressed. 'That's all it was, a stupid accident. I took too much dope and alcohol at a club in the Latin Quarter and my girlfriend took me to my rue Beautreillis apartment to sleep it off. Sometime in the night, I got up to have a soak in the bath and there I died from heart failure brought on by the effects of drugs and alcohol. It wasn't suicide, you ass.'

"'I believe you, but few do,' he muttered. 'Come now, we will walk back together and you can tell me all about it.'

"'Forget it. I've had enough of you. I'm off home.'

"I was feelin' drained and confused. I didn't fancy any more of his company, but still I allowed him to accompany me. We walked back down the hill and before long; he was talkin' and actin' in his usual manner. He didn't mention my death or anythin' to do with it. He seemed oblivious to the fact that he had insulted me in the most offensive way – insulted my music, my poetry, and my followers – completely humiliated me."

Morrison threw his reefer to the ground and closed his eyes. "That's my sorry tale, for what it's worth."

"Didn't I tell you? The man's barmy!" shouted Seurat. "Lock him up. Throw away the key. He's a menace."

"Oh, shut it, will you," cried Marie, ready to throttle Seurat.

"But what's causing it?"

"Search me, Sophie," replied Musset. "But I hope it's not catching."

There was a loud rap at the Divine Door.

"Come in," called a voice.

A small chubby fellow entered and shuffled his way to the large oak desk.

"What is it, Gabriel? I'm rather busy."

"Sorry to bother you, Chairman, but I've just received a disturbing report from the Père Lachaise Reservation."

"About what?"

"That Wilde fellow."

The Chairman raised his head from his paperwork. "What, you mean, Oscar, that sharp Irish wit who thinks he's a genius?"

"The very same, Chairman."

"Well. What is it? What's he done?"

"Our man on the ground is sitting at the Central Reservation at this very moment listening to a bunch of souls discussing Oscar's odd behaviour. By the sound of it, I think we may have a problem."

"You don't mean…?"

"Yes, I'm afraid I do."

"Not another."

"I'm afraid so."

"Thank God they are rare. What's in the report, any clues?"

"It's just a preliminary report but the hallmarks are all there. I can only see one outcome, I am afraid. We should prepare for the worst."

"Could you be reading too much into it? It could be a false alarm."

Gabriel gave a wry smile. "Could be, but I doubt it, Chairman. It may be a rare occurrence but I haven't made a wrong call yet. I have been spot on with all the previous cases. This one, if the reports prove correct and it materialises, will be tortuous and prolonged, like none before, even worse than the Michelangelo case."

The Chairman's face creased at the very thought of it.

"Our man has indicated he'll give another report after the souls have dispersed and a full and comprehensive one once he's made more enquiries. He says the gathering is getting bigger by the minute. It seems like the whole Reservation wants to get on in the act. That Wilde man still has pulling power even though he's not present at the gathering."

The Chairman sat back in his chair, rolling his gold pen around his fingers. "But isn't Oscar one of our Trusted Souls?"

"He is."

"Then how come he's at the centre of this disturbing report? Trusted Souls are usually beyond reproach."

"Well, it seems this one isn't."

The Chairman frowned. "The last report I saw intimated he was the heart and soul of the place, a real pillar of the community. He was writing plays and novels at an astonishing rate. I was only reading his latest last week. What was it called now?"

"*The Chairman of Vice.*"

"Oh yes, *The Chairman of Vice* good title. He seemed to be at peace with his condition. What could have gone wrong?"

"Well, Chairman, I think that will become clear in due course."

"Whose was the last case we had to consider? It's slipped my mind."

"Charles Darwin."

"Ah, yes, Darwin, the fellow who thought he knew it all – thought he knew the secrets of the universe. Thought he knew the secret of creation, even thought he could second-guess God. He was some lad, wasn't he? In the end, it proved quite a straightforward case. He really didn't stand a chance."

"I can assure you, Chairman, that if this Wilde case comes on, it will be far from easy or straightforward. Nothing is straightforward with this Wilde fellow."

The Chairman sighed. "Thank you, Gabriel. Keep me informed and by the way, bring me the Wilde file, will you. I think I ought to review it to see if we've overlooked anything."

"Oscar's behaviour is all to do with his image," Nadar said, as he sat cross-legged next to Marie. Being a superb photographer, he knew a thing or two about image and ego. In his day, he had helped to inflate many. "I've missed most of what you've been discussing, but what I've heard so far only enforces my conviction that our friend has an acute image crisis. Image, was of utmost importance in his life, as it seems to be here. If you look back to his early years, you can see that he carefully constructed an image that was hard to ignore.

"Let's take his dress sense to start with. Now, that didn't come about by accident, I can tell you, it was well worked at and was clearly successful in drawing attention to him, thus satisfying one of his consuming obsessions. He loved himself more than anyone or anything. He had a choice, of course. He could have dressed as most of his peers, as a conservative gentleman, and blended in, but no, he wanted to be different and that is what he achieved. There would be no conservative grey or black suits for him; instead, he favoured colourful tunics of an eccentric mode, fancy cravats, hats, spectacular cloaks and a selection of unusual walking sticks. He became a dandy. He was far from the originator of this style, however, for there were others who had chosen this path, most notably the then British Prime Minister, Benjamin Disraeli, a dandy whom Oscar greatly admired. There was no way that anyone could miss Oscar Wilde. He made sure of that. If they'd seen him walking down a street or making an entrance at some society luncheon, dinner, the theatre or any other kind of gathering, they would remember him, for he stood out from the crowd like no other. His swagger and stance alone would have turned heads. Some called his behaviour eccentricity; he called it style. His image was well planned and executed. This is what he wanted – to be noticed and talked about. As we all know, he certainly was. He was so much into image that he would be photographed in a most provocative way, knowing that remarks would be made about him and his conduct, that there would be gossip that would keep his name on everyone's lips. He loved gossip – the more provocative and scandalous the better. He revelled in his notoriety. He had zest, not just for life, but also for self-publicity that would have left modern exponents lost in admiration." Nadar paused and looked around him.

"Take the matter of his accent and his use of language," he continued. "He developed an accent that gave him that assured air of cultivation. The tones that would percolate around those society dinner tables were not the same as those heard at his family home or around Dublin's Trinity College or at his favourite watering holes in Dublin. At Oxford, he worked at ridding himself of his educated

Dublin accent, to replace it with the tones to which we are now accustomed, tones that would make him more acceptable to the English ruling class than to his Irish kin. You could argue that he was ashamed of his Irish accent and thus rid himself of it, but you would very much be mistaken. What he was doing was using the English ruling class to further his literary career. He used them well. He laughed at them, manipulating them with words laced with hidden meanings. In the end, though, that same ruling class turned its back on him in the most devastating way possible – by socially castrating him.

"He remained very much an Irishman throughout his life – Irish through and through, although many of his Irish brethren would dispute that, calling him a West Brit, a most peculiar term. Even here, he will regularly remind us just how Irish he is."

"Yes. I'd go along with that," said Delacroix. "He often rambles on about Ireland. His favourite reminiscences are mostly about Ireland and her people. I don't know how often I've listened to him talking passionately about Ireland. Sometimes it is hard to get him to shut up about the place. He may have criticised her on occasions, many occasions, but he clearly loves the country. His home here has an Irish name, as does his faithful red setter. He's Irish, as Irish as one could get."

"Exactly," replied Nadar. "When he's himself, he's Irish to the core, but the image he projected to the world was that of an English upper-crust poet, a slick and witty after-dinner speaker who would occasionally knock out a decent play. The press had a field day with him. Yet the more he would see himself set up by them, the better he felt. He really couldn't get enough publicity. He was on a continuous ego trip, on a permanent high."

"So, you're saying there's nothing wrong with him, but an image problem?" Seurat asked, laughing at the thought that his image was the only thing wrong with Oscar.

"No. What I am saying is that one of the symptoms of his problem is manifesting itself as an acute image problem. There's something far deeper causing his distress, as was clear to me when he came to visit my studio a month ago."

"What do you mean? Whatever happened?" asked Jane, feeling uncomfortable at the possibility of further revelations.

"He comes to see me about once a month. I have a lot of time for him. He always leaves me with that special kind of feeling after each visit. He seems to leave his mark wherever he goes."

"I'll agree with that," interrupted Sophie.

"The only mark he makes is a black one, so spare me this 'special feeling' nonsense. It doesn't impress me one iota," said Seurat."

"If you're not happy with what's being said, you can always leave," Jane replied, scowling at Seurat, who ignored her.

Nadar turned his back on Seurat and continued. "At first he didn't seem to be acting any differently than usual. If he had, it would have set alarm bells ringing. To tell you the truth, he was very much his usual self; then began a sequence of events that did indeed set those bells ringing. It was like this. 'My dear, Félix, be kind enough to take some shots of me, will you,' Oscar asked.

"I thought there was nothing wrong with such a request. After all, that is what I did as a profession and he was a customer. Then he said, 'I would like them taken, like these. I should say, exactly like these.'

"He opened an album of photographs and passed it to me. Well, I was taken aback, to say the least. I looked at him in alarm. 'Are you sure?' I asked as I examined the prints.

"'Of course; can you do it?' he snapped.

"'What do you mean, can I do it? You know I can, but why like these?' I asked. 'I don't understand.'"

"Like what, for heaven's sake?" asked Sophie.

"He wanted me to take pictures of him in the pose he'd used in those infamous pictures taken in the 1880s by Sarony. You know the ones. He has his hands on his hips and a sultry look and is wearing a dandyish cloak."

"Oh, those, but they're old hat," said Musset.

"Yes, and there he was with a suitcase containing exact replicas of the clothes he wore then. 'Why bother, Oscar,' I said. 'I can't better them. They are first-class and impossible to improve upon.'

"'Don't be so modest,' he replied. 'Get your camera set and let's start.'"

"Did you take them?"

"Yes, Jane, I did. He went behind the screen to change and came out looking almost exactly as he had in the originals. He then posed for the shots. He didn't need any prompting; he knew each pose by heart. It was as though he was on a stage performing."

"Well, he is a born actor," interrupted Seurat.

"He was happy and looking forward to seeing the finished pictures," Nadar told the circle of friends. "I thought that was it until he began asking questions about others who'd sat for me. He asked about people, like Chopin and Delacroix. 'I believe you took some photographs of a very notorious woman at one time,' he pointedly asked.

"'Did I?' I said. 'You know more than I do – who are you talking about? As I recall, I have taken quite a few of what you call notorious women in my time. Whom do you refer to?'

107

"Oscar gave a loud guffaw. 'George Sand!' he shrieked. 'Who else, she is the most notorious French woman I know of. If there are more, they cannot have been as notorious as she. She was in a class of her own. You photographed her many a time in her heyday apparently,' he said.

"'Notorious! My, my, Oscar, you of all people should know that notoriety is just a matter of opinion. You more than most should be aware of that. Yes, I did take quite a few photographs of Madame Sand,' I said, wondering where this was leading. He had a devilish glint in his eyes.

"'Tell me now, were you two... lovers?'

"'What? I yelled, taken by surprise by his impertinent question.

"'Were you fucking her?' he demanded.

"I took a deep breath. 'For a man of letters, you come out with some oddly vulgar expressions. You're hanging about with that sixties crowd too much. It is ruining your vocabulary. Why ask such a low question?'

"'I was just wondering,' he replied. He was silent for a while then repeated his question.

"'Were you?'

"'Don't be so rude,' I said laughing at the outrageous suggestion that I could have taken advantage of a client. 'Every time someone mentions poor George, you assume they were having an affair with her, or, as you so colourfully say, fucking her. It is so unfair, so unjust. The poor soul – you are demonising the unfortunate woman. History has not been kind to her when it comes to her personal life and your insinuations compound that unkindness. Madame Sand only exposed herself to me at the far end of my lens. She was a good subject. That's all.'

"Oscar began to fold his costumes and carefully return them to the suitcase. 'Are you telling me you didn't fancy her?' he asked.

"'No Oscar, I didn't. To be honest, I found her rather cold and distant. She was not the kind of woman I found attractive, nor ever contemplate making overtures to. I remember her as a talented woman, attracted to the opposite sex, *but not to me*. Now, are you satisfied?'

"'Not really,' he replied as he closed the bag. 'There had to be more than that to your relationship.'

"'Oh, really; what relationship was that? You know more than I do. You're talking rubbish, as usual – why should there be more to our relationship than that of a professional association and friendship?' I asked.

"'Well, it seems highly unlikely that a woman like George, who made a beeline for artistically successful men, would somehow ignore you, the supreme society photographer of your day. The man with the magic touch,' he said.

"'Touch! The only one who is touched is you. Tell me, Oscar, where do you get your information from?'

"He laughed. 'I do keep my ear to the ground. Very little gets past me. I would say I' am pretty well informed.'

"'You're way off the mark, I'm afraid. George may have had a few problems with men, but not in the way you are making out. You are near on saying she was a loose and amoral woman, a literary whore. She was far from that,' I replied, trying my best to protect her reputation. With the likes of Oscar's insinuations, she needed protection. He was out to besmirch her or he had a serious fixation about her.

"'A few problems with men?' he bellowed. 'You are joking, Félix. Do you know how many lovers she had?'

"'No!' I shouted at him. 'And to tell you the truth, I don't care. It is none of my business and certainly none of yours. You are wrong to paint her as a scarlet woman. I say you're doing an injustice to her and ought to cease ridiculing one of France's talented women.'

"Oscar picked up his bag and smiling at me, said, 'Thank you, Félix. You have answered my question.'

"'Have I?' I cried, astounded at his assertion.

"'Yes, my dear fellow. Anyone that tries to defend the honour of a woman with such an appalling reputation must have had an affair with her. It is a simple deduction – good day. Thank you for your time. Let me know when the photographs are ready,' he beamed as he swaggered out of the studio.

"What's this thing about George Sand?" asked David. "He's got it really bad, hasn't he? He seems to be obsessed by her."

"I agree," replied Nadar. "As I said, his problem is all to do with image and his fixation with George is part and parcel of it. Just as he's wrapped up in his own image, he somehow sees a mirror reflection of his life in the life of George Sand."

"It's crazy and so is he," replied Seurat.

"By the way, Félix, did you ask him why he needed the photographs?" asked Delacroix

"No, Eugène, but I'd say he's trying to rekindle a part of his life when he was at his best when his literary talents were at their height and the world was at his feet, a time when he was happy – happy with himself, with the world and those about him."

Chopin gave a nervous cough. All eyes turned on him with looks of anticipation.

"Frédéric, have you something to add?" asked Sophie.

"I have," he quietly replied. Not a man for showing his emotions in public or talking about anything of a personal nature, Chopin seemed to have steeled himself to tell his tale. He cared passionately about Oscar and needed to release his pent-up feelings about Oscar's recent uncharacteristic behaviour towards him.

"You know, Oscar and I, we didn't get on too well when we first met. He was a little too ostentatious for my liking, too full of himself; his outrageously vulgar dress sense affronted my own conservatism. He was a show-off who loved his own shadow. He was too shallow for my liking. He wasn't smitten with me either. He thought I was sour, a prude, but he loved my preludes with a passion and wondered how I ever had the capacity to compose them. We kept our distance for some time. If we did meet, we gave each other the time of day and that was it. Yet gradually over the years, we warmed to each other. Nothing drastic, mind you, just a kind of slow-burn – a very slow one, now that I think about it.

"He would often sit while I played the piano, forever asking questions about every element of my music, wanting to know about my life in the tiniest detail, especially about my relationship with George Sand. I believe this was the beginning of his obsession with her. She was the one subject I refused to talk about to him or anybody else. He tried his best to extract information, which I refused to divulge. He tried every trick he could, but I was steadfast in my determination to keep that part of my life private. It was too full of memories. Try as he may, I refused to give into him. He was good-natured about it, respected my point of view, but still, at every opportunity, he would try to extract information about her. Of course, I talked to him on most other aspects of my life. I must have given him enough material for a biography, albeit minus George. In return, he would talk about his colourful life and its infamous end.

"He'd lovingly reminisce about his mother, Jane, whom he absolutely adored; he acknowledged that it was she who instilled in him his love of life, literature and the arts.

"I didn't find him funny or entertaining at first, but after getting to know and understand him, his wit suddenly came alive and I began to see what it was that made him so special, what made him the success he was in life and why he is so popular here at the Reservation. I also discovered that he was a man with a passion for life, a man with an all-consuming passion for his fellow beings, something I've never seen in any other person, at least not at the same level. If he had any fault, it was that he expounded too much of it.

"Of course, he talked about those darker and disturbing episodes of his life. He was candid about his personal failings, his trials, the disaster of Lord Alfred Douglas, the shattering loss of his children, his exile, of his sexual confusion and, most of all, the loss of his wife Constance and the hurt he inflicted on her."

"So you found nothing odd about his behaviour?" enquired Marie.

"No, not then, or in the years to come – of course, there were odd moments that caused a few eyebrows to rise, but nothing to make me concerned. That was to change, I'm sad to say."

"In what way, man?" asked Morrison.

"Well, about a month ago I was at the Music Academy over on Cloud Forty-Four, overseeing a score of mine which was being rehearsed for May Day's Venetian concert. I was demonstrating to the orchestra the way I wanted my Barcarolle performed when I noticed Oscar leaning against a stage prop. He listened for a while, tapping his fingers in time on the back of a chair. As I played, I looked over at him and there was an odd look on his face. A look I had never seen before. There was something unusual about him that day, but I couldn't put my finger on it. When I was finished, he casually wandered over to me.

"'Fancy a drink, old chap?' he asked.

"'Yes, I could do with one. It has been an arduous day. The orchestra has been a nuisance. I keep telling them how I want my Barcarolle played, but will they listen? A drink would be a blessed relief,' I replied.

"We headed off to the Piano Bar. He had his usual pink champagne and I a Bloody Mary with a splash of vinegar to put an edge to my soul. He seemed a bit preoccupied as he sipped away and diverting his eyes every time I tried to look at him. It was odd because he is one who is keen on eye contact. I knew then, as we sipped away, that there was strangeness about him. He had something on his mind and a feeling of unease about him. I knew something was wrong with him but didn't realise just how serious it was. However, I was soon to find out that it was far more serious than I could ever have imagined.

"'Tell me now, Frédéric,' he said. 'Is it true that once you finished composing a score, you dedicated it to some special person in your life?'

"'Yes, I did – still do as a matter of fact,' I replied, wondering what was on his mind, as he was fully aware of the history of my dedications.

"'You did this for those who were close to you?' he enquired.

111

"'Yes, or ones I admired and respected.'

"'Or… loved?' he asked as he swilled the champagne around the glass, not taking his eyes off it. He said this in an icy tone, his face hard as stone; his eyes glazed with cynicism. There was something about his demeanour and body language that screamed trouble. It made me uneasy.

"'Yes, certainly those I love and loved. That goes without saying.'

'Like… George Sand?' he asked.

"He knew he had hit a nerve. I looked at him. He tried to avoid my eyes but I fixed my gaze on him. He returned a blank stare. What on earth had happened to him?'

"'You know I won't talk about her to you or anyone else. You know that already. You have tried for years to get me to talk about her – tried every trick in the book – and I think it is about time you gave up. It's becoming very tiresome,' I replied.

"'So I take it you did dedicate a composition to her?' he demanded, ignoring my concern.

"I remember him telling me that he had read George's autobiography, *Histoire de ma vie*, her *Journal intimate* and umpteen biographies about her, about me, about our relationship. I was certain he knew a great deal about our relationship but that he was out to irritate me for a reason known only to him.

"'Well? Did you?' he asked again in a cold flat tone.

"'No!' I snapped back.

"'Why not?'

"'Finish your drink, Oscar,' I said, wondering how I was to extricate myself from his intrusive questioning.

"'How odd, how very odd,' he continued. 'You mean to say you never loved her or admired her, that you weren't even close to her?'

"He was trying to draw me out. I ignored him and quickly finished my drink.

"'Did you love her?'

"'You're getting far too personal. You know I won't answer that,' I replied.

"'Are you telling me you weren't even close to her?'

"'Don't be stupid. I lived with her for nine years, you asshole,' I replied. 'Of course, I was close to her. That's rather obvious, is it not?'

"'Come now, living with someone does not necessarily mean you are close to them. Just ask any married couple,' he sneered.

"I ignored him. 'Are you ready to go?' I asked, damned if I was going to give into him. I'd rather put up with the tantrums of the orchestra than his irritating probing.

"'Did you admire her?' he went on.

"'Dear God!' I heard myself say. 'Yes, I admired her. She was a very gifted woman. She may have annoyed some people, but those same people would have probably admired her as well, not just for her literary prowess but also for her feminine independence. She's unfairly demonised by history. She was a caring and loving woman with the flaws and virtues of ordinary mortals. There you are Oscar, against my best judgment I have answered one of your inane questions. Are you satisfied? Now, can we go?'

"I put down my empty glass, reached for my hat and cane and rose to leave, annoyed that I had talked about George. It was time to go and leave him to his demons. 'I'm damned if I know what's wrong with you,' I said. 'I can't even imagine what I've done to you, for you to show such antagonism towards me. I'm off. I don't have to sit and listen to your obsessive nonsense about poor George. You can be a stupid and irritating sod at times.'

"He ignored what I was saying and snapped at me. 'Well... did you, did you?'

"'Did I what?'

"'Did you love her – *stupid*?' he barked, as he stood up, blocking my way.

"I couldn't believe he would talk to me in such an insulting manner. I had never encountered him in a destructive mood before. I was having none of it. 'Out of my way, I'm leaving,' I said as I passed him. 'I've had my fill of you today. You are impossible – now, out of my way.'

"'You either loved her or you did not. Come now, it is either one or the other. Why do you have a problem answering such a simple question? It is not going to tax your brain too much, is it?' he said as he pointed his cane at me in a menacing fashion.

"I pushed by him but he grabbed my sleeve and spun me around. 'Surely you don't live with someone like George for nine years without being close to or in love with. Come now, Frédéric, dear fellow – did you love her or not? It's such a simple, simple question,' he asked again.

"He was becoming tiresome. I tried to push my way past him again, but he wouldn't budge.

"'Come now, out with it,' he demanded as he continued to block my way.

"'For pity's sake, let me pass,' I cried as I tried to manoeuvre around him.

"He pushed me backwards. 'Did you, did you love her?' he screamed, his eyes open wide and sweat streaming down his fat face as he continued to push me until he had me up against the wall. The man was obsessed. His demons were getting the better of him. 'Yes,' I reluctantly replied. I pushed past him and made towards the door, annoyed with myself that I had given in to his bullying. Before I knew it, he was in front of me again.

"'I don't know what's wrong with you. You've got your answer, now get out of my way and let me be,' I demanded.

"He just laughed at me and ran ahead, blocking my way to the door. 'So, you loved her, did you? If that is so, why did you not dedicate a piece of music to her as you did with all the others? Here, look at this.' He took a book from his coat pocket and opened it at the last two pages, to the appendix. It was a biography of me by a chap called Adam Zamoyski. I had read it and wasn't too impressed, but Oscar thought it a bible. 'For the life of me I cannot see the name of George Sand,' he went on. 'Why is that? If you loved her, as you say you did, her name should be here, should it not?' he said as he thrust the book in my face and tapped the page with his index finger. 'Where is her name? Come now, point it out for I am damned if I can see it.'

"'What's wrong with you? I refuse to bow to your outrageous harassment. Now go away and let me be,' I replied as I again tried to push by him.

"'No. No! You are not getting away as easily as that,' he bellowed, again pointing to the dedication page. 'Interesting… I see you have a few dedications to Marie d'Agoult, three to be precise, a few to Maria, the one you once set eyes on and planned to marry but who gave you the cold shoulder. Here is one to Camille Pleyel, and to Julian Fontana, who I am surprised you have included seeing that you treated him like dirt. There is even one here to the besotted Jane Stirling. Oh, who is this? A Mrs Eskine, whoever she was? The list goes on and on – but guess what – no George, no George Sand, not a mention of her – not a hint. This woman, with whom you spent nigh on ten years, does not even get a mention – very strange indeed.'

"'If there's anything strange, it's you being so obsessed by what amounts to nothing but nonsense,' I shouted.

"'My dear fellow, it is far from strange. It is these dedications, or, should I say, lack of them that is strange,' he said tapping the pages again. 'Leaving out the one you profess to love? Well, surely that is strange, but there again life, as well as folk is strange, is it not?'

"I pushed past him once more and made my way back towards the rehearsal room to collect my score. He followed and continued hounding me. He ran in front of me and again thrust the book at me in such an intimidating manner it made me feel faint.

"'Well, why? Why did you not dedicate a score to the one you loved, to dear George, the *love* of your life?' he asked, once more tapping the pages with his fingers.

"I ignored him, but he wouldn't give up.

"'So… it's not true after all that you dedicated your scores to those you loved or are supposed to have loved? It is all a sham, is it?' he asked.

"He had me rattled. I looked at him, as he glared at me, and wondered whether to ignore him or to retaliate.

"'Is it? Is it?' he shouted. 'Is it true?'

"He was really getting to me. I pride myself on my patience but, by God, he really knew how to provoke me. I could feel the anger rising. He poked at me with his cane, repeating over and over again, 'Is it true – is it true?'

"'Yes! It's true!' I shouted at him. 'Yes! Yes! Yes! That is exactly what I did! I dedicated scores to those I loved, to those I admired, those I respected and those I cared for. Do you have that through that thick skull of yours yet? Give me that!' I demanded, grabbing the book from his grasp. 'These are the ones I loved,' I said as I tapped the pages. 'Look – Madame Sybil Style, Marie Dupont, Princess Clara Matao, Marie d'Agoult. It is a long list, Oscar. Yes, these I loved and they loved me – satisfied?'

"He stood there transfixed, his mouth open and sweat running down his face.

"'Satisfied? Never,' he announced. 'You can show me as many names as you like, but where is the most important name? Where is George Sand's name, uh? Answer that. Where is George?' he demanded.

"My mind was swirling as he continued to shout over and over again, 'Where is George?' I couldn't stand it anymore. I needed to escape from his suffocating mania.

"'Her name is not there for a very good reason,' I replied, 'A reason that would be lost on you, especially in your present state of mind.'

"'What reason?' he insisted.

"I tried to ignore him by dashing towards the entrance of the academy. To my despair, he followed me, still brandishing the book in one hand and his cane in the other in a menacing fashion. Most of the musicians were still there and thought I would at least be safe from his harassment, but no, I was not so lucky. He was at it again.

"'This reason – what is it?' he bellowed, brandishing the book as though he were an evangelical preacher.

"All of those present turned and looked at us, probably wondering what the fuss was. I wasn't going to give them the chance of finding out. I decided to ignore him but to no avail. He went on hounding me. I collected my score and made a quick exit from the academy while the musicians looked on in amazement. I made my way up Quaver Hill, with Oscar following me like a lost dog. You know how steep Quaver Hill is, so by the time I was halfway up he was nearly on his knees with exhaustion. Yet he didn't stop running in front of me, throwing questions at me at an alarming rate. He would drop back, gasping for breath, then run ahead of me again, still peppering me with questions.

"'Come now! Come now!' he screamed, prodding me with his cane. 'Come now, if you loved her, why no dedication? It makes no sense. What's the big secret?'

"'You're a bounder, Oscar. You know the reason, so why are you annoying me?' I said through clenched teeth.

"'I *don't* know. Why do you think I'm asking you, you fool?'

"'Asking? That's what you call it? I would call it harassment, intimidation. You are doing this because for some reason you are trying to annoy me. And you've succeeded. Now be content with that and leave me alone.'

"'Nonsense. I just want to know, that's all,' he continued. 'Why omit George from such a loving list? Of all the people, you dedicated your scores to, why didn't you do the same for poor George. It's something I need to know.'

"'No, you don't! That's balderdash,' I stated. 'You are only interested in feeding your pathetic obsession with her. There's no reason for it.'

"'Don't make excuses,' Oscar snapped 'Just answer the question – why no dedication to George? Why? Why? Why?'

"I'd had enough of him. 'Listen,' I said, 'the reason is simple. She was different, so different to any woman I had ever loved…'

"'Different!' he yelled. 'Jesus! I know she was different, you clown. Dressing as a man, smoking cigars and getting through men like a dose of salts. I know she was different. That is well known. So, that is the reason for her exclusion, you loved her because she was different. Not convincing at all.'

"'Yes, I loved her because she was different,' I replied. 'But the reason I never dedicated a score to her was that I didn't just love her, you fool… I was in love with her, madly, passionately in love with her. A love such as I had never known before. Do you understand that kind of love, Oscar Wilde? She was the only woman I had ever loved with such deep emotion. She was so different, so special compared to those listed in that book you have been brandishing. I didn't dedicate a score to her, for, in reality, I dedicated all of my work to her. Not just my work, but also my life – a life, as you know, that fell apart after her departure. Satisfied, are you? Satisfied now?'

"That shut him up. He just stood there, his mouth wide open. 'Good day, Oscar', I said as I continued walking, thinking that was it. I was not to be that lucky.

"He grabbed hold of my coat-tail. 'If you loved her so deeply, if she was everything in the world to you, why, why did you leave her? Unless you're an idiot, you don't leave the person you love.'

"'You did!' I trumpeted. 'You left your wife and children to gallivant with that fellow Bosie and all those other young men. Do not preach at me, you hypocrite. You have had your fill, now let go. Just go, go away.' I pushed his hand from my coat and continued up the hill. I could hear him running after me puffing and panting. With some relief, I reached my home. I opened the door and was just about to close it when I noticed Oscar was flat out on his back in the gutter. I ran to his aid. He was sweating and panting, staring into space. A passer-by gave me a hand and we brought him indoors, laying him on the settee. I gave him a drink of water. He wiped his brow and lay back, gave a deep sigh and within a few minutes was sound asleep."

"Wow!" Seurat said. "Didn't I tell you he's lost his mind? He is madder than I thought. And he's showing a violent streak."

"That's unfair. He's suffering, can't you see that?" replied a tearful Jane.

"So are we, having to listen to this garbage."

"Shut up, Seurat. You're becoming a pain," someone cried.

"What did you do with him?" Sophie asked.

"I sat there for a while, still suffering from the shock of his attack on me, watching him sleep and wondering what had happened to him. Why was he behaving in such a strange manner? I left him resting and retired to bed, but I was unable to sleep. I tossed and turned with my mind in turmoil. I lay there thinking back over all the years I've known him, all those good times as we'd sat and philosophised about life and this, our pink-tinted existence. The first time I came face to face with him was at a dinner given by Alfred."

"Yes! I remember," said Musset.

"It was given to celebrate Honoré's additions to his *Comédie humaine*. You introduced Oscar to me. As I said earlier, we didn't exactly hit it off. But over the years we became very close. I'm a great admirer of his work. I would have loved to have known him in our earthly existence. Ours was a mutual admiration. My work entranced him. It's odd, isn't it, that I've dedicated so many of my scores to souls here on the Reservation, but not to Oscar? Maybe he is in the same league as George, maybe the love I have for him is the same as I had and still have for her.

"I had a woeful night. As I lay there, my mind was racing. What is ailing him? What has caused it and, most important, what could be

117

done for him? I began to think about this place, what's it about, what is the endgame might be. Was Oscar straying from the norm? Was he challenging why he is here? Most of us don't want to know. We just get on with our everyday existence and don't ask too many questions. We would all love to purge our sins and move on. We would if we only knew how. Perhaps Oscar has finally realised it's impossible – that we are damned to this existence forever and has gone mad in the process. Oh yes, it was a woeful night. It reminded me of that long night. When I realised that George, the love of my life, no longer loved me and that our love was at an end. She blamed me. I blamed her – that's the way love goes – no logic to it. We lost each other over being too proud to apologise. That hollow ache returned that night when I gazed into emptiness as it slowly dawned on me that the person I most admired was dying for a second time, this time mentally, and I was unable to comfort or rescue him."

"Well, what do you make of that?" asked Sarah.

"As I said before, it's all part of his malaise. This is just another symptom."

"What malaise do you refer to, Jim?" enquired Jane.

"Dunno what name to put to it, but it's a debilitatin' one, as is clear from what we've heard so far. Whatever angle we come at it from we're seein' the same disease that's eatin' away at him."

"It can't be a disease, as none exist here, so what is it?" Seurat asked.

"Search me," replied a downhearted Chopin, burying his head in his trembling hands.

Jane sprang to her feet. Looking down the steps she cried, "Its Édith. Whatever is wrong with her? Look, she is walking so slowly and seems to be sobbing."

"Édith!" She cried. "What's up, love?"

Édith Piaf looked up as she slowly walked towards the steps. They all stood as the Little Sparrow slowly climbed the steps, her head down and hands clasped behind her back. On reaching the top, they could see she was soaked to the skin and sobbing. Morrison put a comforting arm around her. She laid her head on his chest, her black mascara streaking her face. He sat her down. The others gathered around, wondering whatever could have happened to this delicate flower.

"My God, what's wrong, Édith? Whatever's happened?" asked Morrison.

"It's terrible. It's terrible, so terrible," she sobbed.

"What is? You must tell us?" David gently asked.

Isadora knelt down and held Édith's trembling hands. "Take your time. There is no hurry. Tell us in your own time.'

"That's right. Whenever you're ready," Marie said as she handed her a glass of water.

Édith, shivering, took a sip, clung on to Morrison and closed her swollen eyes. Silence descended as they waited for her to reveal what had caused her distress. David wrapped his coat around her, giving her a comforting pat. Opening her eyes, she surveyed the curious and concerned faces looking down at her.

"It was such a beautiful day," she began. "I was up and about early and decided to practice my singing on a walk through the Cherry Blossom Forest over on Cloud Forty-Nine. As you know, I'm fond of doing this. I'm always happy and relaxed amongst the cherry blossom for my voice is always at its best there. There is something special about skipping through the trees and across the blanket of bluebells with a song on the air. I spent most of the morning there, rehearsing 'Le mauvais matelot', which I hadn't sung for years. I was feeling so happy. I was just starting to sing it again when I heard a dog barking, not a normal bark, but a distressed one. I looked around, but couldn't see any dog. I kept on walking then, suddenly, tearing towards me, was a red setter. It was Oscar's dog, Dubliner. She grabbed my skirt and began pulling at me as though she wanted me to follow her. She ran ahead. I followed. We sped through the clearing that led down to the Lily Lake. She stopped at a rock and barked at me. To my horror, as I stood there upon the rock, I noticed Oscar in the water in a distressed state. I dived into the lake and made my way through the lilies. I managed to reach him. I tried to pull him out, but it was difficult, for he is quite a heavy man and was struggling. Dubliner swam out to us and grabbed Oscar by the collar. Between us, we managed to get him ashore.

"'Let me drown, let me drown. For pity's sake, let me drown,' he spluttered as he struggled to loosen my grip on him.

"'Whatever are you playing at?' I screamed as I laid him on his back. 'Drown? Whatever is wrong with you?'

"'Why did you not just leave me there, leave me to die? That is all I want, to die, to end my misery. Why did you rescue me? Why did you not leave me to drown? Do me a favour, throw me back in, hold me down and end my misery,' he mumbled.

"Oh, I was so furious with him. 'You silly, silly man,' I yelled at him. 'You know you can't die here. Nobody ever does. It's impossible. You know that. We all know it. You can't drown; all you're doing is causing yourself distress and upsetting me.'

"I was so annoyed with him, I shook him hard, but he just lay there mumbling to himself. Dubliner was licking his face, but I don't think he knew she was there. Oh, I was so very, very angry with him, the silly, silly man.

"'You listen to me,' I firmly said, as I tried to get him to sit up, but he wouldn't budge. 'You must get it through that head of yours that this is it. Are you listening to me, Oscar? This is it, for now, tomorrow and forever. You won't die here; none of us will. Try as you may, it won't happen. It cannot happen. It is impossible! Do you hear me, impossible! We're spirits, that's all. Spirits don't die, they only linger. This is it, Oscar, a lingering Purgatory. Get used to it. There is no Paradise or Hell for us, only this, our eternal existence. Accept it. Accept this reality and you'll free your soul.'

"I made no impression on him. He looked so sad lying there, and wishing he were dead, wishing that it were all just a bad dream. It's no dream, as we all know. This is it. This is the reality of our situation and here was this genius lying there, brooding and trying to change the course of his destiny, the silly, silly bugger.

"As I sat there, cradling him in my arms, my mind went back to my teenage days when I was a singer on the streets of Pigalle. There was great pressure on young girls like my beautiful friend Nadia and myself to become prostitutes. She gave in to the pressure, but when she tried to pick up her first client, she failed and, out of fear of her *souteneur*, ran away. The next day, they pulled out of the Seine, her body gnawed by rats. As I looked down at Oscar, I saw the beautiful face of Nadia, eaten away. The difference between Oscar and Nadia was that he couldn't drown but she could and did. She loved life and didn't want to die, unlike our troubled friend, who didn't just want to drown, but to die for a second time – only a special kind of fool wants to die twice.

"I shook him again and told him, 'This is our Destiny. Whatever theatrics you perform, whatever antics you get up to, it will not change your situation and certainly not the course of your destiny. You know that already, yet you act the maggot. What in all that is holy is ailing you?'

"He grabbed my hand and cried, 'Throw me back into the lake. If I stay there long enough I will drown. I know I will. Help me. Help me, Little Sparrow. Help me to die. Help set me free.'

"I was so angry with him. I gave him another shake, which he didn't notice. He simply lay there like a whale washed up on a beach. 'You listen to me, you shit. You are no different to the rest of us. You may think you are special, gifted, but here, you are no different to the rest of us. We are all souls who have fallen short of Paradise. We all have to cope as best we can. You are not the only one with a cross to bear. We all have one to carry. Some are maybe heavier than others but still to be carried. We'd all like to be in Paradise or to wake up and find we are home, in familiar surroundings with those we love, but you, you silly, silly man, don't you see, these are things of a past that will never return? They are gone forever. Don't you understand that? We only have each other. We have to rally round each other on this journey, a journey that may have no end. We don't have a choice in this – we have to help each other. You know it is impossible to purge our sins, so we have to accept we will be here forever. We must take care of each other; we have no choice.'

"'I don't want to be here forever,' Oscar whispered. 'Help me, Little Sparrow. Help me. Set me free,' he pleaded, as he looked at me in absolute despair, horror carved into his contorted face.

"'Oh! Oscar,' I cried as I cradled his head in my arms.

"'Set me free, Little Sparrow. I beg you, set my soul free,' he whispered, as he looked up at me his eyes bloodshot and full of tears.

"'I'm just a singer of the blues, that's all. I can't set you free,' I cried as I held him. 'Only the truth will do that. The truth is, Oscar, this is your home, your eternal home, here with me and the rest of the souls of Père Lachaise. Facing that truth will set your soul free. If you don't accept that then you'll have an existence of torment. It is only your maker in His wisdom who can grant you the freedom you are seeking – I don't have that kind of power.'

"He rolled out of my arms and before I knew it he was in the water again, swimming out into the lake and vanishing under the lilies. I dived in, followed by Dubliner. I made my way through the lilies and found him trying to submerge himself, taking in deep gulps of water. I got hold of him again and he struggled and fought to get away from me. I managed to get a hold of him by the scruff of the neck and, again with the help of Dubliner, we once more dragged him ashore. I lay there next to him, exhausted, my mind racing as I tried to make sense of his erratic behaviour."

Édith began to cry again as Morrison cradled her in his arms.

"My God," cried Chopin. "It's getting worse. There must be something terribly wrong with his mind if he thinks he can die here. He must know that never can be. Surely, he must know we are just spirits without any substance. He is talking as though he were a living creature, as though he was flesh and blood. We may all look as we did in life, but he must know we are only spirits."

The others nodded in agreement.

"I lay there exhausted," Édith continued. "My mind was in turmoil. It had been such a lovely day, now it was turning into a horrid nightmare. I lay his head in my lap and stroked his thick lustrous black hair. He didn't move, just stared into open space. Dubliner was as exhausted as I was and lay next to her master with her head on Oscar's chest. Poor soul, she was shivering with fear, her eyes darting back and forth, not knowing what was going on.

"Oscar opened his eyes, looked up at me and whispered, 'Little Sparrow?'

"'Yes,' I replied.

"'Will you do something for me?'

"'If I can – what is it?' I answered.

"'Sing for me.'

"'Really, Oscar,' I said, stroking his brow. 'I don't feel like singing. I'm feeling too sad to sing.'

"'I need to hear your sweet voice. It always makes me feel secure. Please, Little Sparrow, sing for me.'

"I just couldn't refuse him as I looked down at his sad and tortured face. 'What will I sing?' I asked.

"He closed his eyes and said, '*Marble Halls*'. Yes, *Marble Halls* that will do nicely. I need to hear it.'

"A few years after I arrived here we were discussing our favourite songs and he said he loved this song above all others as it was his mother's favourite and she was forever humming or singing it. He asked me to perform it at a concert I was due to give later that week. It wasn't my kind of song and really out of my range, but I managed to master it. At the concert, I performed my version and he loved it so much he didn't stop talking about it for months. So, as I sat there with him in my arms, he tenderly stroking Dubliner's head, I sang it."

Édith released herself from Morrison's embrace, stood up and sang the song. Her beautiful voice, slightly trembling, wafted about the Central Reservation, bringing more souls to the Laburnum Tree.

Marcel Proust had recognised her voice and came running up the steps to be near her. Ledru-Rollin, Yves Montand and Simone Signoret followed him. They all wanted to be near this heavenly voice. The new arrivals joined the circle, taking their positions on the steps to hear Édith conclude her rendition. As the last notes drifted away across the expanse of the Reservation, she lowered her head and cried for her tortured friend. Morrison reached out to her and brought her back into his embrace.

"When I finished the song," she continued after composing herself, "he looked up at me and smiled, then closed his eyes, as the tears squeezed through his swollen eyelids. I let him rest, thinking he was now settled in his mind and needed some quiet contemplation. I don't know how long we were there but my mind was racing at the memory of our times together. Then, the next thing I knew, he was on his feet and running into the forest with Dubliner hard at his heels. I ran after them, but they were too fast for me. I lost them. I slumped to the ground, gutted and confused. As I sat there trying to regain some energy I recalled how I first met him and how our relationship developed into the strong friendship it is now.

"When I arrived here from Père Lachaise, Oscar was designated my guide.

He was a Trusted Soul. I didn't know what that was, but he soon put me straight. I knew a lot about him, of course, being a regular reader of his works, especially his poetry, and I had attended his plays on many occasions. I was delighted he was the one who would show me around and settle me into my new surroundings. I knew of his past, of his tribulations and the sadness in his life. He didn't talk much about it to me but he was surprised that I could recite so much of his work. Very impressed, he was. And I would often give him a rendition of 'Non, je ne regrette rien', which he drooled over, as he did with many of my songs. I love the man as most of you do, so to see him in the state he is now in is very disturbing. "Not long after I arrived here," she continued, "he found me in very distressed state, lying in the gutter on the Road to Nowhere.

"'What's wrong?' he asked as he gently lifted me up from the stony roadside. I was so distressed I was hardly able to mutter a word. Being the soul he is, he calmed me down, wiping my eye with one of those flamboyant handkerchiefs of his and gave me a warm hug. 'Come now, my Little Sparrow, whatever is it? It cannot be that bad, can it?' he said.

"'It can and is,' I tearfully replied.

"'Come now, you know you can tell me.'

"'I can't find Marcelle. I can't find my lovely daughter, Marcelle,' I replied. 'She's not here. I've searched the Reservation and she can't be found. Where is she? Whatever has become of her? She has to be here, as I laid her to rest in Père Lachaise along with my father, Louis, way back in 1939.'

"He held my hands and, looking deep into my eyes, said, 'No, Édith, she's not here. There are no children here. Your child is in a far better place than this.'

"'Where is she, then?'

"'In Paradise.'

"'My Marcelle, in *Paradise*?'

"'Yes. Where else could she be? There are no children here or in Hell. Innocent souls like Marcelle are spared our fate,' he said.

"'You mean to say my beautiful Marcelle is in Paradise, in the arms of Jesus?'

"'Yes. All children are.' he replied.

"'Oh, I hope so. I loved her so much. Oh, you would never believe how much I loved her. I should have spent more time with her but times were hard. When she died I felt so guilty, that I had somehow let her down,' I cried.

"'Guilty?' he gasped. 'Oh, I know that feeling all too well. It has been my constant companion for as long as I can remember. It has hung about my neck like the hangman's noose. You have no reason to feel guilty. She died because of an illness, not because of your neglect.'

"'Yes, that may be so, but, I should have been with her. She died alone. I didn't even have the money to bury her. My friends at the club in Pigalle managed to raise most of the money. I was ten francs short and didn't know how I'd raise it. You wouldn't believe what I did to raise those ten francs. It shames me to even think about it.'

"He looked at me with tender loving eyes. 'You don't have to tell me. Whatever it was you did, I know it was done for the best of motives and if it was wrong, I am sure you have been forgiven.'

"'Oh! I doubt it,' I replied. 'I'd say my sin was grave enough to have me here at this Reservation, rather than in Paradise with my Marcelle.'

"'We're all guilty of some sin or other. Whatever you did can't be any more sinful than my own antics. When it comes to guilt my Little Sparrow, you are just an amateur.'

"'But mine was unforgivable,' I cried. 'I sold myself for the measly ten francs to bury my child. I was so desperate that I went out that night and picked up the first available man I laid eyes on in return for ten francs.'

"He understood. He just held me and let me cry away my sorrows. I don't know how long I sat there, thinking of things past. I got to my feet and made my way through the forest. It was a waste of time rehearsing any more songs for my heart wasn't in it anymore. I was sadly making my way home when I heard Jane calling me. Oh, what will become of him? We must find a way to rescue him, but how?"

The circle of friends sat in silence as Édith and Morrison, arms entwined, gently swayed back and forth wondering what it could be that was torturing the soul of Oscar Wilde.

Suddenly the silence was broken. "What's so urgent?" Colette asked as she took her place in the circle, breathing heavily after her dash from the Literary Quarter after bring summonsed by a call on the Purgatory Line asking her to come as soon as possible. It had sounded serious so she dropped everything and headed for the Central Reservation. Colette was one of the quieter inhabitants, generally keeping very much to herself, but was still as keen a writer as she had been in life. She had a small select circle of friends, Oscar being one of them. She had clicked with him the moment they met and they held each other in great esteem.

"It's about Oscar," Sophie said.

"How very odd."

"Why?"

"I saw him about two hours ago staggering up Literary Hill, his clothes looking creased as though they'd been wet and with a demonic look on his face. Dubliner wearily followed; her tail between her legs, looking sorry for herself. I called after him, but he ignored me. He looked preoccupied. He was mumbling to himself. He entered Merrion, slamming the door after him. I was thinking of knocking to ask what was wrong but thought better of it. He looked so distracted and angry. But why do you wish to see me?"

"You were seen recently talking to Oscar at the Viewing Platform. We need to know if you noticed if his behaviour was in any way odd or out of the ordinary." Isadora explained.

"I wouldn't say odd, more like strange. I was on my way to the Knowledge Zone when I came upon him at the Viewing Platform. He was peering down over Père Lachaise.

"'Hello, Oscar, what are you up to?' I asked as I gave him a friendly tap on the shoulder.

"'Oh, it is you, Colette. You gave me a bit of a start,' he said looking rather panic-stricken.

"He was rambling on about the cemetery cleaners vandalising his tomb. He was in a desperate state. I did point out to him that what they were actually doing was giving it a good clean. That didn't go down too well with him. He went on about it being sacrilege. I tried to talk some sense into him but to no avail. He had a journal with him. In it, he was making notes on the visitors to the tomb. As you all know, he has this thing about the quality of the kisses planted on his tomb. It is one of his many silly obsessions. He asked me to help him. I had better things with which to occupy my time than gawking over Père Lachaise. It seemed such a pointless exercise, but he asked me in such a pathetic way that I felt sorry for him and said yes. Foolish me –

I took the binoculars from him and viewed the tomb. It seems the cleaners had been wasting their time as it was again festooned with lipstick kisses. Even as I was looking there were quite a lot of women and a few men waiting to leave their mark. I particularly remember a group who looked like seven sisters making a performance of their kissing skills. They even had their photographs taken. I described what was happening – you know the description of the sisters. I then described the other visitors, whether they kissed the tomb or not and, if they did, how they did it and what colour lipstick they wore."

"God, is there no stopping the man?" Seurat interjected. "It's so comical, it's sad."

"I did challenge him on why he wanted to take such detailed notes and he said that there was psychology about the use of lipstick – a very profound psychology."

"Are you serious?" laughed Seurat.

"Very much so, and so was he. He maintained that the colours used by women reflect the extent of their sexuality."

"Good God. Give the man a pill," groaned Seurat. "Lip psychology indeed. Is there no end to his nonsense?"

"You may say it's nonsense, but he puts forward a convincing argument."

"It would need to be," smirked Seurat.

"You're becoming a bore, Seurat. Put a sock in it, will you,' said Musset.

"I'm dying to hear this," said Balzac, who had joined the circle after hearing Édith singing and wondering what was going on. "I must say, dear Oscar certainly knows how to put an edge to his words. Carry on, Colette, let's hear it?"

"Edge, more like over the edge."

"Stop being so cruel," cried Jane. "What's wrong with you? Must you always have a dig at him? Maybe Colette is right – he may very well have a good case to make that could justify what we are calling his odd behaviour."

"Good case?" laughed Seurat. "It'll have to be brilliant to convince me."

"Oscar sees things a lot differently from most of us and this is one of them," continued Colette. "Because I had a beauty-product line in my earthly life he was of the belief I would have understood what he was on about. He was wrong, for until he explained it I hadn't the foggiest idea what he was talking about.

"He maintains that each colour has a meaning and whether it's a gloss, satin or matt finish also has a profound meaning. The way it's applied has an even deeper connotation and effect and, of course, how the lips are used has the most profound meaning of all. As I was writing down the details for him, I did begin to wonder about his mental state, but he put my mind at ease as he explained the logic behind it."

"Logic! Is there any logic behind it, then?" asked David. "It sounds ridiculous to me."

"Of course there is," Colette continued. "At least according to him there is. You should know, David, Ingres and even you, Seurat, that colour has many profound meanings and effects. All of your paintings are expressing those very meanings, their moods, feelings, and visual and mental impact. This is what Oscar was interpreting as he studied the lipstick effect on his tomb."

"He may be an artist, but he isn't a visual one that's for sure if he believes wet kisses on his cold tomb are a piece of art," replied Ingres.

"Maybe so, but this is what he said. This is what Isadora witnessed up at the Viewing Platform. He maintained that women who use scarlet lipstick have a burning passion, not just for life but also for sexual fulfilment, and most are confident, outgoing and sexually liberated individuals. Those who wear scarlet that naturally don't suit them are inclined to be extrovert, self-absorbed and very, very shallow.

"Those who use red are slightly different from those who use scarlet, for they only give the impression that they are sexually liberated. Their passion is hidden and takes a lot of discovering, but when discovered there's no stopping them. There again, those who use it when it clearly doesn't suit them are being sexually teasing, giving the impression they are looking for trouble and therefore attracting the undesirable kind."

"Did you ever hear such shit in your life? God! Do we to continue to listen to this?"

"Oh, shut it, Seurat, will you? This is very interesting. This is Oscar at his most sublime," cried Balzac.

"Those who apply pink do so with a fine touch," Colette continued. "These have a slow smouldering sexuality that is hidden behind a reserved personality. They can hang about waiting too long for the real thing to appear. When it arrives, they are too reserved to grab it. Those who wear pink that clearly doesn't suit them are chancers trying to get the real thing by deception.

"Blue... well, he was very definite about that. He maintained a dark blue, like cobalt blue, represents coldness in spirit and mind and the mark of an asexual woman. A light blue such as azure represents a frozen sexuality that is unlikely to melt, even if she met the man of her dreams.

"Brown represents intellectual prowess. As I see it, Oscar was saying that those who use it could only relate to sexuality in an intellectual context. Those wearing brown when it doesn't suit them are social climbers putting on an air intellectual superiority."

"Jesus, you're not serious, Colette," cried Seurat. "Surely you don't believe it? I've never heard such tripe. Lip psychology my arse."

"I didn't say I believed it, only that it made some kind of sense. Most women would know what he means. It would be lost on most men. It's well thought out, though, you must admit."

Seurat burst out laughing. "You're being taken for a sucker, my dear lady. He must have seen you coming. As matters of interest, what about those who wear no lipstick, what does that idiot say about them?"

"Those, Seurat, are free spirits. They take life as it comes. There is little pretence about them. What you see, is what you get. To be kissed by them is a privilege."

Balzac was fascinated by this lip psychology and could hardly contain his glee. "You must admit it's an intriguing and sensuous subject. Trust Oscar to come up with something like this. I will have to get him to write a paper on it, to explain the whole concept. I'll look at lips in a different way from now on."

Seurat sighed. "You're as mad as he is if you fall for that load of nonsense."

"After he concluded his studies we walked down the hill and headed for the Café Oueurde," Colette said. "Apart from his studying lips, I found nothing in his behaviour that would cause me alarm. At the café, he was in great form, so I can't understand what all the fuss is about."

"Really?" laughed Seurat. "Just hang around here for a while and you'll change your mind. You will soon discover that the man is stark raving mad. He needs locking up – and quickly, so we can all have some peace."

"Marie, you started this," Sophie reminded her. "You said he's been acting oddly. I say it's about time you revealed just what you know."

"OK," Marie replied, standing up. Leaning against the Wisdom Stone, and to the relief of the frustrated Sophie, she finally began her tale. "Over the years I've often visited Oscar at his home in the Literary Quarter on Cloud Fifteen, for afternoon tea or just for a good gossip – gossiping being one of his favourite pastimes – or to many of his social evenings that none of us with any sense miss. These were always the most illuminating experiences, as many here know too well.

"Not long ago, I arrived for afternoon tea. I recoiled as I came face to face with my reflection – not that I usually recoil at such a delightful sight, but coming face to face with it on the way to tea is just too much. I noticed that a highly polished mirror was where a glass pane used to be on his green front door. At the time, I thought nothing of it but that was soon to change. He opened the door and welcomed me in his usual way – a peck on the cheek accompanied by a mischievous wink.

"'Come in, my dear,' he cheerfully greeted me.

"The entrance hall had been changed. There was a large mirror facing the front door and it reflected a portrait of Oscar dressed as a judge – you know, with a wig, gown, and a stern expression. Odd, I thought. I looked around and there hanging on the back of the door was the portrait. It was one of *your* portraits, David. There it was, staring at me. What a peculiar place to hang a picture and what a strange subject matter.

"'Where have you been hiding, you bold one? I haven't had the pleasure of your company for ages,' Oscar teased.

"'Oh, I've been terribly busy working on a venture close to your heart,' I replied.

"'And what would that be, may I ask?'

"'Yourself,' I replied.

"The look on his face was a treat. 'Tell me more. I just love intrigue. This way, my dear, there are fresh crumpets warming. What better way to spend a pleasant afternoon, than talking about oneself, whilst enjoying tea, crumpets, and the company of a gorgeous lady such as yourself,' he said as he led me towards the reception room that led to his delightful sitting- room.

"I followed him into the reception room. On one wall was a mirror that reflected a painting of Oscar, this time dressed like a pompous aristocrat, a marquess or the likes. I could have sworn he posed as the Marquess of Queensbury. I looked around and there was the portrait. A fine one, I must say, this time by Seurat."

"Fine – I beg your pardon, a masterpiece is more like it. I only paint masterpieces," replied Seurat.

"If you say so – anyway, most of the walls were hung with mirrors, all different shapes, and sizes. He took my coat and hung it on the most peculiar clothes-horse I've ever seen."

"But he has a plain wooden one, hasn't he?" asked Musset.

"As long as I remember he has had," added Delacroix.

"He had, but not anymore. He's replaced it with one in the shape of the Scales of Justice."

"What!" exclaimed Chopin?

"The Scales of Justice," repeated Marie. "What's more, it's made of glass – looks rather brittle too."

"Like his brain," Seurat said as he scratched his beard in disbelief. "Has he completely lost his mind?"

"If he has, there's no chance of him finding it again. The malaise Morrison was referring to is far more serious than I had at first thought. Poor soul," Nadir said, shaking his head in disbelief.

"Anyway," continued Marie. "I walked ahead of him into the sitting-room, and to my amazement, the walls here too were hung with mirrors. In the alcoves were two more portraits, both by you, Eugène. The first was of Oscar dressed as the Statue of Liberty. He was standing with his back to me with his head turned gazing at me with a look of disgust on his face. The other depicting Justice, with Oscar lying on the ground, dressed in ragged clothes with a large boot pressing down on his chest. Imprinted on the boot was 'Ignorance' and 'Indifference'. I must say, it appeared to be rather odd."

"Odd. He's odd all right. There is no hope for the fool. Must I say more?" Seurat sneered.

"No. You've said enough," Morrison retorted as he glared at him.

"I'm only expressing my opinion and an honest one at that."

"Is that what you call it? Well, keep it to yourself. You're becoming extremely offensive," replied Jane. "Where were you, Marie?"

"In the sitting-room. Above the fireplace was a Max Ernst depiction of three faces of Oscar within a melon placed atop a pink marble pedestal."

"Very odd," whispered Nadar – "very odd indeed."

"Didn't I say the man has some malaise? Man, the more that's revealed the more depressin' it gets."

"I think maybe you're right, Jim. There must be a name for this malaise – any idea?" Nadar asked.

"None at all, but I'm sure there's one."

"Quite a few, I'd say," Seurat muttered, "Delusion, mania or how about simple insanity. By the sound of things, our errant genius is one

131

big malaise. What about you, Delacroix, do you mean to say you didn't think it odd when he asked you to paint those peculiar portraits. I would have thought that kind of thing wasn't up your street."

"He's a friend of mine. He asked if I would take them and I did. Admittedly, they were not in my usual style but I do experiment now and then. I had no idea what he wanted them for and I didn't ask, at least not until the meeting that I've already recalled."

"You must be as daft as he is."

"That's enough now, Seurat, you're really stretchin' your luck."

"Is that so, Morrison? But not as far as he is, eh?"

"Let me continue, will you," snapped Marie, annoyed with the interruptions. "I sat down and Oscar went to fetch the tea and crumpets. I looked up and to my horror saw the ceiling decorated with mirrors. Replacing his spectacular cut-glass chandelier was a plain round mirror, surrounded by diamond-shaped green-tinted mirrors. Anyway, he returned with the tea tray and set it down on a table with a mosaic-mirrored surface. He didn't seem to notice my surprise and as he poured the tea said, 'Now my dear, tell me of your venture. It has to be good if I am the centre of attention.'

"'It is. You'll recall our sojourn on Cloud Thirty-Seven some months ago?' I asked as I spread butter on a hot crumpet.

"'How could I forget,' he replied, dropping three cubes of sugar in his tea.

"'If you recall,' I said, 'Jane suggested that the centenary of your departure from your earthly life should be commemorated...'

"'Oh yes, the lovely Jane. What a jewel she is. She can always be relied upon to suggest something suitable.'

"'Along with Jane, Balzac, Nadar, Musset and Sarah, we resolved to put on a performance that would be something to remember.'

"'A brilliant idea it was too,' Oscar said, spreading butter on a hot crumpet. 'Not to commemorate a genius such as I would not be proper, would it. Well, come, my dear, what was decided?'

"'After taking into consideration your fascination with the musical theatre we resolved to stage a musical extravaganza based on your masterpiece, *The Importance of Being Ernest*. It has great potential as a musical,' I informed him.

"He nearly choked. 'A musical! Yes, yes. What a brilliant idea,' he said his face aglow at the prospect. 'I had thought of it myself, mind you, but didn't want to appear vain by suggesting it. I will compose some perfect lyrics. They are forming in my mind as we speak. Yes, I can see it all before me – the perfect musical.'

"He was gleaming. How was I going to tell him?

"'Oscar,' I said, tenderly touching his hand. 'You won't be doing the lyrics.'

132

"He was dumbfounded and dropped his crumpet on to his green velvet trousers, his mouth open in disbelief.

"'Whatever do you mean,' he spluttered, 'I won't be doing the lyrics? How preposterous! What do you mean I won't be doing the lyrics to the musical version of my *own* play? Explain yourself. You have me perplexed.'

"'It's simple,' I said. 'This will be an opportunity for your admirers to show *their* appreciation of you and your oeuvre. Nothing personal, mind you, but you will have no part in it. Sorry.'

"'Sorry! Sorry indeed,' he cried. 'Well, I'll be damned! A show about *me*, without *my* lyrics – how could such a show succeed?'

"'Without difficulty,' I mumbled.

"'Never heard such nonsense,' he said, taking a sip of tea to help him regain his composure – 'well, who will be doing the lyrics, then? It will have to be someone with finesse, someone with style – No riff-raff. Who is it, then?'

"'It's a secret.'

"'*A secret!* This sounds more like a conspiracy against me, than an appreciation. Whoever dreamt up such ridiculous nonsense?' he fumed.

"'It's far from ridiculous nonsense. The committee has decided to keep the identity of all those involved, including the lyric writers, the composers, the cast or any others involved in the production an absolute secret. You won't be allowed on the set or be involved in the production,' I informed him as calmly as was possible.

"'For Christ's sake… why not?' he cried.

"'You'll interfere. You will want to do things *your* way. We all know what you are like. This is not your production, but that of your friends. They all want a free hand, not to be tripping over you every few seconds and listening to you complaining because you think they are not doing things your way. You know exactly what I'm on about. You can't be involved in your own tribute and that's it.'

"He sat down and gazed up at the circular mirror, muttering away to himself as he stirred his tea. 'Come now, Marie,' he coaxed, 'who is doing the lyrics? You can tell me.'

"'I've already told you – it's a secret. I won't tell you and that's that.' I replied sharply.

"'Why the big secret?' he groaned. 'There should be no secrets between friends.'

"'Because if you knew, you'd be giving advice and generally making a nuisance of yourself, that's why'

"'Me… being a nuisance?'

"We finished our tea and I excused myself and headed for the powder room, leaving him pondering his next move. As I turned into

133

the hallway, I received another shock, for that too was mirrored. On the walls were two more portraits by David – a matching pair in different shades of blue. Hung all the way up the stairs were different shaped mirrors – triangular, oval, diamond and square? The powder room was an experience. The cheeky beggar even had the inside of the bowl mirrored."

"The kinky sod," cried Balzac.

"The entire floor was a mosaic mirror. As I sat on the loo, I came face to face with Oscar, smiling at me from a portrait by Signac hanging on the back of the door. Well. I was surprised to say the least, for the portrait showed Oscar winking. What was it all about? Had our dear friend gone completely mad?" asked Marie.

"If he has, what better place to do it," cracked Seurat.

"Returning from the powder room, I peeped into his bedroom to see if there were any surprises there. There were. Gone was his sturdy four-poster. It had been replaced by a bed that was shaped like pouting red lips. On the ceiling was a huge oval mirror. The walls were white, as was the shaggy wool carpet. Unlike the others, there were no paintings on the walls."

"Perhaps he's waiting to have some done; that's if he can find an artist daft enough to do them, seeing that most having told him to beat it."

"Very funny, Seurat, you get better by the minute. Now, let me continue if you will," Marie said, agitated at his manner. "When I returned to the sitting-room, I found Oscar parading in front of a large mirror, admiring himself. He continued staring admiringly, oblivious as to my return.

"'Is something wrong?' I asked.

"He turned and looked at me with some surprise. 'Wrong! My dear, what could possibly be wrong? I'm being visited by your lovely self, being honoured by my friends with a musical extravaganza, without my lyrics, may I add. Wrong! Things couldn't be better.'

"'Don't you have something you wish to tell me?' I asked as I returned to my seat.

"'Tell you!' he replied, rather confused by my question. 'Should I?'

"'Oh. It's nothing;' I lied, 'just thinking aloud.'

"'That's a bad habit to get into, you know. It could be the end of your respectability,' he said. 'Ladies of breeding don't talk to themselves.'

"We finished our tea and talked about the theatre, which prompted him to try to wring out of me more information about the musical extravaganza. He made no comment on his redecorated home. I wanted to mention the mirrors but thought better of it. I tried to stay calm so as not to let him know I was disturbed by his bizarre refurbishments."

"He's bloody crazy. He needs seeing to, and quickly. Better still, send him to Cloud Eighty-Seven," Seurat smirked.

Marie tried to ignore him. His continuous ill-humour towards Oscar was as disturbing as Oscar's behaviour. Something, she thought, must be done to see what it was that was bugging Seurat. However, that was for another day. Oscar was her immediate concern. She continued.

"'Like a stroll in the garden?' he said, giving me his hand. 'It's such a fine afternoon.'

"'Why not?' I replied, taking his hand. It would be a welcomed relief to leave his reflective home.

"To get to the garden we had to go through the drawing-room towards the French windows that opened on to it. The room had also changed. The floor was a mirror made in Celtic design. On the main wall was a large painting by Ingres of Oscar as a reclining nude?"

"*That* must be something to see," Balzac exclaimed. "I must get over there and take a good look at it."

"I must say," continued Marie, "I was tempted to ask what was going on, but Oscar seemed oblivious to my sharp intake of breath. There was more to come. As I stepped into the garden, I saw that he had manicured the large privet into silhouettes of his profile. They were repeated every twenty feet or so. When I took my leave I was tempted to challenge him about the changes to Merrion, but was too faint-hearted and simply bade his farewell."

"I don't know about the rest of you, but I feel sorry for him," Édith tearfully said. "He seems to have lost it. But what can we do to help him?"

"What indeed?" Jane sighed.

"Pray," someone murmured.

"What for?" asked Seurat.

"Divine intervention," Édith whispered.

"Huh," cried Seurat, "Divine intervention, my arse. Prayer is a waste of time. He isn't listening. If He is, He is a sadistic bastard, never answering our prayers. It is all a con. I'm telling you, there's no divine Intervention and no divine soul is listening."

"God is," retorted Édith, clearly shocked by such blasphemy.

"Oh, is that so, Little Sparrow? Well, as I see it, we are all kidding ourselves if we believe God is listening to our prayers. If He were, He would be bored rigid. After He realised He'd made a balls-up of us, His supposed Divine Masterpiece, He went off in a huff to some far-flung place, leaving us all to cope on our own, so don't give me this nonsense of praying to *Him*. As for Oscar, lock him up. That's the only decent thing we could do with him."

"God, Seurat, you really are a nasty piece of work," cried Édith.

"I'm only telling you the reality of our situation."

"Was there anything else out of the ordinary, Marie?" asked Isadora.

She shrugged her shoulders. "No. I don't think I could have taken anymore if there had been. When he said goodbye to me, I was relieved to go and get out of the place. I always felt at home there, but not anymore. It was weird, to say the least."

"Like the man himself," laughed Seurat.

There was quite a crowd now gathered on and around the steps of the Central Reservation listening intently to the revelations. Readers will recall the stranger earlier sitting at the foot of steps, scribbling away, taking down every word. He was still there. Musset again noticed this and was curious to know who he was. He thought he would tackle him once the crowd had dispersed. He didn't know it then, but he would have a long wait. There was a lot more to come.

"Is there something wrong?" Sophie asked Jane, who she noticed was weeping.

Jane looked up to see all of then looking at her with concern. Sophie put her arm around her and gave a comforting embrace. "Have you something you wish to say, Jane?"

Releasing herself from Sophie's embrace, Jane stood up and leaned against the Wisdom Stone. She rubbed her eyes, then looked around at the assembled souls.

"Unlike most of you," she said, "I don't have anything to say about Oscar's eccentricities at all. I know he's been a good friend to me and to all of you – even you, Seurat, especially when you were suffering your depression some years ago."

Seurat lowered his head, trying to hide his shame at being reminded of Oscar's kindness to him.

"What has been revealed here today is horrifying? It is heartbreaking, for it is clear that he is suffering dreadfully. What from, I have no idea. I can't even hazard a guess as to what. I see him nearly every day, yet I can swear I've never seen him acting other that he usually does, as a complete gentleman. All right, he's a bit eccentric, but he's always been like that so there's nothing odd in him acting that way. That's how we know him and that's why we love him. I've known him so long, that it hurts to think that if he was having problems he was unable to confide in me."

"Maybe he cares so much for you he didn't want you upset by his troubles," suggested Isadora. "It could be as simple as that."

"Maybe."

Jane looked over at Chopin, depressed by the revelations.

"Your testimony is so sad, Frédéric. You must know that he didn't mean a word of what he said to you. You must have realised that something was ailing him, eating away at him, for him to say what he did – something that was out of his control. He's such a friend and admirer of yours; he wouldn't want to deliberately wound or hurt you in any way. You must forgive him."

"I already have," Chopin admitted. "Yes, he has wounded me… he has caused me pain, but the pain I carry is for him. I forgave him,

Jane, the moment I saw him lying in the gutter. When he was spread out and exhausted on my sofa, I realised that this most generous and loving of souls was dying once more – not in a seedy back-street Parisian hotel but here, surrounded by souls who love and cherish him. I knew he didn't mean a word of what he said. Surely our aim now is to help him through his distress, whatever the cause is."

"Yes,' Jane replied. "That's just what we must do. He has helped me when I needed support and I will repay his kindness. You know, one day, he found me weeping at the Viewing Point. I was very distressed and feeling rather hard done by. He asked what was wrong. 'It looks like I've been forgotten,' I sighed as I pointed down to my grave, bare and unkempt, with the metal surrounds rusted away. 'There's not a flower to be seen. There aren't even remnants of any laid there. Does nobody remember me? Have I really been forgotten?'

"He sat down beside me and held my hands and said, 'No, you haven't really been forgotten. The fact that there are no flowers on your grave doesn't mean a thing. Didn't Toulouse-Lautrec immortalise you in his paintings? Didn't he lovingly put you on canvas for all to see? Your image is known the world over and you are in the annals of French theatre and that of the Moulin Rouge. You are remembered in a different way from the others, but very much still remembered. Everyone is remembered in his or her own way. I, Chopin and Jim Morrison are remembered in different ways, but very much remembered. You are not forgotten, Jane, and never will be. As long as there is dance, theatre, and art in the world, you will be remembered.'

"'Thanks, Oscar,' I said. 'Maybe you're right, but still; it would be nice to see some flowers there just once in a while.'

"He gave a hearty laugh. 'You are rather hard to find down there in Père Lachaise, you know. Your grave is a bit off the beaten track. That is probably a lot to do with it. I wouldn't worry too much about it.'

"He can be very diplomatic at times, you know, and a really smooth talker. He gave me another squeeze and afterwards made sure I wasn't being neglected. He sent flowers to me the next day and has done so every Sunday since and on many occasions delivers them himself. If he hears I'm a bit down in the dumps and need cheering up he's around with a bouquet of flowers and words of wisdom. Even throughout his recent difficulties the flowers still came. That is the measure of the man. He is my guardian angel and far from odd. He's certainly not the kind of idiot Seurat tries to make him out to be."

Seurat didn't respond but again hung his head.

"I originally met him on his first visit to Paris in 1882. He was out on the town with some friends and visited a salon where I was a guest.

He caught my eye and made a beeline for me, introducing himself as a professor of aesthetics. I didn't know what the hell he was talking about but it certainly sounded good. He was full of himself, flashy and pretentious. I thought he was a cheeky beggar for not waiting to be introduced, but, even so, I found him a most attractive man – a bit plumpish – but attractive in a cuddly way. The moment he opened his mouth he had me hooked. His French, like his charm, was beguiling and he knew how to use both to good effect.

"I met him again the following year and he was even more vivacious. He was so elated that I was certain he had indulged in some drug or other. A friend informed me that the only thing Oscar was high on was life itself. Even with all his troubles, he's still my number one, despite what you think of him, Seurat."

"You may well say that, Jane, and I don't doubt your loyalty to him, but you can't ignore the cold facts of the situation. They are clear. In recent months, he has gone totally out of control. Whatever fine words we care to use about him, the reality is, he is mad, not just mad but completely and utterly mad. His behaviour has been bizarre in the extreme. We can't ignore the facts," Seurat said in a smug and self-satisfied way, which cut Jane to the quick. She was furious and let Seurat know it.

"You would say that, wouldn't you? Why such hostility against him – why are you so horrid to him? You are forever having a dig at him. At every opportunity, you have a go. Why? What's he ever done to you to bring out this irrational hostility from you?"

"You tell him, Jane. Let the blackguard have it," cried Isadora.

"He deserves a good verbal bashing," someone shouted.

"You can be a right smart arse at times, too smart for your own liking," Jane said, getting into her stride, determined not to let Seurat get away with his unpleasant remarks. "You should grow up. You are acting like a spoilt child. You criticise Oscar for his behaviour, well, if you think he's been acting bizarrely or weirdly, you should look at yourself. Your behaviour stinks. You two were once so close. I just don't know what's happened to you. It's not Oscar who is odd, it's you."

"Wait a minute," Seurat cried as he sprang to his feet. "That's a bit strong. If there is a spoilt child, it isn't me. It is your hero. The one you think so special. You're all being taken for a ride. And you're being a bit rough on me. Most of what I say is what many of you already think. You all think that he has lost his mind and, regardless, much of what I say is said tongue in cheek. If you can't laugh at our existence and its peculiarities, what can you laugh at?"

"A laugh, that's what you call it? You laugh at the expense of a tortured and sensitive soul. What kind of moron are you? You think

139

my language is strong, do you? Well! Not strong enough, it seems. I won't lower myself to use the language that is needed to show my contempt for you and your behaviour towards Oscar. You need treatment yourself if you can't feel compassion for such a sensitive soul who is clearly suffering in his despair."

"He's not the only one with problems. I have mine too and no doubt, you all have to some degree or other. This Reservation is not the sole preserve of Oscar Wilde and his tantrums. There are other suffering souls, so give me a break."

"If you have something to say that can benefit this unfortunate situation, I suggest you either say it or shut up," Jane blurted.

"Maybe I do have something to say."

"Then say it," Jane said sharply, looking at him with a jaundiced eye. "Then perhaps you can give us a rest from your unrelenting sarcasm."

"If I do have something to say, I'll say it in my own good time. And I certainly won't be cajoled into doing so by the likes of you."

"As I was saying before this ass interrupted me, Oscar has been as normal as he's ever been. Perhaps I'm the only one not to notice any change in him, so if anyone else has anything to say concerning his behaviour perhaps this is the most opportune moment to do so."

"Yes, I agree with Jane," interjected Sophie, who had all but taken on the duties of a chairperson. "If there's anyone else who has something to add, they should let themselves be known so we can determine the extent of his problems before we decide what action we can take to help him."

Marcel Proust jumped to his feet. "I suppose I ought to tell of my predicament."

"And Simone and I have a sad tale to tell too," said Yves Montand, sitting next to his actress wife, Simone Signoret.

"Marcel, let's hear what you have to say first; then Yves, you or Simone can tell your tale."

"That sounds fair enough, Sophie. Marcel, you first," Yves said, indicating to Proust to take the floor.

Marcel Proust was sitting next to Jim Morrison at the Wisdom Stone. He gave a nervous cough as he began to tell his tale.

"Oscar's a friend of mine… a very good friend at that. I would say he's my intellectual soul mate."

"Jesus!" Seurat cried, shaking his head in disbelief. "Don't give me that… intellectual soul mate indeed. What garbage."

"Yes, my intellectual soul-mate," Proust continued. "Perhaps what I'm saying is way over your head. You may think my relationship with Oscar is naff and odd, but there you go. It takes all kinds, even your kind, I'm afraid."

"You're trying to be smart."

"No, just making a point. You were his friend once and a very close one at that, but for some reason, you've turned against him. You haven't just lost him as a friend but you've also managed to lose the respect that others had for you. I don't know how you can justify yourself and your obnoxious behaviour toward him, but whatever it is you should get if out of your system and perhaps give us a rest from your unwarranted sarcasm"

"I may well do that!"

"Well, don't keep us waitin' forever," replied Morrison, handing Seurat his reefer. "Perhaps this may help you."

Seurat pushed his hand aside. "I don't need that weed to help me think straight."

"Well, you ain't thinkin' straight without it."

"As I was saying," continued Proust. "He's a friend and I too have been alarmed by his present condition. From what I've heard so far it seems I was mistaken in thinking that what I witnessed was an isolated incident."

"What incident was that?" asked Sophie.

"It was a few hours after Oscar gave his annual lecture at the Literary Hall last month. If you remember his subject was, Is God a Comedian?"

"He may well be, but Oscar leaves Him standing."

"That's enough now, Seurat, I'm trying to tell my tale," Proust protested. "I admit Oscar can be decidedly mischievous at times and he was certainly stirring at Literary Hall that evening. It was a grand lecture. He was at his best. He had us all enthralled, hanging on his every word. That's what he is all about.

"After the lecture, I went to visit him in his dressing room. As I was walking down the corridor, I saw him hurrying from the dressing room and down the exit steps. He was very nippy on his feet and before I could call out to him, he was gone. As we are all aware, he's not known for hurrying anywhere and so I was curious to discover what was so urgent. I ran after him. Outside, I could see him rapidly disappearing down Literary Hill. I followed as fast as I could. He turned into Comma Lane and slowed down to catch his breath. I ran as fast as I could, shouting as I went. Just as I thought I was gaining on him, he was off again. I was exhausted. At the end of the lane, as you know, the road divides into three, with St Ita's Chapel facing the junction. I stood there scratching my head and wondering which road to take, for I couldn't see which way my friend had gone. I turned left down Scribblers Lane but couldn't see him. Returning to the junction, I took the middle road, Novel View, which twists and turns with all its little diversions. It was hopeless. I couldn't see him anywhere, so I again returned to the junction. I looked down the third road, Prose Grove, that neat, orderly thoroughfare, but no luck. He was not there either. He was gone, where to I had no idea. I thought my quest was useless so I headed back towards the theatre.

"As I was walking past Saint Ita's, I heard someone sobbing inside. Just within the entrance, I discovered Oscar slumped on the ground, his head in his hands, crying his eyes out. Crumpled in his hand was a piece of paper.

"'Oscar. Whatever's wrong?' I asked as I helped him to his feet and guided him into the church and on to the nearest pew. I tried to pacify him but to no avail. He just sat there and sobbed. I thought it best to let him get whatever it was that was causing him such anguish out of his system. Eventually, he wiped his eyes and sat upright, still clutching the piece of paper. 'She said she would meet me here,' he blurted out.

"'Who?'

"'Constance,' he said, holding back more tears.

"I looked at him in surprise.

"'She said she would meet me here, meet me with the boys. She said she would be here,' he sobbed.

"'Oscar,' I said. 'You know she's not here or anywhere else on this Reservation. What makes you think she'd be here?'

"'She left me this message,' he replied, handing me the crumpled piece of paper. 'It was on my dressing-room table when I returned from the lecture. I could not believe what I was reading, could not believe I would see them again. She had forgiven me, Marcel. She had forgiven me. She wanted to see me again. I dropped everything and left immediately, overwhelmed with joy at the thought of seeing them again.'

"I opened the crumpled paper. It was blank. I turned it over – nothing. 'Oscar, the paper's blank. There's no message here…'

"'I know,' he whispered.

"'I don't understand,' I said, as I once more looked at the blank page.

"'When I arrived, I waited at the entrance where she said she would meet me. I was there for some time and as I waited, I decided to read the note again. To my horror, I saw it was blank – not a word. I stared at it in disbelief. I knew I had read it in my dressing room at the hall; I was certain of it. I can remember the exact words: 'My Dearest Oscar, I've returned to you. Meet me at Saint Ita's Chapel. Come quickly. Cyril and Vyvyan cannot wait to see you, your loving wife, Constance.' I couldn't believe my eyes. I looked at the blank paper over and over again. My head felt like it was exploding. I just couldn't fathom what was happening to me. I so much wanted to see them again. I was so certain I would see them again.'

"I put my arm around him as he shook with emotion. I had never seen him in such a distressed state. I hadn't seen him so upset since we first became acquainted in 1922. He was devastated. If there was ever a lost soul, I was looking at it. He just sat there, head bowed and sobbing his heart out over what I was certain was a hallucination.

"'Has this kind of thing happened before?'

"'Yes,' he said wiping his eyes.

"'When?' I asked.

"He stood up, walked over to the font, scooped up some water in his cupped hands and splashed his face. I handed him my handkerchief. He dried his face. He sat down again and said, 'It's only happened once before.'

"'Did it involve Constance and the boys?' I asked.

"'No. Just Constance and Bosie. She had this ferocious confrontation with him. God it was terrible.'

"'Oh! *Him*,' I replied. 'When was this?'

"'About six months ago,' he said. 'I was sitting in my study at Merrion when I heard raised voices coming from the sitting-room. I was startled, for I knew I was alone in the house. I opened the dividing doors and froze on the spot. There before me were the two people who had brought out the deepest feelings I ever experienced going hell for leather at each other. 'Constance!' I called out to her, but she seemed not to hear me. She looked as beautiful as I had ever seen her, full of life and vitality. I walked over to her and went to embrace her but my hands went right through her. I called her name again but she didn't hear me. I turned to Bosie and asked what was he up to, annoying Constance, but he seemed not to hear me. I tried to touch him, but again my hands were grasping at thin air. My mind was reeling as I tried to understand what it was all about. It was clear they could not see or hear me. I slumped into a chair and listened in awe to the nature of their confrontation.'

"'What on earth were they arguing about?' I asked.

"'She was accusing him of being a home-wrecker, morally bankrupt and a spoilt little upper-crust brat. She accused him of being manipulative, a schemer and an out-and-out cad. There was no holding back her pent up feeling.'

"'What did he say?' I asked.

"'Oh. He was his normal petulant self. The more she berated him the louder his laughter became. He was always like that. It used to infuriate me... but Constance was made of sterner stuff. He could laugh as loud as he wanted but that would not deter a woman like her. The more he laughed the more she rattled off his flaws. After a while, he started to panic and his laughter became bitter. He called her a pathetic woman who couldn't hold her man, a weak woman. He declared it no wonder I sought pleasure elsewhere when I had the likes of her as a wife. She just stood there and took it, with her head held high, her pride intact. He tried another tactic, swearing at her and using every expletive he could think of. He wasn't getting the reaction he expected and his anger subsided. He was like a wounded animal. He turned and slowly walked away, glancing back at her with a smirk on his lips. She stood there, quietly contented by her triumph over her adversary, a very sad and pathetic man. This man I had once thought I loved. God, what did I ever see in him? I closed my eyes. When I opened them again, they were gone.'

"I looked down at Oscar. He was a wreck. I didn't know what to say or do. 'Come along. Oscar,' I said as I helped him to his feet. 'You're staying with me tonight. These things happen. You know how fragile the mind is. It plays up at the most inopportune of times. You need a good rest. We'll collect Dubliner and you can have a rest at my place.'

"Before we left the chapel he said he wanted to visit the Lover's Pillar, where he wrote a message amongst all the others sprawled around it. He was very subdued but finally agreed to my offer to spend the evening at my place. We left the chapel and wandered slowly back up towards Literary Hill. After collecting Dubliner, we walked to my home, where we had a good meal and sat up for most of the night talking of things that might have been. When he finally went to bed, he slept peacefully until mid-afternoon. Not long after he woke up he was soon back to normal and seemed to have put the unfortunate episode behind him. Well, so I thought."

"What do you mean?" asked Sophie.

"Well, every time I met him afterwards he always mentioned Constance, saying that she was longing to meet him. I gently told him that that would never be.

"'We will see,' he replied. 'You have no faith at all, Marcel, no faith at all.'"

"Do you know what he wrote on the pillar?" asked Édith.

"I didn't at the time. Some days later, I returned to Saint Ita's and searched the pillar for his message. It was a couplet. It went as follows:

Someday *cherie*,
We will meet and love again.

"Whom was it addressed to?" asked Isadora.

"Bosie. of course, who else?"

"Seurat... are you stupid altogether?" replied Proust. "It was for Constance, not Bosie. It's a love poem to a woman, not a man and especially not to that aristocratic upstart."

Seurat laughed. "God I wish he'd make up his mind. One moment he's a womaniser; the next a pursuer of aristocratic tarts and cheap rent boys. He really is confused,"

Sophie looked over at a couple, sitting arm in arm, hardly taking their eyes off each other. Yves Montand and Simone Signoret were the perpetual lovers of the Reservation.

"It's your turn, Yves, whenever you're ready."

The couple walked hand in hand over to the Wisdom Stone.

"You all know what Oscar's like when it comes to sex," began Yves.

"Don't we just?" laughed Balzac.

"It's his favourite subject, next to himself," Yves said laughingly as he began his recollection. "He is always amusing and great fun to be with. Simone and I can never get enough of his company. He is very addictive. Once he's in your system there's no getting rid of him."

"More like a disease, an incurable one at that," Seurat sneered, continuing to attack his former friend.

"You may sneer, Seurat, but he's worth a hundred of you," replied Yves.

"I met him long before Yves did," interrupted Simone. "Our first meeting was electric. I was on stage at the Blues Bar, doing a revue called 'The Story of the Blues', when he came and sat at a table at the stage edge and eyed me up and down. 'Cheeky bugger,' I thought. 'I wonder who he is.' I soon found out."

"But you must admit, you were teasing him."

"Well, you know how it is, Yves. I can't resist the attentions of a charming man, especially one like Oscar, even though he's not up to your high standard," she explained. "He sat there all evening, watching my every move. At first I thought he was one of those 'observers' that often come to the shows, but there was something about him that made me feel at ease. You know, that warm comfortable feeling. I winked at him. He winked back and blew me a theatrical kiss."

"I know what she means," Yves said, lovingly slipping his hand around Simone's waist. "He's easy to be with."

"After a week or so of his visits to the show, I got Marc, the club owner, to introduce me to him. He was a real gentleman – a charmer with a twinkle in his eyes. He informed me that he had only recently discovered the pleasure of the blues. The music, he meant. He was well acquainted with the other. He said Yves was an excellent singer and wondered why I never sang, for I had the look of a blues singer. He can be a real codger at times. I'm certain he hadn't the foggiest idea about jazz or the blues, but within a few weeks, he had educated himself about them and would converse on the subject as though he had the blues in his blood.

"We regularly invited him down to Drama Row, to our humble abode and, I'm proud to say, he became a good and loyal friend to us. In turn, we would visit him and Dubliner at his Merrion residence. When he visited us, we would sit for hours discussing any subject that came to mind. Once he gets started, he can leave you feeling a little inadequate, for he is so knowledgeable.

"When it came to the arts, in general, we were like identical triplets, the exception being the theatre. He could never win his argument for we were always a step ahead of him. We'd sit for hours discussing theatre. Just because he had so much success with his plays, he thought he was immortal. We'd tease him that he was just an amateur when it came to the theatre, that his success only lasted the few years until he went off the rails. He would take it in good spirit; he certainly knows how to laugh at himself. Many a time he'd crack some really black jokes about his downfall and the events leading up to it. It takes a brave man to laugh at his misfortunes, and none is braver than he. Mind you, I'm not saying we didn't have any real fallings-out, for we surely did. When we got started, Simone would go for a long walk, leaving us to get on with it. It was after one of those rows that Oscar had a visitation."

"Visitation – whatever do you mean?" asked Jane, perplexed at the possibility of another revelation.

Simone looked at Yves. "Do think we should tell them?"

"I'm not certain. It is, after all, very personal."

"I think we ought to, she replied. "It may help. There seems to be a pattern in his behaviour that needs examining. Maybe our contribution may help to understand what is causing his difficulty."

"Perhaps you're right. But I must say I'm a bit uneasy about it. Do you want to tell them?"

"All right!" she replied, looking rather nervous at the prospect of revealing personal details about a trusted friend.

"I arrived home after my walk. Yves and Oscar had finished their slanging match and were sitting cross-legged on the floor singing the blues. I joined them and had a bit of a session. We sat there talking into the early hours. He got on his stride chatting about the theatre and quizzed me about my acting. He wanted to know why I hadn't appeared in any of his plays. He thought I would have made a good Mrs Erlynne. I disagreed and said I'd be better fitted to the part of Cecily Cardew, for it, was the more glamorous of roles. He disagreed, of course; he said I was getting carried away with myself. It was late and we asked him to stay. We said our goodnights and off we went to bed. I don't know if I can go on."

Yves held her hand. "Don't worry, love, I'll tell it. That evening as we warmly snuggled up in bed, and about to drift off to sleep, we

147

were startled by a piercing cry reverberating throughout the house. 'Holy God! What's that?' I cried as I looked at Simone who was shaking like a leaf. There was another piercing scream. We made our way from the bedroom and down the corridor. Oscar was making his way downstairs. He was grasping his hair, giving out a scream every few steps. I was about to call out to him, but Simone restrained me."

"Yes, I did, for I was certain he was sleepwalking."

"As he staggered down the stairs he gave more spine-curdling screams. Once downstairs he slumped on to a sofa, rolling on to his back. We were at a loss as to what to do. Should we wake him or not, if we did would it have a damaging effect? If we didn't, would he do something crazy? As he lay there we realised he wasn't sleepwalking but in some kind of trance. His eyes were open but glazed over. We sat down next to him and I swabbed his forehead for he was perspiring profusely.

"'Why won't you leave me alone? Why won't you go away? Go, go away,' he cried in a sad and forlorn tone. He then sprang up. 'Why are you doing this to me – have you not got your pound of flesh? What else do you want from me? What else can I give?' he cried, as though he was talking to someone. One thing for certain – he wasn't aware of our presence. He grabbed his hair tightly, grimaced and let out another mighty cry – 'blood! Blood! Is that your price, my blood? Is my flesh not enough to satisfy your lust?'

"Suddenly he became aware of us. He looked at us in desperation. He sank back on to the settee.

"'It's all right, Oscar. You've just been hallucinating. Here, take this,' I said, giving him a glass of water, which he gulped down in one swig, reaching out to us with a trembling hand for more. He thirstily downed another glassful, spilling half of it.

"'Where am I?' he gasped, his eyes bulging with fear.

"'You're here at Drama Row,' I said. He looked at us. Suddenly, he realised who we were and where he was. He was horrified.

"'I'm sorry,' he said apologetically, as he jumped to his feet looking terribly embarrassed. 'You must think me mad. Oh! I am so sorry. Perhaps I ought to leave.'

"'No, you're not going anywhere. You're staying where you are,' I insisted. 'It's a hallucination, Oscar. It will pass.'

"He shook his head. 'No, not this one – it will never go away. He will forever haunt me. He will forever crucify me for my weakness. He won't be satisfied until my soul is destroyed.'

"'What is it, Oscar? Whatever is it?' asked Yves. 'Who's haunting you? Who's out to destroy you?'

"'He's driving me mad,' he cried as he wiped his sodden brow. 'I can't shake him off. I can't break free of him. It is the same every time, over and over again. He sneers at me, hounds me and swears at me like some demented demon.'

"'Oscar, it's a hallucination. That's all. You're just allowing whoever he is to prey on your mind,' I said reassuringly."

Jane was on her feet.

"Are you saying you knew he suffered from hallucinations?" she asked, amazed at the revelation.

"Yes," replied Yves. "He told us some months ago that they had been bothering him. They were always about Lord Alfred Douglas. We told him to try not to think about him, but he said it wasn't as easy as that. He said he hadn't thought about him since his nightmares ceased after he was given an antidote to Alfred's potion."

"Dear me," cried Jane, "You had witnessed them before."

"No. No. What happened at our home was the only time we actually witnessed one. It was very disturbing, very much as Marcel witnessed in Saint Ita's Chapel."

"I can very well imagine, Simone. What did he have to say about it," asked Marie?

"Oh, quite a lot.

"'I'm being punished,' Oscar sighed.

"'Whatever for?'

"He hung his head. 'For writing *De Profundis*.' he whispered.

"We both looked at him in wonderment. 'Why, why should you be punished for something that was written decades ago?'

"'It may be years old, Yves, but it seems as though I penned it only yesterday,' he replied. 'According to records at the Knowledge Zone, Bosie hated it. He raged over it, threatening all connected with it. He thought he had the only copy and destroyed it, only to discover that Robbie Ross had had the original deposited for safekeeping in the British Museum. It was years before he realised the manuscript existed. He lost his head and promised to destroy it. He did all he could to retrieve it but failed miserably. Now, he is back, back with a vengeance. Back in my mind, taunting, screaming and spitting venom at me. It was incessant. God, will he forever be a millstone around my neck?'

"We tried to reason with him, but he wouldn't listen. He would not accept our argument that in time the hallucinations would pass. He thought he was doomed, that forever, he would be tormented by that foul-mouthed aristocrat.

"'You would never believe how vivid the images are,' he said. 'It is as though he was here, standing in front of me. I can even smell his stale breath as he screams in my face. No, my friends, I am afraid these images will never leave me. I am doomed. I am paying for my earthly stupidities. Imagine, I thought I loved that man and ruined my life because of him.'

"We managed to calm him down. We sat on the settee with him snuggled between us until the morning; then Yves walked him home."

"Yes, I did, and he couldn't apologise enough. He was very embarrassed. I reassured him that he had nothing to fret about and we would never think any less of him because of his affliction. That's our tale. It seems that our revelation is one of many that clearly show he's in deep trouble."

"Come in!"

Gabriel slowly opened the door, carrying under his arm a purple file that was bursting at the seams. He shuffled up to the Chairman's desk.

"Oh, it's you, Gabriel. What's up? You look a bit glum."

"I'm afraid I've got bad news," he said as he placed the file on the desk.

"What's that?"

"The Wilde file you asked for."

"That's some file, Gabriel. It's rather thick for a Trusted Soul, isn't it?"

"There's more to this Wilde soul than you'd imagine, Chairman. He is a complex fellow, to say the least. He has so many sides to him."

"Let's have a look at it," the Chairman said as he opened the file. He flicked through it, sighing after every page.

"Complex indeed... I think you are right to keep tabs on him. What's the latest?"

Gabriel placed a sheet of paper in front of the Chairman.

"This is the second report. As you can see, Chairman, Oscar seems to be in deep trouble. What's being revealed down there is looking very ominous indeed. Look at the pattern of the revelations. He could be showing the signs of the Syndrome. I'm certain an application will be made. As a precaution, it may be wise to put the preliminary mechanism in operation. It seems we are heading for stormy waters again."

"Are you sure of this?"

"As sure as I can be."

"When will the full report be ready?"

"All depends on what else is revealed at the Central Reservation. There is a crowd there who all seem to want to have a say. It could be some time before our man on the ground can report back."

"Let me have it the moment it's available. If it's as you say, then you can call a meeting of the Divine Privy Council to consider the report and put them on notice of a possible application."

"Very well, Chairman," replied Gabriel as he reached to pick up the file.

"No! Leave it with me," the Chairman said as he placed his bony hand on the file. "I need to give this serious attention. You are right – this Wilde fellow needs careful consideration."

Musset was on his feet. With his hands deep in his pockets, he walked over to the Wisdom Stone.

"What is it, Alfred?" Sophie asked.

"I have something to say," he said as he leaned against the Wisdom Stone. "After hearing these disturbing revelations, I'm afraid I have a confession to make."

"Confession!" gasped Balzac.

"Jesus, this sounds serious," cried Isadora. "Musset and confession don't sit right. Are you sure it's a confession you have in mind?"

"Very much so."

"Are you sure you don't need a priest?"

"No, Jane. You and the rest will be my confessors. I hope you'll grant me absolution."

"Well, come on, out with it, what's the confession about?" asked Balzac, rubbing his hands in the anticipation of some salacious revelation.

There was a deadly silence as they waited for his response.

"I've known about Oscar's problems for some time."

There was a spontaneous gasp.

"Then why the hell didn't you tell us before now? You have sat there listening to our revelations when you knew about his malaise, and you said nought. What kind of an ass are you?" asked an exasperated Isadora.

"Because of the nature of his problems, I thought it best to keep them to myself and perhaps try to help him overcome them. I was clearly wrong, for his problems are more acute and more debilitating than I had first thought. When I arrived here today, and Marie said he was acting in an odd way, I didn't realise it was that serious until you, Jim and Isadora revealed your experiences. Then, as I listened to Félix, Frédéric and Édith's experiences, I realised I had been a fool not to reveal my secret. I think I ought to know."

"Yes, I'd say you'd better," someone cried.

"Some time ago I was up at the Knowledge Zone, where I came across Oscar looking a bit down in the mouth. I had visited the Zone to check if I was still in vogue in France or dumped into life's recycling bin when I came across him sitting under the window of the Puzzle Cone."

"Well, were you?" asked Jane.

"Was I what?"

"Still in vogue."

He gave a half-hearted laugh.

"No, far from it – I'm afraid I'm a has-been. Seems I'm more famous for my dalliances with Madame Sand and a medical condition than for my contribution to French literature. My plays get an occasional outing, and just occasionally, there is a biography. I was far from impressed."

"It's better than nothing," laughed Marie. "My novels are all but forgotten. I'm remembered only as Liszt's lover."

"It was worse," Musset continued, "for although Oscar was a tad glum, he soon started to brag that the public couldn't get enough of him, not simply in England but around the world. He claimed that the Russians were as addicted to him as they were to vodka. He boasted that there were so many books published about him that he had a job keeping up with them."

"Then, why was he so glum?" asked Jane.

"He moaned that it was his sexuality that he's most famous for now. He said that they could put on his plays as much as they like, or quote him left right and centre, but it was of little value to him as an artist if at the end of the day he was seen by some as nothing more than a sexual pervert and by others as a gay icon."

"I told him we could do nothing about history. We can moan and groan as much as we like, but we can't change its course. He didn't take this well, and it certainly didn't improve his humour. He was distinctly out of sorts, and I thought it might be wise to let him be. I rose to bid him farewell.

"'Don't go,' he grunted as he tugged at my sleeve. 'Come and sift through the history pages with me.'

"'Whatever for?' I replied. 'Aren't they depressing you as it is? Why continue looking at them? Why punish yourself?'

"'I need to keep searching,' he replied as we headed for the reference rooms.

"We sat at a table, and he began his search.

"'What are you searching for?' I asked.

"'My lost soul!' he mournfully replied.

"I looked at him. I could see a tear welling up and beginning to trickle down his cheek. I was lost for words. I stayed with him as he scanned the images.

"'You see this nonsense,' he said as an essay on Jim Morrison materialised. 'It says in a report that our Yankee friend did not die and not buried at Père Lachaise, but he faked his death because he was bored with his fame. It claims he is now living a relaxed life in a remote part of South Africa having the time of his life. Did you ever read such journalistic garbage? No wonder he doesn't bother with this place.

"'Look at this one. It is even stranger. This chap maintains that Chopin had gay tendencies. Did you ever hear such twaddle? There is nothing in his nature or actions that could justify such a claim. What a load of drivel. I'm telling you, Alfred, it really isn't a good move to visit this section of the Knowledge Zone. It does one no good at all.'

"'I agree. I rarely visit,' I informed him.

"'How wise you are. I don't know why I came here thinking I might find my lost soul. It is not worth it, is it? My soul is not here amongst these tarnished pages of history. Come, it is time to go. I've had enough. I need fresh air.'

"We made our way down the Zone's steps and into the shade, seeking a secluded spot in which to sit and relax. We settled against an ash tree.

'What is it all about, Alfred?' he forlornly asked.

'Search me,' I replied.

"'What's the purpose of this place? Please, tell me,' he pleaded.

"'I'm as confused as you are my friend. I try not to think about it, but when I do, I end up asking too many questions, and I become depressed. It's hard not to think about it, but I do try. It's the only way to stay sane in this madhouse,' I replied.

"He looked sadly at me and muttered, 'I've been hearing voices.'

"I looked at my friend in amazement. 'Voices! What kind of voices?'

"'Whispers,' he informed me, 'They are just about audible.'

"'What do they say?' I asked.

"'They whisper, "It's all a waste of time, all a waste of time. Do you hear me, Oscar Wilde? It's all a waste of time," he downheartedly replied.

"'That's it?' I asked.

"'Yes. It is always the same voice. It is a woman's voice. I know it, but can't place it, he replied.'

"'How long has this been going on, for Christ's sake?'

"'Oh, a few months. I don't know what to make of it. It's never happened before. It is driving me insane. It's incessant,' he cried despairingly.

"'Where do you hear them?'

"'Everywhere,' he replied. 'When I'm in bed, around the house, walking. I even heard them when I was giving my lecture at the Academy. When you met me earlier she was whispering to me.'

"I didn't know what to say. I'd never heard of this kind of thing before.

"'I try not to think about, but it is not easy,' Oscar continued. 'Sometimes I just pray that this is all a terrible mistake, just one horrendous dream, that suddenly I will awake and find myself

154

snuggled up cosy in my bed in my Chelsea home having my brow stroked by Constance with the world once again at my feet. That my plays are continuing their success with my future spread out before me, full of fortune, laughter, and friendship. I pray that we all wake up from this nightmare and find ourselves back in our old stamping grounds. That you, my dear friend, are once again gallivanting about Paris, wooing the ladies with your verse and having the time of your life; that you continue to be a rising star in the French literary world and don't die in your prime. That Frédéric is back at Nohant composing his nocturnes whilst George looks lovingly on. That she is once more in full bloom, holding her soirees, continuing to attract the best of artistic excellence. That Jim Morrison was once more performing on a stage somewhere in Cincinnati, and living out his life instead of suffering an ignoble exit in a bathtub. That our Little Sparrow is on a stage somewhere in our wonderful world captivating the hearts and souls of her adoring public with her divine voice – that Marcel found love and freedom to breathe and smell the perfumes of life. That Isadora did not die before her time, that she went on to be the great woman of dance. That Honoré went on a diet and lived out a full life, producing more of his masterpieces. That Jane was once more the queen of the Moulin Rouge and sitting for Toulouse-Lautrec. And the Divine Sarah – that she went on to perform in my plays, giving them that extra stamp of class they deserve. Ah, Eugène… that he was once more producing paintings of an even higher standard. The imagination is stupid and dangerous at times.'

"'I won't argue with that,' I replied. 'No soul knows how to control the imagination.'

"'I get so lonely,' Oscar whispered, as he sat twiddling his fingers.

"I was at a loss as what to say. I'd never heard him talk in this way before. I would never have associated him with loneliness. 'It's a pity we can't just die, and that's it, instead, we have to suffer this Purgatory, this intolerable loneliness,' he cried.

"'Come along, Oscar,' I said, as I put my arm about him, 'come, we'll walk you home by the River of Life and reminisce about better days. After an early night, things may be better in the morning.'

"'I doubt it,' he replied as I helped him up.'"

"Had he ever confessed to you before, to being lonely?"

"No, Jane. We'd talked about loneliness on many occasions, but I must say I can honestly say, he never said he suffered from it, nor did I notice any symptoms. I must say, mind you, that after our tête-à-tête, I didn't notice anything odd about him and he never mentioned his loneliness again. He did mention, however, hearing voices, that they were still bothering him. I had put his hearing voices down as an isolated incident, but I was clearly wrong. After listening to the revelations here, it's obvious he has a very deep and disturbing problem."

"You should have told us about this before now. Why did you keep it to yourself? You can be an idiot at times, Alfred, an idiot."

I'm sorry, Isadora, but I'm not the only one guilty of that, am I."

They sat around the Laburnum Tree in quiet contemplation. There had been some peculiar revelations. Morrison, who was still leaning against the Wisdom Stone, lit another reefer. Jane was leaning against the Laburnum Tree. Delacroix sat cross-legged, resting his head in his hand, staring into empty space. Musset stood with his head lowered. Édith was softly sobbing, dabbing her eyes with her silk handkerchief. Isadora was twirling her hair with her fingers. Ingres smoothed his beard. Sophie was resting her head on Marie's shoulder with Marie gently stroking her hair. Chopin was lying flat on the ground, his legs crossed, eyes shut, sucking on a strand of grass. Proust sat with a distant look on his face. Simone and Yves were standing wrapped in each other's arms, gently swaying. Seurat stood with hands in pockets looking out towards the Reservation Gate. Balzac sat on the lower step with his arm around Sarah as she laid her head on his chest. Colette sat leaning against Balzac as she stroked Kiki-la-Doucette. The ever-present Lady in Blue stood at the edge of the steps, observing them as though they had all gone mad, worrying about the likes of Oscar Wilde. Her surly attendance did not affect them, for over the years they had become oblivious to her presence and considered her rather an irrelevance.

The silence was suddenly broken.

"Oscar's suffering must be terrible," sighed Sophie.

"Very much so," replied Édith.

"Perhaps he is lonely, as Alfred says," Chopin said as he sat upright. "Could that be the reason for his behaviour? Yes, that's it, he's lonely?"

"Could be," said Proust. "People act in some odd ways when they are lonely."

"You've put your finger right on it. The poor chap is lonely. There's no doubt about it, why didn't I think of that before?" sighed Balzac.

"But he's surrounded by his friends," Édith stated. "He's involved with us on so many levels I can't see how he could possibly be lonely. He's as involved as ever in his writing, the theatre, the debating circle, and umpteen other enterprises. It seems improbable that he could be lonely."

"You don't have to be on your own, to be lonely, my friend," David informed her. "There's many a lonely soul who's suffered in a crowd, with colleagues or even in the company of family and friends. Loneliness is the curse of the Human Condition."

"How true," sighed Balzac.

"I still can't understand how one can be lonely when surrounded by friends and loved ones."

"I can assure you, Édith, it happens more than you could ever imagine," replied David.

"Maybe he's not lonely at all. Maybe he's having a nervous breakdown," suggested Seurat. "I'm no doctor, but he seems to be showing signs of it. What I say about him, you know, is quite true, whether you like it or not. His recent behaviour leaves a lot to be desired."

"But we can't become ill here," Jane said as she sat upright.

"No! That's not quite true."

"Of course it is, Jim. It's impossible to suffer illness here. God, we all know that. Have you, or anyone else ever suffered from any illness, even a cold? No, you haven't, and for one good reason, there's no illness here. Spirits don't get ill, only perplexed."

"Only physical illness, Jane."

"What are you saying, Jim?" asked Sophie.

"We can't suffer physically, but we can ... mentally."

Everyone looked at Morrison in amazement.

"Can we?" asked Marie, looking rather confused at such a claim.

"It's a rare occurrence, but it can and does happen. Seurat already alluded to this in his remark about Oscar's possible mental breakdown," he replied. "That's what that clinic up on Cuckoo Ridge is for."

"I didn't know that,' said a startled Seurat." I thought it was a bird sanctuary."

"One of many things you don't know," snapped Isadora.

"What about Cloud Eighty-Seven? Isn't that for the mentally ill?"

"No, Marie, it's a sanctuary for those souls who can't adapt to their surroundings here. They're not mentally ill."

"But once sent there, there's no way back. That sounds like a mental institution to me," she replied.

Chopin stood up and sighed. "So, the poor soul could be suffering a form of mental breakdown?"

"Seems likely," said Sarah.

"Sure does," added Sophie.

Édith dabbed her eyes. "God, how terrible," she cried. "I always thought mental illness was only an earthly phenomenon, that here we would be spared it."

"It doesn't seem so. Is there any cure for it?" asked Seurat.

"Yes," replied Morrison. "The cure is simple."

"Is it?"

158

"Yes, lots of love and understandin'. You know — those emotions that we are supposed to possess as part of the Human Condition, which on the face of it has unfortunately passed you by."

Seurat was on his feet, fuming, his fists clenched in anger. "That's a bit low, Morrison. There's no call for such remarks. Are you trying to be smart?"

"No — just stating a fact."

"Well, get your facts right, you smart arse."

"Cut it out, you two," demanded David. "Bickering will not help matters. This is a serious situation and needs clear heads if we are to help our beleaguered friend. We must be focused to be successful in this delicate task."

"Has anyone any suggestions about what we can do to help him?" asked Chopin. "I'm at a loss to know what to do. We can't just sit around doing nothing. If it is a mental problem, then we must procure help immediately. There's no question about that, but how do we obtain such help?"

"I suggest that first, we nominate one of us to go and seek him out and ask what's ailing him," Sophie suggested. "I agree with Chopin. We can't just sit here and do nothing. Someone must tell him that he's ill."

"I'll second that," replied Balzac.

"Who, then, who's going to do the dirty deed?" asked Édith. "Well, there's only one of us whom he would tolerate asking such a question."

"Who?"

"Eugène! Who else?"

They all turned and looked at Eugène Delacroix who had been sitting quietly, plainly disturbed by the revelations about the decline of his friend.

"Don't look at me," he replied. "He'd have my guts for garters if I suggest he sees a shrink. Anyway, how would I approach him? What would I say to him? How would I say it? After all, we are all but saying, as Seurat puts it, that he's as mad as a hatter."

"No! That's not so. We're not suggesting any such a thing. Seurat might, but the rest of us. All we are saying is that Oscar needs help. Do you all agree?" Sophie asked, looking at each of them in turn.

"Yes," they replied.

"I still say I'm the wrong one to approach him. We may be the best of buddies, but I really wouldn't know what to say to him, after all, it is a delicate matter, telling your friend he's mad, that he needs seeing to. No, thank you. I think I'll pass on this one," said a reluctant Delacroix.

"But you're so close. Surely, it's best to be told by a friend that you're mad rather than by a stranger. It would be best coming from you," said Balzac.

Delacroix nodded his head. "No. I would be afraid of having another row with him. Sorry. It's for someone else, someone with a thick skin."

"What about you, Jane?"

"Ah! Sophie, don't be daft. I certainly don't have a thick skin and he wouldn't listen to me – certainly not on such a serious subject."

"Why not?"

"Why? Because we rarely have a serious conversation, that is why. That's the way we are together. It's how it has always been between us. We' are always laughing and larking about, and this is no laughing matter."

"Maybe its humour that is needed," suggested Morrison. "It's often better to laugh than cry at the misfortunes of life, even in the direst of circumstances."

"How on earth do you tell someone in a humorous way they need psychiatric treatment."

"Well, it's like this, Jane. You come straight out with it," Seurat said. "You say, by the way, Oscar, my dear fellow, did you know you're nuts, that you're as loopy as they come and that you're ready for the funny farm, and, by the way, you need to see a psychiatrist. It's as simple as that. I'm sure he'll see the funny side of it"

"Then perhaps you should try it," David suggested.

"Not likely. He won't find anything I'd say funny, and I'd probably punch him if I saw him after what he did to me. That doesn't mean one of you lot can't try to make him see sense."

They all looked at him.

"What did he ever do to you?" asked David.

"Plenty."

"Such as?"

"I don't want to talk about it at the moment. It was too hurtful."

"Take no notice of him. He's rambling again. It's Oscar we are worried about, not that attention-seeking idiot," Isadora reminded the circle.

"I beg your pardon, madame. How dare you talk of me like that?'

"Oh, shut up, will you? How about you, Édith, do you fancy talking to him?" asked David.

"Oh, I don't know. Like Eugène, I wouldn't know what to say to him. You must remember my last outing with him wasn't exactly a success. It was rather torturous, and I have no burning desire to repeat it."

"But you're great at getting him to open up. You've already seen him in a vulnerable state in the Cherry Blossom Forest, so he's more likely to listen to you."

"I'm sorry, Sophie, I don't think I could cope with the task so soon after my trauma. Sorry. I love the fool dearly, but I can't handle this kind of thing. Too heavy for me, I'm afraid."

Silence returned.

"Isadora, what about you?" asked Sophie.

"Oh, no, I don't think so. I still feel a bit guilty after spying on him up on Cloud Nine. I can't see him appreciating any intervention from me."

"You weren't spying on him."

"Well, Marie, it feels like it. I'd say if he knew about it, he'd agree."

Marie looked over at David.

"Don't go looking at me that way," he said. "He has little patience with me at the best of times, so if you're expecting him to take any heed of what I'd have to say, you're in for a disappointment – how about yourself?"

Marie nodded her head. "He'd just laugh at me. He'd think I was having him on. No, I'm not the right one."

Again, there was silence as they contemplated their dilemma.

"What's causing this mental trauma?" Musset asked, breaking the silence. "I must say I'm rather confused by it all. If it is a mental illness, I don't know how he acquired it. I thought it was an exclusively earthly condition."

"For pity's sake, Alfred, we've been over this already. The fact that it's an earthly illness as well is rather irrelevant. It's only mental illness we can suffer from here, and he was obviously already suffering from it on earth, and it has somehow followed him here in his spirit form."

"You can say it as much as you like, Jane, but it just doesn't make sense. I'm confused."

"Likewise," replied Balzac. "I'd speak to him if I thought he would listen. I know he'd tell me to bugger off, so it's a waste of time even trying."

"There may be another explanation for his condition," Édith suggested.

"I'm telling you, it's mental," Morrison insisted. "It's as clear as crystal. If it's not mental, what is it? There doesn't seem to be any other answer."

"Perhaps he's depressed."

"Oh! It is more than depression, Édith. Depression's bad enough but what he's sufferin' from is way beyond depression, somethin' that is exclusive to this place, like a purgatorial mental breakdown," replied Morrison.

"But isn't depression a mental illness?" asked Isadora. "That's what I thought."

"Yes, Isadora, technically it is, but Oscar is more than depressed. As I say, he seems to have suffered a mental breakdown, a purgatorial one."

"Well, let's just presume it's mental and see what can be done for him."

"Yes, Jane, I believe you're right. Before we decide what's to be done, let's first reflect on what has been revealed so far," Sophie said as she leaned against the Wisdom Stone.

"It is clear that Oscar is suffering from some form of a mental aberration, as Jim says. Whether it's unique to our surroundings, I'm not too sure. It must be mental, for, as Jane has reminded us, we can't to suffer any form of physical illness. What is also clear is that those of us who have witnessed his bizarre behaviour kept it to ourselves and only revealed it when we met here by accident. Why? As I see it, we either thought his behaviour was a one-off incident, and not worth bothering about or we were unable to confront him for fear of embarrassing or upsetting him.

"The evidence, so far, is that he first began acting out of character about nine months ago and that eccentricity has intensified over recent months. What Isadora revealed about him visiting the Viewing Platform to gawk over Père Lachaise seems to be the beginning of his problems. We all know he loves to do this and has done so for years without any diverse effect. He's always done so in the most light-hearted way. What Isadora witnessed showed a disturbing shift and was far from light-hearted. His behaviour at Eugène's studio was not just an unjustified attack on his artistic ability but also on his integrity as a friend. His humiliation of Jim Morrison at the Viewing Platform leaves a bad taste in the mouth. Félix revealed Oscar's obsession over his image and his disturbing fixation with George Sand. This fixation alone leaves many questions about his emotional state. His change of attitude towards Frédéric shows serious dysfunction, reinforced by Édith's revelation in the Cherry Blossom Forest. Then Colette witnessed his manic and obsessive behaviour in a most graphic way. His fascination with the quality of the kisses and his philosophy of female sexuality can only give us cause for concern. Then Marie was taken aback by drastic changes in his domestic habits that verge on the surreal, with his mirrors and reflective portraits. What about his meeting with Marcel? He seems to have lost all sense of the reality of his situation and Yves and Simone confirmed the beginning of his hallucinations. Then Alfred's report of Oscar's hearing of voices and his confusion show us that he's terribly unhappy, not just with himself but all about him. Maybe Alfred should have shared his concerns earlier. Something has turned our genial genius into a mumbling and stumbling freak. We must find out what's causing it and, if possible, cure it."

A tall gentleman stood up and coughed to catch the attention of the assembly.

"Ah! Monsieur Torrès, just the man. Perhaps a calm legal brain needs to be applied here. In your opinion, is there a remedy that can be applied to his condition?" Sophie asked one of France's most successful advocates and brilliant legal minds, who, after joining the circle, sat quietly taking in all that was said.

"I'm no physician, so I can't give a medical opinion," he said, "but I'm aware of similar cases in other Reservations. These cases are available for inspection at the Knowledge Zone and are in the same vein as Oscars, and grounded in a medical condition, similar to the symptoms that he seems to be showing. This is a difficult case, a minefield to say the least. As I see it, there is a possible remedy. It's a long shot, mind you, a very long shot, but first, we have to find out the true nature of his malaise, as Jim Morrison rightly terms it. Then, we must convince Oscar to seek professional help, as has already been suggested, for this will be essential if this remedy I have in mind is to be put in operation."

"What kind of professional help?" asked Jane?

"Psychiatric, as already referred to by Seurat."

"Oh, he'd love that. I pity the one who has to tell him. He won't appreciate being analysed by some shrink and pity the shrink that tries it," Balzac laughed.

Monsieur Torrès nodded at Jane. "To save him, one of us, although we're reluctant to do so, must do just that and convince him to be assessed. It is essential that he does so and does so voluntary. Otherwise, the remedy I have in mind will certainly fail, with the possibility of him being in his disturbed state for eternity and a strong possibility of incarceration on Cloud Eighty-Seven with all that that entails. It doesn't bear thinking about."

"*Mon Dieu*," Jane cried, distressed at the very thought of it.

"He's not that bad, surely."

"I'm sorry to tell you, Simone, but he is."

"What remedy do you have in mind?" asked Marie?

"I don't know if you're all aware of it, but there is a legal framework to our existence here," he informed the friends.

"Is there? It's news to me."

"Yeah. Everythin's news to you, Seurat," cracked Morrison.

"Come on you two. Pack it in. Monsieur Torrès is talking about a serious matter. Now give it a rest," insisted Sophie.

Morrison and Seurat glared at each other; there was no love lost between them.

"Everything we do or are allowed to do is governed by this legal framework," continued Torrès. "As I said, it's a very simple framework, but very effective. It's within this framework that I believe we can save Oscar, but some procedures have to be put in train, implemented and adhered to. They are simple to implement, but the results are hard to achieve. We must get this exactly right, for there is no appeal. We can have only one crack at it so we must be focused and not be sidetracked by irrelevancies or stupid arguments," he said, glancing over at Seurat.

"What is this legal framework called then?" asked Delacroix, fascinated at the thought of a legal framework in their surreal domain.

"The Divine Code."

Balzac burst out laughing. "I didn't think there was anything divine about the law – well, not the law I ever had anything to do with or with any of its practitioners. We don't need a legal framework here, for we don't break any laws, as we're not capable of committing any crime – Divine Code, my arse."

"I'm sorry to disappoint you, Honoré, but you are governed by law," replied Torrès. "You may not see it about you, but it is there, keeping us in order in a quiet and invisible way. A law above all laws. That's what makes it divine."

"If you say so."

"I do. Divine Law isn't solely for Paradise. It stretches its divine tentacles here, into Purgatory. The Divine Code is comprised of articles that set out the governing structures and administrative laws of this and other Reservations, and it's within this code, under Article Thirteen, that I believe we have a slim chance of saving the soul of Oscar Wilde – a chance, but a very slim one."

"But what's the law to do with Oscar's condition. He is ill, needing a doctor, not a lawyer. This doesn't make sense to me at all," Jane said, nodding her confused head.

"Bear with me, Jane. As you will see, it has a lot to do with it. There is a chance for him and we must take it."

"How does it work?" asked Sophie, delighted that there may be hope for Oscar after all.

"I'll outline it for you all once we have Oscar's consent to seek professional help, which is essential to put this motion into action. It can only be implemented if accompanied by a psychiatric report. All we need now is for someone to talk to him, but most importantly we must keep this legal avenue from him, for if he is aware of it the process stands no chance of succeeding."

"I'll do it."

They all turned and looked at Jim Morrison.

"Yeah, man. I'll do it. I can understand why you are all so reluctant to approach him. It's not an easy subject to discuss. It is difficult, but I'm up to it. But first, I say that Seurat should try and justify his hostility towards Oscar if that is at all possible. We've all heard many in favour of Oscar, so it's only fittin' that we hear from a dissentin' voice – well, Seurat, you seem to be the dissenter here – are you game?"

Seurat, startled by the sudden suggestion put to him had to think fast. "Yeah, I'll say I am. We all have a tale to tell. I'll tell mine, and then perhaps you may understand my difficulty with Oscar and what has caused my resentment of him."

He looked very nervous as the group looked at him, waiting for his explanation if indeed he had one.

"You all think I'm being unfair to good old Oscar, don't you? Come along. Don't be shy, that's what you all think. Isn't it?" Seurat asked as he took his seat on the Wisdom Stone.

There was an audible assent from the circle, although most were not that interested in what he had to say. "Well, as I say, we all have our tale to tell. I'm no different. This is mine for all it's worth."

They all sat there waiting for this talented artist to reveal why he had an axe to grind against a fellow artist and former friend of many years.

"I well remember the time Oscar arrived here. I was settled in by then and knew the ropes of survival in this semi-Paradise of ours. Oscar, like the rest of us who arrive here, had no idea what this place was all about. Most of us were confused, in a haze and thought it was all a bad dream. Oscar, however, thought it was a horrendous nightmare.

"For my sins, I was nominated as his guide and went to meet him at the Reservation Reception Centre. The Green Door opened, and there he stood, this strangely overdressed man. I had no idea who he was and had little interest in finding out. When I introduced myself, he was delighted to meet me and informed me that he was an admirer of mine. He seemed to know a great deal about my paintings. He rattled off a number of my canvases, especially my masterpiece, *Une Baignade, Asnières*. He gave the impression he was some kind of art connoisseur. I was flattered, of course. Who would not be? It's nice to be appreciated by a stranger, especially for no other reason than they like your work.

"As I said, I didn't know who the hell he was. I was only told to meet a fellow called Oscar Wilde and escort him to his new home at 33 Literary Way, in the Literary Quarter up on Cloud Fifteen. After talking for a while, I had the impression that he thought we were still on earth, that he had just happened to meet me on the way to the theatre or somewhere. I told him to sit down.

"'Do you know where you are?' I asked.

"'That's an odd question. In Paris, of course,' he replied. 'Where on earth do you think we are?'

"'Oh, I know exactly where we are, but you don't seem to.'

"'My dear fellow, whatever do you mean?' he asked, looking rather startled. 'Of course, I know where I am. As I said, we are in Paris, at the opening of your exhibition, are we not?'

"'No! We are not in Paris, or anywhere near it and certainly not at one of my exhibitions?'

"He looked at me, puzzled.

166

"'Then, where are we?'

"'At the Central Reservation of Purgatory.'

"'*Where, where* did you say?' he laughed.

"'In Purgatory, we're in Purgatory, at the Reservation of Père Lachaise, a Parisian division of Purgatory.'

"He stood there, his mouth wide open. 'Purgatory!' he roared.

"'The very same,' I replied.

"'Purgatory? Purgatory? My God!' he cried, his laughter getting louder. 'Are you telling me, I am dead?'

"'Yes.'

"'What do you mean I am dead? For Christ's sake, aren't I here talking to you? Dead men don't talk.'

"'They do here.'

"His face was ashen. He slumped against the wall, sliding slowly to the ground. Taking out a handkerchief, he dabbed his damp forehead. Poor soul, he was taking his transition badly.

"'Stop fooling about. We are here in this exhibition hall, viewing your paintings,' he said, getting to his feet and walking over to the paintings and pointing at them. 'These! These are your paintings, are they not?'

"'Oh! Yes indeed. My paintings are here in this wing of the Reservation Reception Centre. In the next wing, you will see David's masterpieces and next to him, Delacroix's, then there is Ingres, Signac, Modigliani, Pissarro and Ernst. They are all here. All of the artists here have a wing of their own. We artists are well looked after, I can tell you. This gallery would give any on earth a run for its money, even the Louvre.'

"He turned to face me and touched my shoulder. 'You are real. I can touch you. I can even feel your breath on my cheek, for Christ's sake. I can hear and see you, so how could I possibly be dead? I heard you were a bit of a joker, but I must say, Seurat, your humour is rather black, even for me,' he protested.

"'It's no joke. This is Purgatory, and I'm appointed as your guide to familiarise you with your new home and the rules that govern us.'

"He sat down again and stared at me, confusion stamped all over his face. 'This can't be so. I don't feel dead. I don't remember dying, and I don't believe you. This is a setup. A sick joke, concocted by those society friends of mine,' he said, his face now as white as a sheet.

"'Listen to me, my good man,' I said, 'this is no setup or a sick joke. Before you walked through that Green Door, what was the last thing you remember? Think now.'

"He sat there, deep in thought, his eyebrows raised, his face contorted. He wiped his forehead again. 'Wallpaper,' he murmured.

"'Wallpaper?

"'Yes! Wallpaper,' he repeated.

"'Now *you* must be joking.'

"'No. Wallpaper, ugly, ugly, wallpaper. The last thing I remember was looking at the hideous wallpaper in my rooms at the Hôtel d'Alsace. I was lying in bed, covered by a dire-looking brown blanket that had seen better days and looking at the most hideous wallpaper one was ever likely to see. It was beyond description. You wouldn't see wallpaper as ugly, even in Hell...'

"He gasped. His eyes glazed over. You could see in his features, the reality of his situation dawn on him. I let him sit there for some time, allowing him to come to terms with his new reality.

"'I was ill,' he continued in low voice. 'All I had was an earache but before I knew it, I was seriously ill. A few loyal friends surrounded me. There were Robbie Ross and Reggie Turner, good, decent and loyal friends. Then a priest arrived. I thought I recognised his face but could not place it. He looked familiar. They introduced him as Father Cuthbert Dunne, of the Passionist Fathers, a fellow Dubliner, I believe. He asked me if I wanted to be received into the Roman Catholic faith. I indicated that I did and the last I remember was the priest asking me to repeat the Acts of Contrition. I did so as I looked at that ugly wallpaper, and as I closed my eyes, I could faintly hear the priest administrating the last rites and Robbie sobbing. Then, the next thing I knew, I became aware of being transported to a place that looked like a doctor's waiting room. A woman told me to go through a tunnel, for I was marked as a Temporary Tenant and was waiting for a transfer to the Reservation of Père Lachaise.'

"He became quiet and wiped his forehead again with his now-sodden handkerchief. I offered mine. He took it and buried his face in it. It was finally dawning on him that he was no longer mortal. It's not an easy reality to be faced, that one is dead and gone, but we've all faced it and come through the other side. I couldn't help but wonder as he sat there whether this strange fellow would. He seemed by the look of him to be nothing but trouble.

"'God, you are right. I am dead. What an injustice,' he cried, jumping to his feet. 'I am an artist, for Christ's sake and yet to reach my full potential. My best was yet to come, and I go and die in a seedy back-street hotel in Paris looking at ugly wallpaper. What a way to throw off one's mortal coil. Is there no justice in life?'

"'Oh, yes, I forgot, you're a writer of sorts, aren't you?' I asked.

"He looked at me with absolute fury.

"'What do you mean, a writer of *sorts*?' he bellowed. 'I will have you know I am a man of genius, a writer of outstanding ability and achievement. I can't believe you have never even heard of me. Really, you are just too much – writer of sorts indeed.'

"'Sorry,' I replied. 'All I know is what is written on this chit I was given by the Administrator. Read it if you wish. Here, take a look.'

"He snatched the chit from my hand and read it: 'Welcome Oscar Wilde, a writer of sorts, and escort him to his accommodation at 33 Literary Way, in the Literary Quarter on Cloud-Fifteen.'

"'This must be a sick joke,' he howled. 'You don't introduce a genius as I in so off-hand a fashion.'

"'Oh! You're a genius, are you?' I said, wondering who this clown was that I'd had the misfortune to meet. 'Quite a few here profess to be such. Join the club. There are quite a few geniuses here, *all* special and *all* completely misunderstood.'

"'Like whom?' he asked in a surprised fashion, as though he thought he was the only genius about the place.

"'Chopin to start with,' I replied. 'He doesn't say he's a genius – he's far too bashful to say so, but we all know he is – a very stylish soul is our Chopin, so divine. '

"'Really? Frédéric Chopin?' he exclaimed. 'Yes, I would agree with you on that, a genius of the highest order. I must say, I'm surprised he is here. I would have thought that with his contribution to life and music, his divinity and place in Paradise were all but guaranteed. I hope I meet him.'

"'You will, no doubt.'

"'Who else?' he keenly asked.

"'Let's see now… Balzac! I suppose you haven't heard of him – one of France's finest writers; a slave to the written word.'

"He was downright indignant at what I'd said. 'I beg your pardon,' he scowled. 'Do not be so insulting. He is a man of letters held in as much esteem as I used to be. Of course, I know who he is.'

"'All right, no need to get tetchy,' I said.

"'Anyone else of merit?'

"'Certainly… there's good old Musset.'

"He again wiped his forehead. 'Who… you mean, Alfred de Musset, that *enfant terrible*?'

"'The very same,' I replied, 'a genius with words, if there ever was one, and he knows it too. Very popular he is. Can be a bit vain, mind you, but women just love him. His ego knows no bounds. If you happen to be egocentric, you will be in good company. He'll give you a good run for your money.'

"'Will I have the opportunity of meeting him?' he asked.

"'I can't see why not. We are, after all, one big happy family, who live in each other's pockets. You will meet him OK, along with and

Chopin. Balzac. Musset – he's staying not far from you on Literary Way. I'm sure you'll bump into him one day.'

"'*Bump!*' He cried. 'My dear fellow, you employ some odd words. I never bump into anyone or anything; I am, after all, a gentleman of style, grooming and refinement and gentlemen do not bump into anyone, or anything, especially this one.'

"'I'm sure you don't, Monsieur Wilde. We have many here too, who also profess to be gentlemen. This place is a kind of club – a gentleman's club with a perceived touch of genius,' I replied.

"'You seem to have a cynical edge to your words. They seem rather cutting,' he replied, looking down his nose at me.

"'It's just my manner – one of my many redeeming features, so I'm told. I do work hard at it. It isn't easy you know being at the cutting edge of cynicism.'

"'I'm sure it is not. But perhaps you try too hard,' he retorted.

"'Cynics don't try hard – that's why they're cynics,' I replied. 'Come along, I will show you to your new home. It's a good stretch. I hope you are up to it.'

"'Wait a moment,' he cried as I turned to move. 'Have I no luggage?'

"I couldn't help but laugh. What a comical fellow this was, I thought. There will never be a dull moment with this clown around.

"'You need no luggage here, monsieur – all will be provided for when you reach your home. Come along now. Let's not tarry. Eternity beckons.'

"We left the Reception Centre and headed up the steps towards the Reservation Gate and on to the Highway to Paradise, which would take us out across the Reservation to his new home. We had only just begun climbing that steep incline when he suddenly stopped and looked around him.

"'Why has everything got a pink tint to it?' he asked. 'Look at the hill and the clouds – they are all pink trimmed.'

"'Many ask the same question, but nobody knows the answer. It's just one of those things, one of the many things that can't be explained in this domain.'

"'What things?' he asked, concern lacing his words?

"'Ah! Just things,' I replied. 'You'll find out sooner or later.'

"'I would rather find out sooner if you don't mind.'

"'You're a real impatient chap, aren't you?' I said as I continued walking, with him tarrying behind.

"'No. Just curious to know and understand my surroundings,' he replied as he tried to keep up with me.

"'Being curious here is a waste of mental energy. Take my advice – put curiosity aside and take it easy.'

"He looked at me as though I was stark raving mad. 'Take it easy?' he squealed. 'Are you some kind of sadistic weirdo? What do you mean, take it easy? How can I take it easy with you as my guide?'

"'Oh, I'm not that bad,' I replied. 'I know I'm not a genius or a refined gentleman like you, who doesn't bump into things, but really, I'm not that bad. I've acquired a relaxed manner since I arrived here. All I'm saying is that you should do likewise. Take things as they come and enjoy your Purgatory.'

"He stopped dead in his tracks. He glared at me, his eyes near popping out of their sockets. 'Enjoy my Purgatory! Are you mad?' he yelled. 'I don't even know where I am. You say this is Purgatory. I don't know if that's true. This could all be a dream, and I'll wake up in a moment and find I am in my rooms at Oxford, full of the delights of life and never died in a seedy hotel.'

"I took a good look at this clown and it was stamped all over him that he was going to be a real bagful of trouble. I'm always handed the awkward arrivals, and this one had awkwardness radiating from him.

"'No,' I said. 'This isn't a figment of your imagination. This is Purgatory. This is the real thing. Come along. We're wasting time.'

"We continued our journey towards the Reservation Gate. Before us was the splendour of the Heather Moor, a view that astounded him. 'But this place is stunning,' he cried. 'Are you sure this is Purgatory?'

"'Positive.'

"'This could be Paradise itself. Look at those colourful shades of heather on the moor. The view is extraordinary. Yes. This could indeed be Paradise,' he exclaimed.

"'You think so?' I asked.

"'Yes, indeed.'

"'Could be, but it isn't. Yes, it is beautiful, that I agree, but, being a literary genius as you profess to be, you no doubt know the old adage, about beauty being only skin-deep. After being here for a while, you will realise how true that maxim really is.'

"'Whatever do you mean by that?'

"'You'll find out in due course,' I replied. 'All I'll say is that there's many a pitfall amongst all this perceived beauty.'

"'Perceived! Are you saying I am only imagining the beauty before me? That this carpet of heather is not real?' he asked.

"'It's not for me to explain. I'm just your guide. I'm not privy to the workings of this place or for the reasons for its peculiarities and complexities,' I replied. He did look rather perplexed. We continued out through the Reservation Gate with the Heather Moor stretching out before us. When we reached the middle of the moor, he stopped and with hand on hips looked around at the heather-clad hills in all their glory. Colour returned to his ashen face as the sight lifted his spirits. 'So, it is only skin deep, is it?' he sighed. 'What a shame.'

"'You can enjoy the beauty of this place, Monsieur Wilde, and be at peace with yourself and with the souls about you if you are prepared to accept it at face value. It will be a shame if you decide to be a malcontent, become too curious and dig deep beneath the beauty you see. Don't be tempted, for what you'll find, will inevitably devalue your soul, make you more discontent and turn your Purgatory into a living Hell.'

"He turned towards me and, scratching his forehead said, 'What a curious fellow you are. Do you always talk in riddles?'

"'No! Only the truth,' I replied.

"'I haven't been here long, my friend, but it seems that it is not just the clouds that are pink-tinted, but the truth too.'

"'I fail to see what you mean,' I replied, offended that he could possibly imply that I was dishonest.

"'No doubt you'll find out in due course,' he replied, trying to be smart, but failing miserably.

"As we were walking, he kept glancing over to the right.

"'Is there something bothering you,' I asked.

"'Yes, there's a woman, over there. You see her?' he said pointing over towards a woman dressed in blue. 'She has been following us since we left the Reservation Centre. Who is she?'

"'Oh! That. Take no notice. It's only our Lady in Blue, commonly known as Sour Grapes. Don't let her bother you. We don't. Come along now, we are starting to linger.'

"'Sour Grapes? What do you mean?' he asked as he looked over at her again.

"'She's of no consequence; she disagrees with anything and everything. Can never see the good side of anyone – Ignore her. We do,' I said.

"'But why is she following us?'

"'Us? No, no my friend, she is not following us, she is following *you.*'

"'*Me!*' he cried. 'Why me?'

"'Because you're new, that's why. She knows you're a newcomer and she'll cling to you until she can get the better of *you* or until you can defeat her by getting the better of *her*. It's as simple as that,' I said.

"He stopped and looked over and carefully observed her as she stood under a dragon tree. You all know what's she's like – always dressed in her worn-out blue two-piece suit, her hair unkempt, and wearing her usual azure blue lipstick that set off her sour look.

"'Why should she want to get the better of me? I don't even know her, and she certainly not acquainted with me. And why on earth should I want to get the better of her?' he asked.

"'My friend, you do have a lot to learn,' I told him.

"'Why are you talking to me as though I was a child, as though I was an imbecile?' he asked in an annoyed manner.

"'Well, forgive me, but you're far from acting like an adult soul, now, are you? You're whining like a spoilt child.'

"'I resent that,' he indignantly replied.

"'Well, that's tough now, isn't it? Come along, we must keep moving,' I replied as I tugged at his sleeve. He followed, muttering away to himself.

"We passed over the Heather Moor and down towards the Lemon Grove. He kept looking back to see if she was still following. She was and had her cold eyes fixed firmly on him.

"'How far have we to go? I'm feeling jaded,' he panted.

"'Not too far – once through the Lemon Grove we only have to cut across The Plain and will be in sight of the Literary Quarter. Don't slow down now.'

"As we were walking across the Plain he stopped in his tracks and looked over to the Western Horizon.

"'What's up?' I asked.

"'That high, steep hill – it looks so familiar,' he said pointing over towards a towering hill. 'What is it?'

"'Oh that. It's the Moral High Ground – a pitiful place.'

"He looked at me, stunned, then asked, 'The what?'

"'The Moral High Ground.'

"'God,' he sighed. 'I thought I had seen the back of that.'

"'Sorry, we're cursed with it here as well.'

"'Do many reside there?' he asked.

"'Oh yeah, there's never a shortage of tenants. Most of them are the religious, failed politicians and hoards of Puritans of every shade of black.'

"'Do they ever come down?' he asked, not taking his eyes off of the place.

"'Oh! On the odd occasions; of course, the priests come down once a week to attend the places of worship.'

"He raised his eyebrows. 'There are churches *here*?' he asked in surprise.

"'Of course; why shouldn't there be?' I replied, laughing at his naivety.

"'Why? I thought that was obvious.'

"'Is it?' I asked.

"'Yes. What's the purpose of them? What possible use is a church in this godforsaken place?'

"'I don't know,' I replied. 'There must be a purpose; otherwise, they wouldn't be here, would they? Of course, the services are quite different from those on earth.'

"'In what way?' he enquired.

"'Well, there's no communion, no baptism, no weddings, and of course, no funerals.'

"'Then why bother having churches?'

"'There you go again, asking questions that have no answers,' I replied. 'Really, you are a difficult soul. I can see this Reservation will have to keep a sharp eye on you. I hope you weren't this difficult on earth.'

"'I'm not difficult,' he cried. 'I'm just curious. Surely there must be some reason for having churches here.'

"'I'm sure there is, but I don't know what it is,' I replied as I looked up at the Moral High Ground, which was beginning to mist over.

"'Who else comes down?'

"'Oh, you're in for a treat,' I said. 'The Puritans wander down regularly, ready to have a go at any soul, they consider 'adrift'. They can be very overbearing and are likely to tear a strip off you with their acidic tongues if you happen to be "adrift".

"'Don't worry. I will give them a wide berth just as I did in life,' he said. 'I had no time for them then, and I will give them short shrift if they come near me here – who else?'

"'Oh! The Political Animals – You know the kind –devious, deceitful and two-faced as they come. They slither down the hill, wriggling their way into every available discussion. Superficially, they appear to be real ladies and gentlemen but they lace their words with veiled meanings that are in reality nothing more than verbal diarrhoea. They talk down to us, as they did on earth, telling us that they have the secrets to the perfect purgatorial existence. Trust them, and all will be well. I ignore them. Most do.'

"'That is very wise of you,' he said. 'So they are at it here, are they? I thought I had seen the back of them too. So, they are the only tenants up there?'

"'Oh no, there are quite a few other oddments. You'd never believe how many try to scale those dizzy heights,' I said. 'Some run up there with ease. Some do it with difficulty. Others, however, once at the summit, realise it's too dizzy a height and run back down as fast as they can. Then we have the ones who keep falling and running back up again, never getting the message that perhaps those dizzy heights are not for them.'

174

"'Who are they?'

"'Oh! Where does one begin?' I said, scratching my head for inspiration. 'They come in all shapes and sizes. The most regular ones are Social Climbers. They are gluttons for punishment. When they fall they get up and start all over again.'

"'Are there any permanent residents?'

"'Oh, yes, loads.' I replied. 'There are more judges than any other group. Judges seem to scale the heights without difficulty. They seem quite happy to sit up there, casting their judgment on us poor souls below. Most of them have no difficulties with such dizzy heights of morality. It's in their blood – they thrive on it.'

"'Yes, I know precisely what you mean. I knew of such a judge once,' he replied, his eyes glazing over at the memory of whoever that judge was.

"'Ah! Then there are the Masons,' I said. 'The Moral High Ground would be lost without them and their likes. You could call them the godfathers of the Moral High Ground. You must have met them on your travels on earth. They are so trite and shallow. Up there they have Masonic Lodges, just as they did on earth, each with their peculiar rituals. It's said they come down here in disguise and blend in with the rest of us but take note of activities they consider improper and not up to their high standards. Don't know why they bother, for, in reality, they have no power to influence or change matters. They are a defunct entity yet cannot see it. When they return, most of them find it hard to keep their footing. They slither and fall as they climb the hill carrying their Burden of Virtue. Pathetic, isn't it?'

"'Perhaps we ought to give that hill a wide berth,' he said as he turned his back on the Moral High Ground and continued his journey only to be stopped in his tracks again.

"'My God, what's that?' he cried, as he stared at the peculiar – shaped chair that sat amongst a blanket of daisies.

"'Oh!' I replied. 'That's only Morgan's Chair.'

"'Morgan's Chair – what, pray, is Morgan's Chair?' he cried in an astonished tone.

"'That, my friend is the Laughter Chair. You'll find after a while you'll be in need of a good laugh, just to keep you sane. This,' I said, tapping the arm of the highly polished Irish oak chair, 'this is the key to your sanity. If you are ever feeling down in the dumps or out of sorts, this is the remedy. Here, take a seat. Come now, on you get and let yourself go. It's a great tonic to rid oneself of the Purgatory Blues. On you get.'

"He did. Looking out over to the Moral High Ground, he let out a mighty roar. He was howling with laughter, his eyes streaming. He couldn't contain himself. He wiped his eyes; then howled again, shaking violently. I let him sit there for five minutes or so before dragging him off.

"'My, that is some experience. So you are telling me we can use this anytime we like,' he asked as he dabbed his eyes.

"'Indeed, but in moderation. Too much of a good thing is detrimental to the soul. It's very popular, very popular indeed. Don't be surprised if you have to queue. A good laugh, like a good meal, is always worth waiting for,' I reminded him.

"'Who was this Morgan fellow?' he asked as he tapped the chair with his forefinger.

"'A Gaelic clown,' I replied.

"He looked surprised. 'Really,' he said, 'I have known a few Gaelic clowns in my time, and Ireland is blessed with its fair share of them. Alas! I haven't heard of a Morgan.'

"'He was a mimic of the High and Mighty. He was the saviour of Irish sanity.'

"'Wow! That's some saviour,' he cried.

'Oh! He was, but like most saviours, he was crucified for his troubles.'

'What an injustice,' he sighed.

"As we continued our journey he wearily asked, 'Is there no transport here? Must we walk everywhere? I am a refined gentleman and not used to walking for so long. I am shattered.'

"Poor soul, I thought, refined indeed. Who's he kidding?

"'Afraid so,' I replied. 'There are a few carts about the place, and if you are up to it, you can obtain yourself a nag. Most, however, prefer to walk, as they are really in no hurry to get anywhere.'

"'You seem very relaxed and resigned to your situation,' he remarked.

"'I am, and better for it. It's no good trying to change what will be.'

"He was stunned by my remark. I had somehow hit a nerve. 'You can't be serious? What will be, will be! How do you know what will be? What do you mean by such nonsense? Nothing has to be. Are you a psychic or some kind of prophet?'

"'No. Nothing so grand; nothing of the kind,' I replied. 'I'm a realist, that's all. I know my surroundings, and the reason I'm here and whatever I do and achieve here is what is already ordained. Yes, my friend, what will be, will be and there is nothing you or I can do about it.'

"'A realist! Oh! That's what they call it these days. I would call you delusional,' he sneered.

"'Would you now? Tell me, my friend, seeing that you're so smart, do you believe in fate?' I asked him.

176

"'Of course I do. Don't we all?'

"'No. You won't believe how many don't,' I said, 'if you do believe in fate, you must accept your situation, and refrain from asking such awkward questions about this place. You are fated to be here, and that should be the end of the matter. Why are you so awkward a soul?'

"He was dismayed by my remark. 'I am not awkward,' he said. 'I must question what I do not understand. That is my nature. I can't change my nature. I must know all there is to know of this place – whatever it is, good or bad. That is not being awkward. It is being inquisitive, and I can't see anything wrong in that.'

"God, this fellow was serious. He'd soon learn.

"We headed down the last mile to the Literary Quarter. Passing through the Scribbler's Gate, we headed up Literary Hill, and turned into Author's Walk. I stopped and pointed to the yellow cottage before us.

"He looked it up and down.

"'Very nice,' he said. 'This is *mine*?'

"'Yes, this is your allocated abode. Come in, I will give you a guided tour.'

"'If you wish,' he replied.

"I showed him his new home. He was amazed. It had all he needed for a comfortable existence. He was impressed by the library and gave a smile of quiet satisfaction when he saw that all his works were there. Yes, he was quite happy with his new home but was still a little confused. He couldn't quite comprehend that he was dead. We know exactly how he must have been feeling as we have all experienced it. He was now a spirit and must get used to it.

"I handed him a booklet and he flicked through it. "What are these?' he asked, flinging them on the sofa.

"'The Rules of the House.'

"'Rules, What rules?' he enquired.

"'Just rules,' I said. 'We need them to keep society in check. We have to have rules, otherwise there would be chaos. We can't do without them. Society can't function without them. I suggest you read them carefully. Follow them, and you'll have a trouble-free stay.'

"'But rules… that is what they have in the army or prison. This isn't a prison, is it?'

"'Only, if you wish it to be,' I replied. 'Some people are in prison in their minds, some in their hearts. I'm sure you know what I mean.'

"He nodded his head, indicating he understood. I'd say he thought I knew his history, which I didn't at the time. I left him to settle in and told him I'd call around in the morning to see how he was coping. This I did. To my surprise, he was where I'd left him,

177

sitting on the end of his bed. He was in shock. Poor soul, it was just too much for him to take in. His Purgatory was beginning to bother him. I managed to convince him of the reality of his situation and decided to keep an eye on this difficult soul. After the initial shock of his arrival, he seemed to settle down reasonably well. I visited him on a very regular basis.

"When I finally realised who my ward was, I read everything available about him. At first, I didn't like the fellow but got to know him well and soon we were the best of friends. He would often remind me of our first encounter. He thought I was some kind of sadistic weirdo.

"His novel *The Picture of Dorian Gray* fascinated me to distraction, for it, was peppered with references that have many different meanings that set my mind wandering. He would laugh at me when I questioned him about its content, about whether it was a Uranian tale or not.

"'You're reading too much into it. It's just a simple story,' he would say.

"Once I got to know him well we'd have some great intense debates on exactly what the novel was about. The thing was he didn't consider the novel special. He thought it was just run-of-the-mill, not one of his better efforts. I disagreed with him, as I did on many a subject, but I grew to have a high regard for him and, dare I say, respect, not only for his literary genius but also for his qualities as a man. This was to change utterly.

"On many of his visits to my studio over the years, he's dabbled with the brushes and on occasions produced reasonable canvases. Throughout that time, he never once asked to have his portrait painted. I had asked him to sit on numerous occasions, but he'd always refused. When I asked why, he just shrugged his shoulders and said he wasn't interested, which was peculiar seeing he was obsessed with his image. Then one day, about six months ago, he asked me to do one. I was surprised but delighted he asked. I asked why now. He said the time was right. Hadn't a clue what he was on about but I wasted no time in getting out my brushes. I thought I'd better move fast in case he changed his mind. He sat there calmly smoking and was so relaxed I thought he'd fall asleep. He was thrilled with the finished product and said he had the perfect spot to hang it. I thought nothing more about it and got on with my work.

"A week later he was back, this time not looking so bright and sparkling. He seemed agitated and was a bit snappy. He said he needed another portrait and done quickly. I thought it a bit odd that he needed another but didn't mention it to him. I set about my task. He didn't say much throughout the sitting, barely responding to my questions. I thought that strange, as usually, it's difficult to stop him talking. Seeing him in such a sombre mood was worrying.

"The next time we met, he was in sparkling form. Over two months, I did a series of paintings for him, each one representing the months of the year, each with corresponding colours – grey for January for instance, blue for December. I did ask why he wanted them but he wasn't forthcoming about his reasons. Then he asked me to do another. I would have, but his request was so peremptory I refused, and he stormed off in a rage. The next day he dashed into my studio brandishing pieces of canvases. I asked what they were, and he laughed aloud and threw them at me. 'Here, you can have these back, I have no use for them,' he bellowed. He emptied the contents of a bag on to the studio floor and kicked them towards me. 'You are a useless artist anyway, nothing more than an amateur, a Sunday artist of little merit.'

"He then left, laughing, slamming the door behind him. I picked up some of the debris, and to my horror realised that what was in my hands were remnants of the seasonal paintings I had painted for him. I saw red and ran after him, only to discover that he had vanished. I was seething and screamed holy murder. The bastard, I thought – I'm not letting him get away with this. As you know, I haven't. The next day I headed for his home. He knew I was at the door but totally ignored me. I looked through the window, and there he was, stretched out on the sofa, puffing on a cigar without a care in the world. That was the end of our friendship. I can put up with a lot but having my works of art vandalised by a wayward genius is not on. By cutting up my canvases, he was cutting at my very soul. He had let me down and had done so in the most appalling fashion. I haven't talked to him since.

"That's my story. My antagonism is utterly justified. He hasn't apologised, nor showed any sign of doing so. Yes, you go, Morrison, go and talk to him and if you don't believe my account, then ask that twisted genius if what I say is true. Yes, by all means, try to get him to see sense and get treatment, but also remind him of the hurt and suffering he's inflicted on those who are his friends and more importantly, those he professes to love."

There was a hushed silence. The friends stared at each other, reluctant to be the first to speak. Thankfully, Sophie came to the rescue. She thanked Seurat for his contribution and announced that they would assemble again at her home on the following Saturday evening when Torrès would outline his strategy, for Oscar wouldn't be around. He'd be over on Cloud Thirty, knocking the thespians into shape at the rehearsals for his play, *The Chairman of Vice*. They would be safe from any interruptions from him.

179

The group slowly dispersed. Jim Morrison prepared himself to do as he had promised. However, he had to find out where Oscar was.

The circle of Oscar's friends had grown larger, with other souls arriving, having heard about the initial meeting. Joining the celebrated were the ordinary souls of Père Lachaise, who in general thought Oscar was the bee's knees. There was a hum of excitement about the place as they waited for the return of Jim Morrison to give his report if indeed he had managed to find and talk to Oscar.

"Here he comes," Sophie shouted. "Take your seats."

They settled around the Laburnum Tree, with the overflow sitting on the steps and the grass verges. Sophie, now the accepted leader, stood on the Wisdom Stone and brought the meeting to order.

Morrison meandered up, the crowd parting to make way for him as he climbed up the steps. He sat down at the base of the tree. He was his usual laid-back self. He took a reefer from behind his ear, lit it and greedily sucked in the smoke as they all looked at him in anticipation.

"Did you speak to him?" Jane impatiently asked. "What did he say?"

He took another deep drag.

"Stop messing about, Morrison, will you. What did he say?" Isadora asked.

"It's like this," Morrison began. "I had difficulties gettin' a hold of him but managed to get a message to him sayin' I needed to talk to him as soon as possible. I arranged a meetin' with him in the Rose Garden on Cloud Seventy-Five. I met him at the Dreamer's Arch, just inside the main entrance. We wandered over to the far side of Rainbow Hill, exchangin' pleasantries. When we arrived at my patch, I revealed my prize rose. 'This is it,' I proudly said, pointin' to the yellow bloom. 'You won't believe how much time it's taken; how much love and attention has been lavished on it. I'm gettin' very good at it. It's very relaxin' and satisfyin' pursuit, this growin' of roses. I never thought I had it in me.'

"'My, my, you do surprise me. You don't seem the kind of fellow to be interested in horticultural matters,' he said as he carefully examined the rose.

"'Oscar, you know damn well that I grow roses. You've been here umpteen times with me. Every time you need a rose, you wander up here to see me. What do you mean; you're surprised I'm interested in horticultural matters? You know I am.'

"'Oh, I forgot,' he haughtily said, 'but why roses?'

"'Why not, why shouldn't I be interested in roses or any other kind of flower?' I retorted.

"'Well, to start with, it's not good for your image,' he replied.

"'Is that so?'

"'Indeed it is,' he said. 'Growing and talking to flowers is certainly bad for your image. After all, you are a rock star. You have a certain image and ego to maintain. Growing and talking to roses doesn't sound *cool* for a rock star, does it? You must look after your image, it is most important.'

"'Rubbish. What image, what ego? Man, an image is irrelevant here, and an ego serves no purpose whatsoever. We don't have to impress anyone here,' I replied. 'I *was* a rock star. Now I grow roses and make a good job of it too. I'm not interested in imagery or egocentricity in any shape or form, for I know the damage it can do. You should take note.'

"He looked at me hard. 'What do you mean by that?'

"'I don't want you to think I'm interferin', but you seem to have a problem with your image.'

"He jumped to his feet in surprise and said, 'My image? What are you trying to say? My image is second to none. If you wanted to do a thesis on image, you could do no better than studying mine. It is unique.'

"'Sit down, will you? I've somethin' to discuss with you, somethin' of great importance,' I told him.

"He looked serious as he took a seat on the granite wall surrounding the rose bed. The slight twitch beneath his lower lip gave the impression that he was somewhat nervous. He tossed back his hair and said, 'It is my image that my audience knows and love. My image is everything. It has taken a lifetime of dedication to nurture, mature and fine-tune it. You wouldn't believe how much time and effort I have taken in my pursuit of perfection – what would I be, my dear man, without such an image?'

"I placed a friendly hand on his arm and told him, 'Yourself!'

"He pushed my hand away as though it was diseased. 'I am damned if I know what you mean. I am myself.' he indignantly replied.

"'No, man, you're not. You're hidin' behind a mask, behind an image that is not your true self.'

"He was on his feet again, fumin'. With his fists clenched, he was ready for a fight. 'Mask!' he yelled. 'What mask? What do you mean; my image is not my true self? My image is what I am; it's not a mask, but my true self.'

"'Listen, man,' I said, steelin' myself for a verbal onslaught from him. 'You've been way beyond the pale lately in the way you've bin' behavin'. You're now hidin' your real self behind a mask, a mask of insults and downright vulgar behaviour. Surely, you must be aware of how you have been behavin'. Many here love you and express concern and are worried about your recent behaviour.'

"'What recent behaviour?' he angrily replied. 'Who is concerned? Tell me. Come now, who are these concerned souls?' I don't know what you're talking about.'

"'Do I have to spell it out?' I asked.

"'Yes you do because I don't know what the hell you're on about. This growing of roses is not a good idea. It has gone to your head. It is affecting your senses,' he said as he stared at me, his eyes wide and wild. He sat down, again wiping his brow.

"'I know you're goin' to despise me for this, but what I'm about to say is for your own good,' I finally said as I set about sayin' what I had come for.

"'Is it now?' he said, raising his eyebrows as he looked at me.

"'Yes!' I replied as I sat next to him.

"'Well, out with it! What have you to say?'

"'You need help,' I blurted out.

"'Help! Nonsense, what utter nonsense,'

"'It's not nonsense at all. You need help. Not the kinda help we as friends can offer, but good, solid, professional help.'

"He was on his feet again.

"'*What!* he yelled, 'a shrink? You say I need a therapist – to hell with you, Yankee. I know you have a droll sense of humour, but you have overstepped the mark here. I don't think that is funny at all. You are saying I'm insane. That's what you're saying, is it not?'

"'No. All I'm saying is that you need help, good psychiatric help,' I repeated.

"'Rubbish. I don't need anyone messing about with my mind; it's perfect as it is. No one knows the workings of my mind better than I do. I don't understand – what behaviour do you refer to? What 'recent behaviour' are you on about?' he asked. 'Come, out with it.'

"I was regrettin' ever volunteerin' for this task. I took a deep breath and waded in. 'Isadora was takin' a walk up to View Point Hill, passin' the time of day when she came upon you as you were screamin' down at visitors to your grave.'

"'Did she now?' he snapped.

"'Yes, and you were actin' in a strange and disturbin' way. You didn't see her, as she was sittin' behind a yew tree. You were starin' down over Père Lachaise, shoutin' abuse at the visitors passin' your tomb and she said you were talkin' to yourself. She was appalled and very distressed by your behaviour.'

"'So, she's been spying on me, has she?' he said.

"'No. Not quite spyin'.'

"'Sounds like it to me. I can't even look at my own grave without some prissy missy spying on me; it is too much. I am so disappointed in her,' he said. 'I always thought she had class. Shows you how wrong one can be.'

"'That's drivel,' I replied. 'She was only showin' concern. That's what friends do.'

"'Concern! Oh! That is the new word for spying, is it? It is amazing how words change, is it not? I must invest in a new dictionary. I seem to be behind the times on the changing lingo.'

"He was fuming, and I thought he was going to make a bolt for it. I let him calm down then continued.

"'She returned the next day and you were in a rage over somethin' or other,' I continued. 'She followed your gaze and watched as the workers tried to clean your tomb of the lipstick marks and other graffiti. She witnessed you rantin' and ravin'. You were in a foul mood. She couldn't make out what you were sayin'. She wanted to approach you but was nervous in doin' so, for you were really strung out.'

"'Was I now?' he grunted as he slumped down on the granite wall, bowing his head. He gave a long sigh and then buried his face in his tremblin' hands.

"As I looked down at him, I began to question what I was doin'. Had I any right to confront him in this manner, to cause him even more distress than what he was already sufferin'? When he first met me, he thought I wasn't worth the time of day, but over the years we've been gettin' on pretty well. We have built up a decent friendship, so there I was, jeopardisin' the progress we had made. I bit my lip and continued. 'What's it all about? You seem to be lookin' over Père Lachaise quite a lot these days. It can't be good for you; it's obviously causin' you a lot of annoyance. Tell me. What's worryin' you?'

"'You are!' he snapped. 'You nosey little sod.'

"Go on, what happened next?" asked Sarah.

"I sat next to him. I was in two minds about continuin', but I was there and had better finish off what I came to do.

"'Delacroix said you've had stacks of portraits painted, not just by him, but by Ingres, David, Seurat, and even Max Ernst. What's all that about?'

"'It is really none of your business,' he snapped.

"'I'm just tryin' to understand what's botherin' you, man, that's all,' I said, tryin' to reassure him.

"'There is nothing bothering me, except you,' he snapped. 'I'm not the first person to have had their portraits painted, you know, and will certainly not be the last. It does happen.'

"'Don't you know you upset Seurat by your reaction to his refusal to do any more portraits for you?'

"'He gets upset over anything,' he said. 'He's a tetchy one.'

"'He's still annoyed with you. I do know what happened.

"'Oh, he has been telling tales, has he? That's very adult of him. What other tales has he been telling, then?' he asked.

"'Not tales, only the truth.'

"'Which is?' he asked.

"'That you destroyed twelve of the paintings he did for you.'

"'That's not true,' he replied. 'I have one hanging in my home.'

"'What about the rest, then? What happened to them?'

"He was quiet for a while, fixing his gaze at some point way over the rainbow.

"'I destroyed them,' he said, shrugging his shoulders.

"'And you wonder why he's mad at you? Why did you do such a thing?' I asked. 'You of all people should know how attached artists are to their work, and you go and destroy them? That's real mean of you, man, real mean. To destroy an artist's work of art is akin to stabbin' him in the heart. '

"'I thought they were rubbish, and I told him so. I am sorry I did, though. Not a thing one artist should do to another, I agree,' he said bashfully. 'He'll never forgive me. I don't blame him. It was very childish of me. Sometimes I can be a fool. If I am a genius, as some say, then I am a damn fool of one.'

"'What about Delacroix, your dearest of friends?' I asked. 'After all of those years of amity, you have a crazy argument with him. Man, you were at his throat over what seemed to be nothin' of any importance at all. He may not be as touchy as Seurat, but he was annoyed that you could have criticised his work in the way you did. After all, he is a master.'

"'I was making a point,' he replied.

"'You could have been more diplomatic.'

"'I'm an artist, not a diplomat,' he snapped. 'Anyway, it was constructive criticism. There is no harm in that is there?'

"'No,' I said. 'But some might say your comments were far from constructive – more corrosive, meant to wound and degrade, which you succeeded in doin'.'

"'My dear fellow,' he replied. Some may say so, but they are wrong. If I have hurt Eugène, then I am terribly sorry. As for wounding him, I would never deliberately do such a thing. He knows me well enough to know that, and although it is our first serious disagreement, I am sure he knows I didn't mean what I said. He is a gentleman. I am sure he will forgive my outburst.'

"'I'm sure he will, but man, I don't think he'll ever understand the reasonin' behind your subject matter for the portraits. You must

185

admit, they were odd. There seems no rhyme or reason to them,' I said.

"'I have my reasons,' he replied, flicking a fallen rose petal from his sleeve.

"'Which are?' I asked, knowing he wouldn't tell me, which he didn't. He just shrugged his shoulders.

"'Marie visited you. You remember that I suppose?' I asked.

"He nodded his head. 'Indeed I do. How could I ever forget any visit from such a mesmerizing woman?'

"'Marie noticed the portraits on your walls when she visited you not long ago and also the mirrors. What's that all about?' I asked.

"He said nothing. He just sat there, fidgeting with his hands, looking lost and forlorn.

"'She was confused, to say the least,' I continued. 'Why the mirrors? Man, your once-stylish home has been reduced to a tacky fairground attraction that accordin' to her would have been at home on Blackpool's seafront.'

"'That's a matter of opinion,' he mumbled.

"'Come off it, Oscar,' I replied. 'It sounds grotesque, not your style at all.'

"He grunted. 'What would you know about style?'

"I ignored this. 'What about Édith? You won't believe the state she was in after her experience in the Cherry Blossom Forest. You put her through hell with your theatrics. Can you explain your behaviour? Can you?'

"He said nothin', just stared at the ground. I was feelin' uneasy as I was beginnin' to sound like a detective quizzin' a suspect. 'I can't ever remember her bein' so distressed and depressed as she was that day.' I continued. 'You must know that she adores you; that she admires you, and we all know how fond you are of her. It will take her a long time to get over the trauma you put her through – you've wounded our Little Sparrow.'

"At the mention of the Little Sparrow, the colour drained from his face. He put his head in his hands and began to tremble, tears oozin' through his fingers. He sat there and cried. Man, he opened the floodgates. I've never seen a soul weep so much."

"God help him. God help him. God help him," Chopin kept saying as he walked back and forth with his hands clasped behind his back.

Morrison threw the butt of the reefer to the ground, laid back his head against the Wisdom Stone and closed his moist eyes

"Are you all right?" Sophie asked.

He looked up at her, his face ashen.

"Yeah!" he whispered. "I'm fine, but he sure ain't."

186

"What did you do?" asked Isadora.

"Man. What could I do? I put my arms around him and we both cried like babies."

Suddenly Édith burst into tears, as did Jane and Isadora. This set off Marie and Sophie, and Chopin still walking back and forth, wiped his eyes with the back of his hands. Seurat tried to laugh but failed miserably. Delacroix was disgusted with himself for not being the one to console Oscar in his hour of need.

"What did you do, then?" Chopin tearfully asked as he sat next to Morrison.

"He became very quiet. We sat there for some time, and I thought to myself, what now? Shall I continue or call it a day?

"Did you?"

"No, Sophie, I didn't. I thought I'd better continue and do what I had come to do. I said, 'Marie was disturbed by the way you'd transformed Merrion with mirrors and portraits of yourself. She's concerned about your well-bein'. You know what I'm sayin', man? You must have known by her demeanour that she was disturbed by what she had seen.'

"He looked up at me, his eyes red and swollen. He was a pitiful sight. 'To tell you the truth, I didn't,' he admitted. 'All I remember was her discussing my forthcoming centenary. I did not realise she was disturbed. I was so preoccupied with my problems I didn't notice hers.'

"'Can I ask you, why the mirrors and portraits?'

"He gave one of his deep lingerin' sighs. 'I don't know,' he replied. 'I suppose there must be a reason hidden away in my mind that has caused me to act like such a heel.'

"We sat there, silent, for what seemed like an eternity.

"'What about me?' I said. 'You remember when I met you at the viewpoint and you bragged about the visitors to your tomb?'

"'Yes,' he mumbled.

"'I had the feelin' you set out to put me down, humiliate and embarrass me. I know you didn't mean what you said, but it hurt all the same. You remember that?'

"'Yes,' he replied.

"'Why, man, why did you want me to look at my grave when you knew it wasn't my scene?' I asked.

"He bit his lip. 'Yes. You are right. I wanted to see you humiliated. Really, I was so depressed, I wanted to humiliate any soul who crossed my path,' he admitted.

"'Why? Why would you want to humiliate me? What have I ever done to you, to make you attack me like that? I was under the impression that we were buddies, the best of buddies.'

187

"He shrugged his shoulders again. 'We are,' he said as he wiped his eyes. 'I am so sorry. I can't believe I have treated you and others in such a shabby fashion. I am a lost soul. By nature I'm a free spirit; I always was. I need to be free at all times. I am not free here, not free at all. As you know, we have everything we need here, but, my friend, we don't have freedom, and I don't have peace of mind. We are living in this kind of twilight world that is driving me to distraction. We are nothing more than the living dead. We are here for eternity and can do nothing about it. Maybe Hell would have been kinder to us.'

"'Oscar, this is your fate, and you must accept it,' I said. 'It is a waste of time fightin' and frettin' over it. You' been here a long time so I can't understand why you are now havin' difficulties.'

"'I tried to accept my situation,' he cried. 'I did successfully for decades but then one day I arose and had this overwhelming sense of foreboding, of the absolute meaninglessness of my existence. I didn't know what was happening to me. I looked out of the window, and everything was as meant to be. The sun was shining, and the Reservation looked as normal, yet there was something amiss, and I hadn't a clue what. For days, I drifted in and out of this state and thought that maybe it was part of our purgatorial existence and we all suffered in the same way. I was wrong, of course, as I couldn't see anyone else showing any of the symptoms that afflicted me. I should have talked about it with you or with Eugène, but I didn't want to make a fuss. I thought I would snap out of it, but alas, I did not, and I don't see any prospect of ever doing so.'

"'Man,' I cried. 'We were always here for you. I'm here now, and so are others – if you'll only allow us to do so.'

"'But what can anyone do?' he asked. 'I'm a lost cause.'

"'Listen here; you're not a lost cause. We've all had problems copin'. As you know, I've had some bad moments. Every soul has. Even Chopin,' I reminded him.

"He gave a wistful sigh. 'Oh yes, poor Frédéric. Who would have thought he could have had problems, that anything could have distressed him.

"'I remember that moment well, Oscar. It was to you he came for help. When that blackness descended on him, it was to you he poured out his heart,' I reminded him.

"'He did,' Oscar acknowledged. 'After weeks of shutting himself away and refusing to see anyone, he asked me if I would help take his Pleyel piano up on to the Heather Moor. I thought he had lost it. Why on earth did he want to have it up on the moor? He said he wanted to be alone on the bleakest part of the moor, with his music to try and find himself again. We called Jane, and she brought Can-Can and his cart, and somehow we managed to haul it up to the moor.'

188

"'Man, how could I forget,' I replied?

"He gave a wry smile and said, 'After we finally managed to get the piano to sit right he thanked us and asked us to leave. With us were David, Victor Noir, Signac and Jane, who was trying to pacify Can-Can who was distressed after pulling the piano over such rugged terrain.'"

"That was a surreal experience," Jane said, interrupting Morrison. "It was mid-afternoon when we left Chopin alone with his piano. We didn't leave, as he wanted us to do, instead, we hid in amongst the heather and the gullies. Oscar sat next to me, and we looked through the heather as Chopin sat by the piano, dressed in his grey cashmere suit and silk waistcoat. He slowly removed his white gloves and began to play."

"The tones of his masterpieces drifted across the moors and through the valleys," recalled David. "He played all of his works, playing each one better than ever before. His music had brought many to the Heather Moor, and they all crept through the heather to listen to him. Soon there were hundreds hidden from sight soaking up the genius of Chopin. Throughout the night, he played without a pause. When he did, it was to wipe away the tears. He was playing the demons out of his soul, the demons that were causing the blackness of his depression. Just before dawn, he ended with his 'Heroic Polonaise'. The tears fell as his fingers raced across the keyboard, bringing the music to a dramatic end. As the sun began to rise, he stood, replaced his gloves and walked across the Heather Moor towards the Musical Academy. If he had turned and looked back, he would have seen a mass of souls rising from the heather and following him home."

"He had rid himself of his demons," Jane said.

"That's what I reminded him of," Morrison added. "After recallin' Chopin's moors experience and the help he gave him, Oscar's spirits rose, and he seemed more optimistic. I looked at him and said, 'Chopin came out of his black period and so can you if you accept help, just as Chopin accepted yours.'

"'Yes, maybe you are right,' he replied.

"I thought this was the time to put our suggestion to him. He had accepted he had a problem and so I took a deep breath and waded in. 'Oscar, there is help out there for you.'

"'Is there?' he said in a low voice.

"'Yes. I've heard of a professor who can help you. Will you go and visit him? His name is Professor Jude.'

"'I've never heard of him. He must be a quack,' he said, raising his head.

"'He's not a quack.'

"'If he is not a quack, what is he?'

"'He's commonly known as the Divine Psychiatrist.'

"He sat upright and laughed. 'The what?'

"I knew he'd react like that. 'The Divine Psychiatrist – the very best,' I said.

"'He would have to be, with a name like that. I thought all psychiatrists were divine, so they like us to believe, and far from focused. There are all touched, of course, and certainly not by divinity,' he growled.

"'I know you don't think much of them, however, they have a proven record of success over the last century,' I said trying to convince him.

"'Have they now? Didn't succeed with you, did they?' he said with a grin.

"'If I hadn't kicked the bucket they may have. If I'd taken the kinda' advice you're now gettin', I may well have saved my life and enjoyed all those pleasures and experiences that I robbed myself of.'

"He became quiet again, and then, puttin' his arm around my shoulder, said, 'I suppose a session or two will do no harm.'

"'No, it won't,' I said relieved by his response. 'I'll make an appointment then?'

"'You're in a bit of a hurry, aren't you?' he cried.

"'Well, it's no good wastin' time.'

"'I suppose not,' he said. 'You know, you really are a decent fellow after all, not much of a poet, but a decent fellow all the same.'

The friends sighed with relief. None of them had thought Oscar would accept help, but to their surprise, he had. There was hope for him after all.

The Divine Psychiatrist

So it came to pass reader, that Oscar lowered himself to the level of a fruitcake, so he mistakenly thought, and made his first visit to the practice of Professor Jude, the Divine Psychiatrist, at 22 Loose End, on the lower side of Cloud Twenty-Three.

***

The professor, a genial kind of chap, welcomed him and told Oscar how much he had looked forward to their meeting and how much he admired his writing. Oscar was delighted.

"This is more like it," he thought. "At least the man has class and is cultured."

"Take a seat, Oscar. If you feel like stretching out at any time during this consultation, feel free. We aren't formal here."

Oscar sank on to a long couch covered with dark blue satin. Blue carpets covered the floor and the matching walls and curtains were set off by a delicate pink ceiling with its design of wild geese in flight. Oscar was wearing an avocado-green three-piece suit, a cream shirt, and red cravat and felt that he rather clashed with the professor's colour scheme.

"Relax," said the professor as he sat in his rocking chair, facing his patient. "Tell me, how long have you been at the Reservation?"

"Decades," Oscar replied as he looked around the room, admiring its opulence.

"How do you feel?"

"Out of place."

"I see. You feel out of place, do you?"

"Completely – I shouldn't be here. It's one big mistake."

"I see."

"A terrible, terrible mistake…"

"Then, where should you be?"

"I don't know. All I know is that I should not be here, but somewhere else, yes, I certainly feel out of place."

"Can you be more precise?"

"Indeed. Most of my fellow souls at the Reservation seems content with their situation and go about their business without much ado. For most of my time that is exactly what I did. I did it so well they made me a Trusted Soul of the Reservation. Lately, however, I have an irritation eating away within me that makes me feel out of place and ill at ease. I have a feeling of emptiness and there is something in my mind saying that I am not meant to be here."

"Are you saying this feeling has been with you throughout your stay here?"

"Not at all – for the first year or so I was confused, as are most new arrivals. I didn't know where I was, but after talking to Saint Peter, I realised that this was my lot, that the purging of my venial sins was almost impossible. I settled down to make the best of it. I became involved with the artistic life of the Reservation. I loved every moment of it. I gradually regained the writing skills that had deserted me in the years of my exile and once more found satisfaction in all I did. I wrote new plays and produced several evocative books. I even got round to writing my autobiography, something I had been denied the opportunity of doing in life. I had the pleasure of producing some of my plays and had a full and happy social life. I was at home in my Purgatory. That is how it was until last year when a peculiar and overpowering feeling came over me. I was at a loss to know what was causing it. Whatever it was, I just couldn't put my finger on it."

"I see. What were your symptoms?"

"Emptiness, like I was an empty shell of a human being. I was possessed by a feeling of abject worthlessness."

"How long did it last?"

"Oh, for a good while – it came and went and then it became a permanent condition. There was confusion in my mind. However hard I tried I couldn't snap myself out of it. The last time I felt like this was during the first year of my incarceration. God! That was a living hell. Now here I was, a spit away from Paradise, experiencing Hell in Purgatory. That is why I am here professor – to try to make some sense of it all. That is if there is any, which I doubt."

"What was your first impression when you arrived at the Reservation?"

"Oh! I didn't realise it was Purgatory. I thought I was in Paris at an art exhibition of Seurat's recent works. Seurat welcomed me here and informed me that he was to be my guide. I thought he meant that he was to show me around the exhibition, but he soon put me right. I was neither in Paris nor at his exhibition, but here in Purgatory. I was shocked, to say the least. I thought it was a bad joke."

"When it finally dawned on you where you were, what did you think?"

"Is this a dream? If this is Purgatory, why am I feeling like Hell?"

"So you were expecting Hell?"

"No, not at all, I foolishly thought my genius protected me from such a fate. Paradise was my only aim. I never gave Hell a thought. Come to think about it I didn't even give Purgatory a thought. I presumed Paradise was my only destination. To be truthful, I thought

Purgatory below me. I did have standards to live up to, and still do, even in this weird place."

"I'm sure you do. But weren't your standards too high?"

Our out-of-place genius was taken aback. "Dear me, professor, how can one's standards be too high?"

"Often, those with the highest standards don't see the reality of the life about them."

"What? You think I am not aware of my surroundings. That my standards are so high, that I am blinded to what is going on about me."

"Those who presume to have high standards often can't recognise their sins because of the rose-tinted glasses through which they look at life.

Oscar sprang up from his comfortable position. "Are you saying I viewed life through rose-tinted glasses?"

"No, that's not what I mean."

"Then, what are you saying?"

"That your standards were too high. You're taking for granted that you had a place in Paradise, and forgetting that perhaps you had to make amends for past deeds is an example. Your past was not exactly squeaky clean."

"What? You think I'm a sinner and not worthy enough for Paradise? Is that what you are trying to tell me?"

"It's not what I think that matters. Were you a sinner in your earthly life? Are you really worthy of Paradise? You tell me."

Oscar lay back on the couch and looked up at the ceiling, studying the wild geese intensely.

"You have got me there, professor. A sinner – I will have to think about that. It is a tough question."

"Take your time."

He did. He continued looking at the ceiling as the professor sat cross-legged, carefully filing his fingernails.

After a long contemplative silence, Oscar turned to his inquisitor. "Did you know, professor, that in Ireland everything is a sin," he murmured.

The professor raised his bushy eyebrows to this revelation. "Is that so? Tell me more," he said.

"Sin is an integral part of Irish life. It's ingrained in our psyche. Sin... dear me, where does one begin with sin and Caitlin ni Houlihan? She could not function without it. Did you know that some folks feel obliged to visit the confessional every week even though they have nothing to confess? If they hadn't sinned, venial or otherwise, they make one up just to be on the safe side. It is like hedging one's bets. Absolution in Ireland is like a tonic, it beats alcohol by a long shot. I don't know how many Hail Mary's one receives for a perceived sin, but I would say it is quite a few. Sin in Ireland is a kind of genetic necessity. The place would be lost without it, even for those who are not Catholic. That of course, makes me a sinner by birth. So yes, professor, I am a sinner, along with all my brethren – and a regular one at that."

"Ireland. Does she bother you?"

He roared with laughter. "No, not really, but I certainly bother her."

"In what way?"

"Dear me, professor, don't get me started otherwise there will be no stopping me. It would take a lifetime just to outline her paranoia about me."

"Paranoia – what paranoia do you refer to?"

Oscar again stared at the ceiling. "I would rather not say,' he muttered."

"There's no hurry. Tell me when you are ready." The professor put his nail file aside and cracked his knuckles. "Tell me, Oscar. What's the first word that springs to your mind?"

He stared at his inquisitor. "Is that a trick question?"

"…Not at all."

"Reading, the town of Reading," he responded.

"What about Reading? What does it mean to you?"

"Bars," Oscar sighed, "Nothing but bars."

"What kind of bars?"

"Prison bars."

"Go on."

"Bars of injustice; degradation and humiliation – bars, bars, bars, nothing but bars. There have been so many bars in my life."

He was in a sweat and sat upright, loosening his cravat. The professor offered him a glass of water, which he gulped down.

"Oh, how long and tedious the days were behind those prison bars; the nights, a never-ending nightmare. To be behind bars is soul-destroying, an affront to the dignity of life. It would have been bad enough being in prison for something I did, doing my time for my crime, as the saying goes, but to be there, as I was, innocent of any real crime was a nightmare – an injustice"

"You mention injustice. You believe there was an injustice done in your case, that you were unjustly convicted?"

"Yes – injustice of the worst kind – being incarcerated for acting as nature made one is the worst kind of injustice. Today, my dear professor, it would not have been an issue. There would have been no summons, no trial, no prison, no injustice committed against me, and no early demise in a run-down Parisian hotel. Today, in the modern era, I would have been what they call a personality – a star, maybe even a superstar, or, better still, a megastar. I would have been a guest on one of those television chat shows they have or even host one of my own such as *The Essence of Oscar Wilde,* or something like that. Now that would have been something. My personal life would be the subject of talk and speculation in what I believe they now call the Tabloid Press and in those egoistical magazines *Paris Match*, *O.K,* and *Hello!* I would probably be a favourite celebrity, and the nearest I would come to a court would be that of Queen Elizabeth, where I would entertain her with my witticisms and not incarcerated in Reading Gaol or any other of Her Majesty's prisons for just being myself. Ah, but unhappily I was born in a different era, professor, where being different was considered bizarre and peculiar and left one in danger being banged up. Yes, an injustice was done to me. That injustice remains. In my homeland, guilt is still embedded next to my name. The Irish memory of me is concerned with sin, and it is of little importance to them that I was – am – a writer of international repute. I am an embarrassment to them, the black sheep of the family."

"Oh," said the Professor. "Ireland really *bothers* you?"

"Don't get me wrong – I love my country dearly, but alas, she doesn't love me too much in return. I will be forever behind bars in the minds of many of my compatriots. They did erect a monument to me, would you believe? It wasn't erected in some open public place, and easily accessible to the general public. No, it was stuck in the corner of Merrion Square, opposite my old family home. It is surrounded by shrubbery and, yes, professor, behind bars, albeit not prison ones, but railings. The mental effect is the same. The sculpture itself is hideous and has me laid flat out on a rock with my legs apart. They have made me into a sexual icon. Well, I ask you, is it an insult or an honour?"

"It's not for me to say. What do you think?"

"An insult, a gross one at that – maybe it wasn't meant to be, but it is. It was supposed to be an honour, but it doesn't honour me in the least. It fails miserably to show my real worth. It fails miserably to show my real worth. It fails to show me for what I was, from my head to my toes, in every fibre of my being – an artist. In their wisdom, they decided to depict me as a sexual object and ignore my real and substantive worth. Even England, the country of my humiliation and downfall, decided in the end, to honour me – not as some sexual being, but as a man of words. They installed a window to my memory in Poet's Corner, in Westminster Abbey, alongside Dickens; Tennyson, Browning, and Keats. Now, that is an honour from a society that brought me down and sent me into exile – *They* didn't commemorate me for my sexuality but for my real and true worth, that of an artist."

"You feel bitter about the Dublin monument?"

Oscar gave another deep sigh. "No, not really, only sad, But times are changing. Perhaps they may change their opinion of me. I always keep faith with Caitlin Ni Houlihan, no matter what. Ireland today is a young and vibrant country that is throwing off its old prejudices and hang-ups that have blighted it for generations. The Irish are finally breaking free, seeing, and embracing the beauty of life. That is real freedom. Maybe the present generation, who are broader minded, may look on me as a true artist, not as a sex freak and finally welcome me back home. No, I don't feel bitter about the past, only sad, very, very sad."

"Why do you think you ended up here?"

"Why? Because I took a wrong turning…"

"Wrong turning – when?"

"After I left gaol – on my discharge, I was transferred from Reading Gaol to Pentonville. When I walked through those gates I should have turned and headed for the hills, instead I headed for Newhaven and France, Berneval and then on to Paris and my ultimate demise. Bad timing I was a master at it."

"What hills do you refer to?"

"Any. Which ones would not have mattered, as long as they were hills, the bigger the better! It was fresh air I longed for to clear the fog from my troubled mind. I needed space, acres of space. I needed peace, peace without the hassle of the press and that puritan crew who were forever pursuing me. Instead, I was persuaded by well-meaning friends to head for the Continent, to France or Italy – well-intended advice, no doubt, but disastrous as it turned out."

"You regret taking your friends' advice, however well-intended?"

"Indeed. I should have stayed and stood my ground, stood firm against my detractors and accepted the filth and venom flung at me and slowly rebuilt my life. I should have listened to my heart instead of to my friends, for it told me to stay. The heart is rarely wrong."

"You really think you could have rebuilt your life and returned to your literary work after the disasters of your trials, after being demonised as a deviant and turned into a social pariah? Did you really believe that?"

"Yes, I did. It would have been difficult, but with a helping hand and a smattering of luck, I believed I could have made it. When I left Pentonville, friends took me to the home of the Rev Stewart Headlam, who had met me along with More Adley, a dear and loyal friend, one of the best. It seems that plans were made for me, without a hill in sight. They were well aware of my reluctance to go into exile

196

but thought under the circumstances, it was the best, most sensible option, not that they had any other option lined up.

"At Rev Headlam's home, I was greeted by many of the friends I hadn't seen for two years, who came to wish me luck in my exile. I tried to take control of my destiny by writing to the Jesuits at Farm Street, seeking a six-month retreat and had the letter delivered that very morning. The thought of such a retreat and the sanctuary it offered raised my spirits, but they were soon dashed by the return of the messenger with a reply informing me that I was refused. The reply was short and curt. It was not prudent on their behalf to grant my request at such short notice, and perhaps I should reflect on matters and then apply again at a later date. Those gathered were quietly embarrassed and didn't know what to say. For the first time in their presence, I cried bitter tears of regret. I knew all was lost, and exile was to be my fate; that life for me would never be the same again, that my artistic life was coming to a sad and undignified end. Ah, professor, if only they had granted me that retreat, I know for sure I would have recovered my sensibilities and integrated myself back into society. If the Jesuits had taken time to consider my case instead of rigidly adhering to their rules, if they had shown some compassion as you would had expected from them, I would have been saved – that is for sure. In the peace and tranquillity of their surroundings, I would have cleared my mind of all the silt and garbage that had accumulated there. I would have restored my health and regained my mental equilibrium, but sadly, it was not to be."

"Your friends, those who organised your exile, do you believe they were taking the easiest option by sending you into exile?"

Oscar looked strangely at the professor. "My dear professor, these were my friends; these were people who out of loyalty had stood by me. By your tone, you seem to imply that they just wanted me out of the way, that I was some kind of embarrassment. This could not be further from the truth. These were decent and loyal people. When I went into exile, I was broke, bankrupt with hardly any possessions. They were to be my benefactors. They didn't have to support me, but they did. They took an extremely dangerous course when they financed me. You must remember that society at that period was set against me, and those willing to help risked the odium of that very narrow-minded and judgmental society. These were loyal friends that I was blessed to have."

"I admire your loyalty but did they have another option, other than that of exile?"

"That is a difficult one to answer. If there was another I am sure they would have given it serious consideration. Many thought I wouldn't have survived the hard labour of a prison régime and the grind of the treadmill; maybe it was my funeral they had secretly organised and my survival caught them on the hop."

"Do you really believe that?"

"No, not at all, although it did cross my mind after my first six months in prison, that the prison régime would kill me. I was so low, not just in spirit and mind, but physically that it did occur to me that perhaps I ought to organise my funeral. If I was thinking along these lines, there's a good chance that some of my friends were of the same mind. I am certain it must have crossed Constance's mind, although she never mentioned such concerns to me."

"As a matter of interest, where would you have arranged to be buried, in Ireland?"

Oscar smiled. "Not likely! If I wanted peace, I certainly wouldn't have found it there, I can guarantee you that."

"I hear there is a fine resting place at Glasnevin, in Dublin. Would that not have been a suitable place to rest your weary bones?"

He roared with laughter. "Are you serious? The place is full of chancers. There are some buried there that would have loved to have got their grubby hands around my neck and willingly throttled me. I will not name them as I always said I would never let their names ever pass my lips again. If Glasnevin has its own Purgatory Reservation, I don't think I would fancy it."

"There are some good souls there... Parnell, Daniel O'Connell."

"Yes, I will grant you that, but there're too many that are not so good, some who hated the very thought of me or my kind."

"Your kind..."

"You know what I mean."

The professor looked hard at his client and thought he wouldn't challenge him about "his kind" quite yet. There was time enough.

"So where would you have liked to have been buried?"

"Kensal Green in North London."

"Why, Kensal Green?"

"That is where my dear mother Jane is buried. Yes, if I were to have died in prison, it is with her I would have laid my weary bones, not with that shower at Glasnevin."

"When told you would not survive your illness in Paris, did you indicate where you preferred to be buried?"

"Oh, I was never aware that I could die from my illness. I never gave it a thought. I was so delirious. I was thinking and talking nonsense. I have a vague memory of dispatching Robbie off to Père Lachaise to reserve me a spot but I am sure I said it in jest. He was well used to my black humour. I always thought I would recover. If I not, I knew that whatever had to be done would be done by the capable hands of Robbie Ross. He would have done what he thought was my wishes. I always trusted him to do what was right. He never failed me as a friend and, as history has shown, he was loyal to the end – loyal to my memory, to my art, to Constance and our two boys. The best friend a soul could ever wish for."

"You're a great believer in loyalty… in friendship."

"Indeed. I pride myself on my loyalty to my friends. It is what friendship is all about – it is the cement that binds it together. It is what Robbie had in abundance. He organised my life after my release; took care of my finances; organised the funeral, or I should say, two funerals – the first at Bagneux and then the transfer to Père Lachaise. Did you know, he even got into the grave at Bagneux and helped dig me out? That, professor, is real and true friendship. After my demise, he worked hard to get my estate out of bankruptcy and restored the copyright of my plays to give to my boys. He had my works published again and supervised the erection of my tomb at Père Lachaise. Friendship and loyalty – I was blessed to have had them in abundance in Robbie Ross."

"What did you think about ending up at Père Lachaise?"

"What a better place is there? Robbie was well aware of my love of Paris, so he would have had no difficulty in making his decision. I had never discussed this kind of thing with him, so all decisions were his and whatever he decided would have always been in the best interest of Constance, the boys, and my memory. Robbie was the essence of friendship."

Alternative Strategy

Sophie called a meeting at her home at which Henry Torrès would outline his strategy. All the Hugo's of Père Lachaise were there including Sophie's sons, Hugo junior and Charles, along with most of Oscar's friends and associates, including Marie, Chopin, Jane, Delacroix, Musset, Balzac, Colette, Ingres, Sarah, Morrison and, to the surprise of all, Seurat. Although they were optimistic they would find a way to save him, they all agreed that professional help was a necessary first step. They did, however, think it fitting to have an alternative strategy, if they could find one, in the event that Torrès' legal strategy failed.

Sophie served rhubarb tart and clotted cream. As they settled down to enjoy their refreshments, she wasted no time in getting down to the purpose of the gathering. She got their attention by ringing a silver bell she kept on her writing table.

"Let's get down to business," she announced. "What happens if Torrès fails in his task? What alternative strategy do we have?"

"Is there any alternative?" Jane asked as Sophie poured her tea.

"I can't think of one at the moment, but I'm sure there must be. After all, there is always an alternative to whatever we do in life. Well, in general there is."

"I wouldn't bank on it," added Édith. "I can think of a few occasions in my life when there was no alternative strategy open to me and suffered dearly for it. I can't even think of what we can do for him if Torrès' efforts are in vain, apart from giving Oscar love and understanding, and even that may not be enough to save him."

"You could well be right, Édith, but that doesn't answer the question of what we do if our first efforts aren't successful and Torrès is unable to put his legal approach into operation."

"Very little," sighed Balzac as he licked clotted cream from his fingers and at the same time held out his cup to Sophie. "The truth is we don't have an alternative strategy. I don't think there is one. Come, Sophie, you're a wizard at solving problems, so what happens if Torrès' efforts go pear-shaped?"

"We'll think of something. I must say, though, I do have faith that Torrès will succeed. There is no reason why he shouldn't. I do think we should keep faith with him and his strategy, whatever it may be. He is very good at all this legal stuff. He should be here soon, and then he will outline what procedures are open to us. The fact that Oscar has agreed to see Professor Jude makes it possible to proceed."

"That's all very well, but what happens if Torrès has it wrong? What can be done?" asked Chopin.

"Since Jim let Oscar know that we know of his problem, even if Torrès fails, he could very well confide in us more and in the process, he can be healed."

"That sounds wonderful, Marie, but highly unlikely," replied Seurat. "We are being naive in believing he can cure himself, that by some wonderful intervention he will be cured of his ills. Let's be realistic, Oscar's mentally ill and needs proper psychiatric care, love and attention. All we can do is support him. Let's see how he is after his sessions with the professor."

There was a sharp intake of breath from the gathering. Balzac nearly choked on his tart and Chopin almost fainted. Morrison was transfixed.

They all turned and looked at Seurat in disbelief. Was he really talking compassionately about Oscar? Did he really utter the word "*love*"? Did he really have a good word to say about him?

"Welcome aboard, Seurat, my dear man," said a surprised Musset. "Glad to see you're back on side."

The group cheered, raising their cups in celebration, relieved that Seurat's unseemly behaviour was now at an end.

"Well! I can't hold a grudge forever, can I?"

"No!" they cried in harmony. Seurat was back in the fold. He was relieved to have ended his spat with Oscar and the clearing of the air, lifted a burden from his shoulders.

"This psychiatric help – do you think it could be a success on its own? Maybe Torrès' intervention may not be needed?" Jane asked Seurat.

"Can't see why not, seeing that we don't know what Torrès' strategy is yet, we should look at the positive side of the treatment Oscar's receiving now. After all, it is a tried and tested science. Let's hope it's a success."

"I'm confused. What kind of legal move can resolve Oscar's sufferin'?"

"You're confused, Jim?" Ingres said. "Aren't we all? Can't see what legality has to do with his illness. I would have thought if he can't be cured his only destination is Cloud Eighty-Seven."

They looked at each other in despair at the thought of this. Suddenly there was a sharp rap at the door.

"That must be Henri now," cried Sophie, rushing to answer the door.

"About time too – I thought he had forgotten."

"Don't be silly, Eugène," Sophie exclaimed. "There's no soul more reliable that Henry Torrès. After all, he is a lawyer." She opened the door, and there stood Torrès, immaculately turned out as usual in a dapper grey pin-striped three-piece suit with a shirt of delicate pink and dark blue tie.

"Come in, Henry. So glad to see you," Sophie said as she shook his hand, kissing him on both cheeks. "This way – the committee has just been debating an alternative strategy in case your plan fails."

"Fails!" he gasped. "Let's not be negative before we have even begun. I intend to succeed. If I don't, it won't be for the lack of trying."

Sophie introduced the legal bigwig to her guests. He stood in front of the marble fireplace with his hands clasped behind him, rocking on the balls of his feet.

"It's like this," he said in a low but firm voice. "What I have to say to you may sound far-fetched and far from creditable, but I can assure you that it is the only real possibility of saving the soul of Oscar Wilde.

"It may have crossed your minds that perhaps the psychiatric help he's receiving may be enough to save him. I'm sorry to say this may not be so. It could be, but don't put too much faith in it."

"So, you believe he can be rescued?"

"Certainly, Jane, but I must remind you that it is a long shot, a very long shot indeed. This is how I believe it can be done."

He had the group's attention and, opening his briefcase, took out a document and waved it at his attentive audience. "Have any of you heard of the Michelangelo Syndrome?"

They all looked at each other

"The what?" Musset asked.

"The Michelangelo Syndrome," Torrès repeated. The friends looked at each other for inspiration. None was forthcoming. He had lost them.

"You've got us there, Torrès. What is this to do with Oscar?" enquired Jane.

"Perhaps nothing at all, but there again, if it does, then there is hope of rescuing him – not just from his present malaise but from Purgatory itself."

"Sorry, Torrès, you ain't makin' any sense – no soul leaves Purgatory," Morrison reminded him.

"I'm sorry, Jim. I had better explain. Every soul at the Reservation accepts their fate and makes the best of it. Some try to purge their sins, most don't bother, for they know the near-impossibility of doing so. What we have here is a pretty well-regulated existence that sits well with most of us. However, there are souls who suffer trauma because of their inability to come to terms with their new environment. Most of these – poor Maria Callas, for instance – sadly end up on Cloud Eighty-Seven and there is a possibility that

202

Oscar may also become a tenant there if we are unsuccessful." Torrès briefly paused and gazed around the room. "Then there are those rare souls who show symptoms that put them in a special category," he continued. "Those symptoms are extremely rare and known only to the administrators of Paradise and if they are confirmed the sufferers become known as Special Souls – possible sufferers of what is called the Michelangelo Syndrome and therefore they qualify for consideration by the Divine Council for admittance to Paradise."

"Are you serious? Sounds odd to me," Jane said amidst riotous laughter from the friends, who were under the impression that Torrès was there to disclose a serious plan of action.

"Why don't we know what the symptoms are? Why the big secret?" asked Édith.

"As I read it," continued Torrès. "They are secret because of the chance of some souls trying it on to get into Paradise by feigning the symptoms. You know what some souls are like; they try their hand at anything. But if an application is submitted the key to it is a psychiatric report, which can only be given by Professor Jude. It would be near impossible to pull one over him."

"Ah! This is weird. No soul ever leaves here for Paradise," Sarah reminded them. "This sounds like more legal mumbo jumbo."

"Oh, I can assure, it's far from it," he replied.

"You think Oscar is suffering from this syndrome. What's it called again?" enquired Jane.

"The Michelangelo Syndrome," replied Torrès.

"Sounds peculiar to me," cried Delacroix. "It has to be suspect if it is named after an artist."

Torrès knew he would have trouble convincing them. "Yes, Oscar could be suffering from it. If he isn't and Jude fails to control Oscar's symptoms, I'm afraid he will be transferred to Cloud Eighty-Seven. It's as simple as that."

The gathering looked around at each other in despair at the thought of losing Oscar to Cloud Eighty-Seven and all that entailed.

"Are you sure of this?"

"Yes, Jane. This is all down to Jude's report and the wisdom of the Divine Council."

"Divine Council!" Balzac chuckled. "There's no such thing, just as there's no Paradise, Hell or Purgatory."

"Ah, Honoré, don't start on one of your atheistic rants. This is neither the time nor place for it," pleaded Sophie.

"How can there be anything divine in this sphere – sounds insane to me. This Divine Council is the kind of thing Oscar would dream up, like his Lip Psychology."

"I agree, Colette," replied Torrès. "It does sound insane, but I can assure you that such a council exists. It exists between the spheres, between Purgatory and Paradise. It's the very same council that drew up the Divine Code governing us."

The group of friends gave a collective gasp.

"How can it exist between Purgatory and Paradise? And where, pray, does it sit, this invisible Divine Council?" asked a doubting Balzac.

"You've got me there," replied Torrès. "That's another of the many secrets of the Reservation. All I can say is that it does exist."

"So, let's get this straight. You are saying he could be suffering from a syndrome whose symptoms are unknown to us but known only to a mysterious council, that we must put faith in that council, which no soul has seen or knows who its members are – sounds a bit dicey to me. Who sits on this Divine Council, if you don't mind me asking?"

"I can understand your cynicism, Honoré. It takes some believing, as do many things that surround us. We have to accept that there are many unexplained things here. That's the nature of the place. As for the members of the council, my sources indicate that it is made up by the entire conclave of saints."

Balzac doubled up with laughter. Musset tried to stifle his laughter. Sarah was having one of her giggling spasms, her shoulders shaking out of control. The rest looked on in amusement.

"There are no such things as saints," Balzac told Torrès irritably. "They are a figment of the imagination of the deluded masses – saints – poppycock!"

"I beg your pardon," cried a shocked Édith. "Of course there are saints. I have a lifelong devotion to Saint Thérèse de Lisieux. She has been my guiding light throughout my life, throughout all my troubles and sorrows. She is real."

"Rubbish. Saints are man-made, and there's nothing divine about them," Balzac insisted. "If there is a council dictating matters it has nothing to do with saints or divinity."

"Let's not argue over it. Let's hear Torrès out," Sophie said, trying to soothe matters.

"We have to set up a committee which must endorse the application that I have drawn up and that I will submit to the Facilitator at the Reservation Central Office. You can decide between yourselves who the chair and members will be. We also have to submit this petition," he said, waving it at them, "and as many testimonials as possible in support of the application."

"What kind of testimonials?" Marie asked.

"Well, statements from those who know or have any association with Oscar, giving their opinion of him. They are essential in supporting the application in the same way as the psychiatrist's report is. Of course, those who disagree with this approach and don't support Oscar has the right to submit their objections and give their reasons."

"Objections?" cried Édith. "Who would object to Oscar being rescued?"

"You'd be surprised. Just as on earth, he has detractors here. Once this application is lodged, the detractors can file their counterclaim or simply state their objections. As I said, this is not going to be easy."

"If he has detractors, it will be a waste of time even trying," Édith said despairingly.

"No, Édith. You are wrong. The fact that objections are submitted does not necessarily mean they will be upheld or the case will be lost. All objections will be scrutinised to see if they are sincere in their application or if they are just vexatious. There is the possibility that an objection may be upheld, but that's a chance we must take. This is the only chance we have of helping him. All I am doing is outlining to you the legal necessities of this procedure. You may think this is peculiar, but it is all we have. I suggest you set up the committee and send the word about that those willing to give testimonials must do so as soon as possible and without Oscar getting wind of it."

Jane looked around at her companions. "Well, I'm for it," she said. "If there's no other option, then let's go with it."

"All right," said Balzac. "It sounds crazy, but this is a crazy place anyway, so why not try a crazy thing like this? We've nothing to lose."

"Wait a moment," cried Marie. "What if this fails, what then? What about this alternative strategy we were supposed to dream up?"

Torrès gave a gentle cough. "My dear... there isn't one."

"What are you thinking?" Professor Jude asked Oscar as he settled down for his second session.

"Constance."

"Indeed – your wife?"

"Yes. Dear Constance. She was an angel. She was the divine soul I treated like a leper, as though she were a second-class citizen. How I regret it. With Constance, I was always a moral coward. What a sad case I was. I will never forgive myself for what I did to such a beautiful soul, what I put her and the children through by my stupid behaviour. God, I was such a coward, the ultimate moral coward."

"A moral coward. In what way?"

"In many ways. I loved her, of that there is no doubt, but eating away at me was a new love that I couldn't resist. I should have resisted, but I couldn't. I was weak, so very weak, and I led Constance on in the most disgraceful fashion. I lied to her – I violated her trust. I should have told her how I felt, for she would have tried to understand, but instead, I took the coward's way and deceived her. I didn't have the courage to tell her of that other passion in my life, the passion that was a cancer spreading its tentacles in all directions. The more I recollect, the guiltier I feel. I left her alone to cope with the children, and, later the notoriety I brought down on them.

"I remember, not long after I had arrived here, I was looking down over Père Lachaise and thought I had seen her standing at my tomb. Was it her spirit I was seeing, was I hallucinating, was I going mad? She looked so frail and there was sadness etched into her beautiful face. She kissed my tomb but left no lipstick trace. She laid a violet on its lintel, then, turning, slowly walked away. I was never to see her again."

He sat on the couch, nervously wringing his hands as tears rolled down his cheeks. The professor left him to his thoughts, which were clearly disturbing him.

"You often think of her?" the professor asked after a decent pause.

"Oh yes, all of the time," he replied, wiping his eyes with the back of his hands. "When I do, it's mostly the good times that stir my memory. I see her, as she was when we first met – tall, beautiful and serene, with mesmerising dark blue eyes and exquisite brown hair. She was a real beauty. Not many men would saunter past her without a glance. How proud I was when I married her. I see her as she was when she was carrying Cyril, our first son; she seemed even more beautiful then. He was a wanted child, as was Vyvyan. I see her in a London park, playing happily with the boys, or us enjoying each other's company at our holiday retreat in Norfolk. I see her being the perfect hostess at a dinner party we were hosting and I see her quietly reading. I see her in all her glory, arriving at a Society gathering. I can see her making her entrance, turning every male head and causing every woman to look at her in awe and envy.

"She was a dedicated mother and a devoted wife. I didn't deserve her. She put up with my appalling behaviour in a dignified way, and it shames me to recall how indifferent I was to her – to her pain, her suffering and her loneliness. Hindsight has shown to me that my behaviour was not just simply appalling, but also obnoxious and crude and way beyond what one could call decent.

"When she died, I didn't even attend her funeral. Can you imagine that? I was so wrapped up in self-pity, there was no room for sympathy or respect for the woman I loved and who loved me so much – the devoted mother of my children – that most beautiful of souls. What a shit I was. I didn't deserve her love or loyalty. Of all of my misdeeds, of which there were many, my abuse of her haunts me and causes me the most pain and suffering. I will suffer for eternity for what I did to her. I think of her every day and wonder what might have been if I hadn't been such an irresponsible fool.

"As I lay shivering on my prison bed, I thought of her. My first thought in the morning was of her; the last thought before I drifted into sleep was of her. When I walked the treadmill, it was the thought of her that sustained me. When the lights went out, I saw her face in the darkness of my dank cell. I would see her forgiving eyes and feel her mopping my brow, assuring me that all would be well.

"A year after her death, I was shamed into visiting her resting place in Genoa, where she had died after an unsuccessful operation on her spine. As I stood there, I felt my heartbreaking. All of those regrets, my misdeeds and what might have been swirled about me and mingled with my bitter tears of regret. In my shame and despair, I fell to my knees, asking for her forgiveness. I had never felt as low as I did that crisp sunny afternoon. She was the light of my life, and as I looked up at the cross on her grave, I saw that light flicker and die. Although I may have died of cerebral meningitis in that seedy Parisian hotel, it was there, before the grave of that innocent soul, that my time on earth was marked. There she was, far away from home, in a land not her own. 'No! She shouldn't be here,' I cried. 'If only I hadn't been such a fool, she would not be here but at home with me and the children.'

"What a damned fool I have been. If only I hadn't been so vain and reckless, I would probably still be alive, surrounded by a loving family and at the height of my literary career. Ah, but there was that other love, or what I thought was love, eating and gnawing away, devouring and dragging me down to my doom – it was an abscess on

207

my soul that I was unable to shift. It could not have been love, for love would not have been so vindictive, so cruel, so *low*."

"This other love, in hindsight, was it a mistake?"

"Mistake! True love can never be a mistake. However, this was not true love as I soon discovered to my cost. Yes! It was a mistake, the biggest mistake of my life. As for being love, it was nothing more than self-indulgence, an illusion, a farce, a bite from the hedonistic apple – or, to put it simply, it was just sex – a disaster!"

"Did you understand the moral implication of your situation?"

"No, I was blinded by emotion, by desire, blinded by the thrill of it all. It was only as I languished in prison and with time to think that I realised what a mess I was. How could I love Constance, that beautiful and sensitive soul, and be deeply in love with another? How could I have treated her so cruelly by loving not just another woman, which would be cruel enough, but a man? The more I thought about it, the grosser it became. She even visited me in that most dehumanising of places, Reading Gaol, to tell me about my beloved mother's death. Once released from prison, Constance even gave me an allowance to enable me to live during my exile abroad. After being so cruelly treated, humiliated and embarrassed, she forgave me and was more concerned for my well-being than about my treatment of her. That takes a special kind of woman, and she was certainly that. She could have turned her back on me, left me to rot in my infamy, but no, she was there for me when I was on my knees, at my lowest ebb. Oh! That confounded man. What a fool I was not to have seen through him and to imagine the disaster that was to befall me. What a fool I was. What a stupid, stupid, irresponsible fool."

"That man? You mean, Lord Alfred Douglas?"

Oscar again became silent and stared at the ceiling. "Yes…that man," he said with a deep sigh. "He was like a drug to me. I knew he was bad, even evil, but I could not resist him. He had such a hold on me I couldn't see the world about me; I was transfixed by him. Pathetic, is it not? A grown man transfixed by a brute of a youth."

"Tell me, how do you feel about him now?"

"Indifferent. I try not to dwell on him, but he has a habit of coming back to haunt me. I feel nothing for him now. I have felt nothing for him since I lay dying in Paris. The love I thought I had for Bosie was just an infatuation, a passion, a blinding obsession that was to bring about my downfall and hasten the end of my life – a high price to pay for an error of judgment."

"Error of judgment – have you made many errors of judgement?"

Oscar burst out laughing. He sat up, took a sip of water, and smiled. "Oh yes, professor, many, too many to mention, but nothing on this scale. Bosie was the great error of my life. There were many more, but none quite like him."

"Give me an example."

"The Marquess of Queensbury," Oscar snapped. "*He* was an error of judgment if there ever was one." He sank back into the couch and loosened his cravat. "The man was vulgar. He had breeding and class but was a sad excuse of a human being who used his title to give him a spurious air of respectability. He was a shiver looking for a spine to climb. Unfortunately, he found mine and crippled me - physically, financially and artistically. He swaggered about London, running me down in the most outrageous manner. He slandered me at every opportunity. Some say he only acted the way he did because of my friendship with Bosie, his spoilt and manipulative son. My biggest error was in allowing him to get under my skin. I should have ignored him or simply turned my wit on him. Instead, I gave in to the intolerable pressure Bosie was applying on me to sue his father. By doing so I set in motion the wheels of justice that would bring me down and crush me. I headed for the legal process and ignominy, defeat and social castration. What a damned fool I was. Yes, taking on the Scarlet Marquess was a mighty, mighty error of judgment."

"Do you hate him?"

Oscar smiled. "Hate – that is the devil's work, professor. Hatred serves no useful purpose. No, I do not hate him. I disliked him immeasurably, but hate – I will leave that to others. I'm incapable of such a negative emotion."

"Many would say you have every right to hate him."

"Some may, some may not, but I don't care. It's how *I* feel that matters."

"Indeed? What about forgiveness, are you capable of forgiveness?"

"Surely professor, we are all capable of it."

"Even of your worst enemy?"

"Enemy – the only enemies I have are my shadow and those skeletons that rattle around in the attic of my mind. Apart from them, there is nobody I can think of."

"Not even the Marquess of Queensbury?"

"Not even the Marquess?"

"You do surprise me."

"He believed me to be his enemy, but I was not his. To me, he was simply a sad and brutal aristocrat with a mighty chip on his shoulder. He was his own worst enemy, not mine."

"Do you forgive him?"

"Certainly."

"That's very Christian of you."

"Why be so surprised, after all, it is our Christian duty to forgive, is it not, especially the likes of Queensbury. Although I disliked the man, I forgave him. If I had not, what kind of Christian would I have been? Not to have done so would have made me as brutish as him and put me in the sewer of life with him."

"He set out to ruin you – to ruin your art, your craft, your character and your standing in society – and you say he was no enemy of yours and that you have no hatred towards him? Can this really be so? "

Oscar quickly sat up. "Yes, it is so," he cried. "He certainly ruined me, that is true, but is that a reason to hate him?"

"You're must be a very tolerant man."

"I am! He sharply replied. "Yes, he tried to ruin my art, again is that a just reason to hate him? No, I do not think so. Yes, he has ruined my character without doubt and did so with relish, but is *that* just reason to hate him? No, I don't think so. Yes, he did ruin my standing in society and made a good job of it to boot, but professor, is that a justifiable reason to hate him? I don't think so. Do you?"

"It is not for me to say."

"So you keep saying."

"Oscar, I'm here to listen, not to give opinions."

"I may not have hated him, but I intensely disliked him. I disliked him, and all his kind stands for."

"An ordinary mortal would say you have just cause for doing so. Most would have difficulties *not* to hate such an antagonist."

"There you have it, professor. I am no ordinary mortal. I am Oscar Wilde, a gifted soul who lost his way. I have heard throughout my life that I am gifted and special and far from the ordinary."

"You really think you're something special?"

"Don't we all?"

"Why are you so special?"

"You had better ask God that. He gave me my gifts – the gifts that others say are so special that others say have a touch of genius about them. Best to ask Him, He is the one with all the answers, not me."

"Why do you say that?"

"Why? Because He created me, did He not?"

"Did He?"

Oscar sat upright and looked at the professor. "Of course He did. Aren't we all created by Him, in His image?"

"Are you sure you're God's creation?"

"Jesus! That is a crazy question. Are you on something?"

"No! It is far from crazy. How do you know there's a God?"

"I just do."

"What evidence do you have?"

"Evidence!" Oscar sank back on to the couch and sighed. "You sound like a barrister. I thought you said there would be no trick questions."

"I did."

"Then what do you mean, asking if is there is a God? Of course, there is a God."

"How do you know?"

"I just do. I cannot prove any divine presence – nobody can. I do not know who or what God is, what He or She or It looks like. All I know and feel is that God is all around us, in us and about us. I feel His presence. Is that not enough? I believe in God. I have no doubts."

"Evidence, Oscar, what evidence do you have?"

"I don't need evidence. There is a God. That is it. I believe there is a God and I do not need evidence. Why do you have to have evidence to believe in something?"

"You don't, but it does help. You've never doubted your faith?"

"Ah, now, that's a different matter altogether. I wouldn't be human if I had not."

"Does any instance spring to mind?"

"Yes," he replied, sitting up again. "Many a time as I sat in my prison cell, I would stare at those filthy walls and wonder if there really was a God, if there really was a compassionate and forgiving God as we had been taught to believe. I would wonder why, if that was the case, He had given me such talents but then let me suffer the degradation and ignominy of my imprisonment. Why, why did He let me suffer when my only sin was being myself, being what He had made me? Why did He desert me in my hour of need? Why did He deny my two innocent children the love of their father who adored them? On those bare and filthy walls, I would see visions of the streets of London and the downtrodden, the starving young, begging for charity from an uncaring society. I'd wonder, 'Where is God? Where is the loving and caring God who sent His Son to suffer and die for us, who watched over us with love? Where is He?

"I would see the judiciary lording it over the desperate from their perch in the courts, condemning them to inhuman punishments for the most minor offences, sentencing men and women to hang by the neck and doing so in the name of our loving God, and asking that same God to have mercy on their souls. Oh yes, at times I did question the existence of God. I would stare at those walls and think to myself. If there's a God, why does He always let us down when we're in dire straits."

"Does He?"

"Yes! He never fails. But I'm not angry with Him for long. I quickly forget my negative thoughts. It is we humans that are flawed, not God, although why He made us flawed, His so-called masterpiece of creation is beyond me. At times, I doubted His existence, but it was a temporary state of mind. I would often think that if He did exist, He was some comedian. I'd say the best."

"A comedian!!" said the startled professor.

"Yes, He has to be the Original Comedian, the original stand-up comic. Indeed, the Supreme Comedian."

The professor stood up and walked around the couch, scratching his head, bemused by his patient's description of God.

"In what way, in what possible way is God a *comedian*?"

"You don't know!"

"I'm afraid I don't," replied the professor.

"Well, look at the Human Condition to start with – that's some comedy act. You think about it. We are born in a bizarre and often farcical fashion, after being conceived in an even more hilarious way. This, of course, is God's Great Design, that we mate and give birth in this comical fashion to keep his show on the road. And what a show – a never-ending vaudeville experience. He got it right with the birds, arriving in neat little cosy shells, but us, well; He surpassed Himself when it came to us humans. Look at the way we procreate. Look at the process – it is hilarious. Well, it is for the male species with the woman having to suffer for our pleasure. It is hard to keep a straight face when you think of human reproduction and the process of making love. I can't. I become hysterical just thinking about it."

"You seem *easily* entertained."

"Oh, I am. Let me continue. When we are born we are slapped across the arse to let us know what life has in store. As babies we are cute and adorable, the apple of the eye of our delighted parents," he continued. "There we are, soft and delicate in the care of a couple who, chances are, have no training whatsoever for the task ahead. They plod along on a wing and a prayer, hoping they are doing the right thing. It is a kind of lottery for the child concerned. If you are lucky, you may be born to a couple with a natural parenting flair. If you are luckier still, you may turn out to be an agreeable, lovable, well-balanced individual. If you are not so lucky, you could be landed with an unstable, irresponsible and useless couple who succeed in giving you a complex for life, leaving you unbalanced, confused and a social outcast. Then you end up asking yourself those timeless questions: What is it all about? What is the purpose of life? And there are no answers.

"We grow into infancy and experience the wonders about us, the innocence of it all, the wonder of the discovery of ourselves and our surroundings. Perhaps it is the best time of our life. But, before we know it, the Supreme Comedian cracks his best joke of all. He reveals to us that hilarious and addictive fascination, the opposite sex. Then, we have to try to discover what it is about the opposite sex that is so fascinating, that sends the blood rushing through our veins and keeps our minds so preoccupied that we think of it every minute of the day and dream of it at night. When we finally discover the secret, we just cannot get enough of it - if we are lucky enough to get it. If we do, we feel invincible and ready to take on the world. If we are one of the unlucky ones who cannot get it, you go about demented, wondering why spending every waking moment trying to find out how to get it. It is terribly confusing when it comes to sex. Then, before we know it, we discover that crazy thing called love, designed to confuse us utterly. It quickly becomes clear that love and sex are entirely different things. Before we know it, we are in love, and the battle for supremacy begins.

"Once that's settled, we marry or set up home with the one we think we love and then the fun begins. We have children, which to some is a trauma in itself. We raise them as best we can, and the reward for this effort comes years later when they tell us that we botched the job and that they were deprived or neglected children who were unfortunate to have such dull or prudish parents.

"Soon we are middle-aged, and the children are married, and the crazy cycle begins all over again. We delude ourselves into believing we can relax for the rest of our lives, enjoy the pleasures of life, and then, bang, we're dead. Some punch line from the Supreme Comedian.

"That, to me, professor, is comedy at its best, good, solid, black comedy. Only the Supreme Comedian could have dreamt up such a scenario and got away with it."

"Well, if you put it that way, maybe. But if you are a believer, as you say you are and believe in the afterlife, then the life you describe as a comedy act is surely the first step to Paradise."

"Maybe – perhaps life is the first act of a comedy written, directed and produced by God; the second act, death, written, directed and produced by Satan. Maybe it is one of those comedy shows we have to sit through to stand a chance of seeing Paradise or avoiding Hell."

"You really think life is a comedy then?"

"Well, just look around our earthly abode. You must admit, it does have its funny side."

The professor looked at Oscar, sighed, cracked his knuckles and sprang to his feet. "Well, that's it for today, Oscar. It has been very interesting, very illuminating. I would like you to stay at our clinic for

213

a week or so, if you are willing, that is. There is no pressure. You don't have to decide yet. Go home and think about it and let me know tomorrow, OK?"

Oscar stood up, retied his cravat and smoothed out his coat. "Clinic, what clinic is that?"

"Clinic Dymphna."

"Fancy name – what kind is it, it sounds kinky?"

"Oh, it's far from that; just a place to relax and gather your thoughts."

"You think it would be of some benefit, professor?"

"Yes, I believe it would; again, no pressure now. It's entirely up to you. Sleep on it."

"I'll do just that. Good day."

Balzac, a clay pipe dangling from his mouth, leant against the bar of the Café Oueurde, deep in thought. At the far end of the bar sat Musset, gazing at his reflection in the ornate mirror that hung behind the zing-topped counter in this intellectual waterhole as he sipped a lukewarm coffee. Maurice, the café owner was busy polishing the bar that he was obsessed with keeping gleaming.

"Is it going to work?" asked Musset.

"What?"

"The treatment our distracted friend is undergoing with the therapist up on Cuckoo Ridge.

Ingres, sitting next to Musset laughed. "I doubt it. Miracles simply don't happen in this kind of domain and our dear friend is in dire need of one. If any soul can perform a miracle, it's the Divine Psychiatrist. However, as miracles don't happen, he doesn't stand a chance."

"Divine Psychiatrist – you are dreaming again, Ingres. There is no such thing as divinity, never mind a Divine Psychiatrist. It's just a fancy name for a shrink, that's all it is. There is no hope of Torrès' strategy ever working, never was. Oscar's off with the fairies, and there is no miracle cure, I'm afraid."

André Gill, leaning over the billiard table with his cue at the ready, looked over at Balzac. "Now, now, Honoré, there's no need for that kind of talk. Torrès says there's a chance and, even if it's the smallest of ones, it's worth taking and that's precisely what Oscar's doing up at the clinic. Good on him for going through with it."

"I have a dread that he may end up on Cloud Eighty-Seven. It may be known as the place for the restoration of the soul, but the reality is, no soul ever gets out of the place. Imagine him not frequenting this place again. It wouldn't be the same without him."

"You're worrying too much, Alfred," Ingres said as he took a seat at the bar. "There's no chance of him ending up there. He is far from a hopeless case. I'd say his condition is only temporary and after a few weeks at the clinic he'll be back to his normal self."

Chopin, sitting at the piano, stopped playing after hearing Ingres' remarks and said, "I just can't get out of my mind the revelations about his behaviour. How did we not notice? I know my experience with him was odd, but I thought it was a one-off incident. I can't believe I dismissed it as I did. How come we were so blind?" he sighed ruefully.

"I wouldn't worry too much about it, Frédéric. We all did the same," sighed Ingres.

The café door opened.

"Hi, Yves," Balzac said as Yves Montand walked over to the bar, taking his seat between Balzac and Musset. He looked downcast.

"What is it? You look glum," asked Balzac.

"It's this Michelangelo thing – the syndrome Torrès says Oscar might be suffering from."

"Oh, that," laughed Balzac, "it sounds like a load of drivel to me. I might be inclined to believe in it if we knew what the symptoms were but this notion that secret council members are the only ones who know them is too much to take."

"That's exactly what I was thinking. The more I ponder it, the more unbelievable it sounds. I fear Torrès is having us on. He is a lawyer, after all."

"That's unfair, Yves," remarked Ingres. "He was his country's finest legal eagle. His credentials are impeccable."

"I can see you've had little dealing with the legal profession, my friend. If you had, you would give lawyers the time of day. The word parasite springs to mind when I hear the word lawyer."

"I must say, Honoré, you're being rather unfair to the legal profession. They can't all be that bad, surely," replied Ingres.

"They can and are. The best thing to do with any legal eagle is to clip their wings."

"Well. I disagree with you. All the dealings I've had with lawyers were carried out in an efficient and honest way. I'm sure Torrès will behave correctly. You are too much of a cynic Honoré."

Chopin, as he resumed playing, looked over at his pals. "I'm with Honoré on this one," he said. "I've had umpteen dealings with lawyers, and they were all disreputable. You would never believe how much I lost because of their ineptitude. They may very well appear to be caring and compassionate souls, but it doesn't take too long for their true colours to emerge. The fact that there are not many of them on this Reservation goes to show they came from a lower level of life. Torrès seems to be the only lawyer here which suggests he wasn't that bad in his earthly existence."

Musset gave one of his cheeky smiles. "Perhaps they were such an honest crew they ended up in Paradise. Perhaps Saint Peter welcomed them with open arms for all their good deeds and gave them well-padded abodes to rest their weary overworked bones."

"It seems you're the odd one out, Ingres," Balzac laughed. "The chances are they're all in Hell, giving the Devil their legal opinion. They'd be at home there with their black gowns, stale wigs and sinister view of life. The Devil would just love them."

"I still think this Michelangelo notion is a load of nonsense, a load of legal gobbledygook," Yves said as he took a swill of gin to clear his head.

The professor picked up a box from his desk. "A chocolate, Oscar?" he said, offering him a delicious choice. Eventually, Oscar selected a hard-centred one. Laying back on the couch, he slowly sucked away.

"Your wife, Constance. Why did it take you nearly a year to visit her grave in Genoa?"

"I was wondering how long it would take you to get around to that."

"You have a problem with it?"

"Indeed. It is a problem that causes me acute suffering – it is one part of my life I wish I could eradicate. I would rather not remember, or even talk about it, if at all possible."

"What made you finally make that journey to Genoa?"

Oscar sucked away at the remnants of chocolate as he pondered the question.

"Shame – I was shamed into it after an extraordinary encounter with a stranger in Paris, on the steps of the Sacré Coeur."

"I see," said the professor, offering him another chocolate. "How did this shame manifest itself?"

"It was there a long time before my encounter with the stranger. It was only after that encounter that the reality of it hit home. You must remember I was in a state of shock after I was informed of Constance's passing, although it has been written that I was unaffected and indifferent to her tragic end. That was not true, for it drained me. It was a terrible blow, a shattering, unexpected blow. Her passing turned out to augur my own death.

"It was a situation I had never envisaged. Constance was so full of life. She had such vitality. The thought of her dying before her time had never crossed my mind. By the time I had received and absorbed the dreadful news, she was already laid to rest. God rest her soul. What could I do? My boys, my innocent boys, how would they cope without her – without her love and devotion, without the laughter she brought into their lives? I was concerned for them as any father would, how such a loss would affect them. However, I was a prisoner of circumstances, denied access to them. Being unable to comfort them in their time of need was a cruel blow. I needed to let them know that I loved them, that I was there for them. I was denied this because of my so-called crime. Exile is a cruel blow to any soul, as millions of my brethren know so well. Indeed, professor, my shame – a shame I brought on myself – was now complete by my not making the effort to attend the funeral of my children's mother, a wife who'd shown me a beautiful and unconditional love. Although I would have been unwelcome at the funeral, I should have gone and laid her to rest. As I said before, with Constance, I was a moral coward. My shame was like a sheet of steel wrapped around me. It was like being imprisoned in a bell of shame that was constantly struck by metal hammers in the hands of my detractors.

"When did you decide to go to Genoa?"

"After the meeting with the stranger, who, by her humility, by her common decency and humanity shamed me into going, into doing what I was morally obliged to do."

"I see. When and how did this occur?"

"One day in January 1899 I left my lodgings in the Hôtel d'Alsace and was wandering around Paris, just aimlessly drifting, feeling sad and forlorn, full of self-pity, my mind in turmoil as I tried to make sense of my situation, when I came upon the Sacré Coeur, still in the process of being built on the hill of Montmartre. I looked up at that magnificent structure as it soared up into the heavens and thought that during my time in Paris, I hadn't visited it to see how it was progressing. I studied it in detail and wondered at the loving dedication and sheer hard work that was raising this basilica over the Parisian skyline.

"I asked the foreman for access. He obliged after carefully examining me and asked that I take care. Climbing the steps, I entered its sacred heart and walked around watching the artisans at their work and marvelling at the progress they were making. I stood against the right-hand pillar at the rear of the basilica, just in front of the main doors, and took in the magnificent sight, wondering who designed this glorious place. Closing my eyes, I imagined a mass in progress in that magnificent place of worship. I imagined it with worshipers from near and far, with the serene music of the singing nuns, the Little Sisters of Montmartre, filling the basilica, vibrating around its walls. I imagined the morning light penetrating the stained-glass windows, projecting the dancing colours on to its white stone pillars. For the first time in many years, I felt an air of calm about me, a peace washing over me. I imagined the priest, dressed in his scarlet and green vestments, descending from the altar and walking down the aisles, sprinkling the congregation with holy water from a palm leaf that he dipped at regular intervals into a basin carried by an altar boy. I imagined him approaching the aisle where I was standing and flicking the palm leaf in my direction. The cold drops, as they hit my face, gave me a feeling of exhilaration. I don't know what it was, but it was a feeling I'd never experienced before. I imagined the choir continuing to fill the basilica with their angelic tones as four nuns, preceded by a small altar boy, carried the host in gold dishes held high above them up the main aisle then traversed the basilica, returning to the altar, where the priest waited to receive them. It was very moving and had an air of theatre about it.

"I imagined the mass in full flow with a small African serving boy holding up the bible to the priest, who read out the gospel. I saw the multitude filling the aisles to receive communion, returning to their seats, refreshed and with faith renewed. I imagined the crowd, fulfilled, slowly leaving the sacred heart to go about their daily business. I remained standing, not wanting to leave. The feeling of peace and tranquillity was so overwhelming; I didn't want it to end. I didn't want to open my eyes again to the reality of my life, a life of ruin and abject loneliness. I don't know how long I stood there but when I opened my eyes I thought I saw a priest standing in front of me. He smiled, saying, 'All is forgiven, Oscar Wilde. Go in peace.' I blinked, and he was gone. All I could see were the workers busying themselves with their chores. Two stonemasons were looking at me in an enquiring manner, probably wondering who I was and what I was up to, standing there, leaning against a pillar with my eyes closed and a distracted look on my face.

"Outside, I came across a stall selling religious trinkets. There was a selection of medallions, mostly depicting St Christopher. On impulse, I purchased one and asked the seller where I could have it blessed. He pointed towards a passageway that led to the Church of Saint Pierre and suggested I search out Father Stevan, as no priest was available in the basilica that was yet to be consecrated.

"The Church of Saint Pierre was a short walk from the Sacré Coeur. It was crowded with a mass just finishing. Some worshipers were waiting for confession. Some were performing the Stations of the Cross. I took a pew at the left-hand side of the altar to wait for the priest, as the sun shone through the stained-glass window, lighting up the church with a prism of colour. After a while, I heard someone behind me. Turning, I saw an old priest, who looked at me with some curiosity. I asked if he would be kind enough to bless the medallion, which he did. He looked me up and down in a probing manner then bid me a good day."

"Are you religious?" asked the professor, interrupting Oscar's flow.

"Yes, I suppose I am. I am what they call an Irish Protestant, but don't hold that against me. However, I always had a leaning towards the Church of Rome, so I suppose having the medallion blessed was not that surprising."

"I see. What did you do when you left Saint Pierre?"

"By the time I left the crowds were well dispersed. I was feeling far happier in myself and leisurely wandered towards the steps of the Sacré Coeur, taking a seat at the top. As I sat there looking across the panorama of Paris, that city of light, that city of love, the beautiful peace and tranquillity I had felt in the basilica suddenly evaporated, to be replaced with a black cloud of depression and utter hopelessness. I had the Saint Christopher medallion clasped in my hand and, in a moment of despair, cursing my fate, threw it down the steps. Burying my head in my hands, I wept for my lost life. I felt so useless – a failure, an outcast, not just in my homeland and England but also in the city of light. I could see no way out of my depression and realised that my exile was permanent, that I would never see my children again, never again see Dublin or hear the applause of an audience nor have the confidence to write again. I felt my life ebbing away with every passing hour and the cloud of doom hovering over me with the voice of the Grim Reaper whispering in my ears, 'It's time to go, Oscar Wilde.'

"Through the sound of my tears, I heard someone whistling 'La Marseillaise'. I looked up, and there at the bottom of the steps was a vagabond, tap dancing along and up the steps towards me. She was dressed in red, white and blue and wearing a dark blue peaked corduroy cap with a red and white band, her blonde hair tied back in a pigtail with a scarlet ribbon. Her blue jacket and trousers were all but rags. Tied around her left knee was a blue and white polka-dot handkerchief. A bright red scarf, wrapped around her swanlike neck, set off her once white blouse. As she neared me, I observed that she was all but six feet tall and on her dancing feet were a pair of sturdy hobnail boots that gave a sharp crack as she tapped her way up and along the steps towards me. She carried a white cane that she twirled in the air as she whistled and danced towards me.

"'Bonjour, monsieur,' she said cheerfully, as she stood in front of me, giving a theatrical bow. 'Isn't it a glorious day? Isn't it just great to be alive on such a fine day? Oh yes, one of God's good days.'

"'Is it?' I sadly replied.

"She looked at me and shook her head. 'Oh, come now, what do you mean, is it? Look around you; look at this splendid view – look at this glorious city of ours. Does it not take your breath away? Take a deep breath. Take in the pure air around you.' She took in a deep demonstrative breath. 'Yes, it is good to be alive; but monsieur, why such a long and sad face?' she said turning towards me. 'Whatever could it be, that makes you so sad on such a glorious day as this? Surely, it can't be that bad. Whatever could it be, that ails you so?'

"'Life,' I replied.

"'Ah, life,' she sighed as she sat down beside me, untying her boots. 'It takes some living, doesn't it, this life of ours. It is not life that kills us, not life at all, only its living. What would life be, monsieur, without a touch of sadness – how could we appreciate happiness, laughter and the joys of life, if there was no sadness to balance our life? You can't have happiness without a splash of sadness? That's life – that's living.'

"I glanced at her as she took off her boots and placed them between us. 'My feet are killing me,' she complained as she massaged her toes.

"I looked at her ragged clothes and wondered, what had she, a vagabond, to be happy and thankful for. She looked as though she had not a sou to her name, nor had eaten in days.

"She looked at me closely, studying me. She reached out her hand and touched my chin. She moved my head back and forth, looking hard at me, and gave a slight smile that revealed a cute dimple on her right cheek. 'I know you, monsieur,' she informed me.

"'You do?' I replied.

"She looked hard at me with her dazzling light blue eyes. 'Yes, Monsieur Wilde, we've met before,' she said as she resumed massaging her toes.

"Her remark startled me. 'Have we?' I asked, wondering how she knew my name or how I would have known such a creature.

"'Indeed we have,' she said as she stood up, her big toes protruding from her red socks. With a theatrical wave of her hands, she pointed to herself and said, 'What you see before you, monsieur, is just a ragged street dancer, with a dirty face and grubby hands. Someone you don't recognise. I have nothing to give or offer you, nothing but greetings and the time of day. I have nothing in this world, nothing of any material worth, nothing but my memories, my freedom, my peace of mind, and these dancing boots,' she said pointing at them as they sat on the step below. 'These faithful boots of mine dance around these well-worn streets of Paris, earning me enough to sustain myself and give me shelter in a *petit* garret off the boulevard Saint Germain. But monsieur, there was another me far removed from what now stands before you. I was once a woman of means. You may well raise your eyebrows in surprise, but I had wealth, wealth that would have left you reeling in disbelief. I had a position in society that others envied and craved. I had it all. Oh yes, property, jewellery, a wardrobe of the best that Paris could produce, works of art and antiques that furnished my many properties. I had it all. I lived the high life and lived it to the full – no short measures for me, monsieur. I had everything in excess. I had a box at the Opéra as I did at most of the theatres in Paris. As you can see, I am no classical beauty, nothing to write home about, but men ran after me as if there were no tomorrow. They eagerly pursued me. There were so many of them it made me dizzy. They would fall over each other to court and entertain me. They wined and dined me in the best of establishments, festooning me with flowers and gifts. It was my wealth they were after, of course, not the beauty I thought I possessed. I was so naive to believe those handsome and successful men were after me solely to offer me undying love. I once had a fiancé, a handsome man-about-town, who said he truly loved me. More fool me. I believed him. Like many a girl before me, I fell for a cad and bounder, thinking it was true love. I thought my life fulfilled with my future secure, that my life would be one of happiness and pleasure and sadness would play no part in it. Oh, how wrong I was, for my fiancé, who professed to love me, had other more devious things on his mind than love.'

"I couldn't take my eyes off of her. Who was she? I kept asking myself. When she first started talking, I just wanted her to shut up and vanish and leave me to fester in my self-pity, but now I found myself transfixed by her.

"'You see – way over there, near the Église du Dôme,' she said pointing over the Parisian skyline. 'I once had a mansion there, on the far side of it, on the rue Cler, just off Saint Dominique. That was the heart and soul of the social scene of Parisian life. I was hostess of the best salon in Paris. Everyone seeking the pleasures of life would line up to have their names on my invitation list. Everyone who was anyone whiled their time away in my den of pleasure – all had to be seen there – politicians, captains of industry, intellectuals, military brass and ambassadors of every kind. In my mansion, that I called Plaisir, were the most lavish of furnishings. I collected Chippendales, Ming porcelain and any exquisite work of art I could lay my hands on. On my silk-padded walls hung the works of the masters, no rubbish, only the best: Ingres, David, Ruben and even a Rembrandt that I treasured as I did life itself. I had properties in Orleans, Monte Carlo, the Pyrenees as well as a mansion on Richmond Hill in London, where I entertained the cream of the English establishment. I spent a lot of time in London. It was there, in a foggy damp London, that I first met you.'

"'It was?' I said, again wondering just who she was.

"'Yes. It was at Saint James's Theatre, at the opening night of *Lady Windermere's Fan*. I remember it well. It was a fine play, one of your best. If my memory serves me well, the proprietor of the theatre, a Mr Devlin introduced us in the foyer after the performance. When you realised I was from Paris, your eyes lit up. You informed me that it was your intention to return there soon as you had an affinity with the place.'

"'Well, I'll be dammed,' I said in amazement.

"'A few days later, I was invited to a ceremonial dinner at the home of an admirer of yours in Chelsea,' she continued, 'where you were the guest of honour. It was a splendid evening, and you had the guests spellbound by your wit and wisdom. As I recall, you were a bit of a charmer.'

"'I recall that evening, but I'm afraid, mademoiselle, I don't remember you, not in the least.'

"'How could you,' she laughed. 'What you see now is only a shadow of my former self. Then, I was a lady of elegance and style. The only dancing I did was across the floors of the finest homes of Europe in the arms of some of the most eligible bachelors in society. The best coiffeur in town styled my hair in the latest trend. The cut of my costumes was something to behold and my shoes – ah, my beautiful shoes, how I adored them. They were the finest, fashioned by Sèvres of Paris. It is no wonder you don't recognise me. I hardly recognise myself at times.

"'At Chelsea, I wore a sleek royal blue silk gown, plain, without any frills, with an open back. It was a showstopper. You were bold enough to say I was wearing it back to front, which didn't impress your beautiful wife, who thought you were flirting – which you were.'

"I was stunned by her revelations. My mind was in a whirl as she told her story, taking me back in time, a time when I was in my prime with a rosy future ahead of me. A time when I was free, without a care in the world, where everything I touched turned to gold – when nothing was out of my reach. She reminded me of a time that seemed so long, long ago.

"'Yes, I remember you. Of course I do,' I said. 'That dress – how could I forget? As I recall, there were some remarks made about you concerning your daring attire. "A Parisian hussy in blue", someone cried. The hostess remonstrated with that sharp tongue that insulted you. Yes, mademoiselle, I do remember you.'

"'I'm pleased you do. Few do,' she sighed.' If I am remembered these days, it's not with love or affection, but with acrimony and the venom of bitter and acidic tongues. It's nice to be remembered, even by a down-and-out wit,' she laughed.

"'You have me confused, mademoiselle,' I confessed. 'Why and how did you end up dressed as you are – a street urchin?'

"'Ah, that monsieur, is my tale of woe,' she sighed as she again sat down beside me. She held my hand and looked tearfully at me. 'You see, I thought friends, family and the secure society structure that surrounded me would be there to protect me for the rest of my days. Alas, how wrong I was. It was not to be. It was only an illusion, a trick. You see, by a sleight of hand and with the connivance of my so-called friends and acquaintances, I lost everything. I lost my wealth, security and position in society. It was by no fault of my own that I found myself in dire straits. I trusted and loved too freely and paid dearly for it. Like you, I too was socially castrated – deserted by my

223

friends, publicly humiliated and held up to public odium. I too was made a bankrupt and watched helplessly as my treasured belongings were sold off at a public auction for a mere pittance. Like you, I too was degraded and made to feel like a leper, an outcast to be spat upon. Like you, I too lost the one I loved.

"'What was the nature of this deceit that caused such a catastrophe in your life?' I asked.

"'That, monsieur, is too painful to recall,' she whispered, lowering her head. 'All I can say is that my conscience is clear. I played no part in my downfall. If I did have a fault, it was to fall in love. I fell in love with a cad who played games with my heart. Those who put on an air of respectability and decency, like those who surrounded you and I are often the very purveyors of the decadence, corruption and moral decay that they accuse others of. These are often or not the ones who take the moral high ground and we all know where that leads. They stand on their not-too-steady pedestals as the Pillars of Society denouncing the likes of us, but their lofty perch is a very shaky place to be, for only fools have the neck to take such a position, a position that inevitably come tumbling down. It seems so easy to ruin the reputation of others, as we can painfully testify to.'

"'Was there no hope for you? Was there no way back?' I asked as I reached out to hold her hand.

"'No,' she murmured. Suddenly, she sprang to her feet, giving another theatrical wave of her hands. 'But it would take more than those parasites to defeat me. They misjudged me, for I'm made of sterner stuff. I had nothing, nothing in the world, apart from a few items of clothes, including this party-piece suit that I now stand in, twenty-five francs and an uncertain rocky road ahead. After many a fall down that road and a dose of bruised pride, I found salvation and in the most unexpected of places. I walked the streets of Paris, slept in the cheapest *pension* I could find, but I was always hopeful that providence would favour me, and she did. I didn't find the happiness that seems to be the aim of most of us; what I found was something that money, position or respectability could never buy.'

"'Which was?' I asked.

"'Contentment, monsieur, contentment and peace of mind,' she proudly replied.

"I looked at her in amazement and spluttered, 'How could you be content when you have nothing – no home, no wealth, earning your living off the streets of Paris, how could you possibly have peace of mind after what has happened to you?'

"'I'll tell you how,' she said. 'For the first time in my life, I met and associated with those I had despised, taught to dismiss with contempt, not to even give the time of day to. Yes, I mean those at the bottom of the ladder, those in the gutter of life. It was there in the gutter I found salvation and contentment I had never known before. It was there that I found the value of true friendship and the decency of the human spirit. They accepted me without any reservation, without any questions asked. It was obvious by my accent and bearing that, unlike them, I was well educated, refined and had never experienced a hard life. It was there in the gutter that I found my well-sought-after peace of mind, a heaven-sent peace.'

"'How on earth could one find peace of mind in the gutter of life with all the low life that accumulates there?' I asked

"'By looking life straight in the eye, that's how,' she proudly replied.

"'Uh! I have been looking life in the eye ever since my misfortune,' I cried. 'She looks back at me, laughs and spits in my face – it is not peace of mind I find, mademoiselle, only torment and sorrow. All I can see ahead of me is the rocky road to oblivion.'

"She lifted my lowered head and lovingly said, 'You remember your maxim, monsieur, about being in the gutter and seeing stars?'

"'Indeed. One of my best,' I replied, delighted that she was familiar with my words.

"'When I found myself in the gutter, with my world shattered, feeling God and the world had deserted me, I looked up and saw those very same stars, but mine were sparkling and dancing and their wonder brought me back to life.' She looked me straight in the eyes. 'Can you, can you see those same stars from your gutter?' she asked.

"I looked at her. She held my gaze. I lowered my head and said, 'No, I don't. What I see mademoiselle, is the abyss. There will be no stars sparkling where I am going, only darkness and despair. I had my chance at life and ruined it. I envy you your contentment and peace of mind. Now, please, if you do not mind, leave me to my despair and go your way.'

"I don't know why I said that as I never wanted her to go. There was something about her that made me feel there was hope – what it was, I did not know, but she had an air of refuge about her and I was in dire need of refuge.

"'Now, there's no need to get huffy with me. Why would I wish to leave you in despair? Here, take one of these,' she said, offering me a coconut nugget. 'It was hard to come to terms with the loss of what were the essentials of my life,' she continued. 'I had led no other life. The loss of my fortune, the fine clothes, the comfort of my boudoir and my social circle was hard to bear. I didn't know what to do when I found myself homeless and friendless. My mind was in turmoil as I wandered the streets. I had no idea as to what my fate would be. Would I die of hunger? Would I be ravished by demons? Would I be murdered for the few francs I had, or would a knight in shining armour be waiting around the next corner, my saviour on a white steed? For a long time, I slept in the gardens at the entrance of La Trinité. On the odd occasion, I would hide in the church until the warden closed the doors, and manage to get my head down on the red-cushioned pews of the gentry and sneak myself a decent sleep, but in general, I slept under a tree with the other unfortunate ones, many in a worse state than I.

"One morning, after a sleepless night, I left the gardens. I was wandering the streets when I came upon two youngsters dancing as a third played an accordion outside the Gare Saint Lazare, on the corner of the rue de Rome. I watched as they swirled across the wet pavement with elegance and style. They were very good. One of their hats was filling, with coins at a steady pace from the appreciative public. They invited some of the crowd to dance with them. One of the youngsters, a boy of about eleven, held out his hand to me, gesturing to come and join him. I didn't want to, but he was hard to resist. He twirled me around with great dexterity, then, letting go of me, asked me to dance on my own. I looked at the expectant faces of the crowd and thought I'd better do as he asked. I remembered the tap-dancing party piece that I had performed so often at social gatherings. Throwing my hat to the ground, I put my best foot forward and soon got into a good rhythmic stride, accompanied by the young accordion player. I performed all the sequences I could remember. The crowd were soon clapping and humming along to my footwork, and I found I was enjoying every moment of it. It seemed so long ago that I had enjoyed myself so much.

"When I finished, the crowd and the three youngsters applauded enthusiastically. I picked up my hat. To my surprise, there were coins in it. I offered it to the youngsters. They refused, indicating that it was my money, that I had earned it. I, in turn, insisted they have it, but they wouldn't hear of it and told me to keep it. I did. I bid them farewell and headed for the nearest restaurant I could find where I had the first good meal I had had in days. As I sat in the restaurant enjoying my unexpected meal and savouring every morsel, washing it down with some decent red wine, I got to thinking that at least I would not starve. I could always put on a performance of some sort. It seemed that my party piece from my frivolous days was to be my saving grace. Those youngsters saved me. They showed me how I could earn money – not much, but enough to save me from absolute poverty. Of course, others offered me money, but at some price.'

"'What?' I asked, wondering what she was on about. 'What others?'

"'Oh, come now, you're a man of the world. You have been around. Surely you know the kind,' she giggled. 'You know; those men who take advantage of vulnerable women and do so for a few francs.'

"'Oh... I see,' I replied

"'But I can assure you, monsieur,' she proudly announced. 'I'm not that kind of girl.'

"'I have no doubt you're not,' I replied. 'Did you ever contemplate leaving Paris and remaking your life elsewhere?'

"She looked at me, astonished, then smiled. 'Never! It's Paris or nothing for me. Paris is in my blood. I was born here. All the good times of my life, I've experienced here. I have my thumb on its pulse. I need and crave Paris as I do life itself. I'm Parisian through and through.'

"'Ah,' I replied. 'Hasn't it also been the scene of your sorrow and downfall and the backdrop to your broken heart?'

"'Indeed it has,' she sighed. 'But it's better to suffer a broken heart in Paris than anywhere else — it has healing properties that no other city possesses. Paris can heal the most broken of hearts. Even yours will be healed if you let this city envelop you. I need Paris. I can never envisage life without her. Look, monsieur, just look around you. How could I live without this,' she said as she pointed out Paris with her cane. 'Paris to me is Paradise itself. Even my bad experiences can never take away her beauty, her smell —her taste. Yes, I'm Parisian from head to toe. Her beauty is intoxicating and addictive, and I, monsieur, am a slave to her beauty.'

"'There is a beauty about her, I will grant you that. But it is not all beauty, is it,' I pointed out to her.

"She looked at me, perplexed that I could say such a thing. 'Whatever do you mean monsieur? Paris is beauty and beauty is Paris. There's really no argument about it,' she insisted. 'Even a blind man can see her beauty.'

"'Then what about that,' I said, pointing to my right. 'Surely that monstrosity is not beauty in any shape or form.'

"'Ah, now, monsieur,' she sighed, 'how could you say such a thing. That is our Eiffel Tower, a new kind of beauty it is. Surely you can see the majestic beauty in her contours as she soars into the heavens.'

"I turned my head, looking up, pointing to the Sacré Coeur.

"'That, mademoiselle, is majestic beauty.'

"She smiled, wagging her finger at me.

"'No. No. That is divine beauty. That,' she said, pointing to the steel giant way off to our right. 'That's majestic beauty.'

"I laughed. 'We clearly see beauty in a different light.'

"'Maybe, but we still see beauty all the same,' she replied. 'As long as we see beauty, we're alive. These two beauties face each other over the splendour of an even older beauty, that of this great city. I would say monsieur, in years to come, when we are dead and gone and well forgotten, these two structures will symbolise Paris as that grand old lady down there, the Notre Dame does today.'

"She again looked at me closely. 'Even amongst all this beauty, there's sorrow in your life,' she observed. 'A sorrow that is etched deep into your brow, a sorrow that is far deeper and more traumatic than mine. Sorrow is soul-destroying if you don't come to terms with the impostor. Sorrow, she has visited me and left her scar as she surely has on you. I have come to terms with my sorrow. By doing so, I've set myself on the road to freedom.'

"She again touched my hand and whispered, 'I do know of your sorrow.'

"'You do?' I said as I looked into her compassionate blue eyes.

"'Yes,' she said. 'As I walked the streets of this great city, I kept abreast of current affairs. I read newspapers left on seats and often read about you and your misfortune. I followed your trials with a heavy heart and was shocked that you were imprisoned. I often wondered what happened to you after your release, and here you are, sitting on the steps of the Sacré Coeur, listening to my waffle.'

"I looked at her, as she sat there wriggling her toes. Her waffle didn't bother me but soothed my troubled mind.

"'I read with regret that your wife had died in Genoa,' she continued. 'That must have been a great loss to you. It is so sad that your children not only lost you by your forced exile but also lost their mother in such tragic circumstances. It is so unfair. Life, it can be so cruel at times,' she said, as she slipped her feet into her boots.

"'Constance was such a beautiful soul,' I said. 'It's nearly a year since she died. I did a dreadful thing, an unforgivable thing that is torturing me. I have horrendous nightmares as though I'm being tortured for my final insult to her.'

"She recoiled in shock. 'Whatever is it, monsieur?

"I hung my head in shame. How could I tell her? Would she understand? How could I tell this kind stranger what a scumbag I was?

"'Whatever is it?' she asked. 'You can tell me.'

"'I did Constance a wrong – such a horrible, unforgivable wrong,' I confessed.

"'Whatever is it,' she gasped.

"'I didn't attend her funeral. I didn't do my duty and lay her to rest like any decent soul would,' I stuttered, feeling the shame wash over me, the shame of having to admit such a thing.

"There was a sharp intake of breath. 'Oh! How could you? How could you do such a thing?' she sighed, stunned by my revelation.

"'I don't know. What's more, I have yet to visit her grave,' I added.

"There was a shocked silence.

"I looked at her. Her face was that of astonishment and disbelief. What a disaster I had turned out to be, I had even reduced a happy vagabond to sadness. It takes some shit to achieve that.

"'What have you done?' she sighed as she looked at me as tears welled up in her eyes.

I have no excuse for my disgraceful behaviour. I suppose I convinced myself I was unable to attend; the reality was that I could have, but for my own selfish reason I chose not to. The fact that her relatives would have made me unwelcome should not have been an obstacle to me attending her burial. After all, I was her husband and next-of-kin and had an obligation to be there. I found I was unable to face the reality of her death, for in truth I was the cause of it by my misdeeds and my disgraceful treatment of her,' I confessed.

"The vagabond was embarrassed and uncomfortable. 'I don't know what to say,' she said. 'What you say is hard to believe, that you could have slighted the memory of an innocent soul in such a way, of a soul that loved you so much.'

"We sat there for some time, saying nothing, just staring aimlessly out over Paris.

"'Every day, it eats and eats away at me,' I finally said, breaking the uncomfortable silence. 'The one person that loved me truly is laid to rest, far from home, while the person on whom she expended so much love hasn't the common decency to pay his respects to the most honest soul he ever knew. I am a low life, mademoiselle, and not worth your time of day.'

"Looking at me, she gave a deep sigh. 'My time costs nothing,' she said, smiling at me. 'You must put this wrong to right. Whatever your faults, I believe you are a decent soul who's made a few mistakes and lost his way through this strange life, as all of us have done from time to time. We have all made errors and you have unfortunately made a big one. You must go, go without any delay. Go to Genoa, go to the one that loved you and put your mind at rest. She's been waiting a long time for you. If there is a heaven and she's looking down on you, I'm sure she'll forgive you.'

"'I don't deserve her forgiveness, as I never deserved her love, never deserved her as a wife and mother of my children,' I replied. 'I'm one of those bad threads in the tapestry of life.'

"Her sad face burst into laughter. 'Dear me, monsieur, there is no good or bad thread in the tapestry of life, only threads. We all make up the tapestry. Each life is a thread woven into it. Each of us has a coloured thread that is part of its makeup, whether we're good or bad.'

"'Really – what colour do you think I am?'

"'Well… purple, what else,' she replied with certainty.

"'Why purple?'

"'Because that is your colour,' she laughed. 'You have purple written all over you.'

"'Do I? What colour is your thread, then?'

"'Saffron, of course,' she replied with a shrug of the shoulders.

"'Why saffron?' I enquired.

"'Why… it just is. Just as purple is yours, saffron is mine. We can do nothing about our colour. There's a logic behind it, I'm sure, just as there is to most of life, but don't ask me what it is for I haven't a clue.'

"She stood up and straightened out her pants and gave a bow. 'I must take my leave, monsieur. I'm glad I've met you again. It is only a shame it has not been in better times. Maybe the future will bring us together in far happier circumstances. Remember, nothing lasts forever – nothing at all, except love. It is only love that will see us through, only love that will conquer evil and set us free. Beauty fades and the memory dulls. Happiness is fleeting and sex, well; it is just a state of mind. Money devalues and power corrupts. The only thing that is worth a toss in this uncertain world is love. The giving and receiving of love is the essence of life. Nothing, nothing lasts forever, nothing at all, except true love, and that love awaits you in Genoa. Adieu, monsieur.'

"Giving another bow, she turned and danced her way down the steps, twirling her cane in the air. Suddenly she stopped. Turning, she tossed something at me. I caught it. It was my Saint Christopher medallion, which I had earlier thrown down the steps.

"'You'll need that, monsieur, for your journey to Genoa, and the rest of your journey through life. Take care and keep faith,' she said. She gave a half-smile then continued her dancing and whistling of 'La Marseillaise'.

"I got to my feet and watched her vanish out of sight. I sat there for a while, pondering on her words. I walked to the parapet and looked down to the pavement far below and watched as she danced her way across the place Saint Pierre and down the rue de Steinkerque to the delight of the passers-by. It was then I resolved to go and do what decency dictated, what in all conscience I should have done without any hesitation – to visit the grave of Constance, my loyal wife, and beg her forgiveness."

"Did you?" asked the professor.

"I did, but after the stranger left I returned to Saint Pierre."

"What for?"

"To light a candle for the vagabond, whose name I never knew, who on that fine and beautiful Parisian day gave me the will to carry on, to carry on my journey through life, although I had no inkling as to just how short that journey would turn out to be."

Oscar stood transfixed by the overpowering display of flowers that confronted him as he stepped into the clinic from the Boulevard of Dreams. The delectable red-headed Dymphna, his attendant for his stay, greeted him warmly.

"Bonjour, Oscar, my sweet. Welcome," she said, offering her hand and winking at him. Oscar, wide-eyed, stared at this tall slim vision before him, dressed in a pale green kimono adorned with a pattern of orange leaves.

"I'm so pleased you've taken up the professor's invitation. I can assure you that won't be disappointed, no soul who passes my way ever is. Follow me."

Oscar followed her. Dymphna showed him his quarters, painted in delicate shades of green with black and silver furnishings and fittings.

"We've had this library installed for you. I'm sure you'll feel very much at home," she said as she showed him into the room, running her fingers across the beautifully bound books and winking at him. This was to be his home for some time, and its ambience immediately gave him a feeling of peace and tranquillity.

Dymphna rang her bell. A smart, tall, slim man stepped into the library carrying a glass of claret. He was bald with a small triangle of black beard and displayed a scar that ran from his left eyebrow down to his chin. "This, Oscar, is Jean Petti."

"Pleased to meet you," he said as he warmly shook Oscar's hand, offering him the glass.

"Jean is your personal valet for your stay at the clinic. Just ring this bell if you need anything, or if you just want someone to talk to, and he will come running. Isn't that so, Jean?"

"Indeed," he said as he gave a bow to his guest.

"He's a good listener, too, so take advantage of him. I always do."

They departed, leaving him to examine his new surroundings. He looked at the shelves of books and was surprised to see all his favourites there. Outside his bedroom was an ornamental pond surrounded by raised flowerbeds that were in full bloom with a spectacular array of gladioli. In the centre of the pond was a manicured Japanese-style island with blue painted connecting bridges. Oscar spent some time wandering around the garden and was pleased with his decision to take up the professor's invitation. 'Surely things can only get better,' he thought to himself as he sat outside his bedroom on a wicker chair with his feet resting on the pink marble pond wall, puffing away on a Turkish cigarette. This, he thought, was perfect, a place of peace and tranquillity. What else could he need to settle his troubled and tortured soul but this little oasis, with its excellent library, good claret and the soothing hands of a red-headed goddess?

***

"Good morning, Oscar. How do you like my clinic?"

"It is splendid, professor," Oscar replied, walking over to the couch. He was dressed in white, apart from bright red buckles on his shoes. He was relaxed and found he was in the most positive and optimistic frame of mind that he had been in for some considerable time. He once more settled on the couch. He was ready for whatever the professor could throw at him, but taken by surprise by his first question.

"Did you ever think about dying?" The professor asked as he filed his nails.

"Indeed I did, but it never took up too much of my time. I always had far better things on which to exercise my mind."

"Such as?"

Oscar gave the professor a broad smile. "Sex!"

"That's it... sex?"

"Mostly, of course, there were other pleasures of life occupying my mind that had to be attended to."

"Can you give examples?"

"Oh, keeping myself in the limelight, a most important pursuit that became a way of life. There was my work, of course. That consumed much of my time. I spent a great deal of time thinking about my image, but not as much as I did about sex. That was my consuming passion. As for my death, it drifted across my mind now and then. However, I rarely let negative vibes get the better of me. Rather an idle exercise, wouldn't you say, thinking about the hereafter when one is enjoying life?"

"Not necessarily. Did you ever dream of your demise?"

Oscar closed his eyes. The professor had hit a nerve, a nerve he would rather let be.

"Did you?"

"Indeed," he whispered, "Yes, there were a few occasions and one in particular that scared the life out of me. I never revealed it to anyone before because it became a sore point to me."

"Are you going to tell me?"

"Yes... it will do no harm. I feel a need to do so. As you may be aware, I spent a great deal of time accepting invitations to lectures, luncheons, dinners and other social occasions to entertain my guests

233

with my wit and wisdom. I accepted an invitation, not long before my trials, to attend a house party in the small village of Pity Me, not far from Durham City. It was an ordinary affair – drinks, dinner and about an hour of witticism to pacify the guests, the usual mix of the local who's who, social climbers and the likes. I enjoyed most of these events – there is no better tonic in life than laughter, even in the gravest of times.

"After most of the guests departed, I joined the host and his wife and a few of their closest friends in a game of cards. It was rather enjoyable. I won a few guineas. The lady of the house, being a devotee of the Tarot, suggested we have our cards read. I went along with her suggestion as the rest were keen to be entertained by this overrated trickery."

"Trickery! You think it's a kind of magic?"

"I wouldn't call it magic. It's more like a con."

"Had you had a reading before?"

"There was a Mrs Robinson in London who tried her trickery on me on a few occasions. She was far from convincing. I think it's a load of codswallop. Stella – she was the hostess for the evening – set to work on us. I was the last in line. I watched as she read the cards for the other guests. Her revelations caused alarm. I admit I was feeling rather nervous when I sat down for my session. If there was a way of dodging it, I would have done so, but I was stuck there and could do nothing about it. It would have been churlish of me to refuse.

"She shuffled the cards and then gave them to me, saying I should kiss the pack before I made my spread on the green felt table. This I did. She turned the first card of the spread and looked at me, nodding her head with an extremely serious look on her furrowed face. As every card was turned, she repeated the exercise. She looked at them for what seemed like eternity; then sighed, 'I'm afraid you're in for stormy weather, Mr Wilde, very stormy, stormy weather.'

"'Am I! Dear me,' I replied.

"'If you lose direction in your journey through life, it will be very stormy weather indeed,' she said as she touched my hand. 'Success is all around you, and you are gifted beyond belief with the world at your feet. You have a devoted wife, two adorable children and many friends. Your star is in the ascendant, but ahead of you is the crossroads of your life at whose junction your ultimate fate will be determined. When you reach this juncture in your life, you will have to make a choice – a choice only you can make. Which way do you go, left or right? One of those roads will bring you continued success, happiness and long life. The other will bring you shame, financial ruin, the scorn of society and an early grave. You will be shunned and spat upon and become a pariah. You will suffer on the treadmill of life and you'll depart this earth as an outcast with the curses of your once devoted admirers ringing in your ears.'

"I burst out laughing at such tosh, to which she didn't take too kindly. 'Really – tell me, which road do I take to continue my good fortune and a long and fruitful life?' I asked.

"'If I knew that, Mr Wilde, I'd be rich beyond my wildest dreams,' she replied. 'The decision is yours and yours only. Once you choose that road, there will be no turning back. Think carefully. Be wise, Mr Wilde.'

"'Aren't I always,' I laughed.

"'This is no time for levity,' she cried. 'Fate is no laughing matter.'

"'But why, my dear lady, would society turn against me? I have it in the palm of my hand. Society cannot get enough of me, so why would it turn against me?' I naively asked.

"Stella nodded her head in surprise at my remark then continued the reading. She looked at the cards, touched one, looked up at me and sighed, 'Avoid the Lady in Blue, and your future will continue with success and happiness. Tangle with her and society will close ranks and run you into the ground. It will show you little mercy. Be warned," she sternly advised.

"'Lady in Blue! What Lady in Blue?' I laughed, amused at her absurdity.

"'The one that has her eyes on you,' she hissed.

"'If she does exist, this Lady in Blue, how do I avoid her?' I candidly asked.

"'By taking the correct road,' she replied as she gathered up her cards.

"'Ah! My dear lady, haven't I always taken the right road?' I said. 'Isn't my success the result of knowing which road to take? If I ever do come to the crossroads which you say lay ahead of me, I'm certain I'll take the right road.'

"She sternly looked at me. 'Your cards have given notice of changing events in your life. Beware, Oscar Wilde!'

"This woman was serious. She really believed in all that mumbo jumbo. That night as I snuggled up in my bed in that house at Pity Me, I laughed at her physic nonsense. I soon fell into a deep sleep. Suddenly I shot up, gasping for breath and sweating profusely. After realising where I was I began to recall a horrible dream about my demise."

"Was it as it turned out in reality?"

"No! Far worse."

"Worse? Do you wish to tell me?"

"Yes. I was on a stage somewhere in London receiving what I thought was the applause of the audience after the opening

235

performance of my latest play, but instead of clapping, they threw daggers. The first split opened my thigh. This was followed in rapid succession by other sharp instruments that nailed me to the spot. The audience were laughing hysterically, their faces aglow, their eyes bulging with climatic excitement as I struggled for breath. Standing over me was a Gaelic warrior brandishing a rapier. His face was contorted with rage; in it, I could see the images of most of my detractors. He gave a blood-curdling scream; then slit my throat from ear to ear. He faded out of sight as my lifeblood drained away.

"I woke screaming. The din I made had Stella bursting into my room. I explained by dilemma. She was far from impressed. She cursed at me as she mopped my brow and warned me of the dangers of demeaning the practice of the Tarot, for only trouble follows, like night sweats and nightmares. She insisted that I sit with her and reflect on the night's events before I went to sleep.

"After she left I quickly dressed and, without any goodbyes or thank-you note, I headed off as quick as my legs could carry me and did not look back. You won't believe how relieved I was to leave Pity Me and the demented Stella and her demons. Every time I think of Stella, I think of death."

"Did the dream have any long term effect on you?"

"At first it didn't bother me. I just shrugged it off as being one of those odd things we experience in life, but Stella's dream, it was to return to haunt me."

"When?"

"Years later, as I sat in my prison cell at Pentonville, those images of the Gaelic warrior returned and the faces of my detractors, the Marquess of Queensbury, Justice Wills and Sir Edward Carson were superimposed over the features of the warrior and were laughing hysterically at me. The warrior was brandishing the rapier that still had my blood dripping from it. If I closed my eyes to get rid of the images, the only effect was they became more vividly enhanced."

"Sir Edward Carson was Queensbury's counsel in the libel action, was he not?"

"Indeed. He was a fellow student of mine at Trinity College. Who would have guessed that that he was to be instrumental in my downfall? At Trinity, we didn't get on too well. He was such a stern and serious individual. I wasn't surprised he ended up in the legal profession."

"Why did you allow yourself to be drawn into having your cards read if you were of the belief that is was all utter codswallop?'

"I thought it harmless. What danger could there be in the practice of turning cards? It was no more than a party piece. Light relief at the end of an evening's entertainment. Ah, but it was far from harmless, for that evening my destiny was revealed to me, and I failed to see it.

"When I was in Paris not long after the reading, I left a restaurant in the Latin Quarter on the rue Dormat after dining with friends. It was a foggy, eerie night. I made my way along the rue Galande towards my lodgings when a figure stepped out from the shadow of Saint Julien-le-Pauvre. As I tried to pass, it blocked my way. I looked at the figure, and it was a woman dressed in a blue cloak, who in a cold voice said, 'Go to London, monsieur. Go now, for your fate awaits you.'

"I couldn't see her eyes for the hood of her cloak hid most of her face. All I could see was the faint outline of her blue lips. I ignored her and tried to continue my journey. Again, she moved in front of me and repeated her warning. As I tried to push by her she grabbed my arm. I panicked. I turned and ran back down rue Galande. Looking behind, I could see her gaining on me. I turned into the rue de l'Hôtel Colbert. It was dark and deserted. I could hear her behind me crying out her warning. I made a sharp turn and headed down towards the des Grands Degrés, hoping to escape her along the quays. I could still hear her wailing cry.

"As I turned to see if she was near me, I slipped on the wet stones, falling heavily to the ground. I looked up, fearing she was near but there was no sign of her. She was gone. There was only an eerie silence about the place. I got to my feet. I stumbled towards the quays and hailed a cab that within a short time had me back to the safety of my lodgings. I wasn't too worried by what she'd said as I got to thinking that perhaps I had only imagined seeing her, that maybe I'd too much wine. It was when I was in prison that I recalled her and Stella's Tarot-card reading.

"When I did arrive at the crossroads of my life I didn't give it too much thought as to which road I should take. I just turned and thought nothing of it. It was a gamble, a gamble that unfortunately I was to lose."

"When did you reach the crossroads of your life?"

Oscar lay back on the couch and gave his habitual sigh.

"It was at my lawyer's office in London. I didn't know it at the time, but when I instructed them to instigate legal proceedings against the Marquess of Queensbury for criminal libel, that was the moment I came to the crossroads of my life. Unfortunately, I didn't realise it. It was there in that stuffy, airless office that my fate was sealed. I never thought the case through. I was carried away with my self-importance – a bit of a bad habit I got myself into. If I had recalled Stella's tarot reading, I may well have taken a different course. But it's no good regretting it now, for I have nobody to blame but myself. It was solely my decision to head for the courts. Nobody was to blame for that other than me.

"On a table in front of a window of the solicitor's office was a brittle blue cut glass depicting a lady holding the Scales of Justice, the image of the one that crowns the Old Bailey. If I had only recalled the warning, I would have taken to my heels at the sight of the Lady in Blue."

"So dreams played an important part in your life?"

"I wouldn't go as far as that, but they certainly were part of its pleasures. They were inevitably good-humoured. Up until then, I never experienced nightmares. I would say Pity Me was my first."

"What were the dreams about?"

"Oh! You name any pleasurable pursuit and for sure I've dreamt about it."

"So it's safe to say you're one of life's dreamers."

"*Was* is more like it. When I arrived at the Reservation, I was in for a shock. Did I tell you of my inability to dream? "

"No?"

"After being at the Reservation for some time, I realised that I was unable to dream. At first, I thought every soul here suffered the same deprivation, as part of our Purgatory, until our good poet Alfred de Musset, enlightened me. He happened to tell me that he was a regular dreamer, and to his delight, they were all sensual dreams – he never suffered a nightmare.

"I asked around and discovered that all of my fellow souls indulged in this pleasure regularly. I was horrified. Why me? Why was I being denied such a therapeutic release?"

"You're saying you never had even one dream."

"Not one. It seemed that I was the odd one out. Alfred informed me that he could solve my problem."

"Did he now? How?"

"He had some kind of potion that enhanced dreams, which he promised would not just enable me to dream, but to recall them. We sat down under a hawthorn tree, and he administrated the potion. My God, it tasted foul."

"Did it work?"

Oscar gave a regretful laugh. "Yes… but not as I expected it to. That evening, I had my first dream. What a disappointment."

"What happened?"

"Alas, there was no sex, no fun, and no pleasurable activity at all, nothing of the kind. My first dream turned out to be a nightmare. When Alfred asked if his tonic achieved its desired effect, he was somewhat lost for words when I informed him that I had experienced a nightmare. He was adamant that no soul here experiences nightmares as they were reserved for those on earth."

"'What was it about, this so-called nightmare of yours?' he asked.

"'I would rather not say. Recalling bad experiences are not my forte,' I informed him, hoping he would drop the subject. He would not. He insisted I recall the nightmare."

Oscar sighed, and as he gazed at the ceiling began to recall his nightmare. "You won't believe how excited I was, heading for bed after swallowing Alfred's foul-tasting potion. My mind was reeling at the thought of what could be in store. I didn't take long to drift off. How I wished I hadn't."

"It couldn't have been that bad, surely."

"Oh, it was. I dreamt I was the worst for wear after too much liquor on a visit to Paris and found a spot amongst the pansies in the Luxembourg Gardens in which to rest my weary bones. I soon fell into a deep sleep. Someone prodded me in the ribs, waking me from my alcohol-induced sleep.

"'Wake up, Wilde, you feckin' bowsie,' I heard a voice I recognised. 'Come on, up you get.' He continued to prod me as I tried to grasp what was happening. 'Come now, shape yourself up, Wilde, you feckin eejit. It's no good feeling sorry for yourself as nobody's interested in your-self pity.'

"As my eyes focused, there, towering over me was James Joyce and Nora Barnacle. They were looking down at me with sickening contempt.

"'Come, Jimmy, he's not worth getting upset over. He's just a chancer and a pathetic one at that,' Nora said as she tried to pull him away.

"'No, he's not getting away with it, the blackguard. Up! Up you get, you miserable sod,' he said as he continued to prod me with his cane.

"'Go away! Go away and let me be,' I cried as I curled up in a ball.

"'Leave you alone?' he screeched. 'Up, you feckin scumbag,' he screamed as he grabbed a hold of my feet, dragging me out of the pansies and on to the grass. 'What kind of Irishman are you? More to the point, what kind of Dubliner are you, wallowing in self-pity. Look at yourself; you're an out-of-control boozer. So, you've lost everything, that doesn't mean you must lose your self-respect as well. Are you going to drink and screw yourself to death? Is that your intent? Are ye going to continue wasting your talent? All is not lost, you feckin clown. You have the talent to get yourself out of the mess you're in. Why don't you go back to Dublin or London and face the wrath of your peers? Get it over with, it won't last long. After a few

239

weeks, it will be over. It will be old news, and you'll be able to get yourself together. You won't do that here, boozing and sleeping in the park and annoying these good Parisian folk. You're letting yourself and Dublin down.'

"'Don't bother, Jimmy,' said his impatient wife as she tried to pull him away. 'He's not worth it. He's a loser. Just look at him. It's grotesque. Come, let's go.'

"I again curled up in a ball, but he kept prodding me. The next moment I was brought to my senses. He near on drowned me with a water hose. I staggered to my feet. I was drenched to the skin. As my eyes focused, I realised I was surrounded by curious Parisians out on their morning stroll.

"'Why are you doing this to me, Joyce? It's none of your business whether I drink myself to death or wither away from self-pity. Please, just leave me alone,' I said, staggering away from them.

"The next thing I knew, he had his walking stick under my collar and was pushing me through the crowds and up towards the bandstand. I tried to shake loose, but I was so drunk I hadn't the energy to struggle. He managed to get me up on to the bandstand and turned me to face the morning strollers.

"'Tell me, madame, do you know who this fool is?' he asked a woman who was looking curiously at us as she cradled her pet poodle.

"'He's that weird writer from London, the one who thinks he's God Almighty. We have too many here in Paris who think they are God Almighty without having the likes of him joining the bandwagon. What is he doing here? If he is a God, then he looks like a well-pickled one to me. Is he pickled then?' she enquired.

"'Very much so, madame, pissed is more like it,' replied Joyce. 'He's feeling sorry for himself. A right eejit he is.'

"'Eejit! What is an eejit?' a voice cried.

"'My dear madame, an eejit is a man like this,' he said, looking at me as I dangled from his cane. 'An eejit is a man gifted in all possible ways, like this one but too stupid to know it. He's such a feckin eejit; he throws his gifts away for the frivolity of the pleasures of life.'

"'Oh! He's a hedonist as well, is he?' the woman replied.

"'Very much so,' Joyce sighed.

"'Doesn't look like a man enjoying the pleasures of life, does he?' cried a young woman.

"'Indeed, mademoiselle. What you see before you is the result of the pleasures of life taken to excess. Just look at him – he's pathetic. Pleasure is wasted on him,' Joyce sneered.

"I was so tired and weak, I just wanted to lie down, but every time I tried, he held me up with his cane.

"'Pleasure!' the young woman replied. 'By the look of him, it's life that's wasted on him.'

"'You, monsieur, do you know this man?' he asked another passer-by.

"'Oh, yes! That's Oscar Wilde, a once-brilliant artist,' he replied as he studied me in detail.

"'*Once!* How right you are my friend. What has this genius been reduced to – what is he now?' asked Joyce.

"'A bum, a Parisian bum,' an onlooker shouted.

"'Exactly, my friend – a Parisian bum, our once-brilliant artist has capitulated to the gutter. He's a bum, all right – a right eejit of one. What do you think we should do with this bum, this unwanted Parisian bum?' he asked.

"'Ignore him!' shouted a nun.

"'Piss on him!' shouted a young lad.

"'Drown the bastard!' cried an old man as he rested on his cane.

"'Ah, leave him alone,' a small child, with long blonde curls cried as she wagged her lollipop at Joyce.

"Joyce ignored the young girl's plea.

'And you, mademoiselle, do you know this man?' Joyce asked a young woman walking her dog.

"'Yes, she replied. He is a sexual deviant who thinks himself a writer, who sponges off his friends and makes a nuisance of himself along our city's boulevards and scurries through its alleyways seeking out the seedier side of life. He needs treatment. Send him back to where he has come from. He's not welcome here.'

"Nora pulled at Joyce's sleeve. 'Leave him, Jimmy. Leave him to the crowd; they will see him off. Come, we have other business to attend to. We have a train to catch to Trieste,' she said as Joyce let go of my collar that sent me sprawling to the floor.

"'There's no helping the likes of you, Wilde. Right, Nora, off we go. Bye, bye, you feckin' loser,' he cried as he linked arms with Nora and sprightly headed off to their other business.

"I thought that was it. As I attempted to get up, I was kicked to the ground. 'Pervert!' someone cried. Then someone stamped on my hand, and I heard my weary bones crack. 'Ponce!' Another shrill voice cried. As I gripped my injured hand, someone grabbed hold of my hair, yanked back my head and spat in my face. Then someone kicked me in the face, sending my teeth flying.

"'Sodomite!' my tormentor cried and then smashed my face into the ground.

"'Leave him alone, you bullies! Leave him alone,' I heard a child cry. 'Here, monsieur, take my hand, take my hand. I'll take care of you.'

"I grabbed her tiny hand then felt someone sit on my back, shouting, 'Poseur, poseur!' Another sat on my legs; one on my head and before I knew it hoards of them were sitting on me, screaming absurdities. They jumped up and down on me. The pain was excruciating. I held on to the child's hand. She kept on calling to me, but her voice became fainter and fainter. I gasped for air and shouted after Joyce. 'Jimmy, Jimmy!' I cried, hoping he could hear me. Alas, he was gone and left me with the pain splitting me in two.

"'He's gone,' the faint voice of the child said. 'Don't worry, brother. I'll take you home.'

"Her hand slipped out of mine as one final searing spasm of pain finished me off."

"After I finished recalling this nightmare, Alfred gave a wry smile. 'My dear Oscar, how unfortunate you are to die twice. You didn't die with much grace the first time around, and you haven't improved this time. Are you sure it was in Paris? It seems highly unlikely for Parisians to treat an artist in such a vulgar fashion. I am certain your nightmare is a one-off. Things can't get any worse. Trust me.'

"'Trust you?' I cried. 'I don't think so. My next dream turned into a nightmare too. What have you to say about that?'

"'Perhaps my tonic takes longer to work on a genius like you,' Alfred laughed. 'I'll give you a second dose of my tonic. How much fairer can I be?'

"Did it work?" asked the professor.

"I'll put it this way. The day after taking the second potion, Alfred arrived at my home asking if it had worked. He asked me to recall my dream, which I did. He sat there, his face beaming with anticipation. He truly believed in the therapeutic properties of his potion."

"I recalled how after he had administrated his potion, I fell into a deep sleep. The next morning he awoke me with what he called great news. He was excited and babbled on about me finally getting my wish to meet someone I thought I never would.

"'My dear fellow, what are you on about?' I asked.

"'Here, read it.' he said, thrusting a letter at me. I quickly opened it.

"'Go on… read it,' he cried.

"It proved to be an invitation to a soirée at Nohant, the home of Madame George Sand.

"'It's a joke,' I replied, handing him back the letter.

"'It's genuine, you ass. Look at the handwriting, it's hers, distinguished as ever,' he said.

"I realised it was genuine. Was I really going to meet George Sand, the woman that sent Chopin mad and Musset crazy? Did she really want to meet me?

"'Are you coming with me?'

"Musset laughed. 'Not likely! She doesn't talk or even think about me these days. I'm out of favour. If I turned up, she would run me out of the place. I would have loved to have seen you in operation with the Good Lady of Nohant. It would be something to see. You'll have to go on your own, I'm afraid.'

"'I'll survive,' I replied.

"'I'm sure you will, but be aware of her aura. It can be so deceptive,' he informed me. I didn't have a clue what he was rambling on about.

"On the appointed day I set off for Nohant, excited at the prospect of meeting such a fascinating woman. I arrived at her country residence, in a quaint village deep in the heart of the Loire Valley. I rapped on the large doors and was received by her butler. He refused to shake my hand. His appearance startled me for he looked like Mr Justice Wills, my trial judge. 'This way, Monsieur Wilde,' he said. I handed him my hat and coat. He was looking at me with disdain. He showed me into a reception room that was heaving with people. The waiter offered me a drink. I was startled at the very sight of him. I had to look twice. I thought my eyes were deceiving me. He was the spitting image of Carson. He even had his surly look. I was about to turn and run when I noticed Chopin talking to Balzac. I hurried over to them."

"'Thank God you're here, Frédéric old boy,' I said, relieved at seeing a familiar face.

"'Do I know you, monsieur?' Chopin coldly asked as he looked at me with surprise, without any recognition. I turned to Balzac. His reaction was the same.

"'Stop fooling around,' I replied, giving Chopin a playful nudge.

"They looked at each other and shrugged their shoulders.

"'You must be mistaken, monsieur. Like my friend here, I don't believe we've met before. You seem to know our names, however. That could be because we are well known. But you, who are you?' Balzac sharply asked.

"'Stop clowning. It is bad enough Frédéric fooling about without you trying to outsmart him,' I replied.

"Balzac glared at me. 'You insolent man, how dare you speak to me in such an informal manner? Come Frédéric, let's find a more congenial spot and leave this gatecrasher to his fate.'

"I was flabbergasted. There was a tap on my shoulder.

"'Ah! You must be that Wilde chap I've heard so much about,' said a voice from behind me. 'I'm Gustave Flaubert. Pleased to meet you,' he said as he warmly shook my hand. 'I noticed you talking to Chopin and Balzac. They seemed to be rather sharp with you.'

"'They acted as though they never knew me.'

"'But they don't,' he replied. 'When we were discussing the guest list, Chopin, in particular, asked who you were. I informed him you were a writer. He said he hadn't heard of you or read your book and certainly hadn't seen any of your plays.'

"'That's amazing. I have known Frédéric for years. He often visits me at my home at the Literary Quarter on Cloud Fifteen,' I informed him.

"'Cloud Fifteen!' he exclaimed, raising his eyebrows. 'I think, my dear man, you are mistaken. Please, let me introduce you to the guests before Madame Sand makes her appearance.

"Flaubert led me over to a small group of people, amongst them, my friend Ingres. He took my hand. 'Are you a painter yourself? I don't recall seeing you at any of the salons about town.'

"'You're as bad as Frédéric and Honoré trying such a lark – what has gotten into you lot?'

"He and Flaubert looked at each other as though they'd seen a ghost.

"'Who is this strange man?' Ingres asked Flaubert.

"'Monsieur Wilde, he's a guest of Madame Sand,' he replied.

"'How strange… Madame must be under the weather,' he sarcastically replied.

"'What's wrong with you, Ingres? You're acting as though you had never met me before.'

"'I haven't,' he replied, 'and by your manner, I'm relieved I haven't. I have no desire to do so now or in the future. So, if you'll excuse me, I have other guests to talk to.'

"I was hurt and dumbfounded by their positively hostile manner.

"Flaubert put his hand on my shoulder. 'My dear man, you seem to be a little confused. Take a seat,' he said and beckoned a waiter over. 'Get Monsieur Wilde a tonic. He's not feeling himself.'

"The waiter looked down his nose at me. 'Haven't we met before?' I asked.

"'Hardly,' he snapped; his nostrils flared. 'But monsieur does have a familiar look about him, a look I've often seen on the darker side of life.'

"As he turned to walk away I noticed he had the same gait as Carson as well as looking remarkably like him. I began to sweat profusely. I was feeling terribly uneasy and nervous, wishing Alfred would turn up and rescue me. It was not long before the waiter returned with my drink. 'That will settle your nerves,' Flaubert said as the waiter handed me the drink. 'We can't have you being nervous meeting madame. Nervous people make her reserved and stilted in her manner. We can't have that now, can we?'

"I reluctantly swallowed the tonic and sat down. Within a few seconds, my head was swirling, the room spinning out of control as I tried to focus on the other guests. I heard riotous laughter. As my eyes focused, I could see Frédéric pointing at me as tears of laughter streamed down his sallow cheeks. Balzac doubled over, could hardly contain himself, his flabby chin shaking like jelly. Ingres was beside himself, in hysterics. The rest of the guests were pointing at me, screeching in gales of laughter.

"I felt a hand on my shoulder. 'Madame Sand will see you now. This way,' said the butler. I looked about me. The guests were busy talking to each other as though nothing had happened. I looked at Flaubert, who winked at me. 'You can't beat a good tonic, can you?' he said.

"I followed the butler with Flaubert close on my heels. The butler opened the large panelled doors. There stood George Sand, but not dressed in trousers and smoking a cigar as I imagined her. The woman before me was beautiful, dark-haired, and with large dark smouldering eyes. She was wearing a splendid cream dress with a pink carnation pinned to her hair that fell seductively over her shoulders. She slowly walked towards me, extending her hand. It was icy cold.

"'So, you are Oscar Wilde,' she murmured. 'Musset says you are an extraordinary talent. I must say I have not heard of you. Are you famous in England?'

"'Indeed,' I replied. 'Have you visited England?'

"'Monsieur,' she sighed. 'I have better things to do than visit dull and damp places where the populace forever speak in riddles. They are not very nice about me, are they? The newspapers call me a notorious and scandalous woman. I dread to think what they would call me if I actually set foot in the place. Chip-Chip,' she called to Chopin. 'Come here, my pet, there is someone I wish you to meet.'

"He walked over towards us, a deep frown on his brow.

"'Yes, George, my dear, what is it?'

"'This gentleman, who professes to be a writer, is Oscar Wilde, a friend of Musset,' she said.

"'That's no recommendation,' he snapped. 'I have already had the displeasure of meeting him. My dear, he seems to be more trouble than he is worth. He has already insulted Balzac and Ingres. Send him away to wherever he came from.'

"'You don't seem too popular here. Whatever have you done to upset my dear Chip-Chip,' she asked as she flicked a bit of dust from my lapel.

"'I don't know, but he is acting in the most peculiar way.'

"'Peculiar!' she laughed. 'There is nothing peculiar about Chip-Chip. He is such a darling, so divine, so different from Musset. It was from Musset I received your letter of introduction. He holds you in great esteem, not that that is of any value. He seems little changed. Time has failed to mature him. Pity, he was such a fine poet but a ratbag of a man and a lukewarm lover. I hope he is not corrupting you with his indecent habits. They can be very infectious. He can be a bit low. You must always keep a sharp eye on the likes of Musset.'

"'Oh, I do,' I replied as I looked into her deep mesmerising eyes.

"'You play billiards Oscar?' she asked, finally letting go of my hand.

"'Of a kind,' I nervously replied, her very presence making me feel hot under the collar. She gave a tinkling laugh. 'That will do. This way,' she said, indicating that I should follow her. She opened a door on to a room containing a splendid billiard table.

"'I take no prisoners, monsieur,' she announced as she tossed me a cue. 'It is your break. Make the best of it.'

"I chalked my cue and surveyed the table. The balls looked different. I picked up the black and noticed an image of Musset on it. The rest of the balls represented her lovers apart from Chopin, whom she doted on. She took delight in striking all of them but not as much as she did when her cue-ball kissed the black. She was an adroit player. She left me standing.

"George then clapped her hands as she walked into the reception room. 'It is time for a swim. Come, come, all grab a towel. Come along Oscar, join me for a dip in the Indre – it will do you the world of good. There is nothing more invigorating than to dip your soul into cool water. I never miss a day in the Indre. Its sparkling waters set me up mentally and physically for my evening pursuits,' she said, giving me a saucy wink.

"'Is it not rather cold for swimming at this time of the year,' I cried, terrified at the prospect of such an ordeal.

"'Dear, dear, such churlish behaviour. Come now. It will do you wonders and give you an appetite for dinner.'

"I reluctantly followed as the rest of the guests fell in behind her. It was bitterly cold as we wandered down towards the river. At the riverbank, a servant handed each of us a pair of bathing togs, directing us to the changing cabins, each with our names on them. I was feeling sick and nervous as I was far from a decent swimmer.

"'Come, come, in you get,' George commanded, clapping her hands like some schoolmistress. 'Let's have no dithering.'

"I dipped my toe in the freezing river. George dived in without a care in the world. All the guests followed, leaving me on my own on the riverbank, still testing the water with my toes. George noticed me standing on the riverbank and called out, 'Come along! Once in, you'll feel great.'

"Before I knew it, Balzac and Liszt dashed out of the water and dragged me into the freezing river. Once in they let go of me. The effects of Flaubert's tonic caused my muscles to tighten. I was unable to move. I felt myself going under. I screamed for help, but all the others laughed at me.

"'Bye-bye, Oscar,' they cried as they swam further and further away from me. I went under again. As much as I tried, I was unable to rise to the surface. Through the murky water, I could make out the figure of George. She reached out and grabbed my hand. As she tried to raise me, I felt a pull on my legs. Through the murky water, I could just make out the face of the Gaelic warrior from my Pity Me days. He yanked at my legs, pulling me further and further into the mire. George's grasp began to loosen, and with one yank, the warrior dragged me down. My life raced across my mind. In a final act of revenge, the warrior dashed my head against a rock. I woke up in a sweat, my heart beating like a drum.

"So much for your potion, Alfred,' I said after I had recounted this to him

"Alfred sat there speechless. 'I can't believe my tonic could have such an effect. Nightmares are unheard of in Purgatory. I must make a visit to that herbalist on Cloud Eighty-Six and ask her for some explanation. I'm sorry for your troubles, Oscar, really sorry.'"

The professor sighed. "The magic potion was a dud then, giving the opposite effect of what you desired."

"A dud... More like a deception. Poor Alfred, he was so embarrassed, he couldn't apologise enough."

The professor stood up. "It's been a very interesting and revealing session. I'll see you tomorrow.

The Heavenly Saints, the Administrators of Paradise, were sitting around the gigantic circular granite table. They had assembled for a specially convened Divine Council meeting, a rarity in the annals of the council. Once inside the chamber, their saintliness disappeared, and they reverted to their human state. This always led to vigorous and intriguing debates. There was only one item on the agenda: Oscar Wilde.

Gabriel called the council to order and they settled down, opening the folios before them.

"Item one: Oscar Wilde. This is a petition calling on the council to review the case of Oscar Wilde, denied entry to Paradise on the thirtieth day of November 1900, late of the domain of England and exile of his native Ireland and an intern of Père Lachaise in the city of Paris, France. His soul now resides on the Purgatory Reservation of Père Lachaise," the Archangel intoned.

"Thank you, Gabriel," said Peter, the Chairman of the Council. "Read out the petition, if you will."

Gabriel put his wings to one side and once comfortable, began to read.

"This application in the form of a petition dated the thirtieth day of November 1999 was submitted through the office of the Reservation Facilitator, under Article 13 of the Divine Code, by Monsieur Henry Torrès, counsel on behalf of the applicant, Sophie Hugo, representing the Select Committee of the Central Reservation of Père Lachaise. The petition reads as follows:

We, the undersigned, appeal to the Divine Council to reconsider the case of Oscar Wilde, a member of the Reservation of Père Lachaise.
We submit this Petition under Article 13 of the Divine Code seeking a declaration granting him his rite of passage to Paradise.
This petition is grounded on the affidavits and testimonials of the souls of Père Lachaise, the prognosis of the Divine Psychiatrist and the enclosed legal precedents.

Signed: Henry Torrès, Counsel on behalf of the Select Committee of the Reservation of Père Lachaise.

"This is a difficult case," the Chairman said as he looked at the petition. "I say it's only fitting we mention the rarity of this kind of submission. The first considered under Article 13 was that of the artist, Michelangelo. Before we had a procedure that was fraught with difficulties, created disagreement and brought the whole procedure into disrepute. From this came the redrafted structure and procedures we now use to resolve applications under Article 13, to consider souls who suffer the condition now referred to as the Michelangelo Syndrome. We, the Administrators of Paradise, are the only ones with full knowledge of the symptoms of this syndrome and the power to grant entry to Paradise. What is to be determined here is whether Oscar Wilde is suffering from that very syndrome. If he is, then we must apply the articles and mechanisms as laid down.

"It is well established that every soul who arrives at their Reservation realises in a very short period of time the impossibility of purging their sins and subsequently accepts their situation and settles into their new environment without too much difficulty. As you are also aware, those who have extreme difficulties are transferred to the Restoration Quarter on Cloud Eighty-Seven where their special needs are attended to. There are, however, the odd few who suffer extreme difficulties, who are of a different category to those incarcerated in the Restoration Quarter. These are what we know as Special Souls. It is only those nominated as such who can be examined to determine if they are sufferers of the Michelangelo Syndrome. As I have already said, the first time we called a Special Meeting of this kind was in the case of Michelangelo. Since then only twelve cases have came under consideration of which only three have been successful. These were Dickens, Freud and Titian – the others: Galileo, Shakespeare, Einstein, Descartes, Darwin, Van Gogh, Turner, Blake and Mozart, although showing distinct signs of the syndrome failed on the most basic test of all – that of a lack of genuine repentance for past indiscretions.

"Michelangelo's case, as you may recall, was tortuous and the hearing fraught – but was finally resolved after an adjournment to facilitate changes in the rules on voting. A point of order was made that the voting procedure should be changed to take into consideration the fact that the vast majority of council members were Italian and they would block vote in favour of Michelangelo on the mere fact he was also Italian and not give the case due consideration."

"The Italians weren't too happy," Veronica said, interrupting the Chairman.

"Indeed," he replied. "The change from a majority vote to a unanimous one with all members obliged to contribute to the debate was installed, forcing the Italians to argue their case. At the time a suggestion was made that there should be no abstentions, but the Management Committee of the Council in their wisdom decided otherwise. As it turned out the vote was unanimous in Michelangelo's case, and the symptoms he displayed have become the standard for any application made under Article 13, although the voting method used was questionable. This is what the Wilde case is all about. The question is simple – if accepted as a Special Soul, is he, therefore, a sufferer of the Michelangelo Syndrome.

"There are six questions listed on the agenda to be considered, to reach the qualified standard for a debate on the Michelangelo Syndrome to commence. The criterion is that on every one of these questions, the vote must be positive for this petition to reach the final level of qualification. If there is a positive response, Oscar Wilde will be elected as a Special Soul and therefore be in the position to be considered as a possible sufferer of the Michelangelo Syndrome. If he fails, he will take his position as a Guardian of the Reservation of Père Lachaise, the highest honour bestowed on a soul in Purgatory. The final qualification to allow us to vote on his Michelangelo Syndrome status will be whether we consider Oscar Wilde's repentance is sincere. To help you in your deliberations you will have the benefit of Professor Jude's Prognosis on Oscar's sincerity of repentance. This will be of great importance. Please scrutinise this prognosis, for it will be the defining document of this whole process.

"We will begin with the six questions, followed by the submissions on behalf of the souls of the Reservation and Jude's Prognosis. Jude has informed the Registrar that he is at present analysing Oscar and his prognosis will not be available for a while, which gives us ample time to sift through the mountain of the material before us.

"Please read out the first question, Gabriel, if you will."

"Question one: "Is Oscar Wilde unique?""

"Haven't you something easier, Gabriel."

"Sorry Mark, you'll have to tax your mind with this one, I'm afraid."

"He's certainly a gifted individual," Paul began, "although a flawed one by all accounts. Even with all of his talents, he screams flaws. He's unique, but unfortunately, he's a flawed soul."

"Aren't we all, Paul? Especially Mark."

"You're in a bitchy mood today, Veronica, aren't you? Did someone ruffle your wings?"

"You've no sense of humour. You take being a saint far too seriously."

"It is serious. It's a very serious business," Mark stated. "We're being asked to decide the fate of a troubled soul – not just a run-of-mill one, but one who happens to be a genius. You can't get more serious a business than that.

"I agree with you, but allowances should be made for his genius. We must be fair," Veronica stated.

"But why?" Matthew asked. "Tell me, why should any allowance be made for someone who's lucky enough to be gifted with genius? What's fair about that?"

"Why?" said an exasperated Veronica. "Because they are extra sensitive souls, that's why. We all know how sensitive geniuses are. They are touchy creatures and temperamental by nature. On top of that, they are more susceptible to the stresses and strains of everyday life than ordinary mortals are? Why, with their condition tending to make them take offence easily, they are inclined to lose their rag for no apparent reason and are not easily pacified. They are very sensitive souls and warrant special care and attention. They need handled with kid gloves and given free rein to allow their genius to flourish. We must be patient with them and allow them their little indulgences. After all, this is only fair and proper."

"What…That's the reason? A weak argument, wouldn't you say? Are you telling me that because Oscar is supposed to be a genius, and is temperamental and sensitive, he qualifies as a Special Soul? That he suffers from the Michelangelo Syndrome and is entitled to entry into Paradise? No, no, I don't think so. I can't buy that. It's got to be harder than that to rest your bum in Paradise."

"No, Matthew, I didn't say that. What I am saying is that his genius has to be taken into consideration, that's all. You already know genius alone would not satisfy the criteria for granting the status of a Special Soul, so I don't know why you're making a big deal out of it."

"I'm not. I am only pointing out the obvious errors in your argument. Come to think of it your argument is one big error. I don't see any fairness in making allowances for those lucky enough to be gifted. You're confusing genius with indulgence – a common mistake."

"Come now, Matthew, Veronica is entitled to her point of view," the Chairman pointed out.

Matthew looked slyly over towards Veronica. "Of course she's entitled to her point of view, but it's an odd view, to say the least. Oscar may have wasted his life, but he never wasted his talent. I don't doubt the man had extraordinary abilities – it would be difficult to argue against that – but I have to be convinced that he's so unique that he should be elected a Special Soul. Genius is a gift. To accept Veronica's argument that allowances must be made because of his genius doesn't hang well at all. Is he unique? I don't know. Is he out of the ordinary? Maybe. We've been down this road before. Perhaps matters will become clearer when we consider the remaining questions and especially after Jude's report on Oscar's mental state. Perhaps the submissions by the souls of Père Lachaise will cast a more illuminating light on the subject."

"I agree," replied Simon. "On the surface, Oscar fails to reach the criterion. Although I understand where Veronica is coming from, concerning his genius, I'm with Matthew. I need to be convinced. The argument about genius needing special treatment is not grounded on any solid foundation that I could give my support to. I'll hold my counsel on this until I hear a more convincing argument."

"Luke. You have something to add?"

"I do, Chairman. I'd love to know where this idea of allowances being made for geniuses comes from. There is no logic to it. Whoever dreamt up such nonsense?"

"It's one of those sayings that have been flung about in many different contexts. It's been around since time began," replied the Chairman.

"Probably dreamt up by a genius, to justify his outrageous behaviour," said Matthew. "You know what they're like; acting in the most obnoxious way possible and verbal abuse seems to be second nature to them. They are usually selfish, egocentric and vain. Veronica thinks we should give the likes of *them* special treatment. Really!"

"This genius nonsense doesn't stand up to scrutiny. Let's take a couple of cases – how about Chopin, for example? Now he is a genius of outstanding ability, yet his soul still resides at the Reservation of Père Lachaise. No allowances were made in his case," Bartholomew stated. "Matthew may describe geniuses colourfully, but Chopin wouldn't fit that description. Why is he not a Special Soul? Why is he not in Paradise? Chances are it's because there's something in his earthly life that's barred him, something serious enough to override his genius, that same genius Veronica believes should be given special consideration in Oscar's case. She's conveniently forgetting about his earthly vices."

"Could be that Chopin was fiercely anti-Semitic. That was always one flaw in his character that he never apologised for," replied Thérèse. "That in itself would have barred him from Paradise and certainly rule him out of the running as a Special Soul. If you're anti-Semitic, then you can't be suffering from the Michelangelo Syndrome."

"Anti-Semitic – I didn't know that?"

"Well, Bartholomew, if you were into Chopin like I am you'd be aware of it and all his other peculiarities – and there were quite a few, I can assure you, like dabbling with Madame Sand, abusing the good nature of his friends, and let his temper get the better of him. His abuse of his friend Julian Fontana, a fellow musician and compatriot, leaves a nasty taste. He worked the poor struggling musician to the bone – had him running here and there on errands on the undertaking that he would help the struggling musician in his career. He didn't, of course. He used him as a Man Friday, and his so-called friendship was hollow, to say the least. So don't make old Chopin out to be whiter than white, because he's not."

"Don't be daft. Chopin has very few flaws and, as for his peculiarities, you don't know what you're talking about," said Sebastian. "There's nothing crude or peculiar about Chopin."

"Are you saying there is with Oscar?"

"That's a matter of opinion, Veronica. It depends on what angle you come at him from."

"Victor Hugo still resides on the Reservation of the Pantheon," Bartholomew informed his colleagues. "He was a genius, yet no allowances were made for him."

"That's because he was a heathen," interceded Bernadette, "and a womaniser with a fair share of vanity."

"Perhaps that was the case, Matthew. If it was, then an allowance for Hugo's genius was ineffective, just as it ought to be in Oscar's case."

"What about Leonardo da Vinci who resides at the Reservation of Santa Groco; he has to be one of the most outstanding souls ever to have walked the earth and he was elected as a Special Soul but failed the final test on repentance. Whatever he did was touched with genius, yet no allowances were made for him, so tell me, Veronica, why should Oscar be treated any differently?"

"Because he's Oscar, that's why – not Titian, nor Chopin, nor Hugo – not any of that ilk. He's simply Oscar Wilde, that put-upon and misunderstood genius."

"*Put upon* indeed. We are the ones *put upon* having to suffer this," groaned Simon.

"Don't worry about it – she's just rambling. You know what's she's like when she gets started," laughed Matthew.

"I'm far from rambling. What I'm saying is that Oscar is a unique genius, a one-off. We have to view him on his own merits, not those of other geniuses. Allowances must be made for him, not just because of his genius, but also because of his uniqueness."

"Rubbish!" Matthew cried.

"We are getting carried away with this notion of allowances," Bernadette said, showing her annoyance with Matthew. "We can consider his genius, but it shouldn't be the determining factor. It should be remembered that any allowances would have been taken into account when the Divine Scrutinisers drew up Oscar's Credit Book when he arrived at the Reservation Centre. Any allowances would have been credited to him then. I suggest we move on to the other questions on the agenda. Maybe these will help us to reach a decision on this particular question, at a later stage."

"Sorry Bernadette," Veronica replied. "I don't think we should be flippant and dismiss this first question without giving it due consideration."

There was a murmur of agreement from the assembly.

Bernadette was livid. "I'm not being dismissive. We will give it due consideration after we have discussed the other questions. It doesn't matter in what order we discuss them. The important thing is that they are considered and discussed. The order in which it's done is irrelevant. All we have to do when we vote is to do so in the order the questions listed on the agenda. You only have to read the transcripts of other cases, and you'll see that I'm correct."

Paul stood up. All eyes focused on him. "Chairman, we must be sensible about this. Let's just agree to leave this question until last. We must be fair to this Wilde fellow, for if this petition fails, he will not have another opportunity. I fully concur with Bernadette."

"Paul's right," said the Chairman. "I'm adjourning question one to a later date."

The members were not happy with the Chairman's decision, but there were to be no arguments, as his decision was always final.

"Chairman, would it be an opportune time to submit the Credit and Debit Books before we move on to the next question? Paul asked. "It may help us in our deliberations. It may also resolve the argument of whether his genius has been credited."

"Very well, Gabriel, have you the books at hand?"

"I have," the archangel said as placed them before the Chairman, who opened the Credit Book at the biography page. "Remind us of his life, Gabriel."

"Do I have to? There's a lot to read," Gabriel moaned.

"Give us the gist of it. After all, we're pretty well versed on his life and times."

"Oscar Wilde was a lover of life,' Gabriel began. "He lived life to the full and did so with wit, style and literary dexterity. He was born in Dublin."

"Dublin! Great place," Simon said with glee.

"It is. I was there once, you know," John proudly announced. "Had a cracking time, some cool place, a bit ragged at the edges though."

"I was there too. Had a fantastic visit – impossible not to have a good time there."

"Yes, a great place, Veronica. I was on a mission there once, to shelter the downtrodden from that mad Chieftain and his motley crew that corrupted the place. It was a tough assignment. I failed, more is the pity, but I did try. Some fine watering holes there too."

"Do you mind, Simon? I was in full flow?"

"Sorry, Gabriel."

"Where was I, now," Gabriel moaned, clearly annoyed at having his flow interrupted.

"In Dublin."

"As I was saying, he was born in Dublin into a successful middle-class family. His father, William, was a prominent surgeon whilst his mother was a popular poet who wrote under the name Speranza and who won fame in her younger days writing poetry about the famine and emigration. It was from her that Oscar received most of the talents that would bring him fame and success – he also inherited from her the vanity that was to be his downfall. He soon discovered that he was gifted and even at an early age was showing signs that he was no ordinary little fellow but one destined for greatness. Blessed with a cheerful disposition a great future lay ahead of him. He attended Portora Royal School in Enniskillen; then went on to Trinity College."

"Trinity…Now that's a great place," Simon interrupted again.

"Ah, come off it, Simon. I'll never get through this at this rate. You know the rules. Behave yourself."

"Sorry. I just can't help it. I'm a real Dublin obsessive."

The Chairman looked over towards Simon and sighed, "You can say that again. Now, behave yourself. This is serious business. You will have the opportunity to speak in due course. Allow Gabriel the courtesy of being heard without interruption."

"Sorry, Chairman. I have a soft spot for Dublin since my failed mission there. As you know it was one of my great failures. They rejected the shelter I was offering, but it was a great experience all the same. Sorry, Gabriel, carry on."

"Oh, *thank you*, Simon, that's good of you,' he replied, shuffling his papers in agitation. "As I was saying, he attended Trinity College, where he proved to be an excellent student. He was a good debater and a poet of some repute. He read Greek and English and excelled in both. He went on to lecture on aesthetics. He secured a place at Magdalen College at Oxford University, where he won the prestigious Newdigate Prize. It was at Oxford that he honed the skills that were to bring success and, as it turned out, his fall from grace and ultimate demise.

"After university he embarked on a lecture tour of America, which was an outstanding success. This, it seemed, was the beginning of his rise to stardom. He was the best after-dinner speaker of his generation, with a talent for discussing in the most humorous way any subject put before him. That same humour he instilled into his plays, with great skill that brought him deserved success and respect. *A Woman of No Importance*, *An Ideal Husband* and his masterpiece The Importance of Being Ernest followed his first play, *Lady Windermere's Fan*. The plays reached the dizzy heights of success. He also published his only novel, *The Picture of Dorian Gray*, a society romance with homosexual undercurrents. The book caused a storm of controversy amongst the puritans. The most voracious of his critics were those who hadn't even read the novel. He revelled in its notoriety, considering it a badge of honour. The more controversy there was, the more outrageous he became.

"But, at the height of his career, he entangled himself with the Marquess of Queensbury, a minor aristocrat of little importance, over a remark made by him concerning Oscar's alleged behaviour with his son, Alfred, affectionately known as Bosie. Queensbury left an open card at Oscar's club accusing him of posing as a sodomite. Against all advice, he sued the marquess. The outcome was disastrous. He lost the case and there followed a criminal prosecution by the state for indecent behaviour. After two trials, he was found guilty and sentenced to two years' imprisonment with hard labour. He was deserted by many of his friends and society turned against him. He suffered terribly in his incarceration, first at Wandsworth Gaol in London and then at Reading Gaol, where he wrote what most experts accept now as a masterpiece, *De Profundus*, a thirty thousand-word letter to Lord Alfred.

"After his release he was forced into exile, travelling to Paris and other European cities, living off handouts and the goodwill of his small group of loyal friends. He was a vagrant, spending his time wandering the boulevards and back streets of Paris and frequenting her many cafés and bars. The less money he had, the seedier and cheaper the bars became. Oscar became a sad and lonely figure, and the only serious piece of literature he completed during his exile was his famous poem, *The Ballad of Reading Gaol*, which unfortunately was to be his last contribution to the annals of literature. He died a broken man in a Parisian hotel from cerebral meningitis at the age of only forty-four. He converted to the Roman Catholic faith on his deathbed. History has recorded that he is one of the most successful writers of the nineteenth century. Next to the bible and Shakespeare, his are the most-quoted works in the world.

"That, Chairman, is a brief outline to the life of Oscar Wilde. You will find before you a collection of biographies and copies of his entire works for your perusal as well, as copies of his Credit and Debit Books."

"Thank you, Gabriel. Yes, Anthony?"

"Is there any reference to his creditworthiness concerning his supposed genius?"

Veronica was seething. "What do you mean, *supposed* genius? He was and still is a genius."

"If you say so…"

"Gabriel is there *any* reference to his genius?"

"Yes, Chairman. However, he has no credit for his genius but does for how he's used it."

"Well, that blows your argument out of the water, Veronica, doesn't it? If an exception was given for his genius, it's not recorded. By the thin look of his credit book, his genius is an irrelevance."

Veronica glared at Anthony, knowing she had lost her argument.

"I suggest we adjourn," the Chairman said, "and consider the material before us, including the Credit and Debit Books. We'll meet again in a week."

"Gabriel, another question if you please."

"Very well, Chairman. Question two. Is Oscar Wilde a moral soul?"

The chamber gave a deep sigh of resignation.

"This is even tougher than the first," moaned Sebastian. Sebastian was a long-term opponent of the Michelangelo Syndrome nonsense, as he called it, and had little interest in it. He thought it improper for a soul to gain entry to Paradise by default.

"It's always so difficult judging morals, especially those of others."

"You can say that again, Veronica, and especially Oscar's."

"A minefield, I'd say," replied Christopher. "It's not a sensible path to take, being a moralist. Look what happens on earth when people become moralistic. It never works. All it achieves is dissent and bitterness. It's a tough job being a saint these days. I always thought being one would have been a bit of a breeze. I never thought I'd be asked to judge the morals of others. Makes you wish you were a mere mortal. I never wanted to be a saint really. It was down to others who thought I'd performed miracles and I ended up here, a blessed saint. I would have settled for being an ordinary citizen of Paradise anytime. I hate having to judge the morals of others."

"Stop bellyaching. If you enjoy the benefits of being a saint, then you must accept the downside of it as well," cried Bernadette.

"Downside – who'd have thought there'd be a downside to being a saint? You must accept, Bernadette, this Wilde business is tough. I don't know where to begin. I can't see us resolving this in any way whatsoever. It's just too difficult."

"It may be, but we are directed to consider Oscar's fate, and that's what we should concentrate our minds on," the Chairman pointed out.

"Where do we begin then with someone like Oscar Wilde?" asked Bartholomew. "He is a difficult soul to get to grips with. A bit of a slippery character, too many alter egos to grapple with."

"I suggest we get the ball rolling with the Seven Deadly Sins."

"Wait a moment, Chairman. If Wilde had committed any of the Seven Deadly Sins, he'd be in Hell and therefore no concern of ours."

"I suppose so, Bartholomew – unless there is some other *exception* to the rule," Matthew teasingly suggested, casting a sly look in Veronica's direction.

The Chairman peered at Matthew. "Now, now, you know there's always an exception to the rule. The committing of a Deadly Sin would not necessarily condemn one to Hell. It's all a matter of degree."

"Uh! That's news to me," muttered Simon. "We must be singing from different hymn sheets."

"Let's move on. We have a lot to get through," the Chairman complained.

"Wait a moment, Chairman. We can't leave it at that – what about these degrees –You've lost me. Maybe an explanation is in order."

"Listen, Bartholomew, you must be aware of what I'm talking about. I'm not going to waste time explaining divine doctrine. If you don't know it by now, you never will. Let's move on. We have a lot to get through. We will begin with vanity. John! The floor's yours."

"Vanity and Oscar Wilde; Um, where does one begin?" mused John, as he stroked the stubble on his square chin.

"In his genes," suggested Matthew.

"What? You mean it's *sexual?*" asked a surprised Thérèse de Lisieux, fanning herself.

"No! Not those jeans, stupid," he laughed at her one-track mind.

"What other jeans do you mean?"

"Genetic ones."

"Are you saying he's born with it? Born with vanity?"

"Yes, that's exactly what I'm saying. I'd say it's in his genetic makeup. The poor soul can't help it. Vanity is part and parcel of who he is. It is as simple as that. Genetics is what it's all about. It's the very fabric of life."

"Nonsense," Thérèse cried. "You don't half talk a load of rubbish at times. Vanity and genetics; where do get your notions from?"

"It's what you call *knowledge*," Matthew replied with an air of superiority. "When Oscar looks in a mirror, he can't but admire himself. He sees perfection, absolute perfection. He is in love with his own reflection. He's as vain as one gets, whether it's genetic or not."

"If vanity was genetic, then how could it be a sin?" asked Bartholomew.

They all looked at each other, wondering who is going to answer such a dicey question.

"Matthew, you seem to have theories on these matters. How do you answer that?" asked Christopher.

"What I'm saying, is that in Oscar's case it's clearly genetic. His vanity is a genetic hiccup. There can be no other logical explanation."

"Answer the question, will you? Is it a sin or not?" Bartholomew insisted.

"Well, if it's genetic, as I believe it is, then no, his vanity can't be a sin."

"What!" John was on his feet. "Did you ever hear such claptrap? A genetic hiccup – what on all that is holy is a genetic hiccup? How did you ever end up being a saint with that kind of talk?"

"That's enough now. We don't want any personality clashes here," cried the Chairman, wagging his finger at Matthew and John. "Your behaviour is unbecoming. You are saints after all, and apostles too, so start acting as such and pack this nonsense in and concentrate your minds on the task before you."

"There's no such thing as a genetic hiccup," John insisted.

"How do you know that?" snapped Matthew.

"Because genetics are God's perfected blueprint of life, of all living things, and He didn't hiccup in the process. I'm telling you, there's no such thing."

Matthew tapped the table. "What makes you think that?" he asked.

"Genetics is the key to life. They may have just discovered them on earth – you know how slow they can be – but we have known about the mechanics of it since we were canonised. We all know of the genetic defects that are part of the Human Condition. I don't have to list them, as they are numerous, so why can't Oscar suffer from one of them? I'm telling you, his condition is genetic and yes, it could be a genetic hiccup."

"Well," said Bernadette, "surely when God engineered us, he gave us the most perfect structure – one without flaws or blemishes of any kind. Any flaws that we suffer from have arisen from mankind's abuse of nature – not just nature but of themselves. We are all given free will, and I'd say that it's from the abuse of this free will that all flaws emanate."

"How do you work that one out?" asked a curious Thérèse.

"Mankind has free will to do what it likes. Isn't that right?"

"I'd agree with that."

"We're all fully aware of the abuse of this free will since Eve took forbidden fruit from the Tree of Life and tempted Adam with it. She didn't have to take a seductive bite, and Adam could have refused the temptation to share her forbidden fruit. They knew it was forbidden, yet they ignored it and exercised the free will that had been given to them and paid dearly for it," Bernadette explained. "The abuse of nature has been part of human existence down through the ages. Since the beginning of time, mankind has abused everything with which it came face to face with. Think of all the things man has gorged on that were detrimental to health and well-being. Hand in hand with those abuses was mankind's indulgence in interbreeding, which could profoundly affect the genetic blueprint.

"In recent times the abuse has reached more disturbing heights, with chemical interference to the growth cycle. The digestion of these modified crops may have interfered with the genetic makeup of the present population and that could cause untold contamination in future generations.

"The medicines that have been created and the abuse of them could also have damaged the genetic makeup in the most fundamental way. Furthermore, the abuse of natural resources, such as the continuous burning of fossil fuels and the subsequent damage to the atmosphere through global warming has, in turn, interfered with the supply of pure oxygen, which could also have interfered with the human genetic blueprint.

"And what about all those foreign substances humans have pumped into their system: alcohol, nicotine and all the other drugs. Surely, that could have had some influence on the genetic makeup. Free will; humans have it but abuse it. It didn't have to be like this. But it is now they're paying for the abuse of that free will. Before them were all the benefits of what nature had to offer, to either to use or abuse. Of course, having free will and no sense, humans used and abused it. Maybe poor Oscar's genetic makeup had been interfered with, which resulted in his excessive vanity and sexual behaviour."

"Very good, Bernadette – never thought of you as an environmentalist. You put up a good argument I'll grant you that," admitted Christopher. "But let's face it, Oscar suffers from excessive vanity brought on by his uncontrollable ego, and he manufactured that himself. There's nothing genetic in it at all."

"Then let's take it from a different angle," suggested Bernadette. "What about the diseases the world suffers from – like cancer, Alzheimer's and diabetes. Are they genetic? Yes, they are, but were they in the original blueprint? I doubt it. They somehow attached themselves to the original genes then became part of the genetic makeup, interfering with God's original design. Most diseases come about because of man's abuse of nature and each other. If you accept that, then surely someone like Oscar could suffer from this kind of genetic hiccup in the guise of vanity – seems logical to me."

"I can't accept that. If, as you say the genetic makeup has been interfered with and Oscar's vanity could be the result of such contamination then Matthew can't be right in saying it's a genetic hiccup in the manner he implied. If I'm wrong, Matthew, correct me, but I took it that what you were saying is that such a hiccup was there in God's original blueprint."

"Yes, I say there is only the original blueprint, and it's an impossibility to interfere with it. Whatever deformities or deviations there are were there to start with."

Disquieting murmurs permeated the chamber.

"What?" Thérèse cried. 'Do you know what you are saying? You're saying that God engineered all of those horrendous diseases and debilitating disorders, that they are part and parcel of His master plan, His original blueprint?"

"Yes, I do."

A distinct chill ran through the chamber at such a suggestion.

"Why, that just doesn't make sense," Thérèse said, shaking her head in disbelief that any saint could utter such words. "The diseases we have are of our own making. God didn't create them – we as human beings did, we've done so by abusing what we have and by abusing each other. Our interference with nature is the real cause of the diseases that rampage across the earth. Ever since mankind went astray in the Garden of Eden, it's tried to play God, tried in its misguided way to better its creator's work. No! Diseases are not God's doing, they are mankind's."

"I think we are heading for deep and dangerous waters if we continue in this vein. To challenge genetics is to question the very existence of God and His creation," said Veronica.

"Well, we're in the wrong place to do that," Simon cracked.

The Chairman tapped the table with his gavel. "I must agree with Veronica – we don't want to get into a protracted debate on the fine-tuning of God's creation when what is before us is a simple, straightforward question: Did he suffer from vanity? Whether his vanity is genetic or not, we need an answer to this question. If there are no other points to be made about vanity, I suggest we move on."

"I still say it's genetic."

"All right, Matthew, you've made your point," said the Chairman.

"Chairman," said Luke. "I've spent some time studying this Wilde fellow and his scribbling, and it seems to me that he took people's tolerance of his vanity to the limit. Unlike Matthew, I believe his vanity is nothing more than he making light of life is. He tells the whole world he's just magnificent, a grand chap and all that, but, actually, he is laughing at life and how seriously others take it. Nearly all his vain remarks have been made either in the context of his comedies or in some after-dinner speech. He is quite harmless. The only damage he's done is to himself."

"I don't think I can go along with that," replied Bernadette. "What if he used vanity to enhance and promote his literary career and standing in society? Would that not be vanity at its worst?"

"Ah, but did he? Was it all put on, all a smokescreen? It doesn't seem likely," Patrick said as he joined the debate for the first time.

"Come on, Paddy, you can't be objective. You're his patron saint."

"I maybe, but I have as much right to my point of view as you have, Matthew. I have every right to contribute to this debate as fully as possible. We all have. I'm well capable of being objective. Oscar is no vainer than anyone else is. He's just a bit of a show-off."

"Yes, I'll accept that," added Bartholomew. "He's a joker, having harmless fun at the expense of those who think they're high and mighty."

"I still say it's genetic."

"So you keep telling us, Matthew," sighed the Chairman. "I can't see us getting any more mileage out of this. You will have to make your own informed decision on his vanity. There is enough on record about his so-called vanity. I suggest you digest it and make your own informed judgment. Let's move on. We have a lot to get through."

"The next sin if you please, Gabriel."

The archangel paused before announcing "Lust."

"Anyone for lust?" the Chairman asked, with a chuckle, as he scanned the faces of his council, from whom there came an enthusiastic response.

"One at a time," he said, hitting the table with his gavel to bring the meeting to order. "We don't want lust getting out of hand." He pointed at Saint Anne, who had raised her hand.

"The floor is yours, Anne."

"There are certainly elements of Oscar's life that could be labelled lustful. He lusted obsessively after Lord Alfred; he wasn't shy about lusting after many other young men, the more Greek-looking, the better. The reverse side was his obsession with women – Sarah Bernhardt, for example. He certainly lusted after her. He'd have loved to have gotten the better of her."

"He may have, for all we know," Matthew sniggered.

"Chances are, he did and with Lillie Langtry and several others. He seemed to lean towards the theatrical."

"Nonsense, Anne. You are making his life look grubby. You imply that he had no morals and that he was sex-mad. There is more to this complicated and extraordinary soul than his sexuality. We must look at him as a whole individual and not to simply isolate characteristics which chime with our prejudices."

"Your problem, Veronica, is that you can never see anything wrong with Oscar, even when there is clear evidence to the contrary," replied Anne. "He has a lustful soul; it's as simple as that. He lusted after anyone who he thought beautiful that could satisfy his needs, like Lilly Langtry, Sarah Bernhardt, Alfred Douglas, Robbie Ross and all those other young men who crossed his path."

"That's a gross misrepresentation. You are being utterly unfair to him," Veronica replied. "You're letting personal prejudices blur your judgment which is dicey at the best of times."

"I beg your pardon; I'm not prejudiced at all. Just realistic and my judgment is sound."

"Does anyone else think Oscar is driven by lust?" asked the Chairman.

Eager hands thrust the air, waving in an attempt to catch his eye.

"I do," Ignatius Loyola said in a stern voice. "We can argue about how tainted he is by the other Deadly Sins, but I do not doubt that he is guilty of the sin of lust. I must confess I'm no fan of the man. I can't understand what is so fascinating about him. He does nothing for me. Really, what did his earthly existence amount to – as I see it, nothing more than over-indulgence and a never-ending ego trip. A life spent seeking and over-indulging in the pleasures of life. It was his lust that drove him, not just through life, but headlong to his demise. Because he was considered by a few to be a reasonable writer should not blind us to the fact that he was morally bankrupt, a Deadly Sinner."

"How can you say such a thing?" Veronica cried, greatly shaken by Ignatius' opinion. "You seem to have overlooked the essence of the man. What does it matter that he suffered from weaknesses to which all of us are susceptible? So what, that he had an eye for the sensuous side of life? That doesn't mean he's a bad man. Peel that away and you'll find a decent and compassionate man touched by genius."

Matthew burst out laughing. "Touched – you said it."

"It will take more than sweet talk to convince me of your belief in him, in his genius and goodness. I still say he's a lustful soul and not a suitable candidate for Paradise," Ignatius responded.

Veronica shook her head in disbelief at Ignatius's tirade.

"Does anyone have anything else to add?" Gabriel asked.

More hands shot up. The Chairman eyed them up and down. The council members seemed keen to deal with lust. He shook his head. "On second thoughts, perhaps it may be more prudent to allow you to enlarge of this subject through the committee stages."

There was a collective sigh, then silence.

"Let's move on. Gabriel, what's next?"

"Sloth."

"John. You can take this if you like."

"Really, Chairman, I don't think there is any point in discussing this, as it doesn't apply to him. One thing is certain – Oscar Wilde was neither idle nor suffered in any way from indolence. I'd say he didn't waste a moment of his time and if anything was a very industrious individual."

Bernadette tapped the table. "I agree," she said. "There wasn't a lazy bone in his body. I suggest we move on."

"Hold on," cried Thomas. "I'll challenge that. What about his lazing about in Paris – he didn't do much there other than doss around, drink at the boulevard cafés, visit seedy bars and make a nuisance of himself and pursuing street boys. A real industrious fellow, wasn't he?"

"Come off it, Thomas. It is well documented that he was suffering from deep depression whilst in France," Bernadette exclaimed. "He had lost everything. You're just being pernickety, taking one isolated period in his life to say he was a lazy and idle man."

"Three years is more than an isolated period," Thomas cried. "It's a long time to idle about, begging off the public to maintain his decadent ways. What literary work did he produce in those years, nothing – absolutely nothing – why, because he was too lazy to pick up a pen. If he were the true artist he always professed to be, he would have produced something of worth, even in the direst of situations. History is full of artists and writers – Van Gogh and James Joyce, for example – who burrowed away at their art in some run-down-garret, but not him. All he did was wallow in self-pity, sponge off others and screw around. He produced nothing of artistic merit during that time. He's overrated. Not a true artist at all."

"That's cruel, deliberately cutting. What about some compassion for the unfortunate soul?"

"It's nothing to do with compassion. It's all about realism. You go on about Wilde's decadence while he was in Paris as though it were unique, that he lost his way for a while. That couldn't be further from the truth. He was off the rails a long time before he arrived in Paris. His lifestyle in London was far from what most would call decent. Forget about his talent and look at the way he lived his life. He *was* idle. He was even too idle to go to his own wife's funeral. Now, if that is not the action of a sloth of a man, I don't know what is. I'm not examining him through the lens of rose-tinted spectacles as you are. Sloth – he was a master at it and, like his lust, it sent him to an early grave."

"For a saint, Thomas, you can be a right bastard. It seems we are wasting our time debating this as most have him condemned already – if not as a sexual deviant then as a Deadly Sinner."

"That's not the talk of a saint," said the Chairman, alarmed at the language used. "All we are indulging in is a vigorous debate, which is a healthy pursuit. Just because someone disagrees with your point of view, you don't have to get personal about it. Even if someone doesn't agree with you doesn't make you wrong or them right. Even if you're a minority of one, you are not necessarily wrong."

"Does anyone else have anything to say about sloth? No? Very well then, let's move on. Gabriel! The next sin please."

"Envy," the archangel announced.

"I too have spent some time delving into Wilde's literary work and reading the umpteen biographies about him. Throughout my research, I discovered that envy played no part in his life. Many envied *him* but he seems to be devoid of the sin himself. He admired many of his contemporaries but there is no record he was envious of any of them or their work. If anything, he went out of his way to compliment them. He seems incapable of jealousy or resentment of any kind," Simon said.

"But surely he must have resented the Marquess of Queensbury, for the trauma he caused him," interrupted Luke.

"You would have thought so, but as I've already said, there is nothing on record of resentment against the Marquess or of anyone else, and as for envy, there's no evidence of him suffering from it."

"What about that Bosie chap?" Luke asked. "He must have resented him. Resentment oozes from every page of *De Profundis*. If it wasn't for Bosie, Oscar Wilde would probably have lived out a full and fruitful life instead of having it cut short by an act of folly."

"Many would say that Oscar was responsible for his downfall – not Bosie, Queensbury, society or the legal system," added Christopher. "If he had exercised discretion, he could have avoided the disaster that befell him."

"That doesn't answer the question: Did he suffer from envy?"

"I'm telling you, he was a resentful man. He resented the upper class yet made his money by writing witty plays about them. He amused them but behind his mask, he resented them."

"It's nothing to do with resentment," Bernadette responded. "We seem to be interpreting the meaning of words in the most extreme manner. It's envy we're discussing and there is a difference between resentment and envy."

"Is there? I thought they went together like bread and butter."

"You're splitting hairs," Francis said as he joined the debate for the first time. "Let's interpret envy as we see fit. To continue arguing over precise meanings will leave us frustrated, annoyed with each other, and devalue the Divine Code we are obliged to uphold. We can't allow it to be brought into disrepute."

The Chairman waited for more contributors, but none was forthcoming. "Let's remember what Francis has said. Let's stick to the facts and move on."

"The next sin is gluttony," Gabriel said.

"Who's first?" asked the Chairman. "Yes, Mark?"

"Oscar Wilde was a glutton all right," Mark emphatically declared. "But his gluttony was for living – not a sin in my book. If there was excess in his life, it was the excessive pleasure he took from it."

"He was greedy for success," Anne said, looking over at Mark. "Surely that's sinful?"

"Nonsense… I'm sure the gluttony in the sinful meaning describes those who are greedy, who eat more than their fill, who gorge themselves or those who have possessions above their requirements."

"Well, Mark," replied Anne, "he did have *more* than his fill, he wasn't content with literary success; he wanted more. He wanted to gorge himself with success until it made him sick. And he was utterly debauched. He feasted himself on sex of every persuasion. He was a glutton for it."

Sebastian stood up, shaking his head in disbelief. "Here, in this brief circulated to us," he said as he waved the document above him, "is a report on the activities of Oscar at the Reservation of Père Lachaise. What jumps out from its pages is that he is an outstanding soul who shows no sign of what we are debating here. Apart from this report, there are testimonials galore about his earthly and his purgatorial life that confounds most of the negative comments said about him. On balance, I say he is a decent soul who deserves our compassion and understanding. I suggest Anne reads it as her comments suggest she hasn't."

The Chairman sighed, wiping his brow. "Let's move on."

"A point of order, Chairman."

"Yes, Martin, what is it?"

"I don't want to be awkward, but I must bring to the attention of the council the possibility that we may be heading for a breach of Fair Procedures." The whole council glared at Martin as if he were mad.

"Divine Justice and Fair Procedures are the cornerstones of the administration of Paradise and, I must say, Martin, I'm rather surprised that any member of the council could suggest that there could be a possible breach or we could possibly be capable of such a breach," said the despairing Gabriel.

"Yes, I agree with Gabriel, it seems such an outrageous suggestion. You had better state your case, Martin. It had better be good," added the Chairman.

"If Patrick is allowed to continue in this debate or have a vote on this issue it will leave the decision of the council in doubt, for I believe there could be a strong possibility of bias."

"Bias!" cried the chorus of saints.

"How on all that is holy do you work that out?" asked Veronica.

"With the greatest of respect to Patrick, it must be pointed out that he is a compatriot of Oscar and I doubt he can be objective. For him to argue the merits of this case and to vote on it is asking for trouble. Although he will argue in a fair manner, I'm afraid he'll allow the politics of his subconscious mind to rule."

Patrick sprung to his feet, seething.

"Rubbish!" he snarled. "I'm quite capable of being objective, I'm Irish, after all – at least, I'm an honorary Irishman – and we're masters of objectivity – experts."

"That may be so, Patrick," continued Martin. "But your objectivity would surely be compromised by the very fact that Oscar is a compatriot of yours. It's only natural to stand up for one's own. Hidden within your sub-conscience mind will be something tapping away, reminding you of that very fact. I should remind you and the council of the arguments that followed the Michelangelo case. Then, all that was required for him to gain free passage was a majority. Most of us will recall that all the Italians intended to vote in mass, in favour, without even debating the motion. Because of the disquiet, it caused the rules were changed to what we now have, but not quite changed enough to avoid the possibility of bias."

"Let's get this right," the Chairman said. "Are you saying Martin, that all the Irish saints should be barred from participation in the debate and vote, solely based on their nationality?"

"Well, if we want a fair and just result, that's exactly what I'm saying. It's nothing to do with prejudice, I can assure you. It would be no different if he were French, Chinese or any other nationality. It's all about fairness. No soul should be a judge in his own cause. If this council wants to avoid being seen as breaching the Principles of Divine Justice, yes, they should be barred."

The members of the council took a sharp intake of breath at such a suggestion. The Irish saints were very popular within the conclave, and all thought Martin had taken leave of his saintly senses.

"Martin," sighed the Chairman. "How could you say such a thing? That we, your saintly colleagues could come to a decision that wasn't fair or just, that we could be capable of breaching the Principles of Divine Justice. I must say, I'm saddened and disappointed by your attitude, which is unbecoming a saint."

Martin was on his feet, clearly rattled by the council's attitude towards him and the Chairman's slight to his saintliness.

"How can you all turn on me like this, when all I'm doing is expressing my concerns? I must remind you, Chairman and fellow members, why there was a change to Article 13 after the Michelangelo case. As you know, all that was needed then to pass the motion was a simple majority. At the time, the Italian had an overall majority, and it was certain they would vote for Michelangelo for no other reason than he was an Italian. They had little interest in the merits of the case. An objection was raised before the vote, saying that the Italians should vigorously debate the issues before them, as they and all of us are obliged to do, and not take matters as read, as they were intent on doing. It gave the impression that they had already prejudged matters in favour of Michelangelo and all they had to do was rubber-stamp their decision. Veronica, you should know what I'm on about. It was you who filed the objection."

"I'm fully aware of it.' replied Veronica. "My objection was nothing to do with nationality, but with the lack of debate by the Italian members. When the debate commenced, not one of them participated. The issue of bias never occurred to me or anyone else present. If it did, they remained silent. My objection was simply that they had made their minds up well before the meeting commenced. They weren't interested whether Michelangelo reached the desired criteria, only that he was a fellow Italian. I wasn't seeking to have them barred, only to ensure a full and scrupulous debate."

"If the Italians were barred from the vote, the decision would have been more just. The issue of a possible bias should have been addressed there and then, for if it had, we wouldn't have this dilemma now," Martin declared. "Although it wasn't ruled as such the Italians were biased, just as Patrick and the rest of his Irish colleagues will be if they vote on this motion. To any reasonable soul, their decision could be seen as a bias in favour of Oscar."

Bridget was seething. She was on her feet, waving and trying to attract the attention of the Chairman.

"Order! Order!" cried the Chairman. "Yes, Bridget."

"Chairman, it is downright insulting of Martin to say that we Irish could be accused of being biased. I have never heard such gobbledygook. So what if Oscar is Irish. I will make my decision on the merits of the case. I say Martin is out of order and should withdraw his objection."

"Hear, hear," Kevin cried. "Good on you, Bridget. You let him have it. How dare he say we Irish could possibly be biased? Martin. I think you're taking liberties.

"I'm doing no such thing. All I'm doing is making a valid point. It's of great importance that we give Oscar a fair hearing that's in accordance with Fair Procedures and the Principles of Divine Justice and that none of us members of the conclave of saints is seen to be a judge in our own cause. This will be the case if the Irish saints are allowed to vote on the issue of Oscar Wilde, one of their own."

"Martin!" cried the Chairman. "You know we always adhere to Fair Procedures. The Irish couldn't possibly have any effect on the vote as they are in a minority. Why are you making such a big deal about this? If Oscar's case is made an exception, I don't know where it will lead."

"I do," said Maelruain. "It'll lead to chaos, that's where it will lead, to absolute chaos."

"It will lead to Divine Justice," a voice came from the chamber, a lone voice in Martin's favour.

"Nobody's complained about this bias before and I think it's a bad idea to do so now. It's the first time an Irish soul has come before the council, and all of a sudden an objection is raised about those members who are the same nationality as the applicant and therefore considered biased. Well, I'm not, and I'm certain that all of us Gaels aren't either. We will not be sidelined."

"I must say. Martin does make a very good argument. I know exactly where he's coming from." All heads turned towards the speaker. "I think we should give serious consideration to a change of rules, say in a way that those who have a direct interest in the matter should abstain from the vote but be allowed to contribute to the debate," said Valentine. "It makes sense. The revised rules allow abstentions, so it may be wise to ask the Irish members to step aside."

Patrick was raging. He stood up, his fists and teeth clenched. He knew he'd have to keep cool; after all, it wouldn't look seemly for a patron saint to lose his rag. He took a deep breath, counted to ten and continued. "Well, my dear Valentine, you've seen the error of *your* ways and expect *us* Irish to pay for it. You voted for your compatriot, but now you say that was unfair and we Irish should be denied what you were entitled to. Doesn't seem to be much fairness there, does there; seems to be out-and-out prejudice to me."

"Nonsense!" cried, Francis. "This has nothing to do with prejudice. All Martin is saying is that no saint should be a judge in his own cause."

"I didn't think I'd come across prejudice here. I was under the impression that we left that well behind us when we shuffled off our mortal coil. Haven't we Irish suffered enough prejudice on earth without having to suffer from it here, of all places? " replied a disheartened Patrick.

"Yes! Patrick is right. Martin's remarks smack of prejudice," said Kevin. "We Irish have had to contend with prejudice for years. We've had to fight it on earth; now we have to do battle with it here. It is so unfair. Chairman, I suggest you dismiss this application of bias as the frivolous and vexatious nonsense it is."

"I have no axe to grind. I have nothing whatsoever against you, Kevin or any other Irish saint," answered Martin. "All I'm doing is making a good solid legal argument. You're all getting carried away with yourselves in thinking my concerns are based on prejudice. Nothing could be further from the truth. You all know me well enough to know this."

The Chairman tapped his gavel. "This calls for an adjournment. I need to consider this dilemma. I will give my judgment at two."

The Chairman departed to the disgruntled murmurs of his council. The saints made their way out on to the steps of the chamber, where they huddled together in small groups arguing the merits of Martin's objection. Two hours passed. They were becoming edgy when Gabriel's bell rang out, calling them to the chamber for the Chairman's judgment.

The Chairman looked uncomfortable as he took his seat, his broad forehead creased with anxiety. He wasn't having a good day.

"This is the judgment to Martin's objection on a point of order, that order being that all Irish members should be barred from voting as a matter of fairness, in the case of Oscar Wilde. Martin contends that if Patrick and other Irish saints participate, and vote, there could be a case of bias and therefore a breach of Fair Procedures, which would be against the Principles of Divine Justice," the Chairman said as he began to outline his judgment. "There is no divine case history of this kind of objection, and thus all we have to rely on is that of earthly precedent. If you were deciding matters outside this chamber, there would be no possibility of bias, as there would be divine intervention. However, within this chamber, as you are all fully aware, there is no such intervention. Here, you revert to your earthly personalities and prejudices with all the other peculiarities that afflict the Human Condition. Before you are the recent earthly judgments from several countries concerning breaches of natural justice involving bias. Under Rule 99 of the Divine Code, I have discretion on the formulation and alteration to rules and regulations covering voting. Thus, I am making use of this discretion and applying the principles laid out in these earthly judgments in this case. I realise this will not be popular with the Irish members, but I feel this is the only fair and just decision. For this reason, I am ordering that Patrick and his fellow Irish saints be barred from this particular vote."

Patrick was on his feet. "This is unjust! This can't be right! I say you should reconsider your judgment, Chairman. Martin has no solid grounds for his objection. It will be a travesty if this judgment is allowed to stand."

"Hear, hear," cried Bridget and Kevin with others making their objections clear.

"Order, Order!" cried Gabriel as he rang his bell. "How dare you interrupt the Chairman? Sit down and let him continue."

"I'm sorry, Patrick, but that is my judgment. However unfair you may consider my decision, you have to accept it. I'm also making a ruling that in any future applications under Article 13 no member will be allowed to vote if they are of the same nationality as the applicant. However, Patrick, as a concession, you and all the Irish members will be allowed to fully partake in the debate."

Patrick threw his arms up in despair. The Irish saints took their seats, muttering their contempt for the ruling.

The Divine Dictionary

After calling the meeting to order, Gabriel announced the next of the Seven Deadly
Sins to be discussed in connection with the case of Oscar Wilde: greed.

"Who wishes to open the discussion?" asked the Chairman.

Martha put up her hand. The Chairman nodded his assent, and she began to speak.

"Greed has had so many meanings attached to it that it's easy to forget its real meaning," she began.

"I always thought greed was greed. Don't tell me you're going to give us a dictionary definition?"

"No, Matthew, I'll leave that to Gabriel. Chairman, as a matter of thoroughness, I believe a definition is warranted."

"We don't need a dictionary. We know the meaning of greed. We have managed to understand the meaning of vanity, sloth, lust, envy and gluttony without the help of a dictionary. We are not all stupid. Greed is greed, and that's the end of it."

"Sorry, Matthew," the Chairman announced. "I'm going along with Martha on this – Gabriel, out with the Divine Dictionary, if you please."

Gabriel reached for the voluminous book, blowing off a layer of dust. "Let's see, now," he said as he flicked through the pages. "Here we go, Greed: ravenous, covetous, voracious, gluttonous and rapacious. That should keep things simmering for a while."

"There you are," said Martha. "Didn't I say there was more to it than first appears?"

"Greed is still greed," Matthew insisted.

"Yes, Rebecca," said the Chairman, offering her the floor.

"Oscar Wilde and greed; It doesn't sit too well with him, does it? Well, that's Oscar for you – a greedy blackguard if there ever was one. He was always hungry for sex and didn't seem too selective when it came to his prey. He couldn't get enough of it. Yes, it's his sexual greed that condemns him as a Deadly Sinner."

"That's unfair," cried Veronica, visibly upset at Rebecca's tirade.

"Far from it; I'm telling it as it is. Greed was the creed of this diseased soul. I am telling you, Veronica, you've been blinded by his fine words. You are not the first woman won over by a slick tongue, unable to see the deceiver behind the silken words. Whatever angle you come at him from, greed fits him like a glove. One only has to glance at his life to see what a greedy man he was. All the definitions of greed suit him fine. Oh dear, must I say more? If there were a degree for greed, he'd have passed with distinction. He was a master of it, and there was no one quite like him, was there? He didn't just suffer from greed but revelled in it."

"I'm with Rebecca," Matthew said. "And we didn't need a dictionary definition of greed to know whether it fitted him or not."

"Well, I disagree."

"You would, Veronica. You're just a Wilde obsessive who refuses to see any flaws in him even when they are screaming at you."

"No, Matthew, I just see him for what he is."

"It's quite clear what he is?"

"I wouldn't say he's guilty of greed," Joseph interrupted, making his first contribution to the debate. "To me, he's just a gifted soul with a few glitches in his makeup. He's just like the rest of us. On the whole, he was a decent human being, and he's apparently a decent soul in Purgatory. You won't find me saying much against him. Perhaps Matthew should reflect a little, and then perhaps he will see things in a different light."

Matthew laughed. "The man's a Deadly Sinner in every possible way. There is no getting away from it. Sin seeps out of him like liquid from a sieve. He's soaked in it."

"You would say that. You don't give much thought before opening your mouth. Reflection seems a heavy burden to you. How you ended up an apostle, I'll never know."

"Silence," demanded the Chairman. "Yes, Bernadette?"

"Why do we have to sit through this stupid nonsense? Surely, we can relax on the comfort of our clouds and come to our own conclusions instead of this continuous bickering. What we are doing here is serving no good purpose at all. It's a waste of time."

The Chairman wiped his brow and gave a regretful sigh. "Haven't I already stated that the rules dictate that we go through this process? Whether we like it or not, this is the only process open to us. If there's no more contribution to greed, please, can we move on?"

There was silence.

"Right, we're down to the last sin now; is that so, Gabriel?"

"Indeed," Gabriel acknowledged. "Anger."

"Can I begin?"

"Very well, Helen."

"It would have been natural for Oscar to have been angry with society when it turned on him in such a malicious way, or when many of his friends deserted him or when his own country disowned him, but he didn't. He showed no anger whatsoever."

"Be fair, Helen – we don't know that. For all we know he could have been ranting and raving in private and keeping up appearances in public," said Simon.

"Anger's not an emotion one can keep bottled up for long," she replied. "And there's so much written about him, that if there was anger in his life, surely it would have been noted in some biography or other."

"He was angry with Lord Alfred Douglas. He had to have been. I'm certain he vented his spleen on him. Perhaps he privately gave him a good verbal kicking."

"Simon! That's enough," cried the Chairman. "If you're not careful you'll be sanctioned and sent to the Sin Bin."

"Apart from Simon's sentiments there is nothing in all the material before us to show any evidence of any specific act of anger, so I think we ought to give him the benefit of the doubt," Helen suggested.

"I agree with that," said Veronica. "Didn't I say it was a dodgy idea to use the Seven Deadly Sins to judge someone's morals? All we've managed to achieve is disharmony, not such a good thing for the Administrators of Paradise."

"Yes, you did, Veronica," said the Chairman, "but we have to discuss them and the rest of the questions before us. That is our brief, whether we like it or not. We owe it to Oscar to give his case due consideration and that can only be achieved by thoroughly debating these questions."

"You may say that Chairman; it still doesn't seem right."

"I note your concern, Veronica. That's the Seven Deadly Sins dealt with. If you wish to delve deeper into them I suggest you do so at the Select Committee sessions, established for this very purpose. Use these committees and your research to help you in your deliberations. By covering the Seven Deadly Sins, I believe there is enough material for you to judge whether Oscar is a moral soul or not, as asked in question two. This meeting is adjourned – good day."

"Gabriel, the next question please," the Chairman asked as the special meeting reconvened.

"Question Three," the Archangel intoned. "Is Oscar Wilde sincere?"

"Yes, Paul."

"What, Chairman, is sincerity? What exactly does it mean? Sincerity always confuses me. Could never get to grips with it."

"Stop fooling. You may be confused," Bartholomew snapped at him, "but we're not. We all know what sincerity is."

"Do we? I'm not certain we do. Let's be fair. Let's consult the Divine Dictionary for clarification."

"Not again," cried a despairing saint.

"It's like being back at school," cried another.

"Very well," the Chairman responded. "Gabriel, be a good angel and look it up."

Gabriel flicked through the pages. "Sincerity, sincere... let's see now. Oh yes, sincere: free from pretence or deceit; genuine, honest and frank."

"You see, Chairman," Paul continued, "on the surface, sincere would fit Oscar Wilde's image, but if you scratch a little deeper matters become a bit murky."

"Murky! Are you sure you don't mean filthy."

The Chairman glared at Matthew.

"No, Matthew, murky. If it were filthy, he wouldn't be in Purgatory, would he?" Paul replied. "If you want to stretch the truth a bit, you could say he can be honest and frank at times and may be genuine. Free of pretence and deceit – I would question that. If you take his treatment of his wife Constance, for example, you can see that there was a great deal of deceit concerning his sexuality and some would say pretence concerning his feelings for her. He was a lucky man when it came to Constance – she loved him regardless of all his faults, faults he had in abundance. He said he loved her but was that a pretence that enabled him to hide his real sexual orientation?"

"Paul!" interrupted the Chairman. "You know the rules – a soul's orientation cannot be questioned or discussed. You know the reason for it, so why raise it?"

"It will be impossible, Chairman, to continue discussing the life of Oscar Wilde without raising his sexuality. It would be like discussing the sun, without referring to its heat. We should be able to discuss this in detail if we are to come to a fair and honest assessment of his character and nature."

Paul's persistent agitating was annoying the Chairman. He could not recall any other application that raised the sexuality of a soul, and he was going to have problems with this one. He addressed the conclave in a stern voice. "This is the second time I've had to intervene concerning this issue. The rules are clear that discussion of the sexual orientation of any applicant is strictly forbidden and any reference to it is inadmissible. It could not be any clearer. That is the rule and, Paul; you must adhere to it, as you all must. It's Oscar's soul we're concerned with and if it satisfies the criteria laid down. It is about time you got a grip and applied your minds to the problems at hand. Now let's get on with it and stick only to valid points."

"It may be the rule but it's clearly a wrong one."

"It can't be wrong. It's a Divine Rule – now, if you have more to add, get on with it and please don't give me any more grief."

Paul was furious that he was being denied the opportunity to make what he considered a valid point on sexuality, such a crucial element in Oscar's life – it was being blotted out as though it had never existed. Paul continued. "As I was saying, Chairman, all is not quite what it seems, is it, when it comes to sincerity concerning the soul of Oscar Wilde? There's many a dark alleyway to be searched before we find out just how sincere he was in his earthly life. Down those dark alleyways lay the real Oscar Wilde."

"Rubbish!" cried Veronica. "The real Oscar Wilde is out there, out in the open, in the true light of day, not hidden away in the shadows of the darker side of life. Why can't you see the real Oscar Wilde?"

"I can, but I agree with Paul. It seems rather odd not to consider his sexual orientation; it was, after all, a dominant part of him and certainly dragged him down to the seamy side of life."

"My dear Blaise, rules are rules. How many times have I to say it? There'll be no discussing sexual orientation."

"Then, like Paul, I say the rules are wrong."

"Wrong?" cried the Chairman, sweating profusely. "These are Divine Rules. On all that's holy, how can they be wrong?"

"I don't mean to be rude, Chairman, but how can we come to a decision without discussing the facts of the case? It doesn't make sense. After all, sex played such a significant part in his life. I believe sex *was* his life. His life was nothing more than a sexual obsession that led to his undignified demise. All obsessions are a road to nowhere; a road Oscar travelled all his life and by all accounts is wandering down again at the Reservation of Père Lachaise."

"I agree with Blaise," Anne cried. "It's ridiculous to ignore this part of his nature. It dictated his later life and was the precursor to his downfall. Even if we discuss his trials, we can't help but trespass on

278

his sexuality. That, surely, is what his trials were all about. Just read the court transcripts. They ooze with sexuality, with obsession. If we discuss his relationship with Lord Alfred Douglas or most of his male friends, we cannot help but discuss his sexual orientation. Oscar Wilde is all about sex! He is a byword word for it."

"You have it wrong," said the Chairman. "You can discuss his sexual relationships as much as you like but not his orientation. There is a difference, you know. If you wish, you can criticise him over his sexual behaviour but not his sexual nature. It should not be an issue whether he be heterosexual, bisexual or homosexual, for whatever he is, it's what nature made him and therefore out of his control. It should be of no concern of yours and is certainly of no value concerning this issue before us. I will clarify this, so there is no misunderstanding. You may discuss, give opinion and question his sexual behaviour. However, you will not be allowed to allude to, question or comment on his sexual orientation. This is my final ruling on the issue. Now, let's move on."

There were more murmurs of discontent. They all knew it was a waste of time arguing with the Chairman. Even if they had the best of arguments, it was impossible to defeat him. The Chairman wiped his brow. It wasn't one of his better days. With a wave of a hand, he indicated to Veronica that she should get on with it.

"He was sincere in his love for his parents and his love for his friends. I say he's the essence of sincerity. No doubt about it."

"You would, wouldn't you? You seem to have a soft spot for him, so we should take your opinions as coloured, to say the least, and not give much credence to. You're just a saintly groupie."

"Come on, Chairman, you're not letting Matthew away with that, are you," she cried.

"Certainly not – enough is enough. If you continue in this vein Matthew you will be given your marching orders. I'm serious now. You understand."

"Yes, Chairman," he sheepishly replied.

"No! No!" cried Joan, speaking for the first time. "Wilde's *not* sincere. How can he be? Everything goes back to his wife when it comes to sincerity, or should I say lack of it. We can't just skip around his fatal flaws as though they never existed. It's about time *we* were sincere in our deliberations and faced the truth about this Wilde fellow."

"How dare you say we're skipping around his fatal flaws?" Helen called out. "Haven't we been trying to talk about his sexuality and other sensitive matters, although the Chairman has chastised us for doing so? That doesn't sound like skipping around his fatal flaws, does it?"

"Are you saying, Helen, that his sexual orientation is a fatal flaw?"

"Yes, Sebastian. If the Chairman would allow us to discuss his sexual orientation I'd give you a good argument against it."

There were murmurs of discontent and many a harsh word flung at Helen.

"All right, let's calm down," the Chairman said. "I've had enough of this. Well, Helen, you can forget about his sexual orientation, for it will not be discussed. Ignatius, do you have something to add?"

"I do. Joan is right. Wilde's treatment of his wife is the key to this question, without any doubt. We can argue as long as we like, but when it gets down to basics, it's his treatment of Constance that will define his sincerity. Unless something else is revealed that could alter this, I have no hesitation in saying, no; Oscar Wilde is not a sincere soul and to be fair, never was."

"More rubbish," Patrick yelled at Ignatius. After the previous adjournment, he and the other Irish saints decided to rejoin the debate after Gabriel coaxed them to come back to the chamber. "You just dislike him, that's your problem. The Oscar Wilde I know is not the kind you have painted. You either like or dislike him. You dislike him and do so with vengeance. You're just a begrudger, Ignatius."

"Don't be daft. I have never met the soul, so it is nonsense to say I dislike him. As for begrudgery, you are talking out the back of your head as usual. What I dislike is the moral decay he carried about as though it were some medal, yet that moral decay destroyed him and caused distress to his wife and family. Patrick, if you have any evidence to refute my perception of him you had better state it or keep quiet."

"That's enough," the Chairman stated. "We will have a break of an hour to enable you to calm down and get your senses together."

"Why are you here, Oscar?"

Oscar looked confused. "You know *why*."

"Do I?"

"Of course you do, professor. What on earth do you think we have been doing this while?"

"Talking about your past, your life, your regrets, your dreams, and your sexuality, but why are you here?"

Oscar sank back into the couch, giving a deep lingering sigh, again studying the wild geese as he pondered the awkward question.

"I'm here because Jim Morrison asked me to attend these sessions. He did so, on behalf of the others."

"Others? Who?"

"Chopin, Delacroix, Édith Piaf and most of the souls in my social circle – they all thought it a good idea to visit you."

"Why?"

"Why? They believe you're God's gift to lost souls and that I've lost the plot…"

"Have you?"

"What do you think?"

"You know it's not what I think that matters. Have you lost the plot?"

"Probably."

"You're not certain?"

"No, not really, all I know is I have somehow taken my eye off the ball and cannot find it again. They don't say it, but they believe I am mad. They say I'm confused, that my behaviour is erratic and disturbing, but what they actually mean to say is that I am crazy as hell."

"Why do they think you're confused?"

"There has been a series of events that set their alarm bells ringing."

"Such as?"

"The whole business began when Jane Avril reminded me that I was nearing the hundredth anniversary of my arrival at the Reservation. I thought nothing of it at first for time here is rather irrelevant, but one day, when I was relaxing amongst the nasturtiums on the banks of the River of Life, thinking of nothing in particular, my mind was suddenly awash with thoughts of uncertainty. I had an overbearing feeling of foreboding and fear. I asked myself why I was here, what my purpose was, and why I was writing plays when only the living-dead saw them. As I sat there, I felt a heavy depression weighing me down, as if I was carrying my sins on my back and they were becoming heavier, heavier by the day and crushing by night. I had felt sad and depressed on the odd occasion but nothing on this scale. This was different; this was something that was controlling me. The feeling was of absolute depression, blacker than I've ever known."

"You say your friends noticed severe changes in your behaviour. What kind of changes were they that were so disturbing?"

"There's too much to tell. I don't know if you will have the time or patience to listen to them."

"I've lots of time and an abundance of patience. It's the essence of psychology."

"How lucky you are, professor, to be blessed with patience? If I had been more patient, my destiny may have been far different."

"Jane Avril. You have a lot of time for her?"

"Oh, yes. Jane is always a tonic. With her, I can be free to be as foolish and daft as I want, better still, she encourages it. I find her spirit uplifting. She shows me a love that is free and uncomplicated. I knew her before I arrived here. Not very well, I grant you, but I knew her all the same. What a dancer she was in her younger days – very daring and risqué. She caught my eye when I first met her in 1882. It was at a salon on the Left Bank. She was a dream as she glided across the floor, her yellow hair flowing over her shoulders.

"'Hello, my dear, I am Oscar Wilde, a graduate in aesthetics at Oxford,' I told her as I introduced myself. She burst out laughing and asked if it was a medical condition. When I explained what it was, she was rather impressed. The next day I headed off to the Moulin Rouge to see her in action. At that time, the Moulin Rouge was in its infancy. Very revealing it was. The place was sizzling with sexual vibes, as was she. It was there that she introduced me to Toulouse-Lautrec, who later painted my portrait. Not one of his better efforts, but he did try. I again had the pleasure of her company during my next visit to Paris. I ran into her at a reception at some society toff's place somewhere along the Seine. She remembered me, and we spent a pleasant evening together in that not-too-congenial setting."

"When did you first meet her at the Reservation?"

"I didn't come across her for some time. She arrived here in 1947. As I was walking over the Hill of Desire, I noticed a woman sitting cross-legged amongst the rhododendrons. I bid her good day as I passed. I hadn't gone far when I heard a cry. 'Oscar! Oscar! Is that you? Is that you, Oscar Wilde?' She ran towards me, and I thought, 'I know that face; it's the dancer with the yellow hair'. Before I could catch my breath she had her arms around me and fervently kissing me. 'It's me Oscar, Jane, Jane Avril,' she cried. What a delightful surprise that was. We sat amongst the rhododendrons and talked for hours.

"You must have been surprised to see her."

"I was, just as surprised to see Chopin and Sarah Bernhardt. There were so many here whom I had known or admired in life that it became a source of comfort to me. I was pleasantly surprised to meet Jane. There is something about her that is plain, simple, soothing and uncomplicated – there is no soul quite like Jane."

"You remember when Jim Morrison approached you about your behavioural problems that others were concerned about. Do you recall the behaviour to which he was referring?"

"Oh, I do! My behaviour towards them was unforgivable. I can't justify it in any way. It was uncouth and crass; why I insulted them as I did, I will never know. You asked what I am doing here. I am here to try to understand why I acted in the way I did and said what I did. It cuts to the quick now to think of how I treated souls who loved and respected me. I need to find out why I did what I did and to put matters right if it is at all possible. I am confused without doubt and, yes; I have certainly lost the plot. I have made an art of losing it."

"I see. Tell me, of all the residents of the Reservation, who are your closest confidants?"

"Oh! There are quite a few. They are all so different. I receive a different kind of friendship from each of them. I am lucky enough never to be short of friends. Along with Jane, there is Chopin. I often wonder why he is here instead of playing his divine music in Paradise. He soothes my mind whenever I am in his presence, and his acceptance of his fate is inspiring. He never questions why fate has placed him here. He never moans about it. He just gets on with his music as the consummate artist he is. Oh, I have no hesitation in saying I love the man. That is why my recent behaviour towards him is shameful and unforgivable. I cringe at the very thought of it."

"This behaviour, do you mind telling me about it?"

Oscar sat up and bowed his head as he collected his thoughts. "Chopin has one golden rule that we all respect and uphold – the subject of George Sand. He refused to discuss in any way his relationship with her and, over the years, just for a bit of devilment I would often tease him about her. He would sit there either reading or playing the piano and oblivious to my taunts. He never remonstrated with me for he knew I was only having some harmless fun. We both knew that there was no chance of any information about her passing between us. He is a shy, retiring and private soul, so why he gets on so well with me, a loud and opinionated dandy is beyond me."

"Opposites do attract."

"They often do. Our views on most matters don't tally. The only subjects we agreed on were love and art. What I did to him at the Music Academy was cruel. Do you know what happened, professor?"

283

"I did hear – not one of your better days. You insulted quite a few, didn't you?"

For the first time, Oscar detected a note of criticism in his therapist's voice. "I did. How did you know?"

"Very little of the goings-on of the Reservation get past me; I have my reliable sources."

"You must think I'm a bastard."

"Now, now, you're getting carried away again. I try not to express an opinion. I do occasionally get a little judgmental, but it soon passes. As I have said before, my main purpose is to listen to what you have to say."

Oscar looked at him and smiled. "To whom do you talk when you are down?"

"Myself."

Oscar gave a boisterous laugh. "They say there's nothing better than talking to oneself. Nothing beats pretence."

"What caused your altercation with Chopin?" the professor asked.

"I wish I knew. At the time, I had a feeling that I was being driven by a power over which I had no control. Even when I was harassing Chopin, I knew what I was doing was wrong, yet I was unable to restrain myself. I can remember word for word what I said to him. I could see the hurt on his face as I prodded and probed him. Not content with insulting him, I tore into Eugène Delacroix for no good reason whatsoever. He was so shocked. Then I appallingly hounded Jim Morrison. I shudder at the very thought of it."

"What's this I hear about Seurat's paintings?"

"Dear Seurat, he was so good to me. Did you know he was my guide when I arrived at the Reservation?"

"I did. You surpassed yourself when you destroyed his paintings. What made you do it?"

Oscar sighed. "There was no reason for it. God, it really hurt him – cut him to the core. I doubt he will ever forgive me."

"Have you apologised?"

"No. It's been impossible to get near him. He keeps his distance. If he sees me coming, he is off like a shot in another direction. I've written to him apologising, but I've had no response."

"Thank you, Oscar. That's it for today. Have you tried Dymphna's divine massage yet?"

His eyes widened in surprise. "A divine massage," he exclaimed.

"Not to be missed."

"Really… I must try it."

"Do. You won't regret it."

"Question four. Is Oscar Wilde honest?" Gabriel asked as the session of the Divine Council reconvened.

"What, I ask myself, is honesty?"

"Oh God, Paul, not again – we all know its definition," sighed Veronica

"Paul has a point. What is honesty? What exactly does it mean?" asked Valentine.

"Give it a rest, will you," cried Stephen. "Don't encourage him. Honesty means the truth. We all know that. If we don't, we have no right being here."

"It's more than that. One's first reaction to the word would be that of the truth but delve deeper, and it has a far broader meaning."

"You're talking like a wordsmith."

"Far from it, Stephen – you don't have to be an expert to know what honesty means."

"Let's settle this! – the Divine Dictionary if you please, Gabriel."

"Very well, Chairman. Honesty! Honesty – let's see now," Gabriel mumbled away to himself as he leafed through the pages. "Yes! Here we are. Honesty: sincerity, openness, integrity, candour, frankness and truthfulness. That's it – hasn't changed since I last looked."

"There you are," Paul smugly said. "Words are never what they at first seem, are they. We have already dealt with sincerity. What about openness – I doubt if there was ever any genuine openness in his life. If there had been he would never have hidden his true sexuality from the world, would he – especially from Constance. Integrity, I doubt it. If he had a shred of it, he wouldn't have tried to sue the Marquess of Queensbury. Furthermore, if he had integrity, he wouldn't have bummed around Europe, living off others. As for candour, well, it is not worth discussing, is it? Frankness, maybe, especially with his friends, but that is about it. We could go on and on about honesty and Oscar Wilde's lack of it. Overall, I'd say he wasn't an honest soul and certainly not a candidate for Paradise. I say he is lucky even to be in Purgatory. He's such a Deadly Sinner."

"What nonsense, Paul," Veronica cried. "The truth is you're just like Ignatius – you don't like the chap. That comes across loud and clear every time you open your mouth."

"Rubbish! This has nothing to do with whether we like him or not. It's about telling the truth about Oscar and his way of life. Don't know why you're getting so upset over it."

"I think you're being unfair to him. Perhaps we will know more when we have Jude's prognosis. If we study it with an open mind what we know about him, I believe we'll conclude that he is an honest soul."

"Ah! But was he honest about his sexual orientation?" asked Simon.

The Chairman tapped the table. "I can see we are heading back to sexual orientation again. I'm not going to warn you again. You all know the rules, so why are you persisting in pursuing this avenue of argument. It's a dead end."

"The rule is a handicap to our deliberations. It is a strange rule, to say the least. It needs to be changed."

"Listen here, Simon. It's a Divine Rule. It can't be changed. It is there for a very good reason, so I insist that we move on and away from his sexual orientation. There's more to Oscar Wilde than sex."

"Is there?" someone cried.

"Certainly," said Veronica.

"You could have fooled me."

"Now, Simon, stop it. If you've more to contribute to this debate, get on with it and stop wasting time," the Chairman cried as he tried to control his saintly crew.

"All right, then," continued Simon. "Was he honest in his use of the written word?"

"Of course he was. He is a genius of the written word. A true and honest artist if ever there was one."

"I don't think so, Veronica. Most of his works are full of hidden meanings and sexual high jinks. Take *The Picture of Dorian Grey* as an example. Did he mean it to be a tale about image or friendship that went astray or was it about gay romps in low places? I think it's a handbook for a decadent lifestyle wrapped in an opium haze. He wasn't honest enough to spell it out as such; instead, he laced it with double meanings. If he was that way inclined, he should have come clean about it instead of indulging in all that cloak-and-dagger stuff. He was always a coward when it came to honesty about his sexuality. No, I doubt very much if he was an honest soul."

"You can be so ignorant at times, Simon. Do you really think it would have been wise in the Victorian age for him to say he was gay? You are too much at times. If he had 'come out' as they say these days, they would have strung him up. I should remind you that in Oscar's time, it was a criminal offence to be gay. It would have been suicidal of him to have shown his true sexual orientation."

"Listen here," Simon said. "If he honestly thought his sexual orientation was natural, he should have stood up for himself and took whatever dirt was flung at him. It's what's called being a martyr for the cause?"

"You seem to be on the right track. For once, I agree with Simon. Honesty wasn't one of his virtues."

"You've already said you don't like him, Paul, so your opinion is tainted and should not be taken seriously."

"We can't like everyone, Veronica. Just because I don't like the chap doesn't say I won't give him a fair hearing. I can assure you I will."

"I doubt it. Once a prejudice is planted in one's mind, it's odds on that it will grow and fester and be there forever. That's the insidious nature of the beast."

"Give it a rest, will you. You can be so high and mighty at times."

The Chairman glared at them; then nodded at Gabriel. "Right, Gabriel, read out the next question."

"Question five: Is Oscar Wilde a loving soul?"

"This gets better by the minute. How long do we have?" quipped Matthew."

"I'll allow as much leeway as I have on the other questions," the Chairman replied. "All right Matthew, you'd better begin, then."

"No, thank you. I'll pass on this one. Here, Veronica, this one's more up your street."

"There's no need to be sarcastic. If you've nothing to contribute, keep your smart comments to yourself," she replied.

"Do you wish to open on this question?" asked the Chairman, turning towards Veronica.

"Yes! Whom did he love?" she queried. "Let's look at his life. He loved his parents, especially his mother. It is safe to say, therefore, that he was capable of respectful and parental love. He loved his children deeply, so we can take it he is capable of fatherly love. He loved his wife, so it's safe to say he was capable of emotional love..."

Matthew burst into laughter. "Get away with you. Loved his wife – hardly – he used and abused her in the most outlandish and appalling manner, and you call that *love*? Dear, dear – he treated her like shit."

"Matthew!" cried the Chairman. "There's no need for language like that. Remember, you are a saint, not a tenant from the lower side of hell."

"Sorry, I'll rephrase that. He treated her like the dirt on his shoes. He gave the impression that he loved her, but it was only pretence, and he's the master of pretence. He loved himself and nobody else. He was in love with his own image and reflection. Love! He wouldn't have known real love if it smacked him in the face a dozen times. The man was emotionally cold – a misfit hiding behind a mask who happened to write the occasional elegant sentence, the occasional witty epigram."

"Wait a moment. That's a bit strong, isn't it? I say he was very much in love with Constance – in his own way, I grant you but love all the same, and she was without doubt deeply in love with him. You seem to be suggesting that his love for her was somewhat flawed. That he was disingenuous."

"You're easily taken in, Veronica. Why can't you see him for the deviant he was in his earthly guise?"

"Now, now, Matthew, you are out of line again. There's no need to be so hostile," cried the Chairman. "Let's stick to the question before us. Is Oscar Wilde a loving soul? That's the question. Not whether he's a deviant or anything else."

"It's certain that he's shown all that was expected from a loving soul in his time at the Reservation. Apart from his recent out-of-character behaviour, he has shown great affection to his fellow residents at Père Lachaise, to such a degree that he gained the status of a Trusted Soul. That honour is not given to deviants, Matthew, only to loving souls, even if a few doubts are cast over elements of their earthly life," Philip said, joining the debate.

"A few doubts?" Matthew laughed. "Well Philip, you certainly don't know much about this Wilde fellow, or you wouldn't come out with such rubbish. His whole character is in doubt. I agree that his residency at the Reservation has been impeccable, but, Philip, it is his earthly behaviour that we must address."

The Chairman tapped his desk with his gavel. "No! That's not so," he informed them. "We have to take into consideration not just how he acted throughout his earthly existence, but also how he has acted at the Purgatory Reservation of Père Lachaise."

"I didn't know that."

"You can be a bit slow at times, Matthew. Are you telling us that throughout all the other submissions, with the likes of Darwin, Michelangelo, you only considered their earthly lives?"

"Yes, I was under the impression we all did."

"Well, you're wrong, Matthew. You must consider all elements of Wilde's existence. It's the only fair and just way. Purgatory is an extension of life. I thought you knew that."

"Is that so Chairman? Tell me, then, how can Purgatory be an extension of life if its tenants are dead."

"It has to be. The soul and life are one. When life dies, the soul lives on. We can't divide the life from the soul. They are but one. Under this submission, under Rule 13, we must take into consideration the whole being, life and soul. Really, Matthew, I shouldn't have to explain this to you. Let's move on."

"But Chairman, surely that can't be. It makes no sense whatsoever. I must protest. It seems rules are being made up as we go," complained Francis.

"I'm not going to tolerate such insolence. The rules are the rules. Gabriel, please read out the relevant rule. It seems Francis and others have no confidence in our procedures."

Gabriel gave a critical look at Francis as he turned the pages of the Divine Rule Book, muttering away to himself.

"Rule 11, Paragraph 87. When determining the six relevant questions of whether the soul referred to is a Special Soul, all elements of their earthly and Purgatorial existence must be taken into consideration."

"Still sounds crazy to me, seeing souls cannot commit Deadly Sins in Purgatory. Surely its how a soul has behaved when living that is of relevance, not how it's acted as a spirit," groaned Francis.

"You lot can moan as much as you like, but rules are rules and must be adhered to. Now, if you have nothing to add concerning question four, we must move on – next question, Gabriel."

The saints were not happy. The Chairman didn't like these meetings, as the worst elements of the saints' natures always became evident. Even the apostles were too much to take at times when they were in this kind of mood. He understood some of their concerns, but he had a job to do and was unable to alter any Divine Rule. They all knew that, yet at every opportunity were ready to challenge him. It was becoming very wearisome.

"The last question; question six: Is Oscar Wilde a decent soul?

"What is decency?"

"No! Mark. Don't start again. Let's get on with it," insisted Bartholomew.

"It's a reasonable question. What is decency? It means different things to different people."

"Chairman, do we have to go through this nonsense, again and again?"

"I know what it means," muttered Philip.

"Oh, do you? We're not all blessed with such intellectual prowess."

"Perhaps clarification is in order," replied the Chairman "Gabriel, if you please."

A murmur of discontent filtered through the chamber again as Gabriel once more opened up the Divine Dictionary, wearily flicking through its pages. "Here we go! Decency: propriety of behaviour, what is required by good taste, avoidance of obscene language and gestures and undue exposure of person, decorum, modesty, politeness, civility and respectability. That is some list. We'll be here forever Chairman if we let loose on this one."

"Thank you, Gabriel. Now let us proceed. If there is a danger of it becoming protracted, I'll put a time limit on it. You can broaden your arguments at the sub-committee stages. Mark, as you raised the question of meaning, perhaps you'd enlighten us with your thoughts."

"I said there was more to sincerity than first meets the eye and I'm right. Propriety of behaviour – there was no measure of propriety in the life of Oscar Wilde. As for good taste, that is a non-starter. He thought he possessed it, but he's the only one that thought so."

"Now you're being nasty, Mark," said Veronica. "Disparaging words are totally unfair. The question is simple, is Oscar a decent soul. That's what we should be debating, not getting a lecture on the meaning of a particular word."

"We must be fair, Veronica. Mark has a right to have the exact meaning of decency clarified," said the Chairman.

"As I was saying, once you examine its meaning, it becomes clear that he was far from a decent soul. Veronica doesn't seem to think he has any faults, but she's deluding herself. He is a mass of faults and the more you examine his character the more one sees this. It's not a pretty sight."

"Well, you can't accuse him of using obscene language or of exposing his person, can you?"

"I'll grant you that, Veronica, but are you trying to tell me he wasn't the decadent kind, that in reality, he was a model of virtue – someone with whom you would trust your daughter or son? Not likely – he was as decadent as they come."

"What is decadence to one person is decency to another. That's what makes the world tick."

"Only you would confuse decency with decadence," replied Mark.

"I'm far from confused." Veronica insisted. "What about decorum? Surely, you are not saying he lacked decorum. That would really be stretching it."

"I am. What's more, he wasn't modest. Even with all the praise lavished on his plays, he was incapable of any humility. He had to boast about his success and attempt to persuade the world of his genius and virtue. Had to tell the world what a great chap he was and was not the world blessed to have a genius of his calibre. "

Patrick hit the table with his fist. "He never said such a thing. You are painting a portrait of him that is murky and sullied. That is not the Oscar Wilde most people know or know of."

"Chairman," interrupted Sebastian, "this fussing over word definition is getting out of hand. If we keep this up, we'll never see an end to the conclave."

"I did rule that the definitions be readout. It may seem tedious to most of you, but to answer the questions on the agenda in a fair manner, we must scrutinise each. If that includes scrutinising the meaning of the words, so be it. At the end of the day, it's up to you to define the meaning of any particular word and make your assessment accordingly. Mark, have you more to say on the subject?"

"No. I have made my point. I'm happy to let someone else speak."

"I have something to add," Thomas announced. "I'd like to consider Oscar's politeness, civility and respectability... all distorted and undermined by generations of critics and moralists."

"Dear God, you're not going to give one of your political speeches, are you," bellowed Philip. "They're dubious at the best of times."

"They're nothing to do with politics, only good common sense – something you're sadly lacking."

"Stop this sparring. I have had enough of this unseemly behaviour. Stick to the subject and get on with it," demanded the Chairman.

"It would be ridiculous to say he wasn't a polite individual. Even if he suffered from a lack of it on earth, which I don't say he did, then the evidence before us shows he's the essence of politeness at the Reservation. That, of course, is without taking into consideration his recent lapse, which was the catalyst of this submission coming before us."

"Lapse?" cried Matthew, "He insulted every soul at the Reservation with whom he came into contact. Jane Avril was the only one to be spared his nasty tongue."

"Maybe, but isn't that why we have to determine whether his actions show the signs of the Michelangelo Syndrome? Let us just focus on his behaviour at the Reservation. It's only his behaviour here where signs of the syndrome would come to the surface, not in his earthly life, so let's focus on that."

"You're running ahead of yourself, Veronica," the Chairman informed her. "We must first debate and vote on the six questions before we determine if the Michelangelo Syndrome is present."

"But surely, as we are scrutinising his soul, we are all looking for the symptoms. Most of us will notice them if they are present. Some of us probably have already, so it's crazy to say we must separate the two issues."

The Chairman wiped his brow and sighed again as he looked over at her. "I'm sorry, Veronica, that's exactly what we must do. Rules are rules. How many more times must I say it? If we all adhere to the rules, we will get through this tortuous business far easier than this continuous bickering. That's the six questions dealt with. I'll adjourn the meeting to prepare for the presentation of Jude's prognosis."

Oscar was in a pensive mood as he settled on to the couch in his therapist's study and readied himself for another revealing session.

"How are you feeling today?" asked the professor.

"Peaceful," Oscar began, "but I'm also consumed by a sense of deep, sorrowful regret."

"I see. We'll deal with that in a moment but tell me, did you enjoy your divine massage?"

"Indeed, I did. Divine is the word," Oscar replied as he stretched out on the couch. "Dymphna sure has the magic touch – got yourself a good catch there. She certainly knows how to soothe a troubled mind."

"The best... she never fails to impress. It's fine enough massaging the body, Oscar, but to achieve full relaxation and satisfaction one must also massage the mind and there's no better person to do that than the delectable Dymphna."

"How right you are. The moment she laid hands on me, I was in her control, absolute control. Never felt so relaxed in years. Always thought massaging was a load of malarkey – not any longer. It is great therapy. I should have indulged in it years ago. If I had that kind of massage after I left gaol, it would have rejuvenated me. She would be worth a fortune on earth."

"She's been around in the most unlikely of places, but this is where she's at her best. I have never known her to fail when it comes to the laying on of hands. When she was massaging your mind what effect did it have?"

"It was electric. She did something to me that shocked my entire system. She was able to wipe my mind clean, allowing me to experience the feeling of total relaxation for the first time without all that garbage swirling about in my mind. Afterwards, I returned to my apartment and lay down on my bed, sinking into a deep sleep. When I awoke, I had a feeling of peace but also consumed by a sense of deep, sorrowful regret. It was the strangest feeling I had ever experienced, even stranger to experience such extreme emotions at the same time."

"Regret, regret for what?"

Oscar sighed, pausing before responding. "Regret for a life wasted," he said, "regret for a failed life. I regret a life of shame, decadence and waste, not least of the beautiful gift squandered. I regret a life ended before its time. I'm afraid, professor, regret will be the theme I pursue today but thanks to Dymphna, I'm relaxed and ready to face it."

"If it's regret that's on your mind, let's deal with it."

"Dymphna's calm and soothing voice reminded me of those gentle people in my life and the souls I have taken for granted, whom I have abused, insulted and lied to in the most *outré* manner, going out of my way to wound and humiliate them. All those souls of Père Lachaise who I treated so badly have forgiven me, but I still feel a heel. I do not deserve their forgiveness and certainly not their love."

"Now, now, you're being a bit hard on yourself. Chopin forgave you because he is your friend because he loves you. We all deserve forgiveness, even the worst of rogues and scallywags."

"Maybe, but what about Édith, what about our Little Sparrow, look how I treated her. It makes me cringe every time I think about it."

"Édith Piaf. She's an extraordinary performer."

"And an extraordinary soul," Oscar sighed. "I did a terrible thing to her. I put her through Hell in the Cherry Blossom Forest. I can't believe I treated her so badly."

"You don't need to tell me. I do know the details. Just as I knew about your trouble with Chopin, Seurat and Jim Morrison, I know about Édith and the Cherry Blossom Forest. Have you any idea why you treated her so badly?"

"No. I love the woman, of that I have no doubt. I respect her as the consummate artist she is, and why I turned on her, I will never know. Who in their right mind would turn on that most beautiful of souls?"

"Alfred de Musset? You seem to get on well with him."

"Alfred? Oh yes, he is a gem. I always enjoy his company. Of course, he is as vain as I am, yet he is a positive influence. He kept me entertained with his talks about his exploits with George Sand and stories about his erotic dreams on the occasion when he accompanied me on a visit to the Pearly Gates to see Saint Peter."

"George Sand, a very unusual woman."

"Indeed she was."

"You seem to have a thing about her – some would even say an obsession."

"That is an understatement. I was fixated by someone I had never met – don't ask me why, for I am damned if I know. There is something about her that is addictively compelling."

"These dreams of Musset's, tell me more."

"On that journey, he bragged that most of his dreams were sexually explicit and that he could recall every one of them in graphic detail. Of course, this attracted my attention – I had never dreamt since my arrival and was more than curious to know why. He said he had a potion that would help me dream. He was so convincing I gave it a try."

"And you dreamt."

"I dreamt all right, but the dreams turned to nightmares – horrendous ones. I told Alfred that his potion was a dud. He was surprised and told me to give it time, which I did, only to have more dreadful nightmares that increased in their intensity."

"What did you do?"

"I panicked. He suggested I make a visit into the Herb Valley deep in the heart of the prairie, way out on Cloud Ninety-Seven and call on Madame Dandilla. She's the Reservations herbalist, the only one with the antidote to Alfred's potion."

"You believe in all that mumbo jumbo?"

"Only if I can extract something from it."

"Did you?"

"Certainly, but it was hard graft. I arrived at the narrow pathway that took me down to the gully that is the main way into the heart of the prairie. All I had to go on was his description of the prairie and its environs. After days climbing and fighting my way through the thicket, I came upon a chap of oriental extraction with the unlikely name of Yo Soo Floo. He was a devious devil who knew he had the power to help me and made me suffer for the information that would lead me to Madame Dandilla. He said the information was of great value and accordingly I had to do a few tests to fulfil Madame Dandilla's wishes. She didn't like visitors so if you wanted the pleasure of her presence, you had to endure the tests."

"What kind of tests?"

"Tough ones."

"Yo Soo Floo strapped a heavy weight on my back and told me to crawl on my hands and knees across the fallen pampas grass that was strewn before me for about a mile.

"'Do this, monsieur, and you will be a step nearer to your goal.'

"I did so. It was horrific. I felt a mental pain on every move. If we were able to suffer personal injuries, I would have bled to death. When I finished the task, I was exhausted and ready to head back home when Yo Soo Floo pointed to a large tree and said, 'Up you go. When you reach the top, you must walk that tightrope across the ravine.'

"The very thought of climbing such heights brought me out in a sweat. I have always had a fear of heights. I did what I had to do. Every step was mental torture, and at the end of the wire, I thought my tasks were complete – not so. There was one more task to do before I could see the herbalist.

"'You see that rock ahead of you?' he asked. 'You must sit on it, cross-legged, until Madame Dandilla calls for you.'

"I sat on the rock, thinking it won't be too long, only to find it would last for four long hours. Yo Soo Floo would visit at regular intervals to give me some refreshments. When I asked him how much longer must I wait, he would frown and say what an impatient soul I was. Finally, he called me down from the rock. I was as stiff as a broom but managed to stagger after him as he led me through the thicket until we came to a clearing. Before us was a rickety thatched cottage. The windowsills spilt over with a profusion of thyme of every kind. Between the windows were hanging baskets of parsley. A rosemary bush in full bloom surrounded the rickety door. In front of the cottage was a mound of sage with an odd sprinkling of basil.

"Yo Soo Floo rapped on the door.

"'Come in, dearie,' came a croaky voice.

"I entered into a dark passageway. A silhouette of woman stood in front of us with the brightness of her herbal garden behind her. She indicated to me to come forward. I followed her into a blaze of colour. Her cottage was full to the brim with exotic herbs in pots of every shape and size.

"'Come along, come along,' she beckoned.

"She led me out into her herbal garden. Yo Soo Floo indicated that I take a seat. She turned around, and I caught my first sight of her. Her appearance surprised me. She wasn't the old crone her voice and hunched appearance indicated. Rather, she was a beautiful young woman with jet-black hair, eyebrows and eyelashes that set off her sparkling dark blue eyes. She noticed my surprise. She sat next to me and put on her glasses to have a good look at me.

"'Why should I help you?' she asked, peering at me over her glasses.

"'Because I foolishly wished for something and paid dearly for it.' I replied.

"'A foolish thing indeed,' she laughed.

"'I am locked in a nightmare, and you seem to be the only one who has the power to release me,' I informed her. 'Musset gave me the potion which you had kindly given him.'

"She again looked at me over her glasses and smiled. 'This is your lucky day. Yo Soo Floo, bring me potion number 562.' He returned with a small green bottle. She poured some black liquid into a small blue china cup and handed it to me. 'Down it goes,' she said. Don't look at it. Close your eyes and swallow in one gulp.'

"I took a swill of the concoction, and within seconds my throat and eyes were burning. I could see her looking at me as my eyes began to fail. There was a buzzing in my ears, and my body was shaking so violently that my teeth were rattling. I passed out. When I came to, she smiled at me and said, 'You're done, monsieur.' She laughed, slapping me on the back. 'Off ye go now and behave. Tell Musset, he will have some explaining to do if he ever crosses my path again. That potion he gave you was exclusively for his own personal use. It was formulated to his personal needs, not to be given to any wanderer that passes by.'

"'Could you give me a potion specially formulated for my own needs, to allow me to dream as all other souls do?' I asked.

"'Did you hear that, Yo Soo Floo,' she said, nodding her head in astonishment.

"'He obviously thinks you're a miracle worker, madame. I think Musset's been filling his head with nonsense,' Yo Soo Floo he laughed.

"'I don't possess the magical properties needed to produce a miracle,' she informed me. 'I only enhance conditions that are already present in a soul; I don't create them. I have antidotes for my herbal potions. That is all I have. If you don't dream, then I'm sorry for you, but I can do nothing to help you. I'm a herbalist, not a miracle worker. Yo Soo Floo, escort our guest back across the prairie. Adieu, monsieur.'

"That's how I got rid of my nightmares."

"So you haven't had one since?"

"No, thank God. I've accepted that I was destined not to dream."

"Any more regrets?"

"Oh, yes. As we were on the way back to the Literary Quarter after my visit to Saint Peter, we came upon the entrance to the Valley of Happiness. I wanted to go in, but Alfred begged me not to, as a penalty has to be paid if one attempts to recall one's earthly happiness. I ignored him and entered."

"Musset was wise. Not many enter. Why did you?"

"As I say, apart from being one of those curious souls, I also realised that if there was any chance of purging my sins, I would have to travel through this and other similar valleys. I thought what harm would it do? Little did I know! As I made my way into the tunnel, I looked around, and Alfred was calling on me to come back. I ignored him and followed the twisting path until I came to a stile surrounded by briars. To the left was a wooden sign with a notice burnt into it: 'Grab happiness when you can, for it never lasts long.' I looked at it, thinking it a peculiar saying."

"What did you think odd about it?"

"Well, it gave the impression that what happiness I may experience might vanish once I came through the other side. I never believed happiness was fleeting. Happiness, once experienced, is with you forever. All those happy times of my life are stored away ready to be recalled. I can bring them back in all their glory at a moment's notice. I should have turned around and fled but, alas, I did not. Once over the stile, I wandered down the path between the lush pampas grass that gently swayed in the soft breeze. Ahead of me was an archway of bilberries through which I could see a bright blue sky and hear the laughter of children. I saw a meadow, surrounded by copper trees and banks of dandelions. Skipping across the meadow were Vyvyan and Cyril, who was throwing a ball to each other and chased by Constance. I cried out for them to throw the ball to me. They didn't hear or see me. It was as if I was not there. They were clearly enjoying each other's company. They looked so happy, and Constance was blooming. She clapped her hands, calling them to come and have some refreshments. They were at our summer retreat in Norfolk, sipping lemonade in the summer sun. I was a stranger looking on a pleasure that should have been mine. I called out to them again. It was no good. They could not hear me. They never mentioned me. It was as if I had never existed.

"Then, I was drawn along the twisting path until I came across a gap in the pampas grass. I peered through and saw a party at my home in Chelsea. A strapping young lad was thanking all his friends and relatives for coming to his twenty-first birthday. A beautiful woman kissed. It was Constance and the young lad was Cyril. They looked so happy and contented, at peace with each other. He raised his glass and thanked all and sundry for their gifts. There was no mention of me.

"I heard more laughter behind me. Turning, I again peered through the pampas grass and saw myself as a young lad playing with my little sister, Isola. We were laughing and dancing on a fine summer evening, with Mamma and Papa sitting around a table enjoying their children at play."

"You don't have to go on. We can continue at some other time," the professor said, as it was clear to him that his patient was overcome by emotion.

"I have to tell it now," Oscar replied as he took in a deep breath, regaining his composure. "It's no wonder Alfred didn't want me to go in. He did say I would pay a penalty for my troubles. I did. I continued the journey. I could hear in the distant the notes of the Wedding March. Through the pampas grass, I could see a church, and coming down the steps, arm in arm, were a happy couple. I couldn't contain myself. Vyvyan and his radiant bride were beaming with happiness, as was Constance. I was nowhere to be seen. I heard church bells chiming from the other side of the path. I parted the pampas grass and saw Constance arm-in-arm with me as we descended the steps of St James's after our wedding. There was an air of absolute happiness radiating from us. How did it all go so wrong? Why did I not cherish her, the gift I was given. Why did I throw it so recklessly away?

"I turned again to look at Vyvyan and his bride as they made their way down the street followed by guests. I tagged on behind them to the wedding breakfast and listened to the speeches. Vyvyan said he was never so happy and thanked everyone for their gifts and good wishes. He didn't mention me. Had he forgotten me? Had he disowned me? Was he ashamed of me? I withdrew and left heavy-hearted, rejoined the path and continued my journey.

"As I walked down the lane, ahead of me, I saw a couple with a child. They were laughing happily, as the child skipped along in front of them. As they neared me, I realised they were Vyvyan and his wife and my grandchild. Silly me, I called out to them and tried to ruffle the child's hair. Of course, it was a worthless exercise, for they could not see or hear me. They passed by as though I was never there. Of course, I wasn't. I was only a spirit imagining what should have been – what should have been mine?

"I heard more children's laughter on the far side of the pathway. Through the pampas grass, I recognised myself as a child of about six. I was sitting on my grandfather's lap, laughing hysterically as he tickled me. My brother Willie had my shoe off, tickling my foot. Grandmother came out of the house carrying refreshments, calling us to come and get our lemonade and apple tart. How happy we seemed and little did I know what disaster lay ahead for me.

"I continued my sorrowful journey along the Valley of Happiness, feeling the burden of guilt heavy on my tired shoulders. I peered through the pampas at a gathering of happy folk who stood in front of my old home in Tite Street. They cheered as an elderly bride and groom came. I froze on the spot. It was Constance with her new husband. Vyvyan and Cyril were there with their wives and children. Constance was older but still beautiful. As I looked at her, how I regretted that I never grew old with her, that this man, whoever he was had claimed the prize of my life. Happiness was Constance. Alas, I was too blind to see it.

"I wandered further along the path and was feeling like a heel when rapturous applause rang out. I again looked through the pampas to see an audience on their feet clapping and howling. It was the opening night of *The Importance of Being Earnest* and I was the centre of attention. I looked at myself as I stood on the stage, soaking up their appreciation of my masterpiece. I was at my best and as happy as a lark.

"I heard more applause coming from the far side of the pathway. I dashed across and I saw a similar scene. The audience were as rapturous as the last, some throwing their programmes up in the air with delight. On the stage was an old man with grey hair, leaning on a silver walking stick, receiving their approval – it was I, in old age, still producing plays and receiving the applause of the crowd. As quickly as the scene had appeared, it faded away, leaving me distraught.

"I had enough of it. There was no way I was going to reach the end of the valley without losing the little sanity I still possessed. It was too emotionally draining. I could go no further. At the exit, there was a sign asking if I was sure I wanted to leave the Valley of Happiness, for if I did, then my burden would be heavier than when I entered. I took no notice of it and quickly made my exit.

"Alfred was sitting on a rock, clearly worried about my long absence.

"'For God's sake, you've put years on me,' he cried as I staggered up to him. 'Why are you such an awkward sod? Why do you have to go to places no sane soul would?'

"'Because I can,' I said as I slumped down next to him, mentally and physically exhausted.

"'The penalty – what was it?'

"'A guilty conscience,' I said, 'more enhanced than ever. By cutting short my journey, I have put an extra burden on my back. If I ever attempt to make the journey again, the burden will become heavier. It seems I can't win when it comes to purging my sins.'

"Alfred shrugged his shoulders. 'Seems so.'

"You regret your journey through the Valley of Happiness?" asked the professor.

"Without doubt," he replied as he sunk deep into the couch, once more wiping his sodden brow.

"The other place we passed on our way home was the Valley of Tears," Oscar said as he stretched out on the couch for a session with the professor. "I looked through its ivy-clad entrance wondering if I should enter. Alfred looked at me, wagged his finger, clearly warning me not to be tempted again. After the experience of the Valley of Happiness and the look on Alfred's face, I elected not to go in.

"Many years later I returned to that gate, accompanied by Jane Avril, who also tried to stop me entering, saying I'd regret it, that it would only bring me pain and sorrow. I told her I needed to enter and made my way into the valley whilst she begged me to return. To my regret, I ignored her and entered the Valley of Tears."

"Why did you feel the need to go there?"

"I don't know. I do have the knack to go where nobody else wants to venture. I think it is one of my strengths; others, however, look at it as an innate weakness. I had a burning desire to go, although I knew it would be a journey of sorrow. It was part of the purging of my sins, and I had to go and face my demons, whatever or whoever they were – a journey that had to endure."

"Do you wish to tell me about the visit?"

"Yes, I need to," Oscar replied as he settled on the couch. "Once inside the gate I wandered down the steep incline through an archway of cranberries until I came to a pasture of purple tulips. I walked slowly through them until I came to a sudden stop, standing on a precipice, looking down into a deep, dark, brooding lake. I knelt, and as I gazed into the black water, images began to form. Out of the deep, I heard a whisper. At first, I was unable to understand it; then a shiver went through me as I recognised the voice. 'Papa, papa,' it tearfully cried. The whisper became louder as the face of Cyril stared up out of the water. Then Vyvyan emerged. 'Papa, papa,' he cried. They both sobbed, reaching out to me. 'Why did you go, papa? Why did you go and leave us to be tormented, taunted and humiliated? Why did you let us down, papa, why, oh why?'

"They frantically reached out to me. I lay down and tried to grasp their trembling hands, but they were beyond my reach. I stretched and stretched but all in vain. As I continued to grasp at their tiny hands, they sank deeper and deeper into the pond, their plaintive cries becoming weaker and weaker until they vanished into the darkness of the water. I stared into the void and all I could see was my reflection, a reflection of my discoloured and worn-out image and an ego that cried bitter tears of regret. Getting to my feet, I waded through the purple tulips until I arrived at a lane that twisted through clusters of violets that led me to the entrance of a battered old railway station. There was a deep boom of a horn as a huge steam engine approached. Waiting to greet me at the station entrance was the Lady in Blue. She handed me a ticket and directed me to the platform as an announcement blared out, 'The train approaching platform one is the 19.00 through the mind of Oscar Wilde, stopping at all stations to his demise.'

"I baulked at the announcement and looked about. There was no one else on the platform as the train came to a shuddering halt, releasing hisses of menacing steam. The Lady in Blue met me again as I stepped on board. I looked at her in amazement, for she had just handed me my ticket, yet there she was again.

"'This way, monsieur – your seat is number 33,' she said, directing me. As I was about to sit, I noticed the rest of the travellers sitting stiffly upright, wearing pinstriped suits, pink shirts with black ties, monocles and bowler hats. They all sat with their white-gloved hands resting on the handles of their umbrellas. As I sat down, they all turned and in harmony said, 'Welcome, Oscar, my dear fellow, welcome to your journey through Hell.'

"'Take this,' snapped the Lady in Blue, handing me a sheet of pink paper.

"'What is it?'

"'The timetable of your journey through life,' she sharply replied as she sat opposite me, not taking her cold eyes from me. I scanned the timetable. It didn't make happy reading. The important dates of my life jumped off the page. Most were dates I preferred not to remember, events that led directly to my ruin. The train screeched through the darkness, its whistle screaming as we neared the next station. There was another announcement: 'The next stop is Speranza.'

"I couldn't believe what I was hearing. Speranza – that was my dear mother's *nom de plume*, when she was a young woman, full of vim, writing poems about the famine and the diaspora that followed. Why I wondered, is the station named after her? I was soon to find out. The train came to a shuddering halt. The stiff figures stood, looking at me with utter contempt; then departed the train, leaving me alone with the Lady in Blue.

"'This way!' she ordered.

"I followed her. As I stepped down on to the platform, the stiff figures lined up like a welcoming party, only their looks on their faces were far from welcoming. As I walked past them, they sneered at me and smiled at the Lady in Blue as though she was a goddess. I followed her across the road and up a rocky incline towards two huge gates. As they came into focus, I realised they were the entrance to a pauper's graveyard. Chiselled into grey marble above the gates were the words: 'The Paupers of Life'.

"'Mademoiselle, why are you bringing me here?' I asked. 'I don't know any paupers.'

"'Huh! You don't say,' she said, as she scornfully looked at me, ignoring my question. 'Get in,' she snapped, pointing to the open gates.

"I entered and found myself being led up a steep hill as the heavens released a dreadful downpour. As the rain fell on to my face and ran on to my lips, the saltiness of it took me aback. I soon realised it wasn't rain, but tears that poured from the heavens. I slithered in the mud and fell to my knees.

"'On your feet,' she demanded. 'You have further to go.'

"I struggled to my feet and staggered after her.

"'This is it,' she said, pointing to the mound in front of me. I was so exhausted I once more fell to the ground.

"'Where am I?' I asked, looking up at her. She laughed. 'This is the final resting place of your long-suffering mother.'

'It can't be so,' I cried as I looked around at the mound of mud.

"'Oh, it can and is. This is what you thought of your dear mother. You thought so little of her you gave her a pauper's grave – a great reward for all her suffering. She suffered for you, Oscar Wilde, suffered more than you will ever know. You are not a very nice fellow, are you? I'll leave you here to wallow in your shame,' she said and turned away, leaving me in the pouring rain of tears on a muddy pile that was my dear mother's final resting place.

"A hand touched my shoulder. I turned, and a shadowy figure loomed over me. I gasped, for there before me was the ghost of my mother, her face ravaged by sorrow, her cheeks shrunken, worn into furrows from the tears she had shed.

"'Wasn't I a good mother to you, Oscar?' she whispered. 'Didn't I embrace you with love? Oh! How I gave you love. Didn't I do everything for you; giving you a good and loving home, giving you the best of education, giving you the freedom to blossom, to expand your mind to its very limits? Didn't I do all this for you and do it with love?'

"'Yes, mamma, you did. I loved you too. You were the world to me,' I replied as I reached out my arms to embrace her.

"'Didn't I show you the beauty of life?'

"'You did.'

"'Didn't I give you love and understanding in all you did – didn't I put up with your indiscretions and forgave you all your peccadilloes?'

"'You did,' I cried.

"'Then why, Oscar, why did you leave me, a daughter of Erin, to be buried in a pauper's grave in a foreign land?'

"Tears welled up in her sad eyes. I tied to touch her, but she drifted away.

"'Do you know how many tears I have shed for you? These vases of tears are but a drop in the ocean of what I have shed,' she cried as she pointed to the overflowing vases. 'Why Oscar, why did you dishonour me with a pauper's grave.'

"'I'm sorry, mamma,' I cried as I tried again to reach her. 'I was in prison when you died. They wouldn't let me out. What could I do? They sent me abroad when released. I was unable to visit you, to cry and pray over you.'

"'That is no excuse, Oscar,'" she whispered as she began to drift away. 'You have let me down, Oscar. To your shame, you have dishonoured me with your indifference to love.'

"'I'm so sorry. Forgive me, mamma,' I desperately begged of her. I again reached out to her, but she drifted further and further away, crying and whispering. 'Why, Oscar? Why, oh why?'

"She drifted towards me again. 'Here, Oscar,' she cried. 'Take this. Take this token of regret.'

"Something fell at my feet. In the mud was a gleaming coin. I picked it up. It was two-faced.

"'Take this precious token and give it to the boatman who awaits you.' Through the vases of tears, I could see a man dressed in purple, standing in his boat, his oars at the ready. 'He will row you to another world, a world where you may find peace of mind, a peace that will never be mine.'

"I watched as she vanished into the mist. Within a blink of an eye, she was gone. I sank back into the mud, holding my head in my hands in absolute despair. I heard the strains of a violin. I looked up and standing between the vases was a fair-haired young girl, her long curls falling over her shoulders as she played Massenet's 'Meditation'. It was Isola. I tried to get up to reach her, but I was unable to move. I called out to her, but she didn't hear. As she continued playing, images of my mother in her prime materialised on the overflowing vases. I sat and stared at them as her life drifted by. I again held my head in despair as I realised I had dishonoured her. The sound of the violin became fainter. Through my muddy fingers, I looked over to Isola. She was slowly walking towards the boatman, still playing her 'Meditation'. She stepped into the boat and stood as the boatman slowly rowed them into the misty horizon. They were gone as were the vases of tears. There was coldness in my clenched hand. I opened it. The token had vanished.

"'There was a tap on my shoulder. 'It is time to go. This way!' said the Lady in Blue. I sadly followed her, slithering down the hill towards the gates. The train gave out a shriek. It was ready to leave. It hissed as it moved off. It was as though it was cursing me.

"My poor mother, did I really leave her in a pauper's grave? I looked over at the Lady in Blue, who was staring at me with a smirk fixed firmly on her cold lips.

"'Have you no shame, Oscar Wilde,' she said.

"I ignored her and looked out of the window, only to be confronted by images of those I hurt in life. The list was endless. I never thought I hurt so many, but there they were, drifting past the window, their pain written all over their faces. I closed my eyes to block them out – it was no good; the images vividly remained. I was heading at full steam to Hell, with only my demons and the icy Lady in Blue for company.

"As the train came towards the next station it gave out a sharp whistle. An announcement blared out, 'The next stop is Le Coeur.'

"'This way!' said the Lady in Blue, snapping her fingers as she stood up.

"'Where are we going?' I anxiously asked.

"'You'll soon see. Come now, let's not waste time.'

"I reluctantly followed her off the train to be met by a black horse and a carriage with a heart emblazed upon its door with the motto, 'We all die in vain' written below it. The still figures surrounded the carriage. They stared and sneered at me.

"'Get in,' she demanded as she opened the door. I did so. She slammed it shut.

"'Are you not coming with me?' I asked, concerned I'd be left on my own.

"'Hardly,' she snapped. 'This is one journey you must do on your own.'

"The carriage moved off, twisting its way through ruined buildings. The trees around were all but stumps. There wasn't a soul to be seen. The carriage came to a halt and the door opened to reveal a young lad, with a sallow face, his head bandaged, supporting his emaciated frame with a crutch. His eyes were bloodshot, and he wore a torn French military uniform.

"'Bonjour, monsieur,' he whispered, 'this way.'

"I stepped out of the carriage to be confronted by a desolate site. The air had the taste of sulphur to it, and it looked like a scene from Hell. In the distance, I could hear the mournful strains of a cello. I followed the young lad who limped his way across mud that was tacky with the smell of decaying flesh.

"We arrived at a sentry box. Out of it stepped a white-haired old man with hands dripping with blood. I looked at him but could not place his face, although I knew it. He nodded to me, and then walked away, cradling his lowered head in his trembling hands.

"'Who is he?' I asked the young lad.

"'He, monsieur, is David Lloyd George – an unhappy man. He has been through Hell. It is he who you are relieving.'

"'Relieving, relieving him of what?' I asked.

"'His conscience,' he said as he directed me into the sentry box. I turned and looked out. Before me were lines and lines of soldiers who were staggering towards me. There was a multitude of them stretching up and down and over the hills, all going in one direction – towards me.

"'What do I do?' I asked the lad.

"'Just stand here and take what they give and pass it on to your helpers behind you, who will take the burden from you.'

"'Burden, what burden?' I stammered.

"'A heavy burden, monsieur, a heavy burden.'

"'How long will I be here?' I asked despairingly.

"'As long as it takes monsieur,' he replied as he bowed and bid me farewell.

"'Takes to do what?' I asked as he walked away.

"He turned, pointing to his head. 'To clear your conscience.'

"I failed to grasp what he meant. What had these soldiers or David Lloyd George to do with my conscience or me? Lloyd George was after my time, and I had no connection with soldiers. I stood in the sentry box, and before I knew it, the first soldier came staggering up to me, dragging his feet as though they were made of lead. He stood before me, a lad of no more than seventeen years, his face a ghostly shade of grey. He bowed and said, 'My name is Gerard Messine, from the town of Neuilly. I am a fusilier of the Second Leon Infantry Brigade and fought defending the City of Light. Here is my heart, monsieur, a loving heart that died in vain.'

"He handed me his heart and, after taking one last look at it, he slowly turned and with head bowed headed down the windy hill towards the setting sun, as the cello played a French lament.

"I turned and handed his precious possession to my helper, who, to my surprise, was my spitting image. He, in turn, passed it to another of my images, each one a younger version than the one before until the broken heart reached me as a child at the top of the hill. He took it and placed it on the pile of broken hearts. Then the process started all over again. Another soldier walked up to me.

"'Monsieur, my name is Gerard Roule, from Nancy. I am a private of the Fifth Battalion of the Orleans Dragoons. Here is my heart, a heart that died in vain.'

"I took it from him. He saluted, turned and slowly walked towards the setting sun as the cello continued its mournful cry. Coming towards me were two soldiers, both helping each other to stay on their feet. There was horror etched deep into their young features.

"'Are you the one who we must give our hearts to?' one of them asked.

"'I'm afraid so,' I replied.

"'I'm Taffy Jones and this is my buddy, Glynn Drew, from Aberystwyth. We are from the Sixth Battalion of the Welsh Guards. Our war was short. We caught it in the first salvo. Here are our hearts that sadly died in vain.'

"I took their treasure and they turned and, arm in arm, staggered towards the setting sun as the cello filled the putrid air with the strains of 'All Through the Night'. Another young man stood in front of me, his ashen face reflecting all that was wrong with war and the insanity of man. He was so young; his face all pimples and bum fluff – another child, lost and a long way from home. He stood in front of me, his hands shaking as he held on to his heart and cried.

"'I'm Helmut Wise of the Twentieth Hanoverian Hussars and another victim of circumstances. I've killed, and I've died for my deeds. Here, here is my heart, a heart that died in vain.'

"He handed me his heart but was unable to release it. I coaxed him until he finally let go. He took one more look at it and then, as the cello played Brahms' 'Lullaby', turned and slowly walked towards the setting sun.

"A young lad staggered up the path, his head hanging low. As he approached, he raised his head to reveal a deep wound to his left temple. He was crying tears of blood. My heart sank as he held out his hands towards me.

"'Hello, papa!' he whispered. 'It's me. Do you not know me?'

"I shook with emotion as he moved towards me, grasping his heart to his chest.

"'Here, papa, here is my heart, a heart that died in vain. I wanted to be a hero to restore our family name. Alas, it was not to be. I wasted my life, my precious life on nothing but a dream.'

"I tried to embrace him, but a force held me back. He placed his heart in my hands. Out of his pocket, he took an envelope. He placed it upon of his shattered heart and whispered, 'Read it, papa, read it only when I have gone beyond the setting sun. I love you, papa.'

"With that he staggered away down the hill, joining the multitude as they headed for the setting sun. The cello cried out the 'Derry Air' as he turned and looked at me for the last time, wiping away the tears of regret. I stood there, trembling, with his heart in my hands. What is it all about? What did it all mean? I reluctantly allowed his heart to join the mountains of innocent hearts sacrificed in the name of insanity.

"As I stood there, relieving others of their hearts, I couldn't help but wonder at the extent of the horrors of our so-called civilised society. I witnessed the list of horrors here, the list of the horrific wars that wantonly took these mountains of hearts – The Boar War, the Crimean War and the First and Second World Wars. It goes on and on, a never-ending catalogue of man's folly. But what has it to do with me? I had no hand in these obscenities. Most of them were after my time. I just couldn't understand what it was all about.

"An old man who wasn't a soldier staggered up to me, wrapped in barbed wire.

"'My name is Otis Delize, an industrialist. I supplied barbed wire to all warring sides for a healthy profit. I have no heart to give you, for I don't possess one. I sold it for currency many years ago. All I can offer you is regret, regret that I have in abundance, regret that is of little worth to a soul without a heart.'

"He too slowly walked down the hill towards the setting sun, but no cello played for him – just the cry of thirteen ravens that flew about his bowed head.

"I don't know how long I was there, but my mind was numb with the grief of it all. I was wondering when my relief would come when I spied a small figure coming towards me. It was a lad, no older than fifteen years. He fell at my feet, holding his heart in his hands. He didn't say anything, just sobbed, his tears dripping on to his heart.

"'What's your name?' I asked as I knelt before him. "Not raising his head, he whispered in a broad Waterford accent, 'John, John Condon. I'm a private in the Royal Irish Regiment, No. 6322, and I'm far, far away from home.'

"'Do you know why you are here?' I asked as I tried to raise his head.

"'To give you my heart,' he replied as he held it close to his chest. 'Must I?' he whispered, raising his head, his eyes bloodshot, his young face etched with terror.

"'Yes. It seems so, and then you must head for the setting sun with the rest of your comrades,' I replied as I held out my hands to receive his heart that died in vain.

"'I'm too young to face the setting sun; my life has yet to begin. I'm just a kid, a kid a long way from home,' he cried as his trembling hands held on tightly to his heart.

"A hand was laid on his head, ruffling his red hair. Another soldier knelt down next to him and gently said, 'Come, John, we will go together towards the setting sun. Give your heart to this man. He will take good care of it.'

"The soldier looked up at me.

"'I'm Private Frances Ledwidge of the Irish Fusiliers. This is my heart that died in vain, like many an Irish heart before. Come, John, give this man your heart and we'll be on our way.'

"The young boy reluctantly handed it to me. With his eyes streaming with tears, he placed his broken heart in my trembling hands.

"Private Ledwidge put his arm around the boy's shoulders, and they slowly set off towards the setting sun as the cello cried out 'Let Erin Remember'.

"'What is beyond the setting sun?' I heard the young lad ask his newfound brother.

"'A new tomorrow, my lad.'

"'What, you mean better than yesterday?'

"'Without doubt, my lad, without doubt,' Ledwidge said as he hugged the lad. 'A new tomorrow, a tomorrow where we will be given a new heart, a heart that will beat forever to the rhythm of love; a tomorrow where there will be no death, pain or sorrow, only poetry, harmony and love.'

"The young lad looked up at Ledwidge and a slight smile broke on his tortured face. He grasped his hand, and they slowly walked towards their new tomorrow.

"The hours passed slowly as a soldier after soldier arrived, giving me their precious possession. I had never seen so many lost and tortured souls. I began to think I would be there for eternity when I noticed the young lad with his crutch, hobbling towards me.

"'It is your time to be relieved, monsieur. This is your relief,' he said, directing his hand to the stern figure that stood behind him. I looked at my relief. Looking back at me was the old queen herself, Queen Victoria, her face contorted with pain and sodden with tears. As I passed her I noticed she was pulling heavy chains and balls behind her.

"'Follow me, monsieur,' the lad said. 'I'll take you back to your carriage.'

"I followed him, my hands soaked with blood. I had a firm grip on Cyril's letter as I departed. I looked back at Victoria, who was stupefied as she took up her sentry duty. She looked like a woman with a heavy burden, dragging the conscience of an empire behind her.

"'This is her sixtieth stint on duty,' the lad informed me. 'Her burden is heavy indeed.'

"'Are you saying I have to do likewise?' I asked, horrified at the prospect.

"'That's not for me to say,' he replied. 'This way! Your carriage awaits you.'

"As I climbed into the carriage, my heart was breaking for Cyril and all the other lost souls of countless wars. I held my head in total despair as the carriage rattled its way from that field of horror. I looked through my bloody fingers, only to see the Lady in Blue smirking at me. She sat before me and coldly announced, 'Do you wish to go any further?'

"'How many stops are there?'

"'If I knew, do you think I'd tell you?' She snapped. 'My purpose here is not to help you, only to be your guide and nothing more.'

"The carriage made its way down the twisting road towards the station. She didn't take her eyes off of me for the entire journey. As we were about to board the train, she tapped my arm.

"'Over there,' she said, pointing towards the far end of the platform. 'You can exist here if you wish. Every station from hereon has an exit, and you are free to take it whenever you wish. Remember, if you leave, the next time you try to travel through the Valley of Tears your journey will be harder. All that you have already experienced will be vividly enhanced. Remember, as part of purging your sins you must travel the entire journey until the end of the line. Do you understand? Do you wish to continue?'

"I tightly held Cyril's letter as I looked at this dragon of a woman. Could I take any more? How many more stops? What was in store if I continued? I didn't know. I didn't want to know, but I knew I must continue.

"'Yes... I'll continue,' I informed her.

"We boarded the train, and it moved off to God knows where. It screeched, rattled and hurtled through the darkness as she took out some knitting. She reminded me of the women of the Terror who sat at the foot of the guillotine and knitted away as each head fell into the basket. Was she waiting for my head to fall? It seemed so.

"'What's that in your hand?' she snapped.

"'A letter from my son,' I replied.

"'Read it before the next station. You can't take anything from one station to the next, that's the rule,' she snapped. 'Read it! Aloud!'

"I tore open the letter and read it, ignoring her demand. 'My dearest papa,' it said. 'Oh, how life could have been so different. If only you had realised the value of what you had, if only you had taken a different path when you came to the crossroads of your life. If only you had valued all that life and success had brought. You left us all in want of love. If only you had taken that path, we would have been happy, mamma would still be alive, and I would not have joined the army and wasted my precious life. Vyvyan and I would not have had to bear the taunts of our childhood days, and mamma would not have had to suffer the ignominy that your behaviour brought and her early death. If only, if only, if only you had treasured what you had, if only papa, if only – your loving son, Cyril.'

"The Lady in Blue snatched the letter from me and scanned it with her jaundiced eyes.

"'It's no good moping. You are not the only loser in life. This place is full of them,' she screamed and then flung the letter out of the window. She was only a slip of woman, but she put the fear of God in me.

"The train screeched to another halt.

"'This stop is Foolsville,' an announcement blared out.

"'Out you go,' she snapped.

"Outside, the sky had a dirty yellow hue. There was a putrid smell. I was regretting not taking the exit at the last station.

"Another carriage pulled up in front of us.

"'In!' she snapped, as she opened the coach door. As the coach rattled its way down the hill, she stared hard at me. 'You're rather a fool, aren't you?'

"I wasn't going to rise to her bait. I refused to answer.

"'You are now entering the Sphere of Mankind's Foolishness. You should feel quite at home here,' she informed me. 'Here we are. Out you get,' she said, kicking open the door.

"I stepped down into what I discovered was a sludge of excrement.

"'Don't look so shocked. I'm sure you've been deep in it before, as most of us have,' she said.

"I followed her through mounds of excrement and upturned soil. The smell was overwhelming. Before me was a large red tombstone with tears chiselled into it, along with an inscription that read, '*Here lies socialism: died at an early age from acute indifference to the Human Condition. May it never rest in peace.*'

"'Why am I here? I'm not responsible for mankind's foolishness and certainly not for the mistakes and follies of socialism,' I protested. 'What's this to do with me? The excesses of socialism came about after my demise.'

"'All souls are responsible for some excess in life, some more than others, so spare me your indignation. It doesn't impress me. Keep on moving.'

"I did, but tripped over, falling face-first into the filth. Cleaning the muck from my face, I looked up and staring down at me was the Statue of Liberty herself. She looked haggard and battered, with parts of her cracked or broken. I had tumbled over her severed right arm. Even in this state, she was still impressive, but she clearly wasn't impressed with me. She showed little pity, as she looked down at me as I knelt in the slime. Written on her plinth was, '*Did Someone Cry Freedom?*' If someone did, I didn't hear it.

"'She's a pitiful sight. She was once a fine lady until the likes of you dishonoured her,' said the Lady in Blue.

"I was shocked. Whatever did she mean the likes of *me?*

"'You may look at me like that, but you know exactly what I mean,'

"'Damned if I do,' I retorted.

"'You're telling me you never treated Lady Liberty with contempt? You didn't sully her – you didn't stretch your luck with her?'

"I ignored her. I continued to follow her through the slime. The stench was unbelievable. Although my feet were deep in it, she seemed to hover above the foulness. We passed the tomb of fascism, oozing blood through the cracks in its loose and unstable structure.

"We came to a deep hole. I looked into it. It seemed bottomless.

"'Who or what is being buried here?' I asked.

"'Globalisation!' she said. 'It is taking time to die, but its end is nigh, I can assure you.'

"'Globalisation, what is that?' I asked.

"She looked good and hard at me. 'For a soul who spends so much of his time at the Knowledge Zone, you can be quite ignorant. Globalisation is life's latest folly,' she informed me. I hadn't an inkling as to what she was referring.

"We made our way down the slimy hill towards our waiting carriage.

"'One moment! There's one more tombstone you must see – you can't leave here without seeing why you were brought here,' she said as she pointed towards a cracked and brittle tombstone that read, 'Here lies the wasted talent of Oscar Wilde'.

"Ingrained into the stone were the titles of all the novels, poems and plays I should have written, if I hadn't wasted my talents, hadn't thrown my life away – five novels, seven plays, four volumes of poetry and three volumes of autobiography. By the looks of it, I should have lived a long and fruitful life. I read out aloud the titles.

"'Novels: *The Elevation of Little Miss Nobody; Vibrations; The Last Man from County Down; Tiptoeing Through the Bedroom of Life; The Caretaker of Cantankerous Lovers.*

Plays: *The Chairman of Vice; The Making of Hay; Invitation to a Soirée; Some Ladies Do, Some Ladies Don't; The Making of the Male Species; Men Looking at Women, Women Ignoring Men; The Whispering of Women.*

Poems: 'At Home with the Jesuits of Farm Street'; 'I Didn't Think I'd Live This Long'; 'Vanity in a Vacuum'; Travels with my Ego'.

Autobiography: *My Life: Volume One; Still My Life: Volume Two; What a Life: Volume Three.'*

"I reached out and ran my fingers over the words, the words of my lost life, and sighed at what might have been. The Lady in Blue sneered at me, as I turned away from the tomb.

"'You're not as smart a fellow as you thought you were, are you? I doubt if you could have turned out a fraction of that.'

"I ignored her but she continued to goad me.

"'And you're far from the great talent you thought you were.'

"Again I ignored her but she still went on.

"'And your genius – a bit of a myth, isn't it?' she said. 'This way, we are not finished yet. There are more stations for you to visit.'

"She passed me by. I slowly followed her to the carriage that took us to the station. The train was waiting, hissing, ready to take me to more horrors.

"'In you get,' she said as she opened the door.

"I was about to get in but thought better of it.

"'I'll exit here,' I sharply informed her. She didn't look too pleased. She slammed the door shut.

"'So, this is the end of your line, is it? The moment I set eyes on you, I knew you wouldn't have the backbone to see the journey through. You have weak stamped all over you,' she said. 'Your fate should have been the Conciergerie or La Force and an appointment with the sharp blade of death rather than a quiet death in your bed. Well then, if this is the end of your line, follow me.'

"I did. As we left the platform, I noticed all of the stiff figures had disappeared. She led me outside to a waiting coach that took me to the stile.

"'Get out!' she snapped as the coach came to a halt. I did and walked towards the exit, relieved by the prospect of seeing the back of her.

"'Loser,' she called after me. 'If I have the misfortune of seeing you again, your journey through this valley will be a journey through Hell. Be warned.'

"With that, thankfully, she was gone. Ahead of me were the archway and the lovely Jane, a welcome sight indeed. I stumbled through it, relieved to be out of the valley. Jane was sitting under a sycamore tree, waiting patiently for me. I fell into her arms as she sprang to her feet to welcome me and wept for all the regrets of my life. She understood the sorrow of my life and didn't reproach me for ignoring her advice to stay away from that dastardly valley. "

314

The professor cracked his knuckles, stood up and slowly walked around the couch.

"If you had gone through the entire Valley of Tears when you arrived at the Reservation in 1919, do you think your stay would have been any better?" he asked.

"I doubt it."

"Could it be Oscar, that this experience was the catalyst to your recent behaviour?"

He sat up and looked at the professor. "Maybe – I don't know, but it could very well have been."

"Think about it. That's all for today, your next session will be your last."

"I must say, professor, you've been a tonic."

"There's nothing better than a tonic, is there?"

"Certainly, as long as it's not one of those dished out by Flaubert or Musset."

"Sexuality."

"What about it?"

"You tell me," the professor said as he began his final session.

"What is there to say?"

"Plenty – your sexuality has been a matter of speculation, has it not?"

"Has it?"

"Now, now, Oscar, you know it has. You do have to talk about it; it has to be confronted one way or the other."

"Does it?"

"Yes. Your sexuality – you must deal with it. You didn't address it or attempt to address it on earth, but it's imperative you do so now."

"My sexuality seems to be of more importance to others than it ever was to me. It is not as riveting as you might think. What do you want to know about it?"

"The truth."

"Come now, professor, you have something on your mind, so why not say it. I can take it. If you want the truth from me, it's only fair I get it from you."

"Very well, then."

The professor pressed a button on the arm of his chair.

"Jesus! What's going on?" cried Oscar.

The curtains closed. The ceiling parted as the wild geese took flight, to reveal a large circular mirror. As the walls slid away, more mirrors appeared. Wherever he looked, Oscar could see his image. He looked at the professor, seeking an explanation. He was about to get it.

"Now, Oscar Wilde, let's face facts – the facts about your sexuality."

"Whatever do you mean?"

"This is the moment to face up to just who and what you are, to reveal your true self. To expose what is behind your mask. You understand?"

"Certainly not!" he gasped, as he loosened his cravat.

"Very well, I'll come straight to the point. I want you to look at yourself in these mirrors throughout this consultation. I want you to look good and hard at yourself and face the reality of your sexuality."

"Are you serious?"

"Very much so. I have listened very carefully to you over our many meetings without giving any opinion on your conduct, your morality or your sincerity. Now it is time for me to test you on these. Are you ready?"

"Test! Is this some kind of examination?"

"Yes, you could say that. You could say it's the ultimate test. Are you ready?"

"Yes, I suppose so," he dolefully replied, looking suspiciously at his interrogator.

"What are you?"

"Whatever do you mean?"

"Are you gay, straight or bisexual?"

Oscar sighed deeply as he looked at himself in the mirror above, then to his side, then straight ahead. This was not going to be easy. There was nothing else to look at, only his own reality, a reality he'd rather not face.

"Who am I?" He asked himself as he stared at the plump figure stretched out on a psychiatrist's couch.

"That's a difficult question, professor. It is extraordinary that you use the modern terminology "gay". In my day, to be gay was to be happy, carefree, to have a good time, to be full of life and the likes. It is odd how words can change to have a completely different meaning in such a short span of time. You take 'straight'. It is amazing how it has ended up as a word defining sexuality. If you accept 'straight' representing those being heterosexual, and 'bent' as representing homosexuals, then that term in itself smacks of something deviant and not natural, yet it's used now in everyday conversation. As for 'bisexual', there was no such word in my day. If there were, it was never used, and it was certainly not part of my vocabulary."

"Come now, Oscar, you're blustering. Are you trying to avoid the question?"

"No, far from it, I am just fascinated by your use of words. I am a man of words, after all. We must get our words right for they could be a matter of life or death. Words made me the artist I was, and words sadly killed the artist in me."

The professor looked at him in surprise. "What do mean by that?"

"It was my artistry with words that gave me the success that I craved and gave me the standard of living I enjoyed. Words made me an artist, an artist of the highest standard. I used that very artistry to try to outsmart the courts, but it ruined me, it ultimately killed the artist in me. When you throw words about like 'gay', 'straight' and 'bisexual', I automatically dissect their meaning. Words, they are like people – not quite as they first seem."

"Well then, what is it to be?"

Oscar was quiet for some time, as he looked himself up and down. "The truth is, professor, I don't know."

"Let's put it this way. Have you ever been in love?"

"Of course."

"How many times?"

"Three!"

"I see. You seem very definite about it."

"I am. But I thought I was in love umpteen times: Florence Balcombe, Bosie, Robbie, Sarah Bernhardt and many others."

"So you were confused by love."

"Aren't we all?"

"No… not all."

"Well, I was and still am."

"Who would you say truly loved you?"

"I've spent my whole life believing that the whole world did. It seems I had that wrong."

"Are you saying nobody truly loved you?"

"No. Constance loved me. She loved me so much that it hurt; she forgave me the dreadful emotional injury I inflicted on her, the shame and disgrace that I piled up at her door. She forgave me all. Now that is love. She was a saint.

"Robbie, I'd say he loved me – loved me for what I was, loved me for myself. Yes, he loved me as a good friend he was. He spent so much time looking after Constance and my children's interests when I was incarcerated, then when I passed on he worked so hard to free my estate from bankruptcy and restore my copyright for my children. He showed a beautiful love, not just to me, but also to the children and Constance.

"Oh! Then there was my mother's love. She didn't just love me – she adored me, thought I was special. She believed she had produced perfection. How wrong she was. Oh, yes, she loved me.

"Yes, Constance, Robbie and my mother, they were the ones who truly loved me. Others were fond of me, some of whom I thought loved me, but they didn't. I often confused fondness with love."

"Whom did you love?"

"In my earthly life?"

"Yes. We'll deal with that."

"Are you talking of love in general?"

"No! Passionate love, those you were *in* love with."

Oscar was quiet for a few moments as his eyes filled with tears. "Constance. Yes, I was very much in love with her."

"Were you really?"

Oscar shocked by the professor's comment. He wiped his eyes and turned towards his inquisitor.

"Yes! I did love her. Why – do you think I did not?"

"Well, how could you have loved her if you had a relationship with Bosie and other male friends like Robbie Ross?"

"I loved her *and* Robbie. I loved Florence Balcombe, too, but she didn't love me. Bram Stroker was the one who won her heart. These I could honestly say I was in love with. As for Bosie, he was an irrelevance. You see, my love life is not as exciting as history makes it."

"I see! I'd say it's time you answered the question. Are you gay?"

"Oscar looked at the professor but didn't answer.

"Are you straight?"

Oscar again looked at his inquisitor but still didn't answer.

"Are you bisexual?"

Still looking at the professor, Oscar didn't answer but looked at himself in the mirrors. This was it; this was his moment of truth.

"If it's down to labels, then I'm bisexual," he blurted out.

The professor took out a nail file and started to give himself a manicure. He didn't immediately reply, but allowed Oscar time to reflect on what he had disclosed.

"How do you know that? How do you know you are bisexual and not entirely gay?"

Oscar smiled, one of his reflective smiles. "One thing I do know is that I could not have lived my life without women, mentally or physically. I can't imagine my life without Constance, without the Divine Sarah, or Florence, or Ada Leverson, whom I called the Sphinx. I could go on all day listing women who have been important in my life. I cannot imagine my life without their physical intimacy and presence. Because of that, I could not be completely gay. On the other hand, I could not imagine my life without Robbie Ross or John Gray and the physical intimacy I shared with them and many others. Because of that, I know I could not have been completely heterosexual – straight as you called it. Therefore, when it gets down to labels, there's only one that could be stuck on me and that is 'a bisexual genius'."

"I see. You didn't include Bosie in the list of the ones you couldn't imagine life without."

"The only list I would include him in is one of the blackguards and cads of life. I could have comfortably sailed through life without him in tow and the trouble he brought."

"If you had to choose a life without men or women; which would you choose?"

"My, my, professor, that is a weird question, even to put to me. What you ask is impossible to answer."

"You mean to say, you'd prefer not to answer it."

"What I'm saying is I can't."

"So, all in all, you are bisexual. Are you happy with that label?"

"I wouldn't say *happy*, but yes, I'll settle for bisexual."

"Have you ever admitted being bisexual before?"

"No! I have often thought about it but never really asked the question. I don't like tags or labels of any kind, other than that of an artist. When it comes down to it, I would rather say I am a sufferer from the Human Condition, a sufferer like any other soul, with all those symptoms that afflict or enhance that most peculiar and perplexing of existences."

"Do you think your condition is natural or deviant?"

Oscar gave a deep lingering sigh as he looked at his questioner filing away at his nails.

"Well, I hope it's natural, or I will be in big trouble with my conscience. If it's deviant, I'd dearly love to know what the cure is."

The professor smiled and put away his nail file.

"That's it, Oscar. Your treatment is at its end. I don't think you need my help anymore. I will miss having your company. Spend a few more days at the clinic to ponder on what we have discussed; then you are free to go. I hope these sessions have been of some benefit."

Oscar stood up and warmly shook the professor's well-manicured hands.

"Indeed, they have. More than you would ever imagine. Thank you, professor. Good day."

Well, reader, our errant genius had finally come to terms with his sexuality and was at ease with what fate had meted out to him. We join him as he is sitting in the clinic gardens, on the last day of his stay at that most congenial of places. He was feeling relaxed and pleased with himself.

Suddenly, he was aware of some other presence. Turning, he saw a stranger with a very familiar face walking towards him. Standing before him was a young woman with exquisite striking blue eyes and a smile he knew but couldn't place.

"Bonjour, monsieur," she softly said with a smile in her voice as she looked at him, wide-eyed.

He sprang to his feet. "Do I know you, mademoiselle? You look so familiar."

"No, monsieur, but you do now. I'm Margaret Windermere Sèvres," she announced, offering him her hand. "And I've been just dying to meet you."

He was amazed by her announcement. Was he hearing things? Taking her hand, he found he couldn't help but stare at her.

"Wherever, my dear, did you get such a name from?"

She laughed and said, "Oh! That is another story. It goes back well before my time."

"Come. Sit with me. I am just about to have tea. You're welcome to join me."

He led her over to the table, noticing she couldn't take her eyes off him. Yes, he thought, there was something about her that was pleasantly familiar.

Sitting down, she looked around the garden; then said to Oscar, "You've been difficult to pin down. For the last six weeks, I have been searching for you high and low, from one end of the Reservation to the next, but all to no avail. I even visited the Café Oueurde, where you had not been seen you for some time. I asked so many where you were. They all knew who you were, of course, but couldn't say just where you were. You seemed to have vanished. It was becoming a bit of a mystery. Then I was directed to Marie d'Agoult, who after hearing who I was sent me to this clinic."

"Who are you?"

She gave an infectious laugh. "I'm the daughter of Aimee Sèvres, whom you once knew."

"I'm sorry. You must be mistaken. I don't know any Aimee Sèvres."

"Oh! How silly of me. Of course, she never did tell you her name. She always regretted not doing so. She told me so much about you and about your plays. I know your poems by heart and can reel off pages of *Dorian Gray* at the drop of a hat. As for your maxims, well, without being boastful, I would say I am an expert. My mother was a great admirer of yours and taught me all there was to know about you."

"Did she now? Your name – how did you acquire it? It is unusual. Margaret Windermere. I'm sure you know she's a character in my play *Lady Windermere's Fan*."

"Oh! I know that. It was all Mamma's doing. If she had been blessed with any more children, I would dread to think what she might have called then. She was a great one for the unusual, as you must be aware."

He looked at her in amazement. He hadn't a notion of what she was on about. He stared into her eyes. There was something about them, a gleam that stirred something deep within. Where had he seen them before, and the smile – there was something about it, something special, something that touched his very being. And her pout, where had he seen it before?

"Your mamma – are you sure I have had the pleasure of her company?"

"Oh, yes indeed, monsieur, you surely have. It was a long time ago. She recalled her meeting with you in great detail. She always talked about you with passion."

"Did she now?"

"Oh yes, Mamma was into passion in a big way."

"Where did she meet me?"

"In Paris, on a beautiful sunny day – they met on the steps of the Sacré Coeur."

He dropped his cup. He was as white as a sheet, as though he had seen a ghost. Her sparkling eyes set his mind aflame with memories of his lost Parisian days, of the kindness of a vagabond who danced across the streets of Paris.

"The vagabond!" he cried as he looked into her eyes.

"Oh! Monsieur, forgive me," she cried as she stood up as though ready to leave. "I didn't mean to startle you. I have long wanted to meet you, to meet the man my dear mamma thought so much of. She never ceased talking about you. Oh! Forgive me. I've somehow disturbed you."

He looked at her as she stood there, the image of her mother – the same eyes, the same nose, the same lips and the same dimple in her chin, and that laugh, that infectious laugh. How did he not recognise it?"

"My God – the vagabond of the Sacré Coeur."

"Yes. I'm her daughter."

He couldn't help but stare at her as his mind filled with memories of that fine day so long ago in Paris when he was down and out when out of the blue a stranger tried to save him from his despair. He held out his hand to her, which she grasped tightly. They embraced like long-lost friends.

"I have so much to tell you, monsieur, so much."

"Oscar, you must call me Oscar and tell me, what became of your dear mamma? Come sit with me."

Sitting down, she removed her bonnet, releasing a swirl of blonde hair, the same blonde hair her mamma had tied into a ponytail as she stood before him on the steps of the Sacré Coeur.

"After she bade you farewell," she said, "Mamma continued earning her living as a street dancer. She became famous and on several occasions had the opportunity to leave the streets, but she felt it wasn't the right time to do so and continued earning her crust entertaining the public. One day after collecting coins from her hat, she picked up a copy of *Le Figaro*. She was saddened when she read that you had died. She told me that she had forlornly made her way up to the Sacré Coeur and sat on the steps and cried her eyes out. She had only known you for a short while but her sorrow was that for a lost friend. She was saddened that you had not found a way of rehabilitating yourself and regaining your literary career. Oh, she thought fate would be kind to you, but it was not to be."

"Indeed," he sighed.

"Some years later, after being drenched to the skin, she made her way to her garret off the boulevard Saint Germain and fell into a fever. The next morning she was unable to rise from her bed. The fever became severe and she was near to death. A friend found a note with the address of a Monsieur Sèvres, the shoemaker who kept her dancing boots in good order. She knew him from her days as a socialite when he supplied her with the most fashionable shoes of the day. Her friend Lorrette Jouy hurried to his home on the rue de Rennes. He immediately had Mamma transported to his home, where he and his wife, Victoire, nursed her back to health. It was touch and go, but their love and attention saved her. Mamma didn't want to intrude on them for longer than was necessary and prepared to leave and return to her garret. They would not hear of it and insisted she stay. They offered her a job in the design shop of their shoe manufacturing company, one of France's finest. She was an excellent artist and the Sèvres' begged of her to stay and become part of the company. Thankfully, she did and that brought her days on the streets to an end. She became very successful with her designs and within a few years became a household name – even some of her former friends and socialites, who scrambled to possess her latest designs, tried to renew their association with her. Of course, she declined. She had long forgiven those who had treated her so shabbily but was reluctant to relive the experience and found she no longer had anything in common with them.

"The Sèvres were decent folk and extremely fond of Mamma. She adored them. Ah, but monsieur, you know what life is like. Sorrow was not far behind. Dear Madame Sèvres died. Monsieur Sèvres was devastated, as was Mamma, who loved her so much. They had no children and Mamma was like a daughter to them. Madame Sèvres had suffered terribly during her illness, and when she was near the end, she begged mamma to look after Monsieur Sèvres, for he would be lost without her. He took her death badly. Mamma took charge of the business, allowing him to recover from the shock of his loss.

"Mamma was thirty-three at the time and thought both marriage and motherhood had passed her by. Ah, but life is full of surprises, is it not, monsieur? After Madame Sèvres died, Mamma, as well as looking after the business also spent a great deal of time nursing Monsieur Sèvres. He suffered terribly from depression and drowned himself in the demon drink. But with Mamma's love and care, he was gradually restored to his normal self. The business became even more successful, and they were spending more and more time together. They would be seen at the theatre, the opera and many social gatherings. Of course, there was talk about their liaison, she being a young woman and he a man well past his prime. The gossip didn't bother her, but it did him, as he thought it was unfair to her. Ah, but being thrown together as they were, the inevitable happened. One evening, after they returned from seeing *Madame Butterfly* at the Opéra, he proposed to her. Being the gentleman he was, he told her not to decide there and then, but take her time to think it over. She didn't need any time to consider his proposal as she had fallen in love with him a long time ago. She didn't keep him waiting for long, and they were married in Saint Germain-des-Prés in the summer of 1910. To their delight, I made my appearance eighteen months later."

Oscar gave a broad smile. "I'm delighted that your dear mamma found love after the turmoil of her life. And look, look at what that love produced."

"Oh, it was true love indeed. She was unable to have any more children and, as I was an only child, she spoiled me. She hadn't expected to be a mother, never thought she could ever trust or love a man again, but she did, so I was a great bonus in her life, so she said. When I was fourteen, she took me to the Palm Sunday mass at the Sacré Coeur and afterwards sat me down on the steps of that beautiful place and told me about her days before she married. She told me everything; spared nothing. She told how she was orphaned then inherited a fortune. She talked about the events that led to her downfall and the people involved. She swore me to secrecy, making me pledge that I would not reveal it to anyone. She held my hands and told about her lost fortune, lost respectability, and her life on the streets of Paris as a street performer. It took some believing that my sophisticated and elegant mamma could have been a vagabond and lived in a cramped garret. To think that she lost so much, and treated so badly, yet still kept faith in the goodness of people. I could have survived such an ordeal.

"You'd be surprised what the Human Condition can endure," Oscar replied.

"She told me about your meeting with her in Paris. Did you know that she had seen you on several occasions before meeting you that day?"

"No. I did not. Where did she see me?"

"One morning she'd seen you sitting outside the Café de Paris, sipping a coffee. She remembered it so well, for you were sitting there sad and forlorn, with your collar turned up against the world. Your once-stylish clothes were all shabby, worn out and grubby. She recognised your face but just couldn't place it. Again she passed you as you were leaning against the parapet of the Pont de Sully, as you stared into the swirling Seine bellow."

"Oh! I often did that, wondering if it would be kinder to jump and end my misery."

"That's what crossed Mamma's mind. She stopped and looked at you, but you didn't see her as you seemed far away, in a different world, in a world of your own. She still couldn't place your face. Then, some months later, as she was dancing her way towards place de Tortro, she noticed you sitting on the steps of the Sacré Coeur and throwing something down the steps that landed at her feet. She picked up a Saint Christopher medallion and as she looked up, she noticed you had your head buried in your hands and seemed to be weeping. She continued dancing up the steps towards you. She was in two minds whether to talk to you, but your weeping disturbed her, so she stopped, and you know what happened then."

"Indeed. I often wondered what became of her. I couldn't believe that her future was on the street. She seemed a survivor, one who would always find a way back. It seems I was right. I'm delighted that life turned out well for her."

"When Mamma realised she was expecting me, she was thrilled. Papa was concerned at the prospect of becoming a parent at his age, but those concerns soon drifted away when I arrived. He became a devoted and loving father who doted on me. She said that when she suggested Margaret Windermere as my name, Papa near on had a seizure. Being the conservative gentleman he was, he was thinking more on the lines of Marie or Martha, but he eventually warmed to the name. It wasn't long before he would be proud of such an unusual name for a Parisian. At school, I received a bit of a ribbing. They called me Windy, but I didn't mind. At least I didn't have to worry about anyone forgetting my name. Life was good to us, and we lived a happy and rewarding life. I went on to marry Andre Amelot, a botanist, whom I had met at the Sorbonne. We had a good marriage that produced a daughter we called Gwendolyn after another of your characters."

He smiled at the very idea of it. "When did your mother pass away?"

Margaret hung her head, dabbing her eyes. "Oh, monsieur, that is the one deep sadness in my life."

"You don't have to tell me if it's too distressing."

She was quiet for some time, and then looked up at him, her eyes filling with tears. "I must tell you. I must complete the story of her life."

"Indeed, but only if that is what you really wish to do."

"I do. I was eighteen when papa passed away. Having an elderly father means you don't expect him to live long, but dear God, I missed him so much. Mamma was devastated but she once more reorganised her life. She ran the business so well that it blossomed and became even greater than she could have ever imagined. Men were always trying to win her heart but none succeeded, for none could replace my papa in her affections. However, she still adored the attention they lavished on her. She had many interests. One of her consuming passions was travelling. She travelled the world. She did this at every available opportunity and many a time took me with her to exotic places. Her last journey was to America. The ship was off the coast of Spain when a German submarine torpedoed it. All on board were lost.

"She would not want me to feel sorry for her as she believed she lived a full life, a life where she had known love, had received, given and shared it. We can't wish for more than that, can we? How sad, that she, a woman of peace should die from an act of hatred. Even with the sadder parts of her life, she believed she was lucky and was always thankful for the life given to her. She was such a good Parisian. It is so sad that her final resting place is not here in Père Lachaise but in the blue seas beyond her beloved city. Paris was engraved on her kind and loving heart."

"Thank you for allowing me to ramble,' she said as she stood up her leave. "I hope we will meet again now that we have found each other. I know this is no Paradise, but to know you are here will be of comfort. We will see each other again, won't we?"

"Of course. You'll never know just how comforting it's been to me to have the pleasure of meeting you. Now, my dear, don't leave. Let us sit here and pass the rest of the day together."

Oscar spent his last day at the clinic in the most unexpected way, with memories of the past and the prospect of a brighter future.

"Order! Order!"

The meeting reconvened and the conclave settled down in anticipation of the appearance of Jude, the Divine Psychiatrist. Before them was a copy of Jude's report, a thick volume providing a study of the mind and character of Oscar Wilde. Jude entered the chamber and took his seat next to Gabriel, placing his copy of the report on the desk in front of him.

"Thank you, Gabriel," said the Chairman. "Before we retire to consider the six questions on the agenda, we must listen to Jude's assessment. You have the full text in front of you for your perusal. Jude, if you please."

"Thank you, Chairman. Like most of you I have read and enjoyed the writings of Oscar Wilde and been impressed by his undoubted genius. However, I've been disturbed and saddened by the chaos of his personal life, which led to his humiliating fall from grace. He is different. He's certainly special, but is he so special as to merit the status of a Special Soul? It's a difficult question, but it has to be answered objectively. The ultimate fate of Oscar Wilde lies exclusively with us.

"Oscar accepted an invitation to visit me at the request of his friend Jim Morrison and others concerned about his recent peculiar behaviour. He was reluctant at first, but in deference to them, he arrived at my clinic for a consultation. I must point out that it was difficult for him to do this, for he had deep reservations about the practice of psychiatry. He arrived at the clinic dressed to the nines. Read nothing of importance into this, for he was a man of style and elegance in his earthly existence, so for him to continue this practice at the Reservation is no surprise. I decided to let him talk. This seemed to be the most sensible way to approach him – simply to let him chatter away and see where it led, asking a few questions to keep things moving.

"He covered every element of his life in great detail. He pulled no punches. He was more open and forthright than I had imagined he would be. He had a lot to say and did so with gusto. He was in need of releasing all his frustration and my clinic was the perfect place to do it. The soothing hands of Dymphna, to whom he reacted positively, helped him. You have before you the entire text of all of the sessions I had with him as well as Dymphna's assessment. Attached to it are her assistant Jean Petti's observations, which I recommend you to read. This will give you valuable information and insight into the mind of this complex and unique person that will aid you in your deliberations. His detailed account of his humiliation and ruination after the disastrous trials is compelling reading, as is his account of the loss of his wife, his children, his exile and his ill-fated relationship with Lord Alfred Douglas. His prison experience was difficult for him to recall, as was the whole matter of his downfall. His confrontation with his sexuality was painful but very revealing. He was at first reluctant to discuss it, but in the end, knew he had to face up to it. He made no apology for his sexuality but expressed regret for the effects it had on those he loved.

"You will have a difficult task when making your deliberations, and I believe the text of our sessions will be of great value to you. I believe he is truly repentant and sincere in his regret. It is difficult not to like him, but I must add a word of caution. It would be unwise to allow his overwhelmingly lovable personality to cloud your judgment. You all know the high standard to be met to reach the criteria as laid out in Article 13 –This standard must be adhered to. The task to decide the ultimate fate of Oscar Wilde rests solely with us, so we must be scrupulous in our deliberations. We must do what is necessary. If you decide he's a Special Soul you then have to decide whether the Michelangelo Syndrome applies in this case. If it does, then there is only one outcome."

"Did he know who you were?"

"No, Paul, he only knew me as Professor Jude, the Divine Psychiatrist. He didn't question me on my title, only its divinity, which he thought hilarious. He was only interested in discovering what was ailing him and I was there to allow him to do just that. He's a very astute individual, and I suspect he knew who I really was."

"Do you think he should be made a Special Soul?"

"You know better than to ask me such a question, Paul. I will cast my vote, as we all will, in secret. I still yet haven't decided how I'll vote."

"Had he any inkling that his friends had a petition?"

"No, Veronica. If he had, he may have reacted differently and not opened up the way he did."

"Thank you, Jude," said the Chairman. "To conclude, we will deal with the testimonials submitted by the souls of Père Lachaise. All the testimonials have been randomly spread amongst you, so it's reasonable to say there is a good cross-section of opinion within each of your bundles. I have taken two testimonials from the thousands submitted by the souls of the Reservation of Père Lachaise to read into the record. These are not from what we call personalities but from ordinary tenants. Then I will take one from Anthony to read into the record. To balance matters out, I have a dissenter's submission. Although most submissions are in Oscar's favour, I believe it fitting that I read into the record this dissenter's views. This I will do after the rest of the submissions are read into the record.

"The first testimonial is from a pauper from Paris' Latin Quarter, interned at Père Lachaise on the nineteenth day of December 1832. She died from rheumatic fever at the age of eighteen in the gutter of rue Beautreillis.

"'My name is Leonino Thierry. I was a pauper, as were most of my acquaintances – all buried without ceremony, without a prayer, in unmarked graves, some in the murky depths of the Seine. We had much in common – nobody to worry over our fate or shed a tear for us at our departing. We came from the same downtrodden side of Parisian society and we all passed away from the likes of tuberculosis, diphtheria, and cholera, or, as in my case, rheumatic fever. Few of us could read or write; the only education we had was from life in the gutter and sewers of Paris. I thought fortune had been unkind to me and after suffering a tough earthly life perhaps the next would be kinder. Alas, it was not to be, for providence turned her back on me for a second time. I found that my existence here was little different to that of Paris. I was still 'a nobody', marginalised and put upon, kept in the gutter by indifference. The gutters and sewers are the same wherever. All I did was exchange one gutter for another, only this one had no foul smell. I may not have suffered illness or starvation, but mentally I was in the same gutter with that same feeling of being a waste of time and space.

"'One day I was sitting on a rocky crag looking over the Desert of Indifference, towards the Moral High Ground that peered down over our humble domain, when someone tapped me on my shoulder. I turned. Standing before me was a man dressed like a dandy. He looked like the kind of person that always looked down on me on earth, so I ignored him as I always do with that kind.

"'He sat down and lit a cigarette, offering me one, which I declined.

"'"Tell me, monsieur, have you ever been up that hill?' I said, pointing over towards the Moral High Ground.

"'He laughed. "No, but I did have ambitions to climb such a hill once. Every time I tried, however, tumbling down I came before I got halfway up. After several attempts, I gave up, as it seemed that I was destined never to climb to such dizzy heights. I settled for being a wit instead."

"'"I tried once," I said. "I was curious to know what went on up there, so I walked over the Desert of Indifference, a feat in itself, to have a look at the place. When I arrived, I looked up, and there seemed to be a multitude trying to reach the summit. Many were sliding down after falling on the climb; others were pushing their way through as though they had a divine right to be a step ahead of others. I began to climb but didn't get far. Each time I reached the first ledge, I lost balance and tumbling down again. After the fourth fall, I was confronted by a very sour-looking woman who angrily pointed to a notice board."

""'Can you not read, you fool?' she yelled. 'Can't you see the warning? It is clear as day that you and your kind are not welcome at the summit of this hill. Go away. This is the preserve of those who know the value of morality and the importance of decency and decorum, which you don't. You are not welcome. Be on your way.'

""'With that, she pushed me and sent me tumbling down the ridge to land at the foot of the Desert of Indifference. With the little pride I had dented, I wandered back across the desert to my hovel at this craggy knoll to lick my wounds."

""'Why would you want to climb a hill of that sort?" he asked. "What were you expecting to find?"

""'I wanted to know why so many souls were keen to climb it, and why those who settle there didn't want others to join them. It was the oddity of the place that fascinated me."

""'Believe me, madame; you've had a lucky escape. Sometimes it is best to leave odd things alone – there is nothing fascinating about that lot, I can assure you. As a matter of interest, what exactly did the notice say?" he enquired.

""'I can't read, monsieur," I confessed. "Not a word."

"'He gave a smile and touched my hand. "There is no shame in that. It can be solved."

""'How," I asked.

""'I could teach you," he replied.

""'Monsieur,' I replied, "why would you want to do such a kind act for someone like me, someone you don't even know, someone of little importance, who is clearly of a different class from yourself? Why would you want to help a Little Miss Nobody like me?"

"'He sighed at my remark.

""'You are far from a Little Miss Nobody, you're as special as the next soul," he informed me.

""'But I'm in the gutter," I exclaimed.

""'Let me lift you out of it and teach how to read and write. I have time on my hands," he replied.

""'Who are you?"' I asked

""'I am Oscar Wilde."

""'Oh! I've heard of you before. You're a writer, aren't you? You have better things to do than to waste your time with me. I have nothing to give you in return for such a kind offer."

""'Your company will do," he replied.

"'Very few people have ever wanted my company and here was this famous writer wanting mine. How could I refuse?

"'That very day, sitting on the rocky crag, be began to teach me the basic rudiments of reading and writing. It was to be the beginning of a journey that would open my eyes to a different world, a world I'd been robbed of by my earthly circumstances. I was to have my mind broadened, stimulated and liberated. This stranger was to elevate me from the gutter to a height I could only have dreamt of. He was a patient and considerate teacher who spent days on end teaching me the wonders of another world and opened my eyes to the seductive beauty of the written word. He visited me for a few weeks; then arranged to take further lessons at his home up in the Literary Quarter. I had rarely left the Rocky Crag and was nervous about leaving my safe environment. He put me at ease. I was in safe hands. I read every book I could lay my hands on and studied his literary works and the story of his life. He then informed me I was ready for the Knowledge Zone.

"'I remember well, the day he escorted me there. When he explained what the Zone was all about, he said it was the redeeming feature of the Reservation. I didn't understand what he meant but soon found out. I was nervous as we climbed the steep hill towards the large brass doors that was the entrance to a new and better world. As I stepped inside the sight of the massive round room with its acres of books made my heart skip a beat. He escorted me through the umpteen passageways. At the end of each passage was another room to discover, with more passages leading to even more modules of knowledge.

"'In that wonderful place I set about to discover a world that I had previously been oblivious to. All the time I have been here, I had never shed a tear, but I cried for Oscar Wilde. I lost out in life. I had nothing of value to lose, but he did. He lost all that was of any value to him − his wife, his sons, his friends, his reputation, his freedom and, most sacred of all, his literary career. It was such a waste that he died so young. I couldn't help but cry as I read about his life. He should have been valued and appreciated by his peers rather than treated as a leper and cast aside as though suffering from some infectious disease when all he was suffering from was a natural condition.

"'To conclude, I believe that Oscar Wilde is an honourable soul who went out of his way to help me and many others for no other reason than to offer help and friendship to those less fortunate than himself. I wholeheartedly support this petition.

"'Signed: Leonino Thierry.'"

"She seems focused," said Thérèse.

"Focused; more like delusional."

"All right, Matthew! That's enough," said the Chairman.

"I agree with Matthew," Timothy said as he nodded his head. "The poor creature is demented. She's as daft as he. Why should we take ant notice of her?"

"Why not, her testimony is as valid as the next."

"About as valid as yours."

"Matthew! That's enough," the Chairman muttered, fed up with the bickering coming from his council.

"The second submission is from Daniel Gaite, buried as an unknown soldier. He died on the battlefields of France," announced Gabriel. "It reads as follows.

"'When I heard that Oscar Wilde was in difficulties and submissions needed in support of a petition organised by the Central Reservation Council, I immediately put pen to paper in support. In France, I am one of the many unknown soldiers, buried with full military honours, one of the Republic's unknown heroes who gave his life for the glorious cause. In reality, my name is Daniel Gaite, a native of Bonnac on the outskirts of Limoges. They inducted into the army trained me as a fusilier to fight in that War to End All Wars. I had better things on my mind than an unglamorous end in a war about whose cause or reason I hadn't the foggiest idea. I left behind my true love, my darling Louise, with a babe in arms. I had been a blacksmith by trade and had plans to build a future for my family. Instead of being a provider for my family, I became a hero, so they say, a lad who sacrificed himself for the glory of France.

"'I remember the day I died. It was early December day. The air was crisp, and the snow was up to my shins. The enemy was on the far side of a ridge, blocking our advance. We lined up and rushed the enemy's defences. Our commander had miscalculated. He sent us to oblivion. All Hell let loose as we fell like matchsticks. I was shot in the leg and fell into the snow in excruciating pain. I looked up, and a German, even younger than myself, was staring down at me with his bayonet at the ready. "I'm sorry, monsieur. Forgive me," he cried as he thrust his bayonet into my heart. As I felt my precious life ebbing away, my enemy's tears dripped on to my brow. He was just a kid as lost as I was. Within seconds, I was dead. I was a hero. I would rather have been home with my wife and babe than a dead hero without a name. They robbed of my precious gift of life, not by my young enemy but by the stupidity and the ignorance of politicians and military strategists who brought us face-to-face on that bloody battlefield.

"'When the war was over they selected me, as I had no identification and transported to Paris as one of the many unknown soldiers. I was buried at Père Lachaise with full military honours. All fancy stuff and to a certain extent an honour, but I would rather have been laid to rest with my kin at Bonnac and remembered with my name on a stone instead of a forgotten soul of Père Lachaise. When I arrived at the Reservation, my nightmare began. My father was a committed non-believer. A naturalist he called himself and instilled in me the view that religion was a load of rubbish. Really, the word he used was *merde*. I followed suit, although I had the highest of respect for those who had a religious faith and never challenged them on their convictions. Being a non-believer, I never gave the prospect of an afterlife any thought, so my arrival here came as a shock. It soon dawned on me that my father had been wrong as here I was in another life, such as my father said never existed. After my stint at the Reception Centre, I was directed towards the Green Door. I opened it and stepped through. Standing waiting for me was a fellow who introduced himself as Oscar Wilde. He extended a friendly hand and welcomed me to the Reservation. I had heard of him as an infamous man who shamed himself and threw away a talent, ending his days wandering around Paris begging from strangers and making himself an ass. He escorted me to my new abode at the Military Academy of the far side of Cloud Eighty-Nine. I was nervous about him at first, as his reputation didn't inspire confidence. However, I soon found him a good listener. I had a lot to say, especially about my reluctant military service, in which he took a deep interest. He was my constant guide and helper. For the first year, he visited me every so often to make sure I was coping with my new surroundings.

""So you were a soldier," he forlornly sighed one day as we looked over Père Lachaise.

"That I was,' I replied, "but I didn't last long, I had only finished my basic training, and before I knew it they sent me off to war, to the green fields of France – such a fine-sounding description, masking its real horror." The mention of the green fields of France caused him to sigh, and his eyes misted over. "It was a horror beyond belief. It was as if all of mankind had gone mad. The generals would lose ground; then attempt another advance with horrendous casualties. Then they would call a retreat and thousands died in the confusion. Not content with their losses, they would order another run at the hill, with more senseless killings – madness, monsieur – absolute madness. This would go on for days on end. Then, it started all over again. If we didn't die from our wounds we died from disease. The trenches were swarming with rats; they had a field day gnawing at the dead and spreading disease. It is hard to describe the waste of human life. The mutilated bodies I saw were soul-destroying. Severed limbs lay strewn about; there were shattered heads and guts wherever one trod. At times, I was ashamed of being part of the human race, ashamed that I didn't have the strength to say, No! No! No! I won't fight in this stupid war.'"

""'Indeed. I know exactly what you mean," he said as he wiped his eyes.

""'Monsieur, why are you so sad?" I asked, concerned by his demeanour.

""'I had a son once," he softly said, "who like you went to fight a war for all the wrong reasons. Alas, he died at the hands of a German sniper. You remind me of my son."

""'In different circumstances I could very well have been his killer," I said.

""'Indeed,' we wistfully sighed.

"'All of my time here he has treated me as his son. To me, he's a good sort, a man I wouldn't have minded having as a father or . brother. I can see no wickedness in Oscar Wilde. All I see is a kind and likeable soul, who, in his earthly life suffered for nothing more than being himself. Whatever critics may say about him, his real value is in his just being, Oscar Wilde.

"'Signed; Daniel Gaite.'"

"What a load of twaddle."

"You're not letting Matthew away with that, are you, Chairman?"

"Certainly not! A bit of respect won't go amiss. If you insist in this vein, I will ask you to leave the chamber. Do you understand?"

"Yes, Chairman," Matthew sheepishly replied.

"Let's continue," the Chairman said. "Anthony! Please read out your selected submission."

"Very well, Chairman. I have managed to get through thirty-two of them. They were of a high standard. The one I have selected is from Yvonne Monlessan.

"'My name is Yvonne Monlessan, a native of Biarritz. I spent most of my life in Paris as a waitress in the Café Due, in Montmartre. I never married for I was unlucky in love. My first love was a bum who treated me like a tart. I gave him his marching orders, and in return, he kicked and punched me from one end of Paris to the other. It took eight years to get that scumbag out of my life. Then I fell in love with a policeman. More fool me. He ended up being another bum who left me with the pox and a soul full of sorrow. I gave men the elbow and settled for a life of peace and tranquillity in my apartment, with my cats and books. To my surprise, I found love when I reached my forties, not with a man but with the lovely Capucine, a ticket collector at the Bastille Metro. We lived a blissful life until she died. I didn't last long. Within the year, I followed her.

"I never gave men much time, as they all seemed mental. I thought they weren't worth the energy needed to love them and, by God, it takes some energy. That is how it was until I came across Oscar Wilde. Now, here was a man I could gladly have fallen for in life. When I first met him at the Reservation, he had me hooked. They say he was gay in his earthly existence, but that didn't deter me. If he was, he never showed it – there again, there is no sex here so it is hard to know just what a soul's sexual orientation is. I get on well with him. I can't remember the last time I could have said that about any of the male species. Who is Oscar Wilde? What is he all about? Is he real? These were the questions I asked myself when I heard he was at the Reservation. I knew who he was, for at the time of his trial he was the talk of the Paris cafés. Sadly, talk of his talents was soon replaced with gossip about his sex life. The English seem hung up about sex and because of it ruined a good man. I soon found out who he was and got to know him very well, and within a short period realised he was not the deceitful deviant history painted him as. What I found was a decent soul. I was one of the nominators of Oscar Wilde as a Trusted Soul of the Reservation. I did so because of his ability to show love and tenderness to umpteen souls who have crossed his path. He is special, and I fully endorse this petition.

"'Signed: Yvonne Monlessan.'"

"Thank you, Anthony. We have only one more submission to be read into the record – it is that of the dissenter," said the Chairman, as he prepared to read it out.

Matthew was up on his feet. "Are you saying that in all of the Reservation there is only one dissenter?"

"No, Matthew. This is just one of a few. If you're unhappy about it, you are free to look through them all."

"How many are there, then?"

"Gabriel! How many dissenters are there?"

"Thirty-three, Chairman, all men."

"Now, are you satisfied, Matthew? Can I continue?"

Matthew threw his hands in the air.

"Very well. This is the selected dissenter's submission.

"'I'm Eugène Pottier, a reluctant tenant of the Reservation of Père Lachaise. I object to this Oscar Wilde being given any kind of preferential treatment, and he is certainly not a Special Soul by any possible stretch of the imagination. I objected to his elevation as a Trusted Soul as I do to this outrageous attempt to have him elected as a Special Soul. There has been much said about his so-called goodness and that he is a genius of good standing. I disagree. To me, he is a second-rate writer who plagiarised most of his works. His poetry is quite moderate; his plays are at the best mediocre. He was a parasite in life and is an even bigger one here. He is a deviant with little regard for the moral sensitivities of others.

"Forget about his earthly life and look carefully at his tenancy here. Look at how he has treated those he calls friends. He says he loves Édith Piaf, yet he put her through hell in the Cherry Blossom Forest, causing her distress and hurting her deeply by his antics. If he loved her or had any respect for her he would never have treated her so cruelly. It is the same with Chopin. I say in reality he despises him and puts on an air of admiration and respect as part of his warped sense of humour. If he had any respect for him, he would never have harassed him as he did at the Music Academy. When informed that he had destroyed Seurat's paintings, I was far from surprised.

"'He's a monster and seeking Special Soul status for him should not be entertained. There are far worthier souls, like, Chopin, Ingres and many others, who are deserving of that special honour than the likes of Oscar Wilde. Forget about him and put an end to this nonsense of him becoming a Special Soul. He would be more at home on Cloud Eighty-Seven. I know I'm out on my own as most of you have been hoodwinked by this most dishonest of souls. I say this petition be dismissed as the irrelevancy it is.

"'Signed: Eugène Pottier.'"

"I must say, that's a bit rich. I hope you're not going to take any notice of such trash and it's withdrawn from the record of this chamber," cried Veronica.

"Eugène Pottier is entitled to his say. You may not agree with his sentiments, but you must accept that he and others who disagree with your point of view are entitled to have their say."

"Anyway," replied Veronica, "There are only thirty-three dissenting submissions – not many to be concerned about when you count the number of endorsements on hand. There are thousands of them."

"Yes! They are all available for you to peruse. Make good use of the time available and study Jude's prognosis and the rest of the documentation. Familiarise yourselves with every element of this case and remember – the destiny of a soul is in your hands. Jude, I look forward to reading your prognosis, as do the members. Now, this meeting is adjourned – we will meet in six weeks to cast your votes."

The Sunshine of Love Café

Rehearsals being over for another day, the ladies of the cast retired to the comfort of the Sunshine of Love Café to rest after the exertions of trying to get the better of Oscar's extravaganza. It was more difficult than they had envisaged. The café was the preserve of the women of the Reservation who wished to relax, reflect or just to chill out. It was always well patronised by those wishing to be intellectually stimulated without the tedious intrusion of the male. The place was a kind of woman's liberation café, Purgatory style, where customers were free to take the male apart or forget about them altogether. It was great therapy. Jane flopped into a chair, tossing her hat aside.

"I hope Oscar will appreciate our efforts. I've never worked so hard. I'm whacked."

"Of course he will. After all, this is all about him, and so it's guaranteed to please him. It won't do his ego any harm either. It needs to be stimulated and kept in peak condition."

"Well, I hope you're right, Isadora. I hate to think what effect it would have on his already delicate state if it went pear-shaped on the night."

"Relax, He'll love it," Édith declared, as she took a sip of pink champagne. "Stop worrying. It's impossible to disappoint him when it comes to his work and ego. He thinks he's divine, touched by genius and all that waffle he goes on about. Isadora's right – he'll love it as long as it concerns him. He's easily pleased. He's like most men I've known. Just appeal to their ego and you can wrap them around your little finger. I did that with all the men in my life. I had Oscar hooked within days of meeting him. Men are so shallow. It's a kindness to show them contempt. I can never understand why we sisters put up with all of their nonsense."

"I can," replied Colette as she touched up her mascara.

"Oh, can you now," laughed Isadora. "You'd better enlighten us."

"Sex! Yes, we put up with men for one reason and one reason only: sex. It's all they're useful for. Well, some are. Most we can happily do without."

"Did someone mention sex?" Sarah asked as she entered the café.

"Indeed they did," Isadora answered. "Colette says men are good for sex and nothing else. I kind of agree with her."

"And for buying us diamonds," Sarah said as she sat next to Colette. "If there were no men about who would buy us diamonds? We couldn't buy them ourselves – that would be tasteless. The problem with men is that when they give you diamonds, they expect sex in return; the more sparkling and valuable the diamond the more erotic the sex. They are crass and have no taste, no style; no romance and fail miserably to understand us. Men…"

"Oscar, he's different. He's *all* style."

"How right you are, Jane. He's an exception to the rule, isn't he?"

Édith sniggered. "He may be, but he's still as sex mad as the rest of them. They can't help it. It's an incurable disease."

"You can say that again," laughed Marie. "He may well pretend he's in touch with his feminine side, but it's all a load of bull. If he were in touch with it, he would know that love is more important than sex. He doesn't. He is like all other men – sex-mad. It's all about sex with him, male or female, but we love him all the same."

"Here, have a cream cake and stop talking about sex."

"Really Jane, didn't you know a cream cake is like sex itself."

"Simone, you're incorrigible. Anyone else wants one, one of these delicious, sexy cream cakes?" asked Jane as she handed around a large platter laden with creamy delights.

They all took one and sat back and enjoyed it. The café was quiet apart from the licking of the cakes. Édith looked curiously at Simone, who was deep into her cake, and asked, "Excuse me for asking Simone, but what have cream cakes to do with sex?"

"Oh! Everything."

They all looked over their cream cakes at her.

"Tell us more," someone laughingly cried.

"There was this Geordie fellow from Newcastle, in England – you know that cold and windy place way up there towards the Scottish border," Simone said as she took a break from her cake. "Well, he maintains the satisfaction you get from a cream cake is equivalent to good sex – that the chemicals released by the body during sex, is the same as devouring a good fresh cream cake. He was forever going on about it. I met him when I was filming *Room at the Top*, way back in the 1950s, with Lawrence Harvey. Lawrence, so taken by it was devouring cream cakes at every opportunity. Don't know why, as he had hoards of women running after him, offering him far more than tasty cream cakes."

They all stopped licking their cakes and looked at Simone, who was finishing off hers, licking her fingers as the last morsel vanished out of sight.

"Are you serious?"

"Well, Jane, that Geordie was very serious indeed. He was always serious about sex. He was all talk. No doubt he was probably a dud and wouldn't know what to do with a woman if she offered him something tastier than a cream cake, so he put it about that cream cakes were as good if not better than sex."

"Don't fellows talk a load of crap?" laughed Isadora.

"Especially about sex," Jane said, as she looked at her half-eaten cake, in two minds as to finish it off or not.

"Did I mention I met a young one looking for Oscar the other day?" Marie said, getting away from the subject of sex a subject that always unnerved her at the best of times. "I hadn't seen her before but, my God, she was keen as hell to meet him. She'd been searching the entire Reservation for him without any luck. I asked her name. She called herself Margaret Windermere Sèvres, would you believe? She said that her mother once knew Oscar. Well, that got me curious. I asked her this and that, hoping to extract some information about who she was, but she was reluctant to say anything, except that she had to see him. I was in two minds in letting her know he was at the clinic, but she seemed such a devotee of his, I directed her there. I'd never seen a soul as delighted as she was at the prospect of meeting him."

"Never heard of her before – I hope she wasn't one of the objectors trying to get at him and annoy him about the petition."

"God, Jane, she couldn't be, could she?"

"You never can tell, Édith. We'll soon find out if she is."

"Ah, we're getting carried away with ourselves. I'm sure she's harmless. Are there any more of those cream cakes left?" Isadora asked as she licked her lips at the prospect. "I've taken quite a liking for them."

It was a full house when the Divine Council met for the final time in the case of Oscar Wilde. Every scintilla of evidence, for and against, had been gathered, read, scrutinised and argued over. Almost the entire membership of the Council was present for this rare occasion. It seemed every member wanted to be involved. Although Oscar didn't know it, this was the day that would decide his ultimate fate.

Gabriel called the meeting to order in his usual efficient manner. Very few of the members were absent. Only those on assignment would miss the occasion. Even the Irish members were there, for, although denied the opportunity to vote, they still wanted to have some input.

The atmosphere was tense as Gabriel addressed the council. "This is the case of Oscar Wilde. The procedure will be as follows; you will first vote on each of the six questions on the agenda. If the there is a positive vote he will be elected a Special Soul. You will then vote on whether you consider Oscar Wilde to be a sufferer of the Michelangelo Syndrome. If the vote is positive, his rite of passage will be granted. The revised rules state that only a unanimous result from those casting their vote will suffice. One vote against and the motion will be lost. Those who wish to abstain, please leave the chamber now. If you do abstain on the first vote, you will not be allowed to vote on the second."

Those abstaining slowly made their way outside. There was just a handful of them. The Chairman raised his eyebrows in surprise. This did not bode well for the destiny of the unfortunate soul. A hush descended over the chamber as the Chairman rose to address the council. He looked jaded. This had been the most argumentative and protracted of all sessions he had dealt with concerning Article 13. All the previous cases had been thorny enough, but this one was fraught with difficulties that had not been present in the others. The question of Oscar's sexuality was particularly vexing. Although according to the Divine Code, discussion about sexual orientation was barred from any submissions coming before the Council, the Chairman was certain it would be taken into account in this case. It had become clear to him throughout the debates that Oscar's sexuality would determine how they would cast their votes.

"We have come to the decisive moment," he began. "We have spent a great deal of time and energy on this motion, and the fate of this soul depends on your decision. You all know the rules and procedures. You will cast your votes now," the Chairman announced as he handed the Golden Key of the voting booth to Gabriel, who walked slowly towards it and opened its golden door, to reveal a rare sight – the Divine Ballot Box. Ringing the bell, Gabriel motioned the voters to proceed with their task. As the Divine Scrutiniser, he stood guard over the ballot box to ensure all was above board. He would not tolerate any unsaintly shenanigans took place. The members collected their ballot paper and, after ticking the six boxes, placed it in the Divine Ballot Box. After doing their Divine Duty, the members left the chamber and gathered on the marble steps to await the outcome of the count. For the sake of accuracy, the vote would be counted three times. The saints gazed up at the chimney for any sign of white smoke, the indication of a positive result.

They muttered amongst themselves, wondering why the announcement was taking so long.

"Look!" cried Veronica, "White Smoke!"

"It doesn't look white to me, more a dirty grey," observed Simon.

"No, Veronica is right, it's white. Who would have thought he'd have made it?" Matthew sighed.

There was a welcome relief, but a look of resignation on the faces of the abstainers.

Against all the odds, Oscar had won the first round. However, would he win the next? They returned to the chamber. Now deemed a Special Soul, it was down to the serious business. Was Oscar a sufferer of the Michelangelo Syndrome or not?

Gabriel called the assembly to order.

The Chairman looked around at the members, surprised by their vote, for after all of the hostile remarks made at the debates he thought it inevitable that Oscar was doomed to Cloud Eighty-Seven. He knew that the sub-committees had dealt in detail with the questions under consideration by the members, but had serious doubts about the outcome of the second vote.

"Now that Oscar has been elected a Special Soul," he said, "you must vote on the matter of the Michelangelo Syndrome. Off you go and vote as your consciences dictate."

Arising from their seats, the council members slowly made their way to the lobby. After collecting their ballot cards, each went into the booth to vote on the ultimate fate of Oscar Wilde; then assembled outside to wait the outcome. Meanwhile, the archangels locked themselves away to carefully count the votes. It was the charge of Gabriel to hand the results to the Chairman, who, before the change of rules, would have had the casting vote in the case of a tie. He felt a bit out of it, as the new rules debarred him, and he was now obliged to be a neutral observer, a position he believed to be of no value. His sole purpose was the good government of the council and its procedures.

Suddenly the door of the chamber flung open, and Gabriel appeared, looking decidedly harassed, with his wings all a-flutter. He rang his bell to bring the members of the council to order.

"What's wrong, Gabriel?" asked Paul.

"You look as though you've seen a ghost," cried Simon.

"You must all return to the chamber. There's a problem with the count."

"Problem… What problem?" Veronica cried.

"You'll find out once inside."

They made their way inside, wondering what could possibly be wrong. It was a straightforward vote: yea or nay. What could have gone wrong?

"One of the papers hasn't been endorsed," Gabriel announced after he had closed the doors behind them. "You know the rules – they are quite clear. Any spoilt votes nullify the result. All ballot papers must be endorsed. The rules state in this situation, there must be a second vote without undue delay. I am afraid you will have to vote again. The ballot papers have been destroyed, collect your new ones and this time *please* remember to endorse them."

"Which silly saint made a mess of his vote?" laughed Matthew.

"Probably Simon – you know what he's like. His mind's always anywhere else but on the task before him."

"Nothing to do with me, Christopher, I do know how to endorse a ballot paper. I cast mine correctly."

"I did too," said, Christopher.

"I certainly did," muttered Ignatius.

"Well, someone didn't and it certainly wasn't me."

"Oh! We all know how perfect you are, Bernadette," laughed Matthew.

"Who was the culprit, Gabriel?" asked Christopher.

"How would I know? I'm not psychic. It's a waste of time speculating who the culprit is. Even if I knew I've no intentions of embarrassing anyone," he replied. "Now, in you go and please, get it right this time. I do have other important issues with which to deal."

This time there were no problems. The Divine Scrutinizer was happy. There would be a result.

"Dear God! Look!" cried Veronica. They all gazed in amazement towards the chimney, now bellowing smoke.

"Surely not," a saint cried as he wiped his brow.

It was over. There would be no further meetings. The decision would be posted on the basilica's Divine Notice Board, and the Chairman's messenger would inform the Reservation Council of Oscar's fate. As the Chair of the Council, the decision was Sophie

Hugo's as to who was to inform Oscar. If she wished, an intermediary could do the task. It was her decision and hers alone.

With the roll of drums, the lights of the Comédie Française dimmed. This was the show of the year and tickets were like gold dust. Opening night was a glamorous affair, with the theatre full of Oscar's friends and admirers from every quarter of the Reservation, all decked out in their best glad rags for the occasion. The theatre had witnessed many excellent shows, from the best of French theatre to Édith Piaf's musical spectaculars, but this evening promised to be something completely different and would stand apart from anything previously presented. There was a second roll of drums, and the audience settled for the big event.

The programme was an impressive publication, designed by Modigliani. It was unusual. None of the performer's names was printed, simply those of the characters. There was a brief itinerary of the event, and to his delight, Oscar noticed that the musical score was by Jim Morrison, with additional lyrics by Musset. He had a feeling it was to be an evening to savour. A shapely leg in red tights protruded from behind the dark blue stage curtains as another roll of drums stifled the hum of the expectant audience. Oscar was in his element, sitting between Sophie and Marie, relaxed and at peace after his stay at the clinic. He was looking forward to the extravaganza. He was curious to know how his work would translate into what the programme called *A Musical Extravaganza, or, The Importance of Being Earnest in a Pink Purgatory*. He was soon to find out.

A white-gloved arm reached seductively out from behind the curtains, followed quickly by a head of golden locks. Another roll of drums and the curtains opened to reveal Jane Avril, resplendent in a green dress and holding a black cane with a silver handle and tip. There was a gasp of delight as she stepped into the spotlight. Tapping the stage with her shoe, she pointed her cane at George Bizet, the conductor of the Reservation Orchestra, who gave the signal with his raised baton that set the orchestra alight. Jane twirled across the stage to set in motion the Reservation's tribute. The stage quickly filled with the Cucumber Dancers, dressed in delicate satin shades of green as they performed the opening act with Jane, in the role of Amour and the evening's raconteur, swirling in between them. The set, a backdrop of iced tipped cucumber leaves, designed by Max Ernst with additional trappings by Modigliani. The dancers came to a sudden halt and fell spread-eagled around the cucumber, which split open to reveal Miss Bunbury, aka Chopin, dressed in a black bodysuit, pink wig and white gloves. Oscar failed to recognise his friend until he turned and looked directly at him. He squealed with laughter as the composer stepped out of the cucumber and sang and danced his way through the opening number, "Algy, My Lad". The audience roared their approval as he made his exit, and the theatre fell into darkness.

The only sound came from the gentle beat of a snare drum. Suddenly a blinding flash of orange-yellow light and the heightened beating of the drum made the audience jump. The drumming reached a crescendo and came to a sudden end. The lights came up to reveal a set depicting a morning room in a flat in Half Moon Street, the home of Algernon Moncrieff. The room, entirely decorated in shocking pink, set off the black furniture. Seated at a grand piano, wearing a royal blue dressing gown and smoking a Turkish cigarette through a silver holder was Algy, played by Simone Signoret. At the far end of the room, dressed in a black and white morning suit, stood Lane, Algy's manservant, played by Leonino Thierry, who, as the scene began, burst into song about "The Science of Life and Regret of Lost Champagne." Algy's friend John Worthing skipped into the room clad in an orange suit launched into a duet with his friend.

"Heavens," Oscar cried, turning to Marie, "that's Sarah."

Oscar was enthralled as his play *The Importance of Being Earnest* unfolded before him in a show, unlike anything he could ever have imagined. Musical versions of the play had been staged, the first as early as 1927, and there had been versions in French, German and Italian. He fondly remembered an all-male production staged in Berlin in 1998. However, the extravaganza on stage before him surpassed anything previously conceived. After all, Purgatory had access to performers, musicians and designers who could not have worked together during their time on earth.

Entranced by the sheer outrageous spectacle, Oscar couldn't believe that his friend Balzac, his heavy body tightly squeezed into a frock, was playing Lady Bracknell. It soon became evident that the entire show was nothing more than a saucy and suggestive spectacular given an elegant and witty transvestite slant. Alfred de Musset followed on stage as a most fetching Gwendolyn Fairfax. Oscar roared with laughter as he realised the pretty miss tiptoeing on to the stage was the *enfant terrible* himself, who gave a sly wink to the guest of honour. Musset made a good-looking woman. Oscar wiped away the tears. He hadn't laughed so much for a long time, not since his last visit to Morgan's Chair. He couldn't contain himself as Lady Bracknell sang the "Bunbury Lament" and Gwendolyn seductively eyed Jack. Gwendolyn burst into song with "The Essence of Being in Love". This made little impression on Lady Bracknell, who exited the stage, leaving the lovebirds together. Gwendolyn held Jack's hands and serenaded him with the seductive notes of "The Ideal Name for Love is Ernest". Jack danced around her, trying to confuse her, which he did, then confused her further by his not-too-well constructed song

"Real Love Oozes out of Anyone Called Jack". The stage, lit in bright yellow light as Jack declared his love for Gwendolen, who then informed her aunt, Lady Bracknell she was engaged. Lady Bracknell blows her top with a high-pitched voice version of "We'll Inform You Who You Are Engaged To".

Act Two opened with a spectacular dance by the Schoolgirls; all dressed in short black and white spotted uniforms and red cricket caps. Édith Piaf materialised as the girls' headmistress, dressed in a white gown and black mortar hat and outlined the setting of the next act. The Schoolgirls formed an archway, and Miss Prism made her appearance, singing, "The German Tongue is Good for You". Oscar roared as it dawned on him that Miss Prism was his old pal Seurat. He smiled with delight for he was certain that Seurat had now forgiven him. Édith and the dancers exit the stage.

Sitting in the corner, diligently writing in her diary was Jack's ward, Cecily. When she burst into song with her rendition of "Dear Diary", Oscar knew in an instant that it was Delacroix, minus beard, strutting around as an eighteen-year-old girl. He couldn't believe Eugène had been persuaded to shave to play the part. Colette, disguised as Canon Chasuble, joined the couple, singing "Let Me Hang from Your Very Lips", to the disbelief of Miss Prism. Isadora, playing Jack's butler Merriman, informed Cecily that Wicked Uncle Ernest has arrived. She burst into a chorus of "Someone Wicked at Last". Jack entered, dressed entirely in black, singing a lament, "My Brother Died of a Chill in Gay Paris". Miss Prism cynically replied with "So! He Reaped What He Sowed, Didn't He, The Cad?" as Jack, surrounded by six dancers dressed as ravens, did a dance in homage for his lost brother.

Jack's dead brother Algy appeared, his resurrection sending Jack into a fury. Cecily declared that she loved Ernest, in the song "The Secrets of a Diary. Jack showed his surprise and then professed his undying love for Cecily, who says she couldn't love anyone if his name wasn't Ernest. As Algy exited, the stage was awash with dancers who made way for the entrance of Gwendolyn. She and Cecily introduced themselves with the words of an upbeat melody, "Sisters Forever". Act Two concluded with Cecily and Gwendolyn adjourning to the morning room, arm in arm, leaving Algy and Jack eating muffins.

Act Three began with the Muffin Troupe, dressed in yellow and black diamond-patched body tights. They swirled across the ochre-lit stage with their "Dance of the Muffin Eaters", followed by Gwendolyn and Cecily giving a delightful rendition of "The Art of Preserving a Dignified Silence" as they gazed out of the window in the morning room at Jack and Algy, who were wiping their faces after devouring the last of the muffins.

Jack and Algy entered the drawing-room and asked the ladies for forgiveness, which they gave, but were held back as there was still a serious barrier to their future happiness, that of Ernest. They sang a dirge, "That Insuperable Barrier of Christian Names". Jack and Algy happily replied that they were prepared to suffer the ordeal of being christened to secure the ladies' affections and did so with their duet of "Let's Change our Names for the Sake of Love". Lady Bracknell made another appearance. She turned to Jack and asked after the health of Bunbury. Algy sang in deep sorrowful tones of "Poor Bunbury's Explosion", as a Cucumber Dancer waltzed across the stage carrying an urn with the ashes of Bunbury. Lady Bracknell noticed Cecily for the first time. Jack announced their engagement. Lady Bracknell sings with gusto, "Hertfordshire's Disturbing Marriage Statistics". Dr Chasuble pranced on to the set, announcing it is time for the christenings, only to be disappointed that none will occur. Distressed, his mind turned to love, and he sang "Miss Prism in the Vestry Waits for me".

Lady Bracknell, aghast at the mention of the governess, angrily sent for the unfortunate Miss Prism, who rushed on stage and screamed at the sight of Lady Bracknell, who screeched out a high-pitched hysterical song, "Where is the Baby, Prism?" The Pink Baby Dancers dashed on stage and surrounded Miss Prism, protecting her from the wrath of Lady Bracknell. Miss Prism confesses that she mislaid the baby at Victoria Station.

Jack cries out, 'Who is my mother, then?'

Lady Bracknell bellows. "Your mother is Algy's mother."

Algy and Jack, delighted to be brothers, give a dancing display in celebration. When Jack delves through the army lists, seeking his father's first name he finally realised he was Ernest after all. He burst into the final song of, "Thank God for Army Lists". The Cucumber Dancers filled the stage led by Jane, who brought the show to its conclusion. The curtains fell.

The crowd went wild as the cast took their first curtain call to rapturous applause, followed by curtain call after curtain call. It was an absolute success. Oscar was delighted by the tribute,   although he had no involvement with it. He loved the lyrics, adored the music, admired the set, and the transvestite element gave the show that extra edge. He couldn't have done better.

So many of his friends whom he'd insulted and embarrassed had turned out to perform and he was humbled by the love and devotion shown to him. For most of the time he was away at the clinic, they had been slaving away over staging this tribute to him. It was obvious that a lot of hard work it had been put into it to make it a success. He would be forever grateful to those decent souls whose friendship and loyalty he did not deserve.

"I'm the Messenger of the Keeper of the Gate," a voice boomed out across the theatre as the audience were preparing to leave after their exquisite evening of entertainment. There was nervous laughter from the crowd, and they looked at each other in bewilderment before seating themselves again and gazing up at the stranger on the stage. "My purpose here this evening is to deliver the judgment of the Divine Council," the messenger coolly announced.

The audience fell silent.

"This," the messenger said, brandishing a parchment scroll, "is the divine judgment on an appeal submitted on behalf of Oscar Wilde by the council of the Reservation of Père Lachaise?"

They continued staring at the stranger. Most wondered what he was on about. He seemed extremely solemn, as though he was about to dish out bad news.

"This appeal," he continued, "seeks the rite of passage to Paradise of the soul of Oscar Wilde."

There were gasps of astonishment. Some of the audience fanned themselves with their programmes.

Oscar leapt up from his seat in absolute shock. The colour drained from his face. He stood rigid, his mouth open and beads of perspiration forming on his brow. The audience turned towards him. The extravaganza had been a surprise, but this was alarming. He had a terrible sinking feeling that his newfound joy was about to evaporate.

The fair-haired messenger, dressed in magnolia satin, waited for the audience to settle down and once there was silence began to speak.

"This is the case of Oscar Fingal O'Flaherty Wills Wilde, author, dramatist, essayist, and Trusted Soul of the Reservation of Père Lachaise," he said in a clear voice.

Oscar wiped his brow, loosening his cravat with his trembling hands.

"This is the Judgment of the Divine Council, to a petition submitted by Sophie Hugo and seconded by Marie d'Agoult under Article 13 of the Divine Code. It reads as follows:

JUDGMENT OF THE DIVINE COUNCIL
Dated the 25th day of July 2001
Petition
Seeking the rite of passage of the soul of Oscar Wilde to
Paradise.

"'After long and considered deliberations it is the Judgment of this Divine Council that the above-mentioned petition is granted in the case of Oscar Wilde.

"'It is Ordered that he be given unhindered the rite of passage and has been granted seven days to prepare for his departure and to say his final farewells to the souls of Père Lachaise.

"'A copy of this Judgment will be posted on the Notice Board at the Central Reservation.

SIGNED:

The Chairman of the Divine Council

"So be it," said the messenger. Bowing, he turned and left the stage, leaving the audience stunned. None had expected anything like this when they had taken their seats for the evening's festivities.

Oscar was shocked into disbelief.

After a stunned pause, the audience erupted into applause. Cheering, they turned to the balcony where Oscar was standing being hugged, kissed and congratulated by Sophie and Marie. He was overcome, confused, elated and, most importantly of all, only a step away from absolute freedom. Sophie had arranged to have the judgment read out in front of his friends as she thought it the most appropriate course to take. She was delighted with the success of her decision.

Adieu to a Tortured Soul

Now, reader, it is not every day you have a soul with an open invitation to Paradise. There was no way the tenants of the Reservation would allow Oscar to leave Purgatory without some kind of farewell revelry. It was time for a party to salute Oscar and his elevation to Paradise. This was to be Oscar's Purgatory Party, and all were welcome.

***

An event of this kind would take a lot of organising and a committee was set up, chaired by Jane Avril. She wasted no time in galvanising the committee into action. There was much to do and little time in which to do it – only six days to put together the biggest party the Reservation had ever seen. It would have to be special, for nothing else would be appropriate. Unlike the *Musical Extravaganza*, in which Oscar wasn't allowed any participation, this time he would be consulted on what he wanted – the menu, the music, the general tone of the event. The day after the announcement, Jane visited him at Merrion and was delighted that he had restored to its former beauty. Gone were the mirrors and the paintings were stacked up against the wall, wrapped, labelled and ready for dispatch. She found him calm and serene. At first, he was reluctant to have a party for he thought it might seem in bad taste to have one to send him on his way to Paradise. Jane told him straight that there was no way the Reservation would allow him to depart to such a destination without a feast and a good knees-up. It was a rare occasion, she told him, and *not* having a party would be inappropriate. Once Oscar had warmed to the idea, he made a few suggestions himself, which she took on board. Once armed with her party list, Jane set to work, first by nominating herself to organise the guest list. Isadora would arrange the dancing; the music was in the hands of Chopin and Morrison, with speeches by Musset and Proust. She approached Pierre Desproges and offered him the position as the master of ceremonies, which he accepted with pleasure. Raymond Oliver, the Reservation's celebrity *cordon-bleu* chef, offered to take care of the culinary arrangements. He promised to do something special to fit this semi-divine occasion. André Gill offered to bring his cabaret from the Lapin à gill to perform something fitting the occasion.

Jane and the committee decided to have the party on the Reservation Green that spread out in front of the northern steps. They worked hard to make sure every aspect was covered. The list of those wishing to attend grew larger by the hour, and she was delighted at her choice of the venue, for it was large enough to accommodate the vast crowd who wanted to attend this one-off event. The tables were set out in a zigzag design across the expanse of the Green and around the stage and dance floor at the foot of the steps. The tables for Oscar and his special guests were arranged in a semi-circle around the Laburnum Tree. The tables were covered with shocking pink cloths, and black serviettes set off by royal blue candlesticks and chairs.

Édith had carefully arranged the seating with cards especially made by Max Ernst that matched the design of his invitation cards. On the right-hand side of Oscar would be Marie, Musset, Édith, Balzac, Isadora, Ingres, Colette, Morrison, and Leonino Thierry – to his left Margaret Sèvres, his special guest, followed by Sophie, Delacroix, Chopin, Jane, Seurat, Sarah, Proust, Simone, Montand and David.

In the meantime, Oscar, slowly recovering from the shock of his elevation, was preparing for his departure. He called on Musset and asked him if he would accompany him to Cloud Nine, for he would like to look at the expanse of the Reservation for one last time. Musset agreed and thought of the umpteen times that had visited the place since they made their first sojourn to the place together way back in 1919. As they headed off, Musset was aware of an aura emanating from his friend, showing a soul at peace with himself, his demons and his fellow souls. There was no comparison between this journey and their first one all those years ago. There was neither talk of sex nor dreams of George Sand nor any other nonsense. Throughout the journey, Oscar was tranquil and talked of only the positive side of all the good he had experienced and the decency of those he had met. They passed the Valley of Tears without giving it a second glance, but a single tear trickled down his face as he glanced over at the entrance to the Valley of Happiness. At the summit of Cloud Nine, they sat under the oak tree and gazed out over the reservation.

"What do you think Paradise will be like, Alfred?" he asked as he fixed on the far horizon.

"I haven't the foggiest."

"They say it's something one could never imagine, something beyond comprehension. I'm a bit nervous, you know, as though I was about to face an opening-night audience."

"That's no sin, my friend. Its nerves that give life the edge, that makes us aim for goals we thought beyond our reach."

"I can't help thinking that I'm a bit of a fraud."

"Fraud! You are no fraud, Oscar. Frauds don't get into Paradise. If they did, there would be standing room only. If you're a fraud, I'd hate to think what I am."

"Do you think I will look odd or out of place in such an exalted spot?"

Musset gave a hearty laugh. "Paradise is supposed to be beyond that, beyond petty prejudices and narrow-mindedness. There will be nothing odd about Paradise or any soul privileged to be there. There will be no bitterness, backbiting or nastiness, or persecution because of sexual orientation or physical and mental handicap. Paradise is a perfect state of mind."

"Pity we don't get an introduction book, though – you know the kind, telling us what to expect, how to behave, that kind of thing. A rulebook, you know – etiquette for Paradise."

Musset burst out laughing. "Dear me, Oscar, you're going to Paradise, not Oxford University. You will need no rulebook or any kind of aid to help you. Paradise is Paradise. You need to think on a far higher level. You are heading for the real thing. I'd always imagined Paradise to be supreme in every way, where you always do the right thing, for that's all you'd be capable of doing – you and your rulebook."

"I'm going to miss you, Alfred," Oscar said. "I'll miss your colourful philosophy... did you hear that?"

"Hear. Hear what?"

Oscar sprung to his feet. "That singing, can't you hear it? It is Maria, is it not? Come, Alfred, I must see her one more time. I must say adieu to that tortured soul."

"You know how difficult it is to get through to Cloud Eighty-Seven," Musset reminded him as Oscar helped him to his feet.

"I know, but I must try and see her one more time."

They ran up the slope towards the rugged rock face that separated Cloud Eighty-Seven from the other quarters. The last time they climbed it, it had been tough going to reach the Slit, a narrow gully that allowed souls to look over into the forbidden domain where tortured souls who couldn't cope with Purgatory were incarcerated. The Slit was the only place from which to view this place and was difficult to get to as it tapered off to a small gap that one could just about see through it. As they neared it, the classical tones of a heavenly voice became clearer. They looked through to see the beautiful lavender-clad valley amongst a spattering of poplar trees. He scanned the landscape to see where the voice came from.

"Look, Oscar, over there. That's her."

On a cliff edge, overlooking the fields of lavender stood Maria Callas, dressed in a white tunic with white roses entwined in her long black hair that fell on to her bare shoulders. She was singing Puccini's "O Mio Babbino". Her pitch-perfect voice drifted across the valley. It was purity. They rested against the rock, closed their eyes and let the magical tones engulf them.

"Do you think her soul will ever be free?" Oscar asked Musset as he tried desperately to hold back the welling tears.

"I'd like to think so, but it seems unlikely. I can feel her pain. It's in her voice, in her stance and it wafts across the valley as clearly as her voice. As beautiful and serene as her voice may be, the torture of her soul is in every note. It's the love of a past life that's eating away at her, eating away at her soul – a soul it seems, that will never be free. The beauty of her voice is a beauty compounded by lost love and sorrow."

"Even so, hers is a voice for Paradise just as Chopin's music is," Oscar said as he looked at her, her arms outstretched as she reached the high notes, as though she was reaching out to the love that turned its back on her for another dark-headed beauty.

"Both would cause their maker to weep with pleasure at the realisation of creating such perfection. How can she be denied Paradise, when a sinner like me, a scribbler of wit, with a dicey background and without a note in his head is given that honour? It seems so unjust."

"Surely there's no injustice in Paradise. It has to be just, for its divinity that calls the tune. It's a waste of time speculating on the working of this place or Paradise. It's all a mystery, a mystery, and destined to remain so."

When Maria ceased singing, Oscar called out her name. She turned and threw a kiss, then vanished out of sight.

Oscar and Alfred headed back to the Literary Quarter to prepare for Oscar's departure with Maria's music still ringing in their ears.

The Wilde Party

It was a warm, moonlit night. The partygoers began to arrive. They took their seats and waited for the revels to begin. Jane had little idea of how many would eventually turn up, but the tables soon filled up, and those who were unable to find a seat settled down on the surrounding grass or between the trees on the fringes of the Cherry Blossom Forest. Anticipating a large crowd, Raymond Oliver had arranged a buffet at areas beyond the tables. A fanfare sounded, and the crowd cheered wildly as Oscar, the guest of honour, with Dubliner at his heels, arrived arm in arm with Jim Morrison. As he reached the top of the steps, he took a deep intake of breath as he realised the extent of the celebration was far beyond his expectations. He was delighted as the crowd cheered at his arrival. This was more thrilling than any opening night of his plays. He took his seat between Margaret and Marie. The master of ceremonies, Pierre Desproges, dressed in an orange suit, with green shirt and black dickey bow, tinkled a spoon against his glass and called the revellers to order.

"Welcome all. This is a special occasion, to enable us to say our farewells to that soul of wit and wisdom, Oscar Wilde." They were up on their feet, howling and cheering, clapping and stamping their feet. He paused to acknowledge the applause and cheers. "We all know he's been difficult at times," he continued. "A pain in the neck, one might say, but it's impossible to remain angry with him for long, for essentially he's a caring, loving and decent soul. We all love him. We will miss him terribly. It will be sad to see him go, but our loss is the saints and angels gain. Here's to Oscar, the Wilde soul of the Reservation." He raised his glass towards Oscar, and the revellers followed suit. They all stuck into the delicious fare prepared by Oliver and his chefs. *Hors d'oeuvres* were a choice of Hampshire salad, Bunbury mushrooms in Salome sauce and crispy Algies. The main dishes: roast chicken with Erlynne stuffing, roast pork with saucy Cecily sauce and Oscar's fried rump with Greek dressing. Desserts were Gwendolyn's apple-eye tart, cold Dorian platters and Windermere treacle. The best Purgatory wine complemented the meal.

Pierre was up on his feet again, ringing his bell to get the attention of the diners. "We have a lot of entertainment for you this evening, but this, my friend, is just for you," Pierre announced. "Give a big hand to the band especially formed for this evening, the Purgatory Blues Band."

The partygoers enthusiastically applauded as the band climbed on to the stage. Gilbert Bécaud, the leader, introduced the band: Stephane Grappelli, Mez Mezzrow, Ginette Neveu, Gabriel Pierné and a recent arrival at the Reservation, Michel Petrucciani. The delectable Yvette

Guilbert provided vocal. Within a few beats, they had the Reservation swinging as their music filled the air. The dance floor was soon heaving with everyone intent on having a good time. Oscar took Margaret's hand and the crowd parted as they made for the dance floor. They swirled across the floor to the applause of the onlookers, each of whom was waiting for their turn to dance with him. He was wondering whether he had the energy to continue, when Gilbert Bécaud, who, with the clap of his hands, brought the revellers to a standstill, rescued him. Gilbert had something to announce.

"It's time for a song from our Little Sparrow."

Édith climbed the steps to the stage and walked towards Chopin, who was waiting with his white-gloved hands outstretched to welcome her. There was a scream of delight as he escorted her to the piano. She stood at the side as Chopin took his seat. The applause subsided as he played the opening notes to Édith's song. She turned towards Oscar and with her exquisite voice filled the air with *"Non je ne regrette rien"*. The revellers fell silent. They all turned towards her as the passion in her voice engulfed them. The tears ran down the Little Sparrow's cheeks as she sang for Oscar for the very last time. Her words were crisp and clear as they drifted around the Central Reservation and through the Cherry Blossom Forest, as the final note died away the partygoers rose to their feet in rapturous applause. The Little Sparrow took her bow.

The Purgatory Blues Band returned to the stage, and the revellers wasted no time in taking to the floor and filling it until the early hours. After the band had played the final number, it seemed the party was at an end with the revellers preparing to leave when Pierre once again demanded the partygoers' attention.

"It's not over yet, folks," he beamed. I've kept one more act for the finale. I had to do a lot of coaxing to put this act together, believe me. Let's have the lights down for a minute or so."

The lights dimmed, apart from the candles dotted around the tables that flickered in the gentle breeze as darkness descended.

"This is for you, Oscar – ladies and gentleman, the one and only Jim Morrison with his New Doors. Let's hear it, boys!" A flash of purple light lit up the stage. There was a mighty blast from electric guitars and keyboard and pulsating drums as Jim Morrison strutted his stuff for the first time since his demise. He was his old self. Grasping the mike, he belted out "Riders on the Storm". On the keyboard, changed into tight blue jeans and tee-shirt, was Chopin and, on the lead guitar, Gilbert Bécaud. Oscar had always wanted to see the rose grower in action, and here he was in full flight, doing his thing. Turning to Sophie, he said, 'This is cool, real cool. Look at Chopin, as cool as they come.'

Margaret nudged Sophie and laughingly said, 'Listen to him. He's the last of the cool dudes.'

Morrison performed "Light my Fire", followed by "Break on Through" and finally, "People are Strange". He was surprised to find he was enjoying every minute of it. After taking his final bow, Pierre thanked him and then, looking at Oscar, offered him the floor. The crowd went wild with anticipation of a dose of Wilde wit. He slowly rose and looked around him at the expectant audience who waited to hear what was to be his last performance. He climbed on to the stage, shook Morrison's hand, thanked him for his performance and kissed Chopin. He stood for a moment, as he scanned the masses before him.

"What can a man say when he's about to leave his friends forever?" he began. "They say one should have no regrets, that what has been was meant to be, so regret is of no value. Maybe that is so, but as I stand before you, regret is whispering in my ear. I can feel it tugging at my heartstrings and plucking at my soul. I will say goodbye to you not with a long-winded witty speech but with regret and a single word. Adieu."

There was a pregnant pause. They expected more. Then they were up on their feet, applauding him for the last time. They may well have expected some great speech from the genius of words, but it didn't matter. They were just happy that he was on his way.

Pierre got them all up, and for the remainder of the evening, they danced. Oscar danced with anyone who asked. He hadn't enjoyed himself so much for such a long time. He couldn't help but think that soon he'd have to say farewell to all of these partygoers, farewell to all his friends and colleagues and farewell to Père Lachaise.

The party was over. There had never been one to match it and unlikely to be another. The crowd drifted away at the end of a momentous evening glad that he was on route to Paradise, but sad at the parting.

The next morning Oscar awoke with a feeling of peace and satisfaction. As he lay on his bed, his head was full of beautiful and happy memories of the good times in his life. The unhappy and ruinous moments found no way into his mind. The love and affection showed to him at last evening's banquet were overwhelming, and time was quickly approaching for him to take his leave. What lay ahead for him he could only imagine. Perhaps Paradise, as many have speculated, is a place beyond our comprehension. The day was to be one of mixed emotions. It disturbed Oscar to think he would never see his friends again, but then, he thought of those he may see again – Cyril, Vyvyan, Isola and Constance, his mother, his father and, maybe with some luck, Robbie. The thought that he may embrace and breathe the same air as they, filled him with delight. Maybe, he thought, he should not daydream of such things and just accept whatever was to come.

Although he'd be going to where he had always wanted to be, there was a tinge of sadness as he looked out of his bedroom window over the Literary Quarter, his home for so many years. Alfred de Musset's home was a few doors down. He smiled at the thought of the times he had enjoyed his hospitality and all the laughter they had enjoyed together. Opposite Musset's home was Balzac's shabby run-down abode with its rickety fence and gate. A fleeting feeling of sadness came over him as he realised he would never enjoy the writer's companionship again. They didn't hit it off when they first met, but all of their sessions at the Café Oueurde cemented an understanding of each other.

Oscar looked up the hill to Proust's townhouse, neat and tidy like the novelist himself. Proust was an intellectual soul mate who knew his every thought. It would be odd not to have him at arms' reach. Across from Proust's home was the Café Oueurde itself. How he would miss it. Maybe Paradise has its own divine Café Oueurde where great literary souls meet. The café had been a central part of his existence and a reminder of his life around the boulevards of Paris in happier times. What of Colette – he could see the gable end of her home at the back of Proust's house. No more would he listen to her crystal-clear philosophy or see her walking sprightly past his window without a care in the world, followed as always by cheeky Kiki-la-Doucette. Yes, he would certainly miss her.

Between the houses, he could see in the distance the Thespian Quarter and the road that twists its way up towards Comédie Française, where he had seen all his plays performed in so many different forms and where was staged the Musical Extravaganza with such stunning success. He could just make out the corner of the cottage of Sarah Bernhardt, where he enjoyed the pleasure of her company. The thought of not seeing her again saddened him, but he had memories that would never dim.

He looked out of a side window over towards the Musical Academy and sighed at the thought of Chopin. How many times he had wandered over there to hear him perform or just to seek out his company. He could just see the tip of the gable end of his home at the top of Quaver Hill. What two unlikely soul mates they were. How they ever got on together, he would never know.

He would miss all his friends he had made here, friends who loved and cared for him, with whom he had laughed and cried, with whom he had argued and fallen out with but with whom he had always made up. He would miss those good souls who had gone to the trouble to submit a petition to save his troubled soul and save him from the humiliation of expulsion to Cloud Eighty-Seven. He sighed at the thought he would never get to know Margaret Sèvres better. He had known her for such a short time. Whenever he looked at her, he could see the vagabond dancing up the steps of the Sacré Coeur, dressed in red, white and blue rags.

There was a rap on his door. Musset stood there with a broad smile. "Good morning, my friend. You have seven hours left. What do you want to do?"

"I was thinking of making one last visit to the View Point. What do you think?"

Musset raised his eyebrows in surprise. "Whatever you wish, come on then, let's go."

As they walked towards Cloud Eight, all that passed by gave him a wink, or a smile, or an acknowledgement of some sort. At the entrance to the Viewing Platform, Oscar suddenly stopped.

"What am I doing?"

"What's wrong?"

He looked at his bemused friend. "Why on earth do I want to look down over Père Lachaise? Has it not been the cause of my confusion, the cause of my depression and the cause of my delusions? Does it really matter, Alfred, how many strangers visit my grave? Is it really of any consequence how many kiss my tomb or leave mementoes? Does it matter at all? No, it does not and what a fool I was to think it. There is nothing there for me to see. Come. Let us go back. I have something waiting for me with a far better view."

"Wait a moment, my friend. Père Lachaise has also been your saviour. It's the souls of Père Lachaise that have seen you through and showered you with their love and friendship. Take one more look; there you will see not just a graveyard, but also the resting place of lovers of every kind, shape and style, of philosophers, artists, writers, singers and ordinary decent skins. That's a special place down there, Oscar, very special."

Oscar looked down over the cemetery. Standing in front of his grave was a couple with their young daughter who held a bunch of sweet peas close to her.

"Who are they, Alfred?"

Musset had a look. "They're an Irish family on a visit to Paris to see the sights."

"I wonder why they have visited my grave."

"Because you're a sight to see, that's why."

Oscar roared with laughter. "How right you are. You know, Alfred, there was a time I would have thought her existence was a sheer waste of time. Why bother, I once would have thought? All she would have to look forward to was a life of suffering and sorrow with just a dash of pleasure and a glimpse of happiness to keep her company. All she would learn and experience would be a waste of time, and it would have been kinder if she had never been born, but how wrong I would have been. She is the future. It is that little girl and all the others like her who will continue the cycle of life, who will continue to enhance what Mother Nature has created. Maybe she will grow to be a scientist who discovers the secrets of creation or an astute politician with foresight and commitment to ease the burden of those less fortunate, or an extraordinary artist. Or maybe she will simply grow into an ordinary individual and take her part in the continuation of life."

"Ah, but Oscar what a wonderful part to play."

"Indeed."

"Are you ready to go?"

Oscar stood for a quiet moment, looking down. "Yes. I'm as ready as I'll ever be," he said as he turned his back on Père Lachaise for the last time. "There's only one more place I wish to visit."

"Where?" asked Musset.

"Saint Ita's Chapel."

They made their way towards the Literary Quarter. Outside the chapel, Oscar asked Musset, "Do you mind if I go in on my own?"

"Not at all."

Oscar walked slowly into the subdued light and sat for a while near the Lover's Pillar. Taking a pencil from his pocket, he walked over to it and began to write. What did he write? That is a secret, but you can take a good stab at it if you have managed to get into the mind of Oscar Wilde. He emerged from the chapel looking peaceful as if the final oppressive cloud had drifted away to leave him completely free.

On Route

The Central Reservation brass band stood to attention. They were a smart-looking lot, ready to lead the grand parade. They were in their best tangerine uniforms with black lapels, and light green peaked hats. Behind them were the Fiddle Band of the Dancing Souls, from the Thespian Quarter, dressed in crimson tights and black and white polka tee shirts. Tucked in behind them was the Physiological Quarter's Trumpet Troupe in white suits and black ties and gloves. On their heels were the black and white outfits of the Political Hot-Air Blustering Troupe playing their cheap penny whistles. The rest of the bands lined up for the parade across the Reservation to escort Oscar to the Pearly Gates and his eternal home.

The festive atmosphere was building up as the bands tuned up their instruments. There had never been a gathering quite like this, and every musician had arrived to take his or her part in the unusual event.

The brass band gave a roll of the drums and the parade began. There was a lot of preening and posturing between them as they tried to secure the status as the premier band.

Putting his best foot forward, Paradise-bound Oscar headed off behind the bands. Ahead of them was the broad boulevard lined with popular trees and banks of aubrietia that stretched from the Central Reservation to the gates of the Philosophers' Quarter. This joined the heather and daffodil-clad Highway to Paradise that wound its way over and across the entire Reservation to the Gates of Paradise itself. Dubliner trotted at Oscar's heels as he headed off on this final journey with Sophie and Marie linking arms with him.

The administrators of the Reservation abandoned their desks and, along with the rest of the inhabitants, followed the parade. It wasn't long until there was a steady stream behind them and the atmosphere tingled with every beat of the drums. When they approached the Reservation Gate, they saw that Jane Avril was waiting with a cart and her favourite mule, Can-Can. The cart was loaded high with bunches of forget-me-nots. To all that passed she handed them a bunch of forget-me-nots, mostly blue, but some with a sprinkling of pink and white. They headed off towards the Philosopher's Gate where they were joined by the tenants of the Philosophers' Quarter, led by the Comte de Saint, who accepted his bouquet from Jane as they passed through the gate. A few philosophers who disagreed with Oscar's elevation stayed behind in a huff. As in life, there always has to be a political angle to everything and this event was no different. The parade passed through the Cherry Blossom Forest and down along the Lilly Lake towards the Political Haven on Cloud Thirteen. All shades of political opinion lined up at the Political Exit, waiting to join the party of well-wishers, along with the party faithful who were forgetting their differences. With their forget-me-nots, they stepped out and followed the crowds as though they were on a political rally.

The parade of marchers grew steadily longer and Oscar, striding out in front, felt ten feet tall. They turned towards Primrose Valley, which was in full bloom and led to Cloud Fifteen and the gate to the Literary Quarter that was swarming with well-wishers. Jane kissed Balzac as she presented him with his flowers. Musset would not be outdone by his friend gave Jane a passionate kiss in return for his. Climbing over the Literary Stile, they joined the parade.

The parade continued down and across the poppy fields up towards the Arch of the Thespian Quarter, where Isadora, Sarah and Simone were waiting. As they moved through the arch, the denizens of the Thespian Quarter followed them. The parade wound its way around the twisty highway leading to the gateway to the Music Academy where they were met Chopin and the entire academy. Grasping their forget-me-knots, they happily joined the parade. The ever-growing throng continued through the Ravine of Dreams with its carpet of snowdrops mingled with purple petunia cascading on either side. There Max Ernst, Delacroix, Seurat, Modigliani, David and the entire Artists' Colony watched as the crowds climbed the steep hill leading to the Colony Gate. Can-Can, coaxed by Jane, struggled up the hill. Jane presented the artists with their flowers, which they gratefully accepted, and fell in with the crowd, who were now in full voice singing along with the bands.

It was a day to savour. The parade was all happiness and jollity and the Reservation was in full bloom, but alas, there is always a downside. Not long after they passed the Artists' Colony they came within touching distance of the Huff Club. The tenants of the club stuck their bare backsides to the crowd in protest at Oscar's elevation. The crowds, being in a jovial mood, just laughed at the Huffers for the killjoys they were. To let them know there were no hard feelings, some patted or placed forget-me-nots between the cheeks of the swaying posteriors.

Finally, they came to the summit of Cloud Ninety-Nine and, stretching before them was the last mile home, and in the distance, the glow of the Pearly Gates. Oscar looked over his shoulder to see, stretching away over the horizon, the multitude that had escorted him to his final home. Humbled he was by the response of what seemed like the entire Reservation of Père Lachaise was there to see him on his way. Taking one more look out across the Reservation that had been his home for so many years; he followed the bands on the last leg of his journey. The bands arrived at the gates, making a large semi-circle around the Mount of Saint Peter. They fell silent as the following multitude gathered behind them. Then the murmur of the crowd died away until there was absolute silence.

Stephane Grappelli took his position on the Mount of Saint Peter, in front of the massed bands, as the multitude of well-wishers watched. There was an uncanny silence. With his violin at the ready, Stephane struck up the opening bars of *Molly Malone*. The sweet notes drifting over the crowd broke the silence.

It was time for Oscar to leave. It was time to say his final farewells. There would be no more speeches, just a quiet goodbye to friends and colleagues. Through the gates was liberation. Although he had yearned for this moment, his heart was heavy as he looked into the faces of the friends and companions who had worked so hard to exorcise him of his demons and set him on his final journey. He embraced Sophie, who had mothered him ever since his first week at the Reservation and who had been the prime mover in setting him free. Turning, he embraced Marie, the beauty with a heart of gold, who understood his moods and swings and often soothed his troubled mind. He ran his fingers through her lush golden hair for the very last time.

Parting from Chopin was just too much for him. Oscar loved this man, probably more than he loved any other, and he was saddened he would no longer have his companionship nor be able to listen to him play. Deep down he knew Chopin should be on the road to Paradise and not he. Chopin was far more deserving of such an honour. His music was Paradise itself, its natural background music. They embraced without saying a word, for what more could they say? Bending, he kissed the brow of the Little Sparrow. She looked up at him, her dark eyes filling with tears, knowing they would never see each other again. He would never hear her beautiful voice again wafting across the Cherry Blossom Forest or see her bringing the audience at the Comédie Française to their feet in absolute rapture with the beauty and passion of her voice. He wiped her eyes, and she sent him on his way with a bow. Ingres gave him a warm handshake, kissing him on both cheeks without saying a word. He could find no words to transport his feelings. Delacroix, too, was lost for words. They embraced for what seemed like an eternity.

"God, I'll miss you, Oscar Wilde," Musset said as he embraced his friend. "No more sharing our dreams. You will have no need for them now. Off you go, behave yourself and keep your eyes and hands off those angels."

Jim Morrison held out his hand. Oscar took it and embraced the rose grower. There was no need for words between the two poets. Their eyes said it all. Isadora held out her hand. He took it and gently kissed it. He turned to Balzac and bade him adieu. He looked at

Seurat, his former antagonist, who stood tall before him. Here was the soul who had welcomed him to the Reservation, his guide to its peculiarities and complexities. Seurat held out his hand to his former foe. "I welcomed you here, my friend, all those years ago, now I humbly bid you farewell."

Simone and Yves wrapped their arms around Oscar and whispered their private farewells. Proust embraced Oscar for the last time and cried.

Margaret Sèvres could hardly bear this parting. She had only known Oscar for such a short time, now it was goodbye forever. He held her and whispered something in her ear. She smiled and let him go. Colette, standing with Kiki-la-Doucette in her arms, kissed him on the cheek, leaving her lipstick trace as a reminder of their crazy association. Jane, the woman who loved him unconditionally had the honour of being the last to say goodbye. She stood in front of her friend, dressed in her yellow dress with her red hair falling over her black jacket. She held out a bunch of forget-me-knots, her eyes puffed, her face streaked with tears.

"Remember me, Oscar; remember all of us when you're in Paradise. Remember those who loved and treasured you, those who worried and cried over you," she said, falling into his arms. After kissing her, he took the orchid from his lapel and placed it in her hair, and she threaded the forget-me-knots into his lapel.

Turning, he looked over towards the Lady in Blue, who was standing beneath a weeping willow. She looked at him, smiled, bowed her head and turning slowly walked away. She was no longer the sour-faced creature he usually saw her as, but simply an ordinary woman.

The Pearly Gates opened. He took one more look at the souls of Père Lachaise then calmly walked to his destiny.

The crowd moved towards the gates and showered him with their forget-me-knots as he passed the threshold and into the golden glow.

Oscar stood proudly amongst the children of Paradise. They gathered around him, each with a welcoming smile. Isola, a blonde, blue-eyed child held out her hand to him. "Welcome home, brother," she said as he took her hand. Gently squeezing it, he turned towards the closing gates. He noticed that Dubliner was no longer at his side. Isola, realising his concern, gave a sharp whistle. Dubliner let go of Kiki-la-Doucette, with whom he had been playfully fighting, and ran past the waiting crowd, squeezed through the closing gates and ran to his master's side. Isola knelt and wrapped her arms around the devoted dog's neck.

Oscar, trying to hold back his tears, looked on as the gates receded into a golden haze. He could see the blue hue of the thousands of forget-me-knots that lay strewn around and the faint outline of the multitude that had escorted him to his final home. He stood with a tear of regret trickling down his face, knowing he would never see the souls of Père Lachaise again. He had been blessed and allowed to move on to a better place. It was love that had seen him through. It was love that had saved his soul. The vagabond of the Sacré Coeur was right – love was everything. Nothing but love lasts forever, the same love that the souls of Père Lachaise had unreservedly showered on him. Taking the flowers from his lapel, he raised the bunch of forget-me-knots to his lips and, smiling, whispered his sweet goodbye.

'Adieu, good souls of Père Lachaise.'

It was another fine Parisian day as I sauntered down the boulevard de Ménilmontant, towards the source of my dream, the cemetery of Père Lachaise. Cradled in my arms was a bunch of crimson roses.

Fully recovered from the illness that had left me in a coma for almost a year; I was now strong enough to face the force of my dream, to put to rest the secret of Père Lachaise, a secret that has been a lifetime obsession.

At the corner of the rue de la Roquette, I looked over at the ruined building on the corner where my family's legal practice once stood. It was there, when I was young girl, that Grandfather revealed to me the odd story of the stranger buried in Père Lachaise at the turn of the twentieth century, a soul buried in such mysterious circumstances.

I had turned my back on the legal world and set my sights on a career as a historian, because of my grandfather setting my mind aflame with his tales about the souls of Père Lachaise and the stranger buried there. He refused to tell me who the stranger was, or the secret of Père Lachaise. He said it was a mystery that I could spend my life solving and when I did I'd find the most precious gift of all; he only hoped I'd find it sooner rather than later.

I entered the gates as curious tourists arrived with maps in hand ready to wander around the maze of cobbled pathways, seeking out the famous and infamous residents. They were about to try to seek out the secret of Père Lachaise, a secret I had been fortunate enough to discover.

I visited all of the resting places of the souls in this tale, leaving a rose on each. On reaching Chopin's grave, I encountered a group of Polish children from Zelazowa Wola surrounding the graceful figurine that adorned his resting place and, on the direction of their teacher, humming his Prelude No 6. When they were finished, I placed a rose through the arm of the figurine.

Finally, I reached the tomb of the stranger. There was graffiti daubed on it and smothered with lipstick traces. There was not a soul in sight as I placed a rose on to the plinth. It was odd, for I had no feeling of the presence of his soul as I had on previous visits. Even the lipstick traces seemed to have lost their passionate sheen. It was as though his soul had flown.

"It's such a pity, Oscar," I said aloud. "Such a pity it's all just been one big, crazy, psychedelic dream. You must admit, it was stretching it a bit to think that you, even with all your charms, could have hoodwinked those good saints into allowing you into Paradise.

You would have had the angels perplexed and the saints running for cover if my dream had come true. They had a lucky escape, didn't they, Paradise and Oscar Wilde. I don't think so – do you? But it was worth a dream, all the same, wasn't it?"

"Are you all right, mademoiselle?"

I turned and there, leaning against a tree, was a Greek god with a copy of *The Little Prince* tucked under his arm. An aura about him transfixed me. Within a moment, I knew I had met the love of my life, the love I had spent my life looking for. Here he was standing before me in the afternoon sun with a glimmer in his eyes.

"I'm fine, monsieur," I replied. "I was only talking to my dream."

A smile spread across his chiselled features as he eyed me up and down, sending my pulse racing.

"Really... and what, may I ask did your dream say?" he asked, not taking his sparkling eyes off me.

I walked towards him and placed my last rose in his wavy blonde hair, which wafted with the perfume of love. I brushed a fallen petal from his broad shoulders, and looked deep into his cool blue eyes and whispered, "It said that to give and receive love is the secret and essence of life."

"Ah! And what else did your dream say?" he asked as my heart beat like a drum.

"That nothing lasts forever other than the gift of love."

His eyes twinkled. "Then, mademoiselle, I had better have a taste of this gift of love before I expire from the lack of it."

He held my head in his well-manicured hands and, looking deep into my soul, kissed my welcoming lips and sent me on an uncontrolled spiral of desire.

Here, in this place of past dreams and hope I discovered the secret – not just of Père Lachaise, but life itself. I discovered the real thing: love.

Made in the USA
Monee, IL
06 July 2020